TKO STUDIOS

SALVATORE SIMEONE - CEO & PUBLISHER

TZE CHUN - PRESIDENT & PUBLISHER

CARA MCKENNEY - TALENT RELATIONS

SEBASTIAN GIRNER - EDITOR-IN-CHIEF

JEFF POWELL - PRODUCTION MANAGER

ROBERT TERLIZZI - DIRECTOR OF DESIGN

THE BANKS #1-6.

Published by TKO Studios, LLC.
Office of Publication: 450 7th Ave., Suite 2107. New York, NY 10123.

ISBN: 978-1-7327485-5-2

TKOPRESENTS.COM

TKO PRESENTS A WORLD BY:

ROXANE GAY
WRITER

MING DOYLE
ART

JORDIE BELLAIRE
COLOR ART

ARIANA MAHER
LETTERER

SEBASTIAN GIRNER
EDITOR

MING DOYLE
COVER ART

JARED K FLETCHER
TITLE & COVER DESIGN

JEFF POWELL
BOOK DESIGN

SPECIAL THANKS TO ERICA HENDERSON

The Bank$

CHAPTER 1

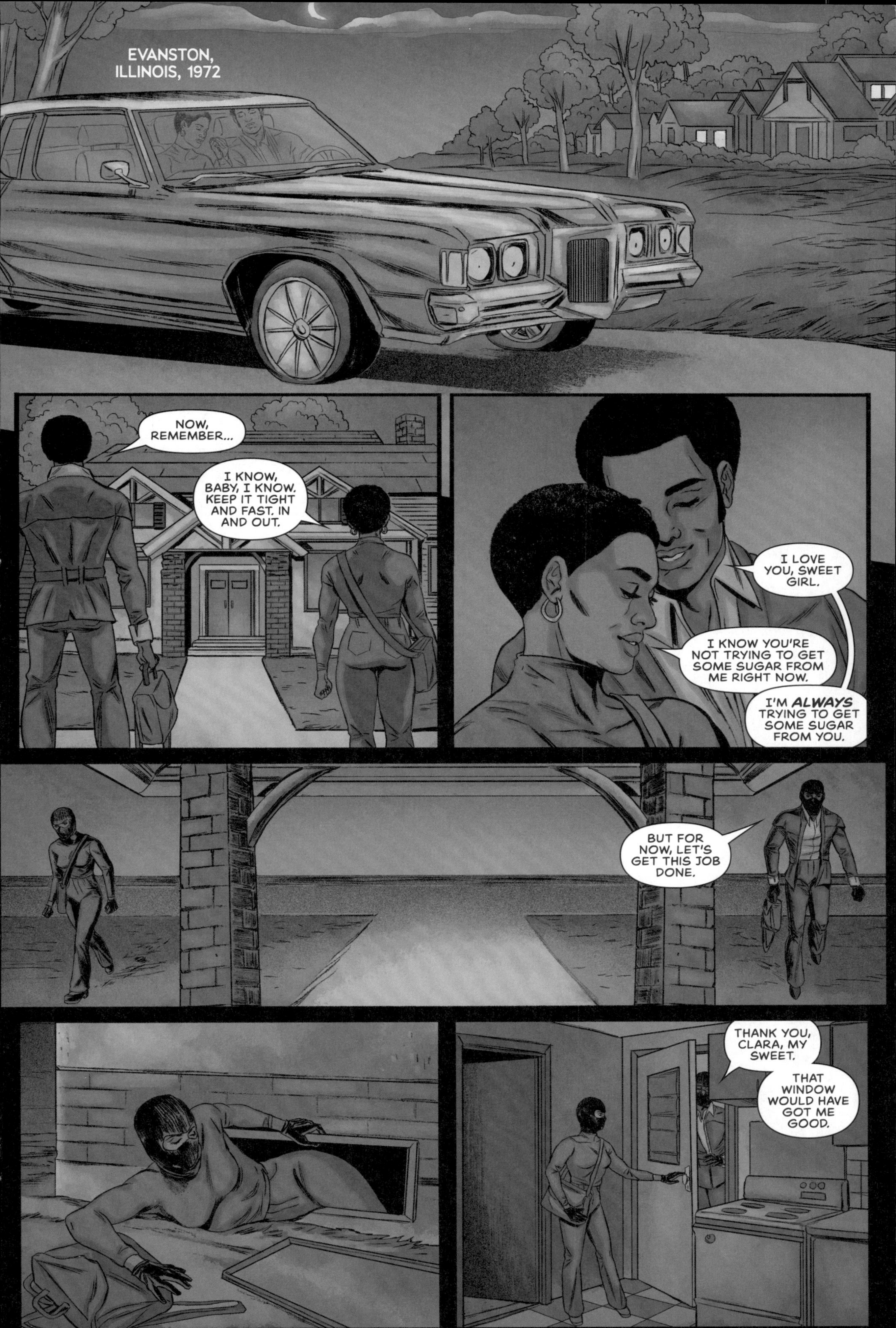
EVANSTON, ILLINOIS, 1972
NOW, REMEMBER...
I KNOW, BABY, I KNOW. KEEP IT TIGHT AND FAST. IN AND OUT.
I LOVE YOU, SWEET GIRL.
I KNOW YOU'RE NOT TRYING TO GET SOME SUGAR FROM ME RIGHT NOW.
I'M ALWAYS TRYING TO GET SOME SUGAR FROM YOU.
BUT FOR NOW, LET'S GET THIS JOB DONE.
THANK YOU, CLARA, MY SWEET.
THAT WINDOW WOULD HAVE GOT ME GOOD.

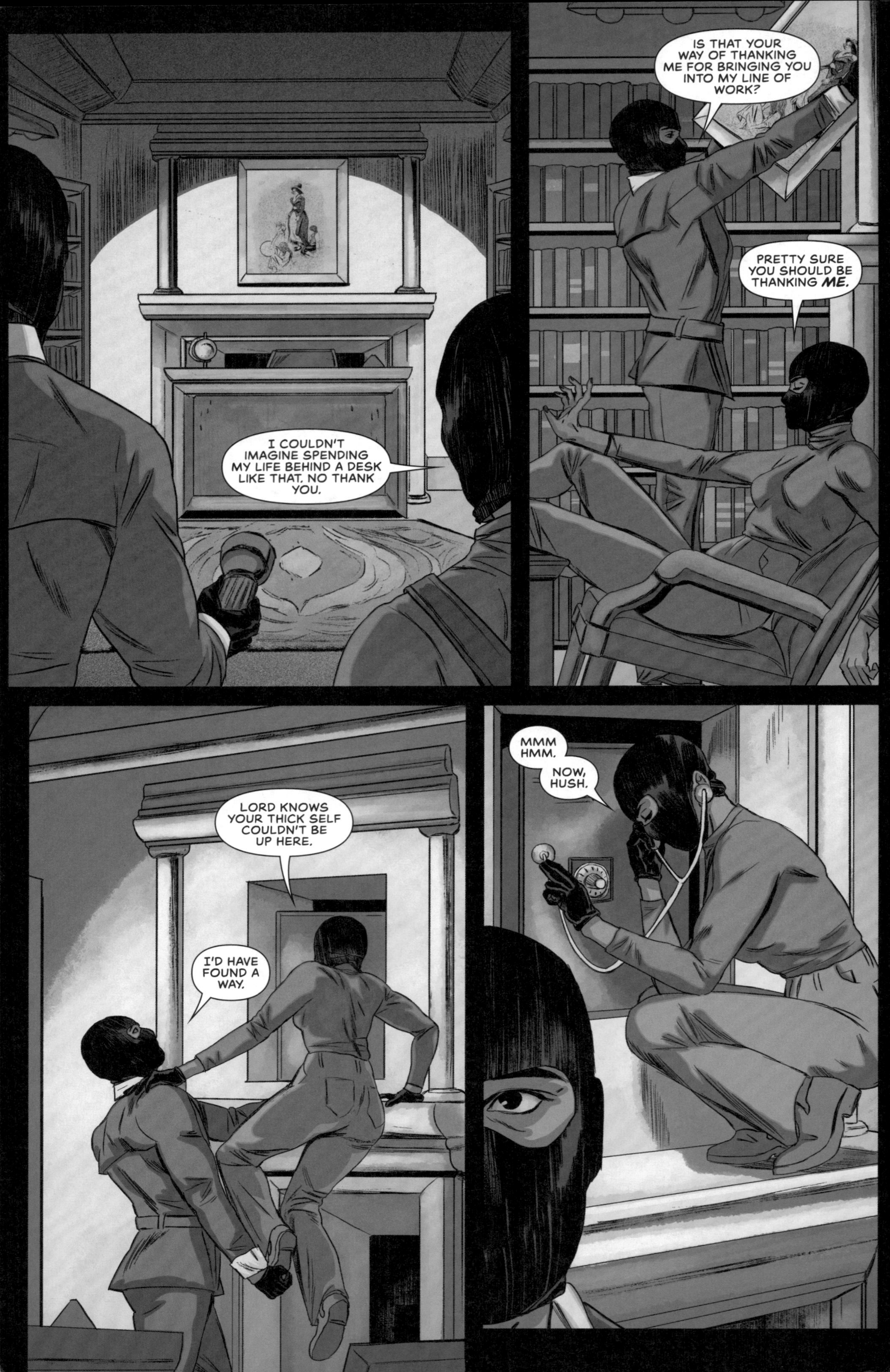
I COULDN'T IMAGINE SPENDING MY LIFE BEHIND A DESK LIKE THAT. NO THANK YOU.
IS THAT YOUR WAY OF THANKING ME FOR BRINGING YOU INTO MY LINE OF WORK?
PRETTY SURE YOU SHOULD BE THANKING **ME.**
LORD KNOWS YOUR THICK SELF COULDN'T BE UP HERE.
I'D HAVE FOUND A WAY.
MMM HMM.
NOW, HUSH.

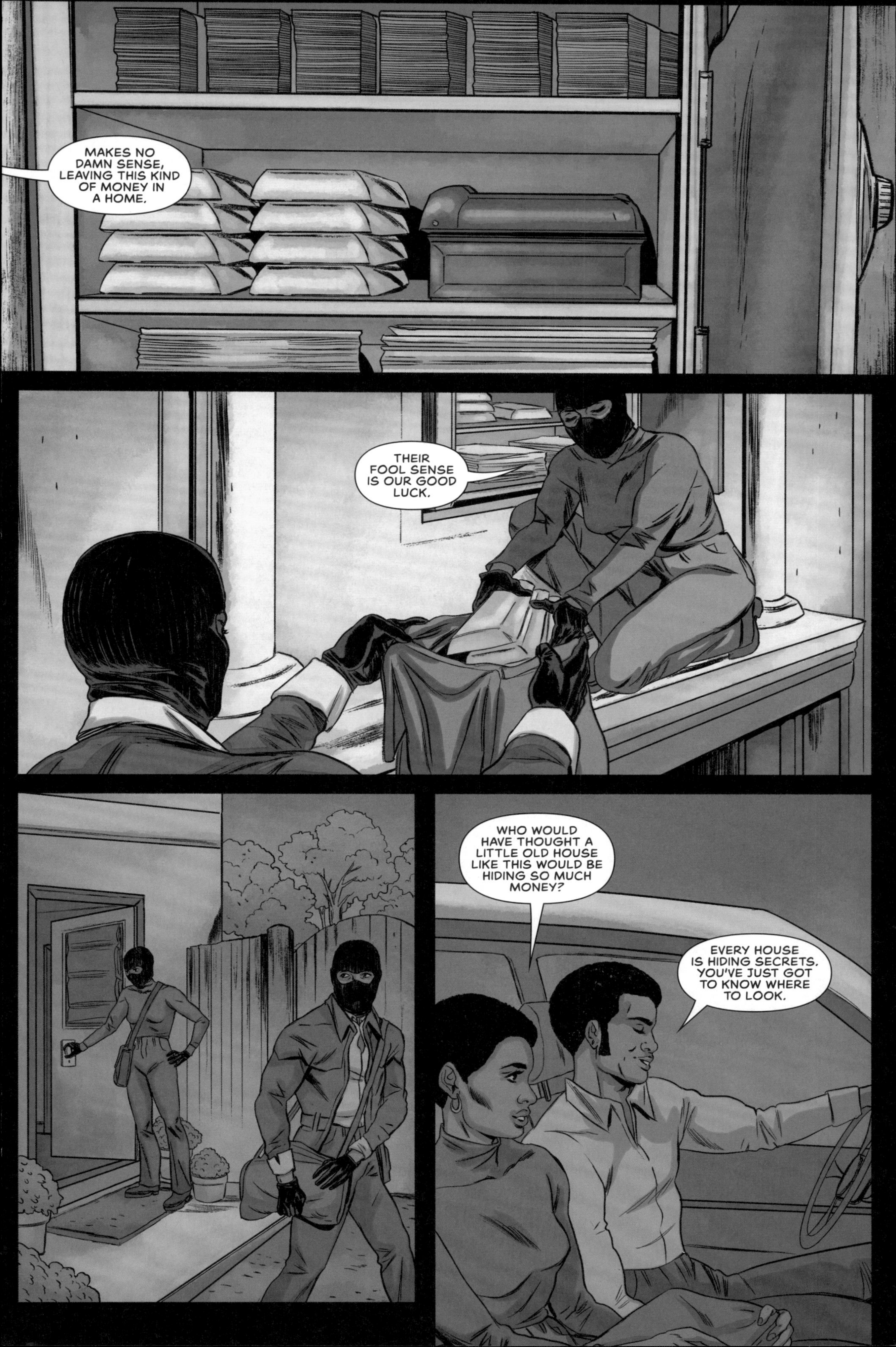
MAKES NO DAMN SENSE, LEAVING THIS KIND OF MONEY IN A HOME.
THEIR FOOL SENSE IS OUR GOOD LUCK.
WHO WOULD HAVE THOUGHT A LITTLE OLD HOUSE LIKE THIS WOULD BE HIDING SO MUCH MONEY?
EVERY HOUSE IS HIDING SECRETS. YOU'VE JUST GOT TO KNOW WHERE TO LOOK.

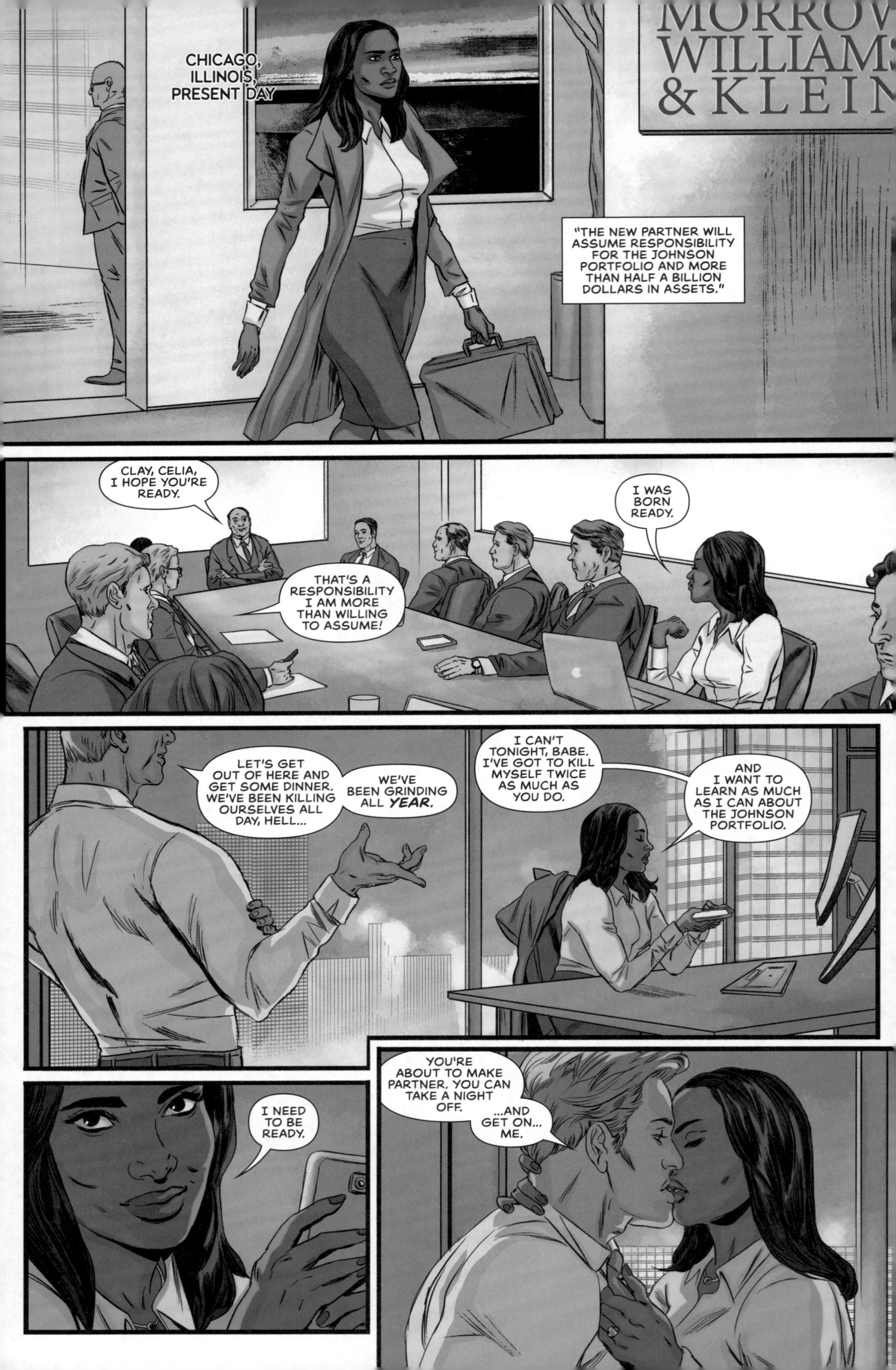
CHICAGO, ILLINOIS, PRESENT DAY
MORROW WILLIAMS & KLEIN
"THE NEW PARTNER WILL ASSUME RESPONSIBILITY FOR THE JOHNSON PORTFOLIO AND MORE THAN HALF A BILLION DOLLARS IN ASSETS."
CLAY, CELIA, I HOPE YOU'RE READY.
THAT'S A RESPONSIBILITY I AM MORE THAN WILLING TO ASSUME!
I WAS BORN READY.
LET'S GET OUT OF HERE AND GET SOME DINNER. WE'VE BEEN KILLING OURSELVES ALL DAY, HELL...
WE'VE BEEN GRINDING ALL *YEAR.*
I CAN'T TONIGHT, BABE. I'VE GOT TO KILL MYSELF TWICE AS MUCH AS YOU DO.
AND I WANT TO LEARN AS MUCH AS I CAN ABOUT THE JOHNSON PORTFOLIO.
I NEED TO BE READY.
YOU'RE ABOUT TO MAKE PARTNER. YOU CAN TAKE A NIGHT OFF.
...AND GET ON... ME.

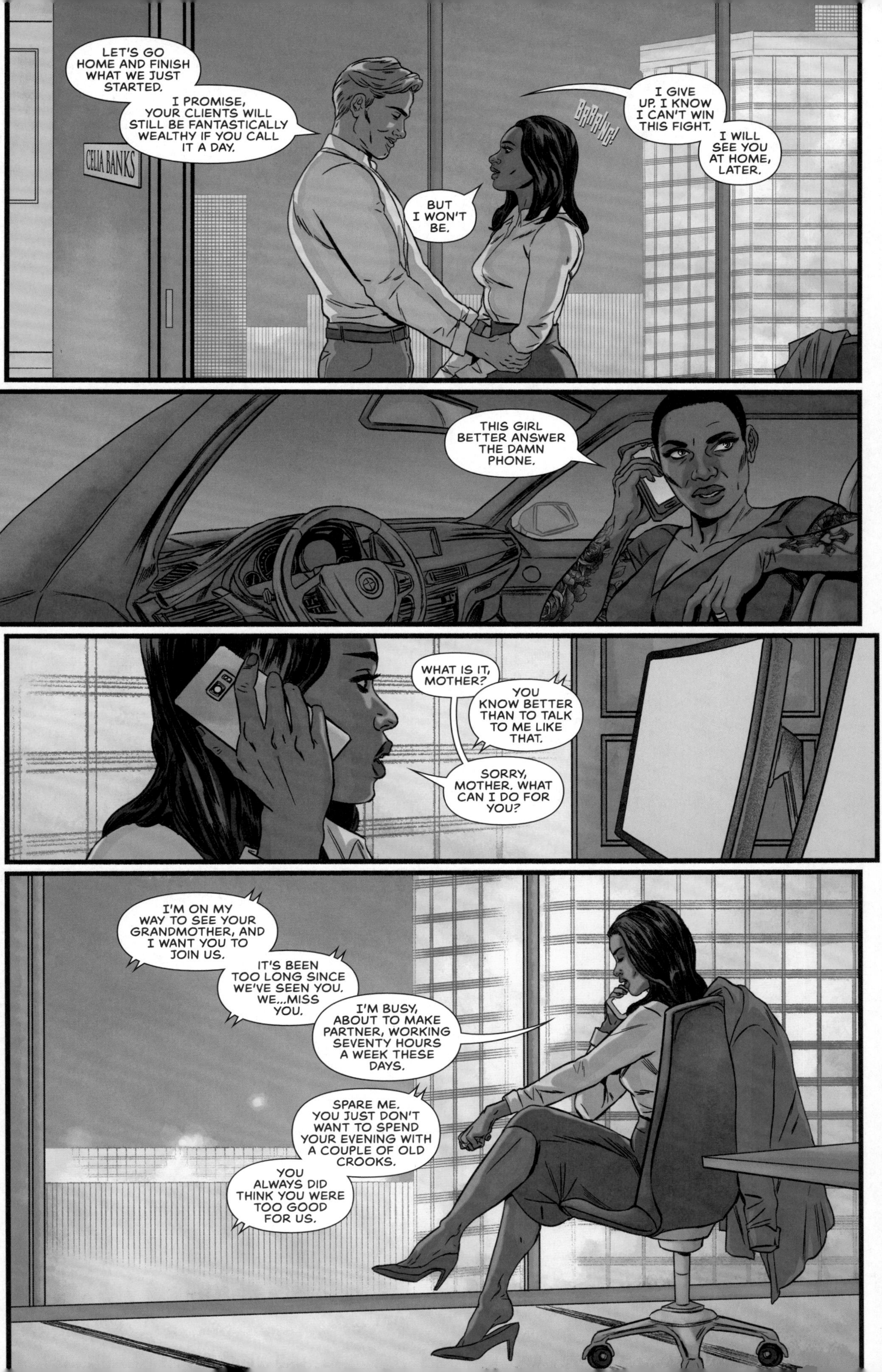
LET'S GO HOME AND FINISH WHAT WE JUST STARTED.
I PROMISE, YOUR CLIENTS WILL STILL BE FANTASTICALLY WEALTHY IF YOU CALL IT A DAY.
CELIA BANKS
BUT I WON'T BE.
BRRRING!
I GIVE UP. I KNOW I CAN'T WIN THIS FIGHT.
I WILL SEE YOU AT HOME, LATER.
THIS GIRL BETTER ANSWER THE DAMN PHONE.
WHAT IS IT, MOTHER?
YOU KNOW BETTER THAN TO TALK TO ME LIKE THAT.
SORRY, MOTHER. WHAT CAN I DO FOR YOU?
I'M ON MY WAY TO SEE YOUR GRANDMOTHER, AND I WANT YOU TO JOIN US.
IT'S BEEN TOO LONG SINCE WE'VE SEEN YOU. WE...MISS YOU.
I'M BUSY, ABOUT TO MAKE PARTNER, WORKING SEVENTY HOURS A WEEK THESE DAYS.
SPARE ME. YOU JUST DON'T WANT TO SPEND YOUR EVENING WITH A COUPLE OF OLD CROOKS.
YOU ALWAYS DID THINK YOU WERE TOO GOOD FOR US.

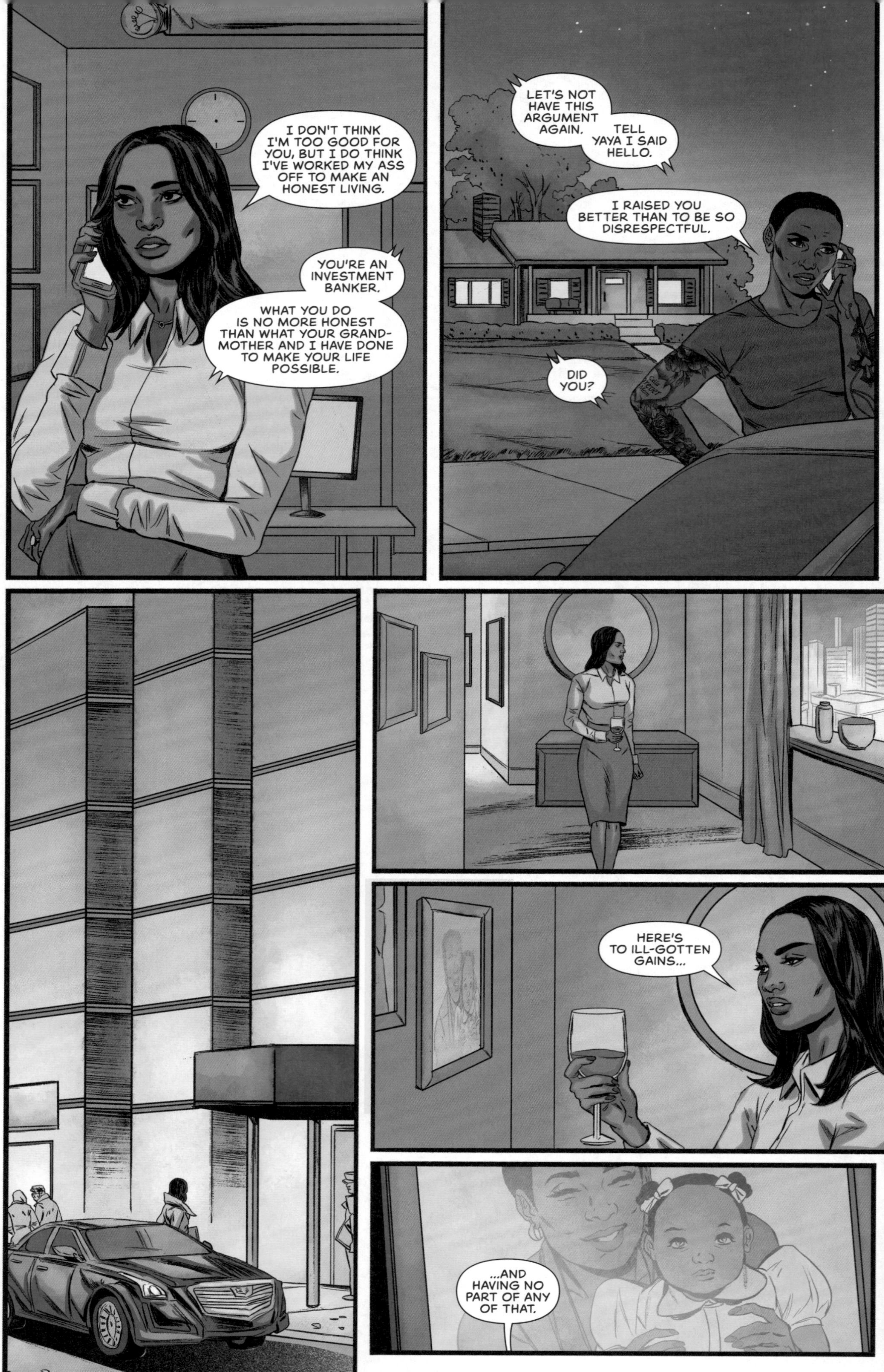
I DON'T THINK I'M TOO GOOD FOR YOU, BUT I DO THINK I'VE WORKED MY ASS OFF TO MAKE AN HONEST LIVING.
YOU'RE AN INVESTMENT BANKER.
WHAT YOU DO IS NO MORE HONEST THAN WHAT YOUR GRAND-MOTHER AND I HAVE DONE TO MAKE YOUR LIFE POSSIBLE.
LET'S NOT HAVE THIS ARGUMENT AGAIN.
TELL YAYA I SAID HELLO.
I RAISED YOU BETTER THAN TO BE SO DISRESPECTFUL.
DID YOU?
HERE'S TO ILL-GOTTEN GAINS...
...AND HAVING NO PART OF ANY OF THAT.

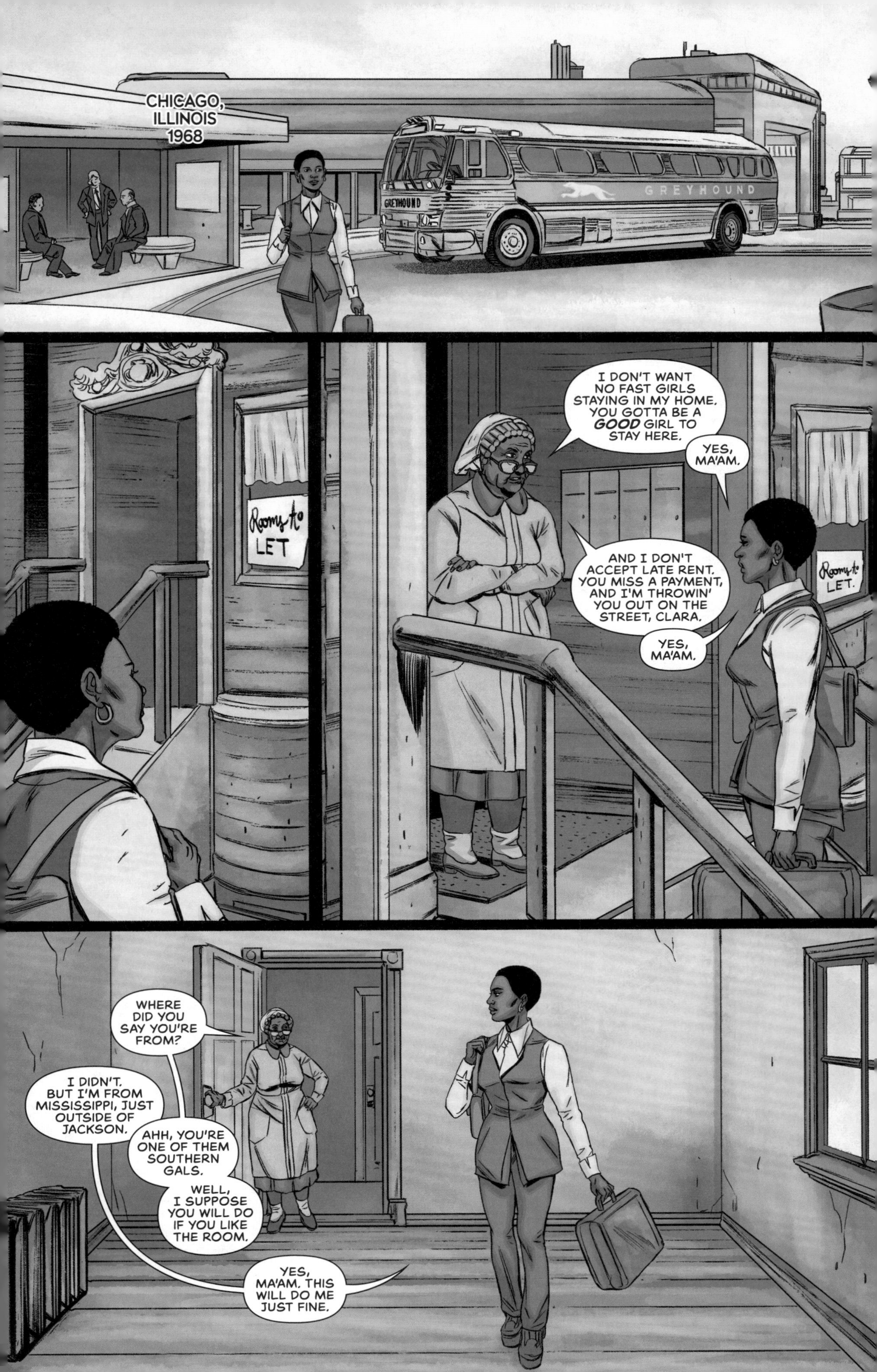
CHICAGO, ILLINOIS 1968
GREYHOUND
GREYHOUND
Rooms to LET
I DON'T WANT NO FAST GIRLS STAYING IN MY HOME. YOU GOTTA BE A GOOD GIRL TO STAY HERE.
YES, MA'AM.
AND I DON'T ACCEPT LATE RENT. YOU MISS A PAYMENT, AND I'M THROWIN' YOU OUT ON THE STREET, CLARA.
YES, MA'AM.
Rooms to LET.
WHERE DID YOU SAY YOU'RE FROM?
I DIDN'T. BUT I'M FROM MISSISSIPPI, JUST OUTSIDE OF JACKSON.
AHH, YOU'RE ONE OF THEM SOUTHERN GALS.
WELL, I SUPPOSE YOU WILL DO IF YOU LIKE THE ROOM.
YES, MA'AM. THIS WILL DO ME JUST FINE.

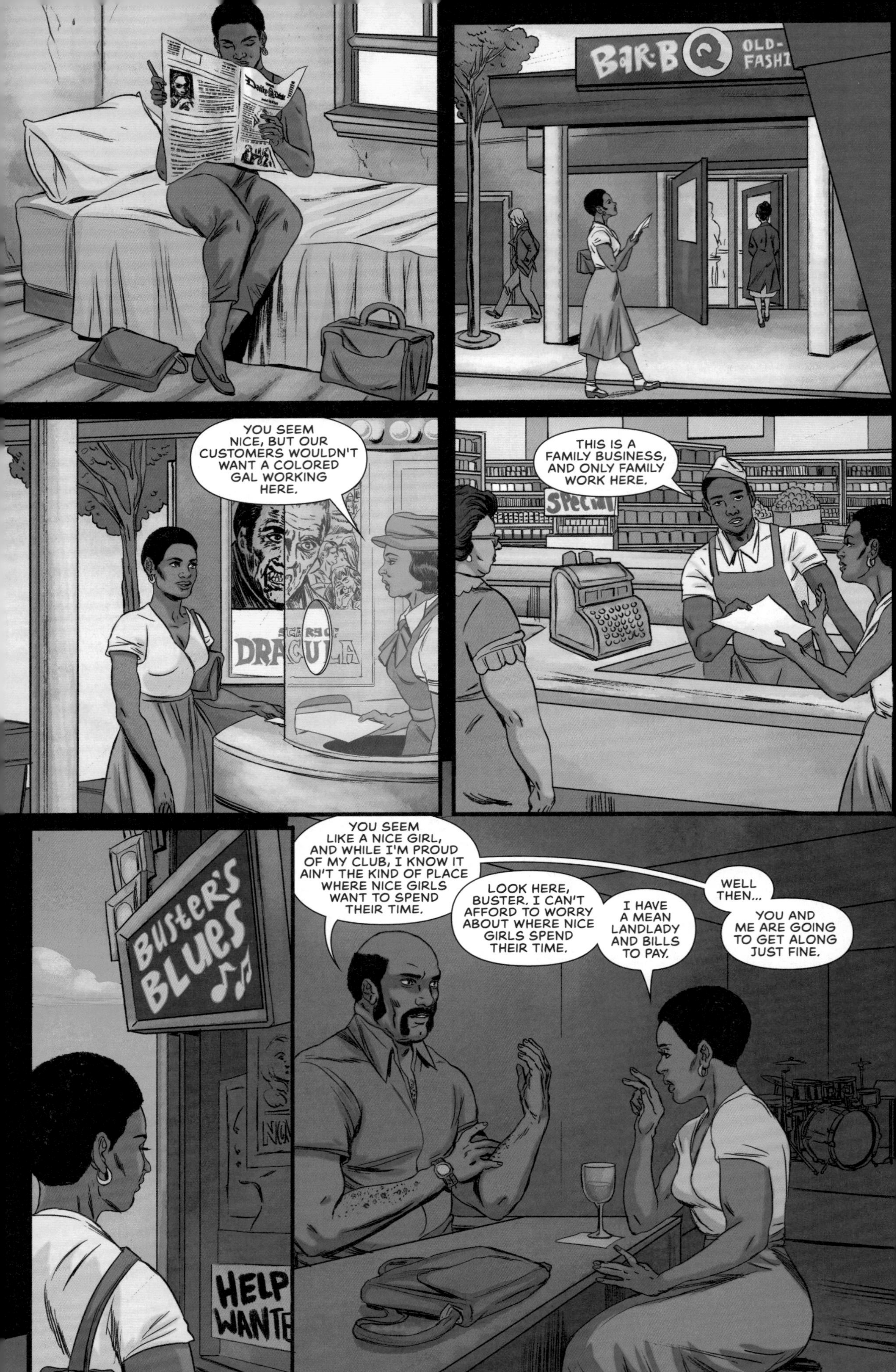
BAR-B-Q
OLD-
FASHI
YOU SEEM NICE, BUT OUR CUSTOMERS WOULDN'T WANT A COLORED GAL WORKING HERE.
SCARS OF DRACULA
THIS IS A FAMILY BUSINESS, AND ONLY FAMILY WORK HERE.
BUSTER'S BLUES
HELP
WANTE
YOU SEEM LIKE A NICE GIRL, AND WHILE I'M PROUD OF MY CLUB, I KNOW IT AIN'T THE KIND OF PLACE WHERE NICE GIRLS WANT TO SPEND THEIR TIME.
LOOK HERE, BUSTER. I CAN'T AFFORD TO WORRY ABOUT WHERE NICE GIRLS SPEND THEIR TIME.
I HAVE A MEAN LANDLADY AND BILLS TO PAY.
WELL THEN...
YOU AND ME ARE GOING TO GET ALONG JUST FINE.

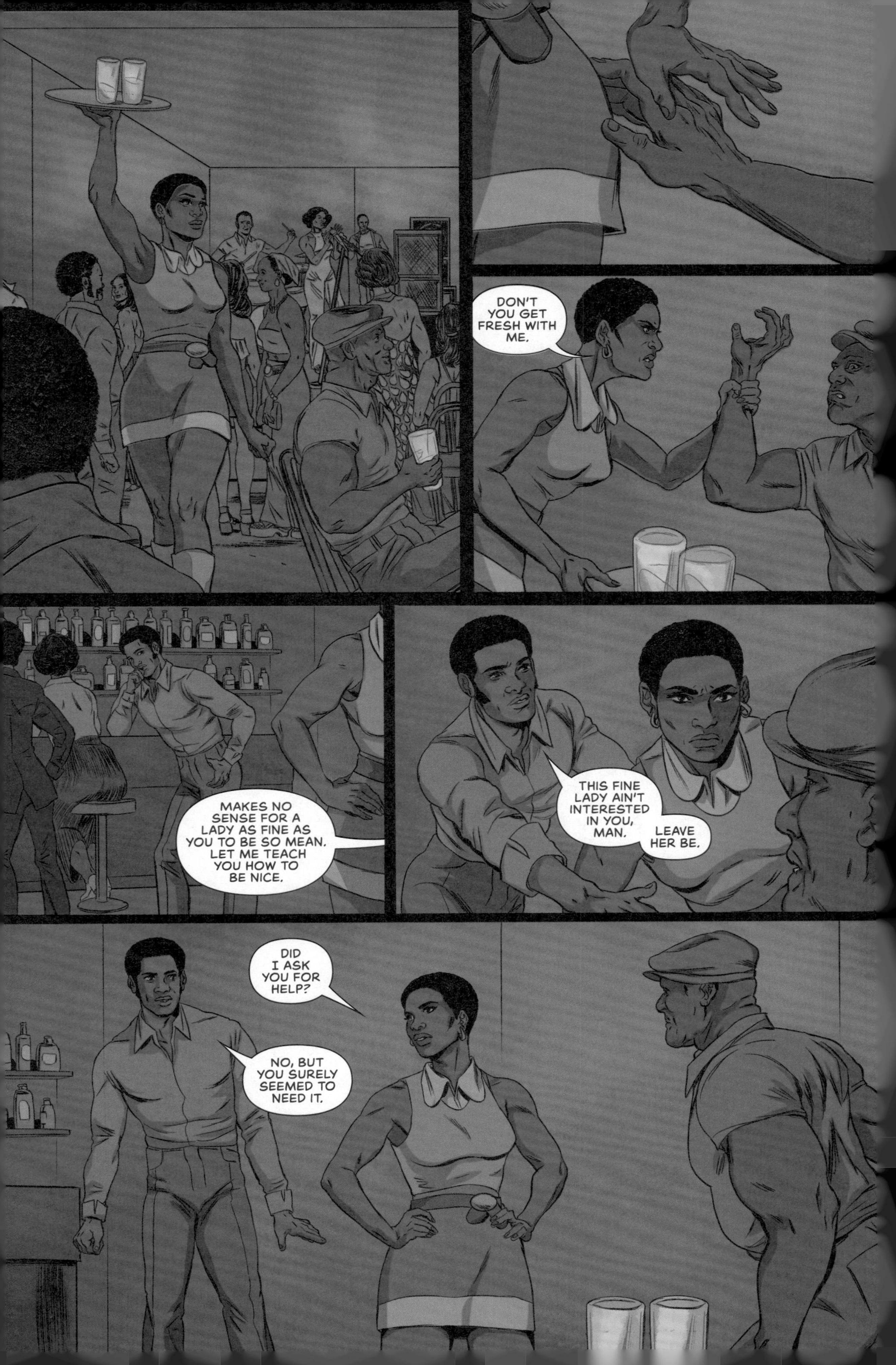
DON'T YOU GET FRESH WITH ME.
MAKES NO SENSE FOR A LADY AS FINE AS YOU TO BE SO MEAN. LET ME TEACH YOU HOW TO BE NICE.
THIS FINE LADY AIN'T INTERESTED IN YOU, MAN.
LEAVE HER BE.
DID I ASK YOU FOR HELP?
NO, BUT YOU SURELY SEEMED TO NEED IT.

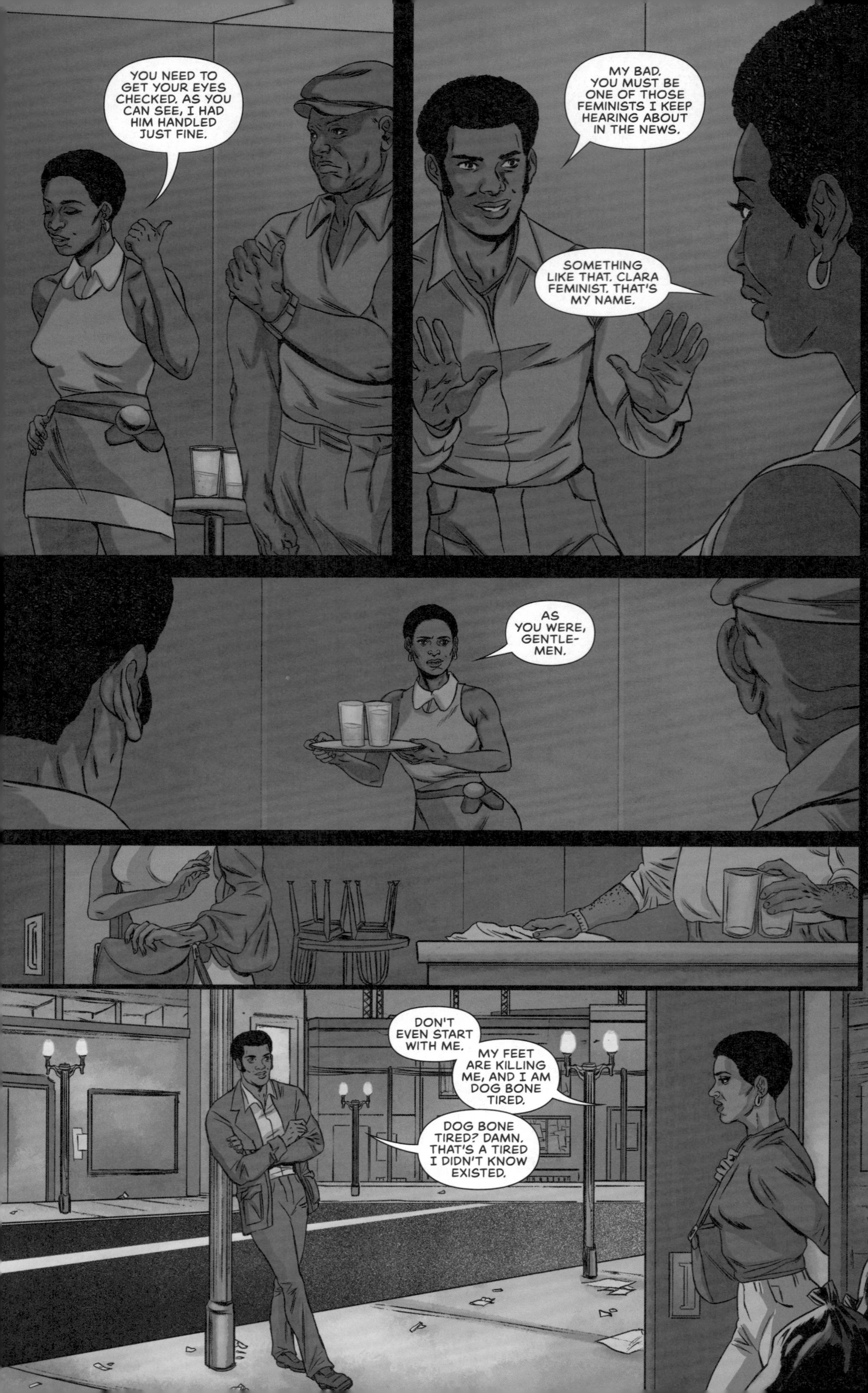
YOU NEED TO GET YOUR EYES CHECKED. AS YOU CAN SEE, I HAD HIM HANDLED JUST FINE.
MY BAD. YOU MUST BE ONE OF THOSE FEMINISTS I KEEP HEARING ABOUT IN THE NEWS.
SOMETHING LIKE THAT. CLARA FEMINIST. THAT'S MY NAME.
AS YOU WERE, GENTLE-MEN.
DON'T EVEN START WITH ME.
MY FEET ARE KILLING ME, AND I AM DOG BONE TIRED.
DOG BONE TIRED? DAMN. THAT'S A TIRED I DIDN'T KNOW EXISTED.

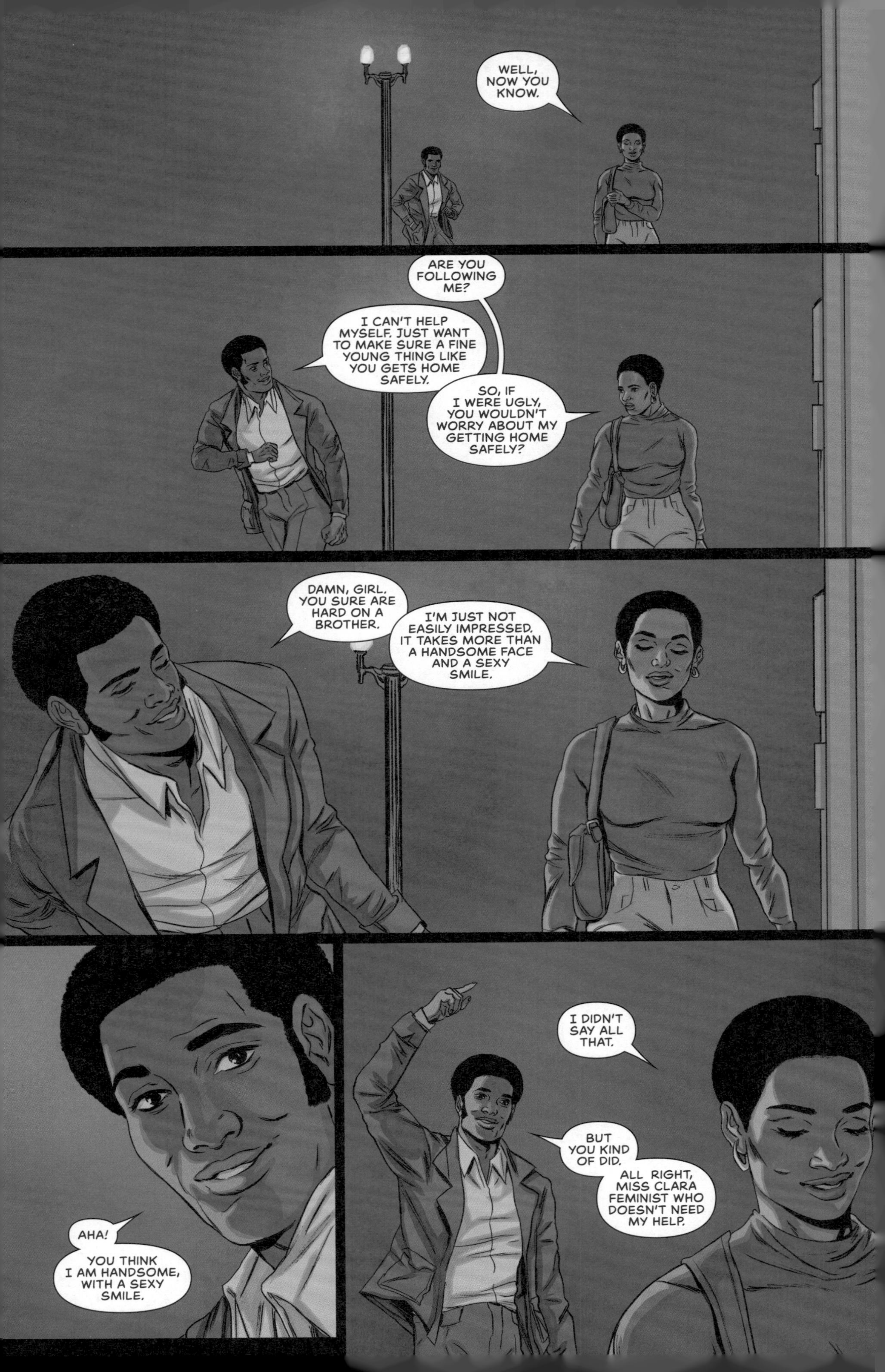
WELL, NOW YOU KNOW.
ARE YOU FOLLOWING ME?
I CAN'T HELP MYSELF. JUST WANT TO MAKE SURE A FINE YOUNG THING LIKE YOU GETS HOME SAFELY.
SO, IF I WERE UGLY, YOU WOULDN'T WORRY ABOUT MY GETTING HOME SAFELY?
DAMN, GIRL. YOU SURE ARE HARD ON A BROTHER.
I'M JUST NOT EASILY IMPRESSED. IT TAKES MORE THAN A HANDSOME FACE AND A SEXY SMILE.
AHA!
YOU THINK I AM HANDSOME, WITH A SEXY SMILE.
I DIDN'T SAY ALL THAT.
BUT YOU KIND OF DID.
ALL RIGHT, MISS CLARA FEMINIST WHO DOESN'T NEED MY HELP.

"I'M GOING TO SEE YOU AGAIN."

CURTIS MAYFIELD
Advance Sale
1971 7:00 P.M.
Gen Adm. $3.00
TOTAL $3.00
ADVANCE SALE
0880
0881
085104

I SEE YOU AND THAT MELVIN BANKS MAKING EYES AT EACH OTHER.

WHAT ABOUT IT?

I JUST WANT YOU TO BE CAREFUL, THAT BOY IS A *THIEF* THROUGH AND THROUGH.

HE HAS THE STICKIEST HANDS IN ALL OF CHICAGO.

HIS SAVING GRACE IS THAT HE ONLY STEALS FROM WHITE PEOPLE.

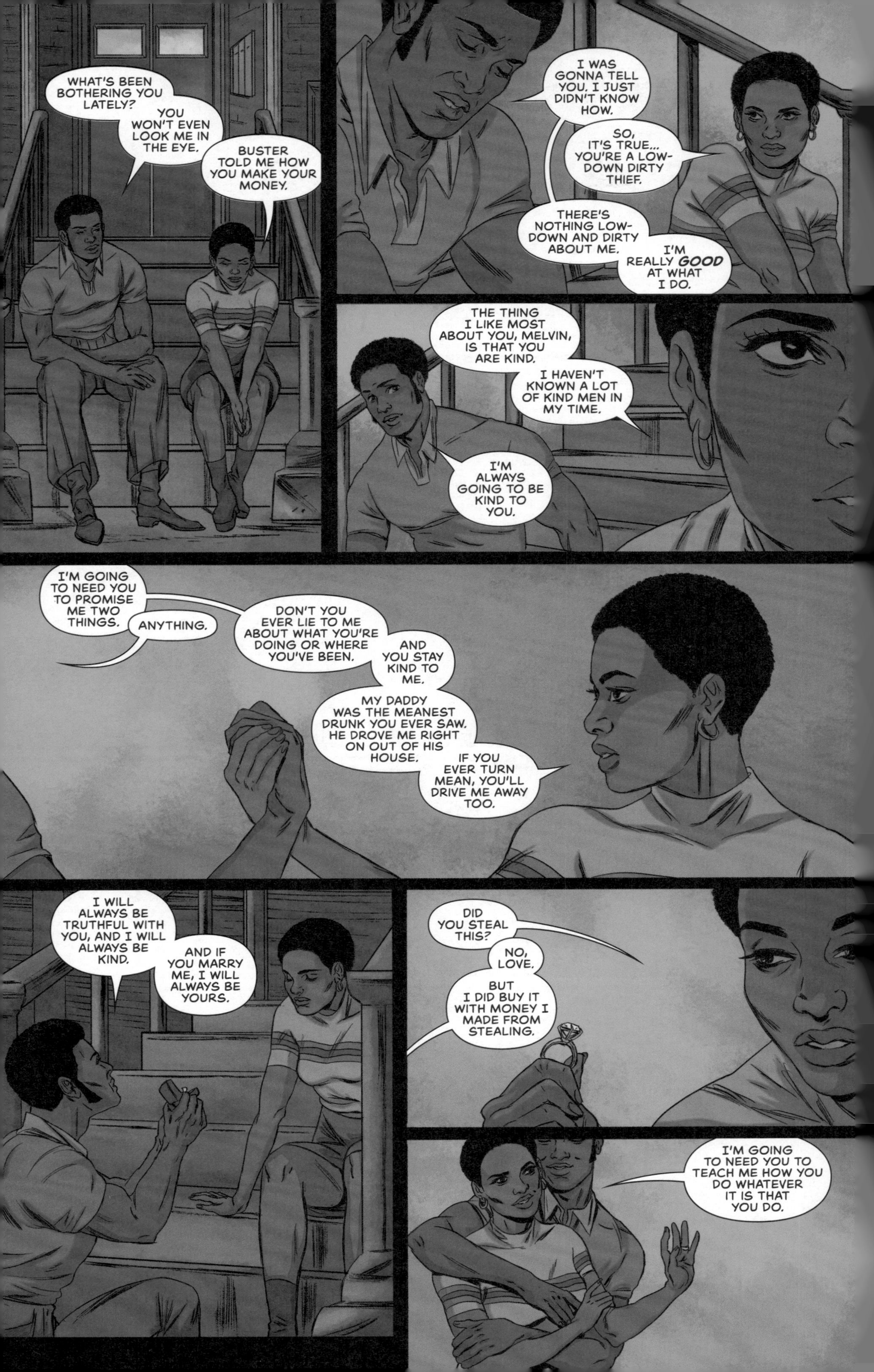
WHAT'S BEEN BOTHERING YOU LATELY?
YOU WON'T EVEN LOOK ME IN THE EYE.
BUSTER TOLD ME HOW YOU MAKE YOUR MONEY.
I WAS GONNA TELL YOU. I JUST DIDN'T KNOW HOW.
SO, IT'S TRUE... YOU'RE A LOW-DOWN DIRTY THIEF.
THERE'S NOTHING LOW-DOWN AND DIRTY ABOUT ME.
I'M REALLY GOOD AT WHAT I DO.
THE THING I LIKE MOST ABOUT YOU, MELVIN, IS THAT YOU ARE KIND.
I HAVEN'T KNOWN A LOT OF KIND MEN IN MY TIME.
I'M ALWAYS GOING TO BE KIND TO YOU.
I'M GOING TO NEED YOU TO PROMISE ME TWO THINGS.
ANYTHING.
DON'T YOU EVER LIE TO ME ABOUT WHAT YOU'RE DOING OR WHERE YOU'VE BEEN.
AND YOU STAY KIND TO ME.
MY DADDY WAS THE MEANEST DRUNK YOU EVER SAW. HE DROVE ME RIGHT ON OUT OF HIS HOUSE.
IF YOU EVER TURN MEAN, YOU'LL DRIVE ME AWAY TOO.
I WILL ALWAYS BE TRUTHFUL WITH YOU, AND I WILL ALWAYS BE KIND.
AND IF YOU MARRY ME, I WILL ALWAYS BE YOURS.
DID YOU STEAL THIS?
NO, LOVE.
BUT I DID BUY IT WITH MONEY I MADE FROM STEALING.
I'M GOING TO NEED YOU TO TEACH ME HOW YOU DO WHATEVER IT IS THAT YOU DO.

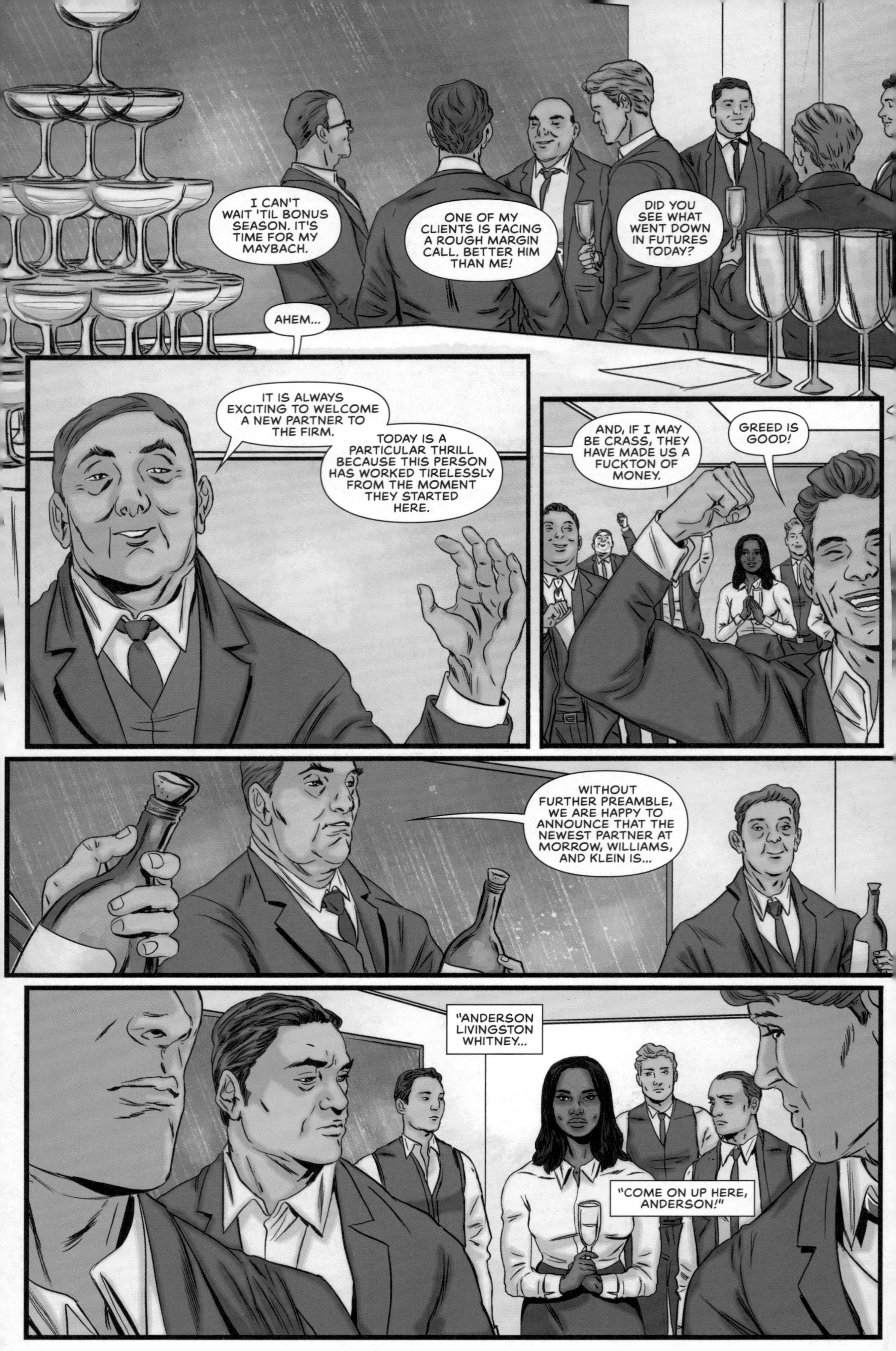
I CAN'T WAIT 'TIL BONUS SEASON. IT'S TIME FOR MY MAYBACH.
ONE OF MY CLIENTS IS FACING A ROUGH MARGIN CALL. BETTER HIM THAN ME!
DID YOU SEE WHAT WENT DOWN IN FUTURES TODAY?
AHEM...
IT IS ALWAYS EXCITING TO WELCOME A NEW PARTNER TO THE FIRM.
TODAY IS A PARTICULAR THRILL BECAUSE THIS PERSON HAS WORKED TIRELESSLY FROM THE MOMENT THEY STARTED HERE.
AND, IF I MAY BE CRASS, THEY HAVE MADE US A FUCKTON OF MONEY.
GREED IS GOOD!
WITHOUT FURTHER PREAMBLE, WE ARE HAPPY TO ANNOUNCE THAT THE NEWEST PARTNER AT MORROW, WILLIAMS, AND KLEIN IS...
"ANDERSON LIVINGSTON WHITNEY...
"COME ON UP HERE, ANDERSON!"

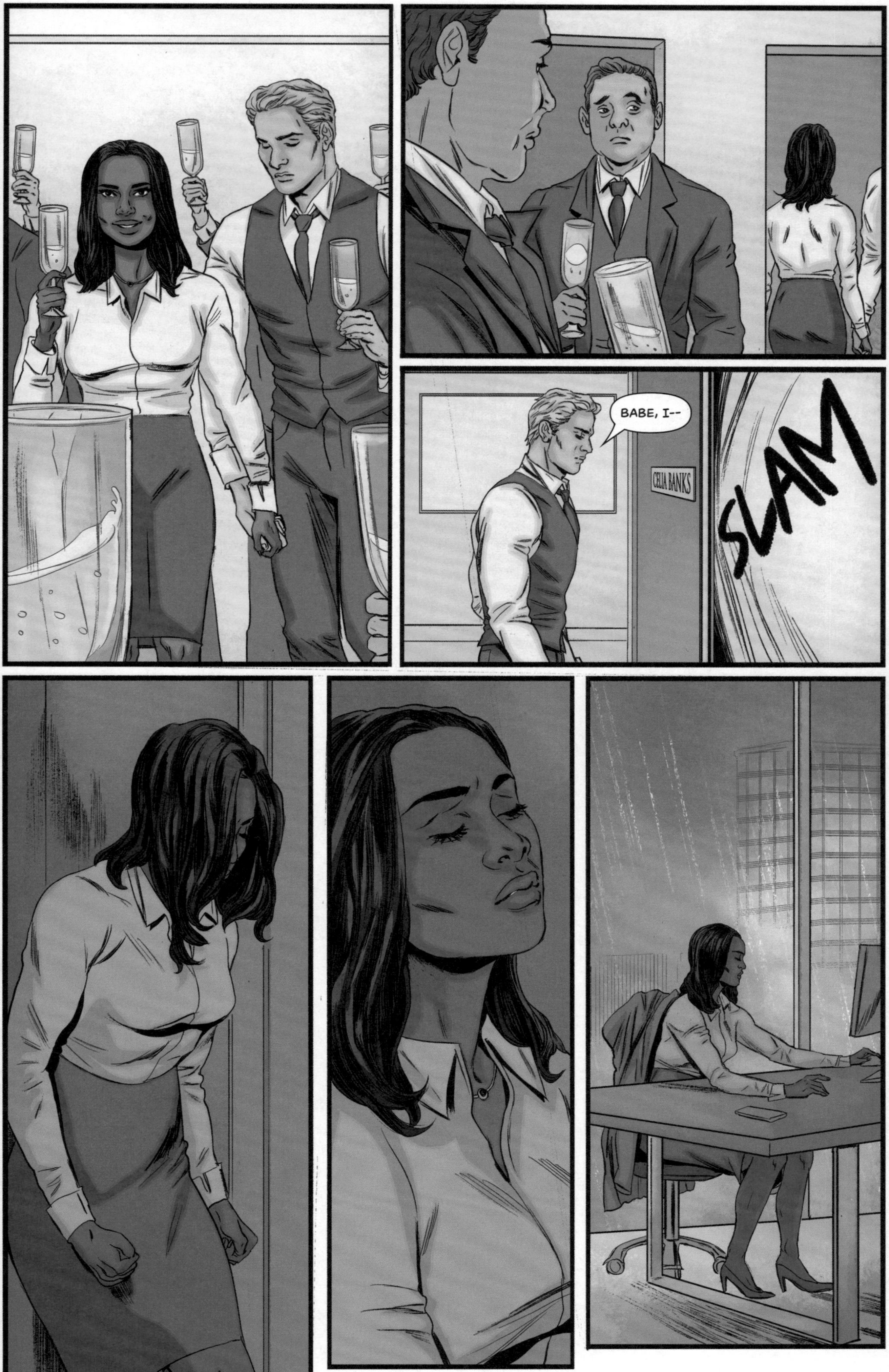
BABE, I--
CELIA BANKS
SLAM

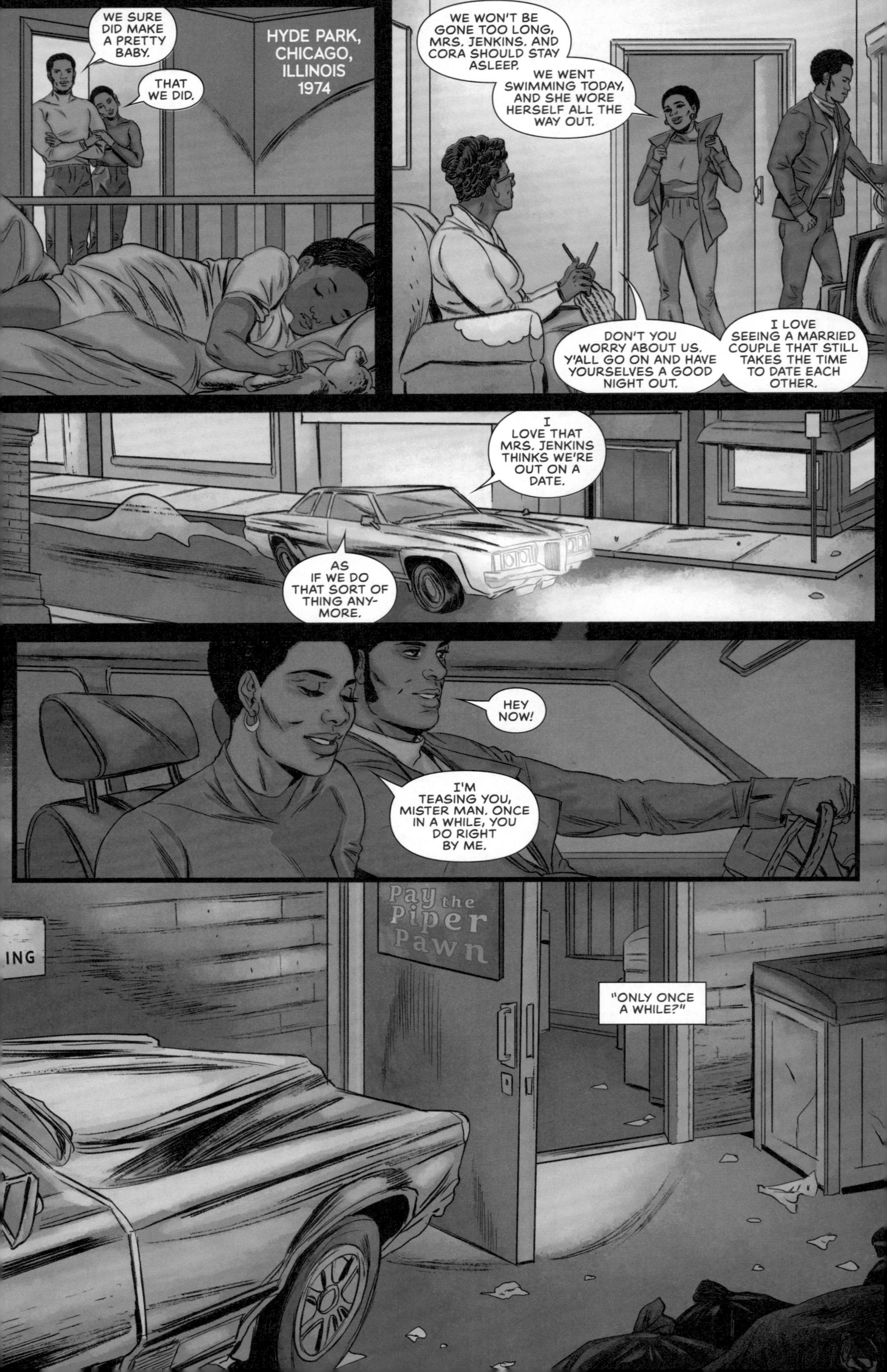
HYDE PARK, CHICAGO, ILLINOIS 1974
WE SURE DID MAKE A PRETTY BABY.
THAT WE DID.
WE WON'T BE GONE TOO LONG, MRS. JENKINS. AND CORA SHOULD STAY ASLEEP.
WE WENT SWIMMING TODAY, AND SHE WORE HERSELF ALL THE WAY OUT.
DON'T YOU WORRY ABOUT US. Y'ALL GO ON AND HAVE YOURSELVES A GOOD NIGHT OUT.
I LOVE SEEING A MARRIED COUPLE THAT STILL TAKES THE TIME TO DATE EACH OTHER.
I LOVE THAT MRS. JENKINS THINKS WE'RE OUT ON A DATE.
AS IF WE DO THAT SORT OF THING ANY-MORE.
HEY NOW!
I'M TEASING YOU, MISTER MAN. ONCE IN A WHILE, YOU DO RIGHT BY ME.
Pay the Piper Pawn
"ONLY ONCE A WHILE?"

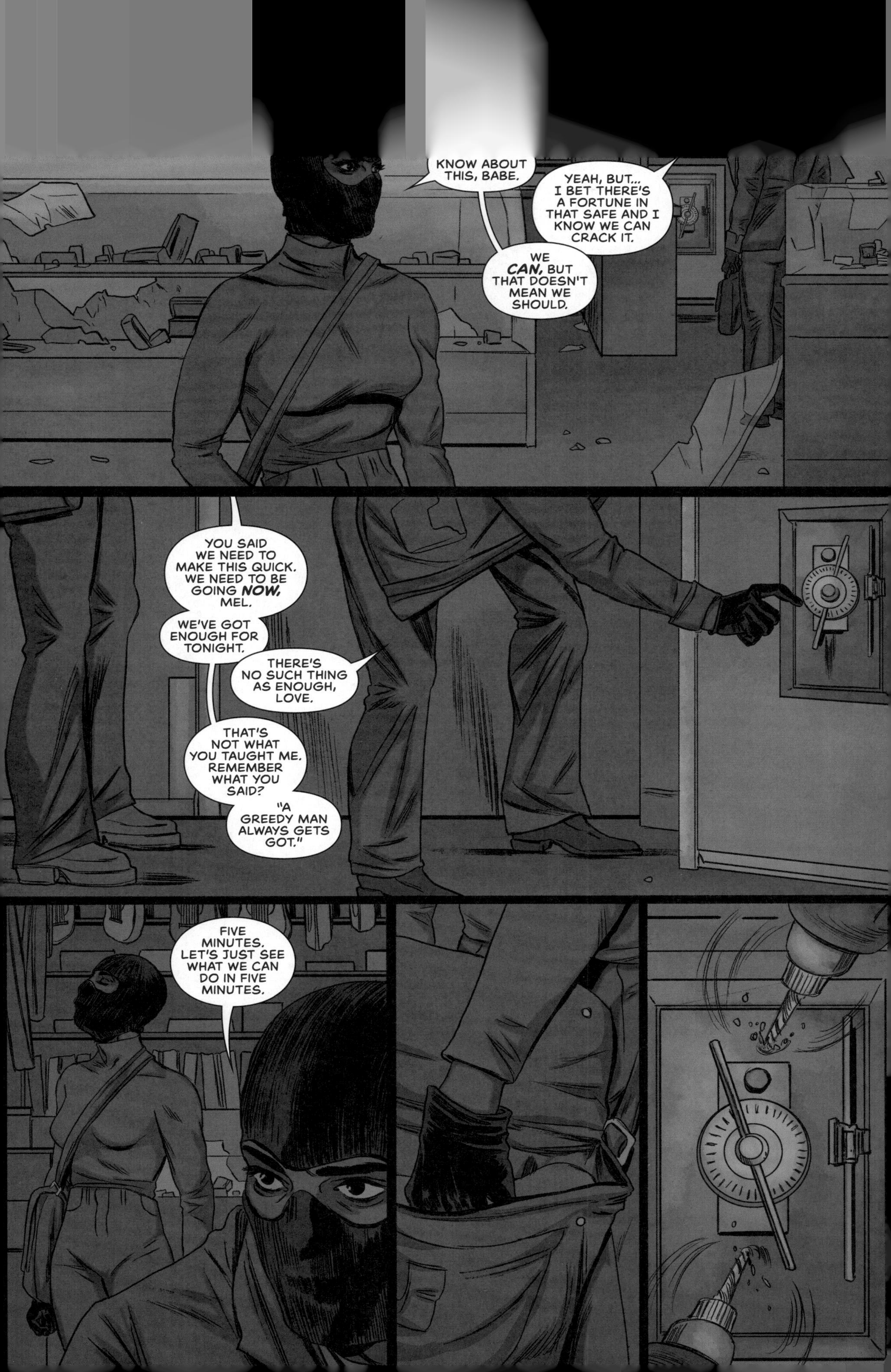
KNOW ABOUT THIS, BABE.
YEAH, BUT... I BET THERE'S A FORTUNE IN THAT SAFE AND I KNOW WE CAN CRACK IT.
WE CAN, BUT THAT DOESN'T MEAN WE SHOULD.
YOU SAID WE NEED TO MAKE THIS QUICK. WE NEED TO BE GOING NOW, MEL.
WE'VE GOT ENOUGH FOR TONIGHT.
THERE'S NO SUCH THING AS ENOUGH, LOVE.
THAT'S NOT WHAT YOU TAUGHT ME. REMEMBER WHAT YOU SAID?
"A GREEDY MAN ALWAYS GETS GOT."
FIVE MINUTES. LET'S JUST SEE WHAT WE CAN DO IN FIVE MINUTES.

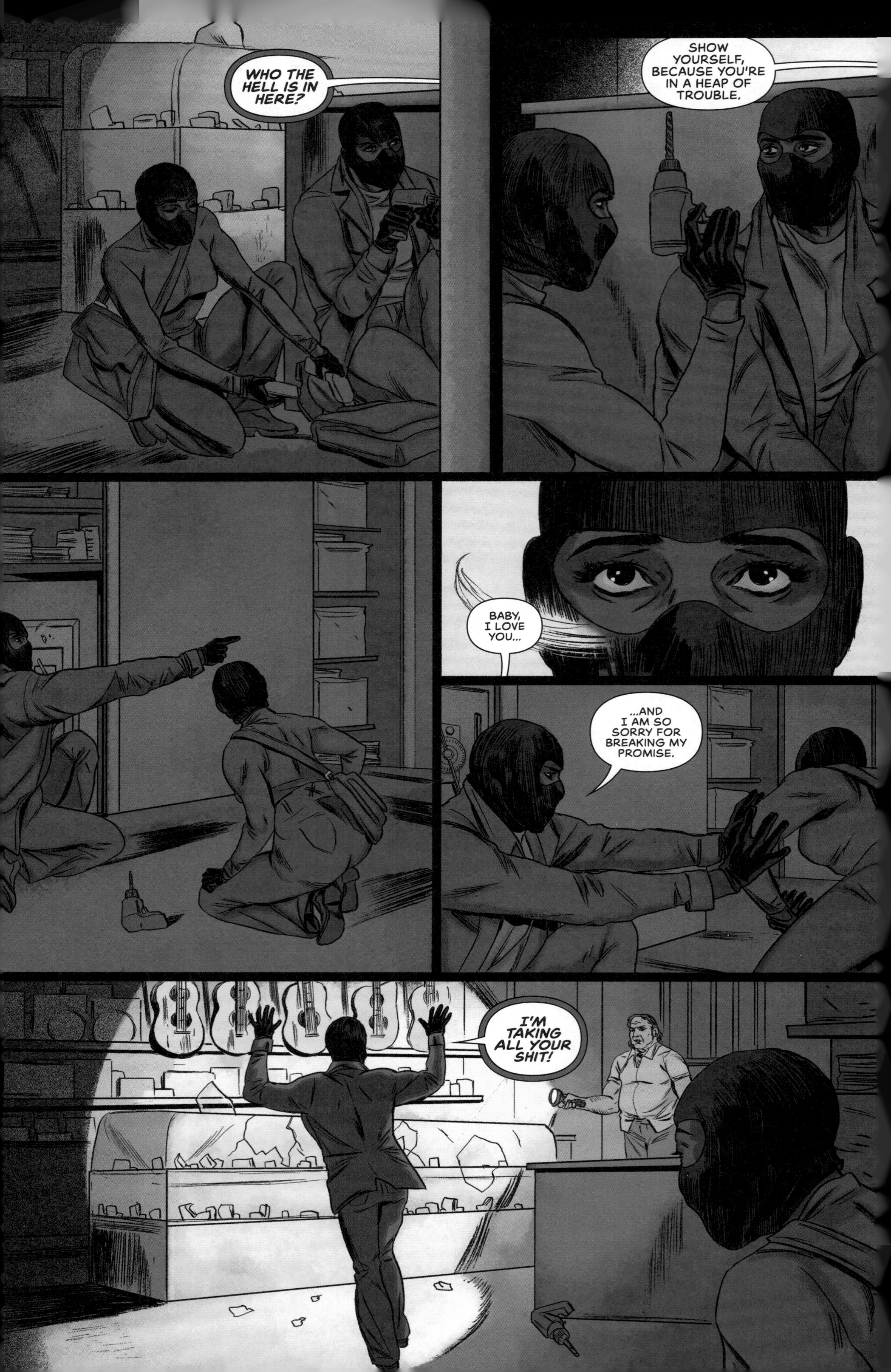
WHO THE HELL IS IN HERE?
SHOW YOURSELF, BECAUSE YOU'RE IN A HEAP OF TROUBLE.
BABY, I LOVE YOU...
...AND I AM SO SORRY FOR BREAKING MY PROMISE.
I'M TAKING ALL YOUR SHIT!

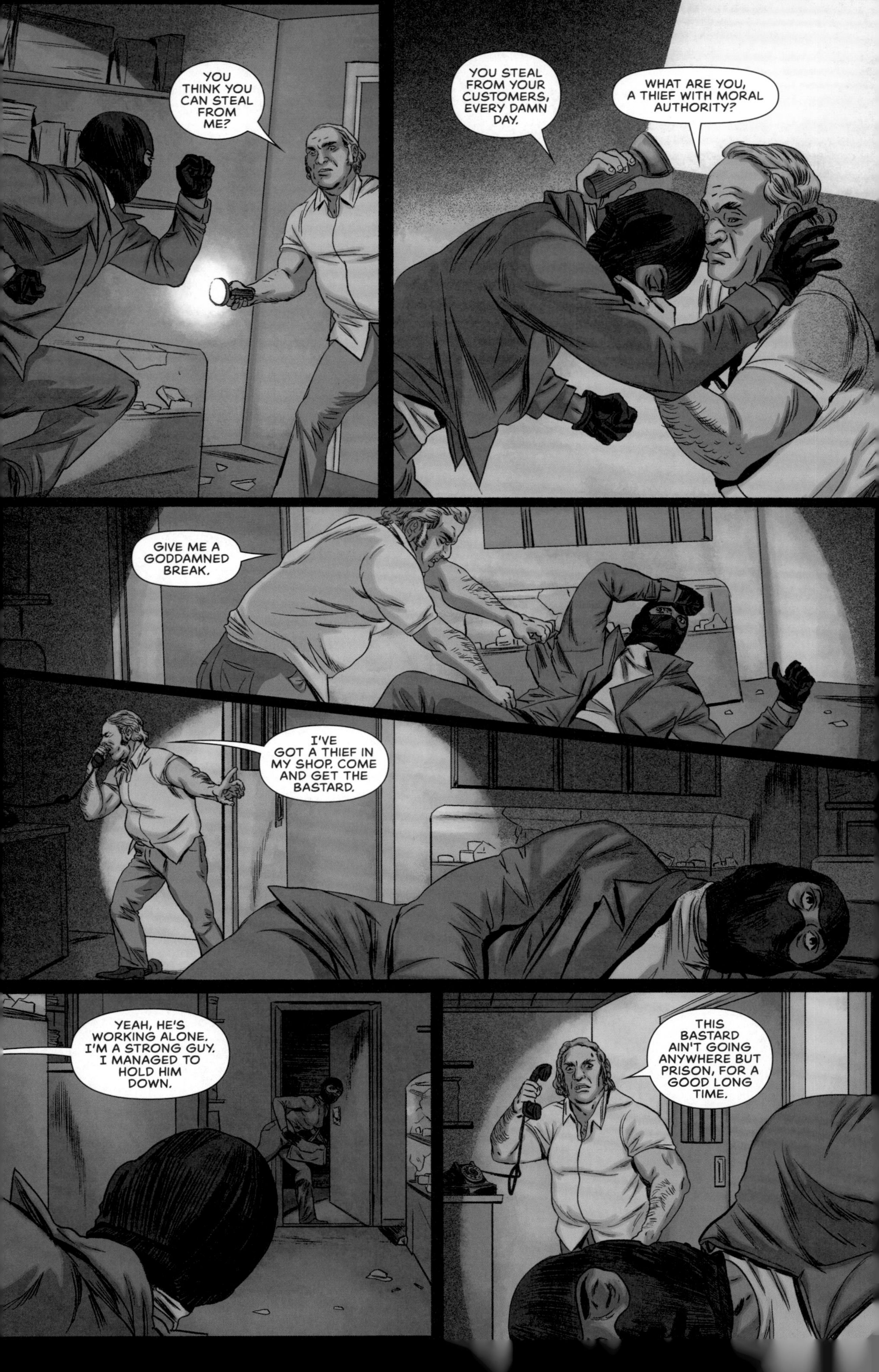
YOU THINK YOU CAN STEAL FROM ME?
YOU STEAL FROM YOUR CUSTOMERS, EVERY DAMN DAY.
WHAT ARE YOU, A THIEF WITH MORAL AUTHORITY?
GIVE ME A GODDAMNED BREAK.
I'VE GOT A THIEF IN MY SHOP. COME AND GET THE BASTARD.
YEAH, HE'S WORKING ALONE. I'M A STRONG GUY. I MANAGED TO HOLD HIM DOWN.
THIS BASTARD AIN'T GOING ANYWHERE BUT PRISON, FOR A GOOD LONG TIME.

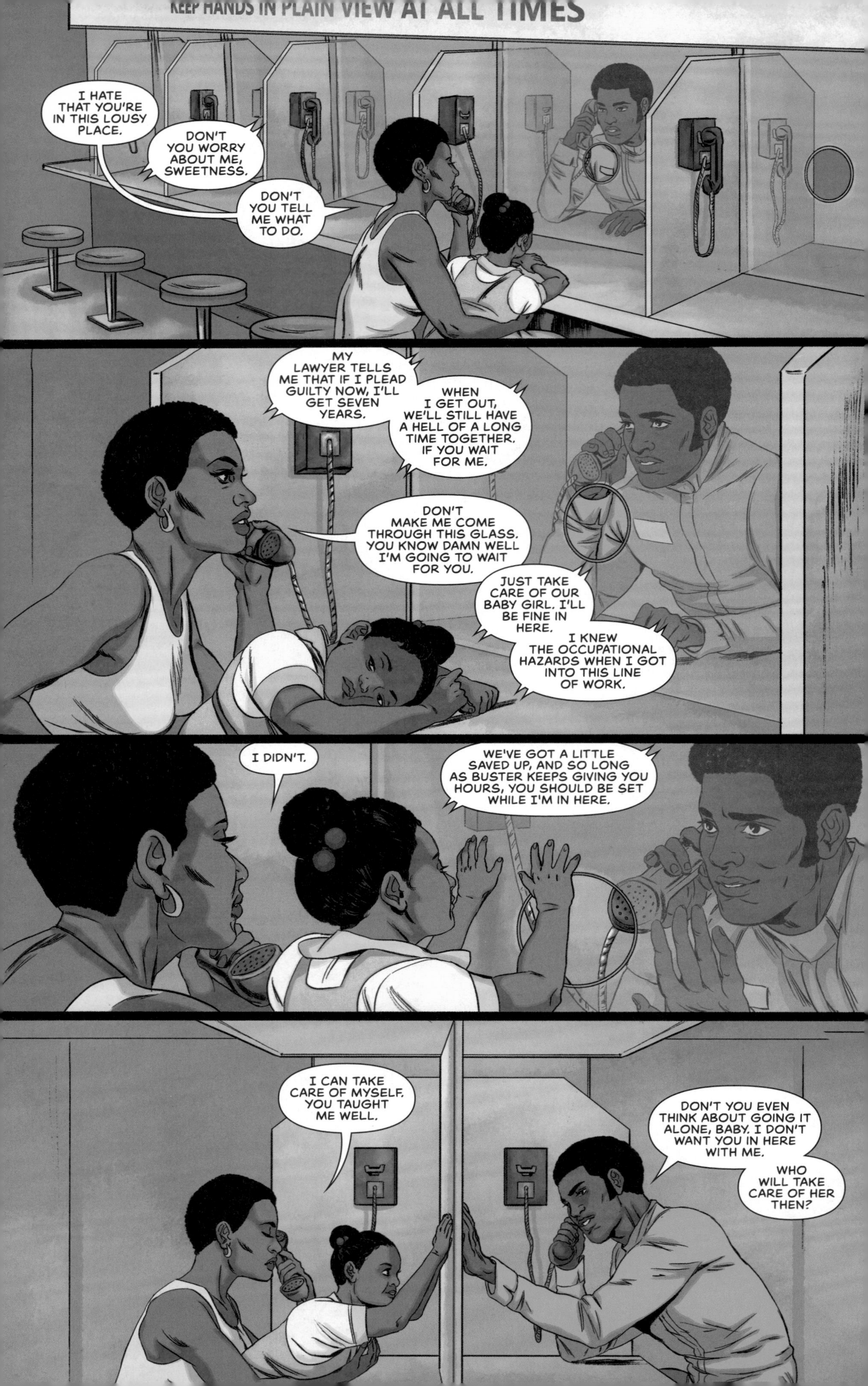
KEEP HANDS IN PLAIN VIEW AT ALL TIMES
I HATE THAT YOU'RE IN THIS LOUSY PLACE.
DON'T YOU WORRY ABOUT ME, SWEETNESS.
DON'T YOU TELL ME WHAT TO DO.
MY LAWYER TELLS ME THAT IF I PLEAD GUILTY NOW, I'LL GET SEVEN YEARS.
WHEN I GET OUT, WE'LL STILL HAVE A HELL OF A LONG TIME TOGETHER. IF YOU WAIT FOR ME.
DON'T MAKE ME COME THROUGH THIS GLASS. YOU KNOW DAMN WELL I'M GOING TO WAIT FOR YOU.
JUST TAKE CARE OF OUR BABY GIRL. I'LL BE FINE IN HERE.
I KNEW THE OCCUPATIONAL HAZARDS WHEN I GOT INTO THIS LINE OF WORK.
I DIDN'T.
WE'VE GOT A LITTLE SAVED UP, AND SO LONG AS BUSTER KEEPS GIVING YOU HOURS, YOU SHOULD BE SET WHILE I'M IN HERE.
I CAN TAKE CARE OF MYSELF. YOU TAUGHT ME WELL.
DON'T YOU EVEN THINK ABOUT GOING IT ALONE, BABY. I DON'T WANT YOU IN HERE WITH ME.
WHO WILL TAKE CARE OF HER THEN?

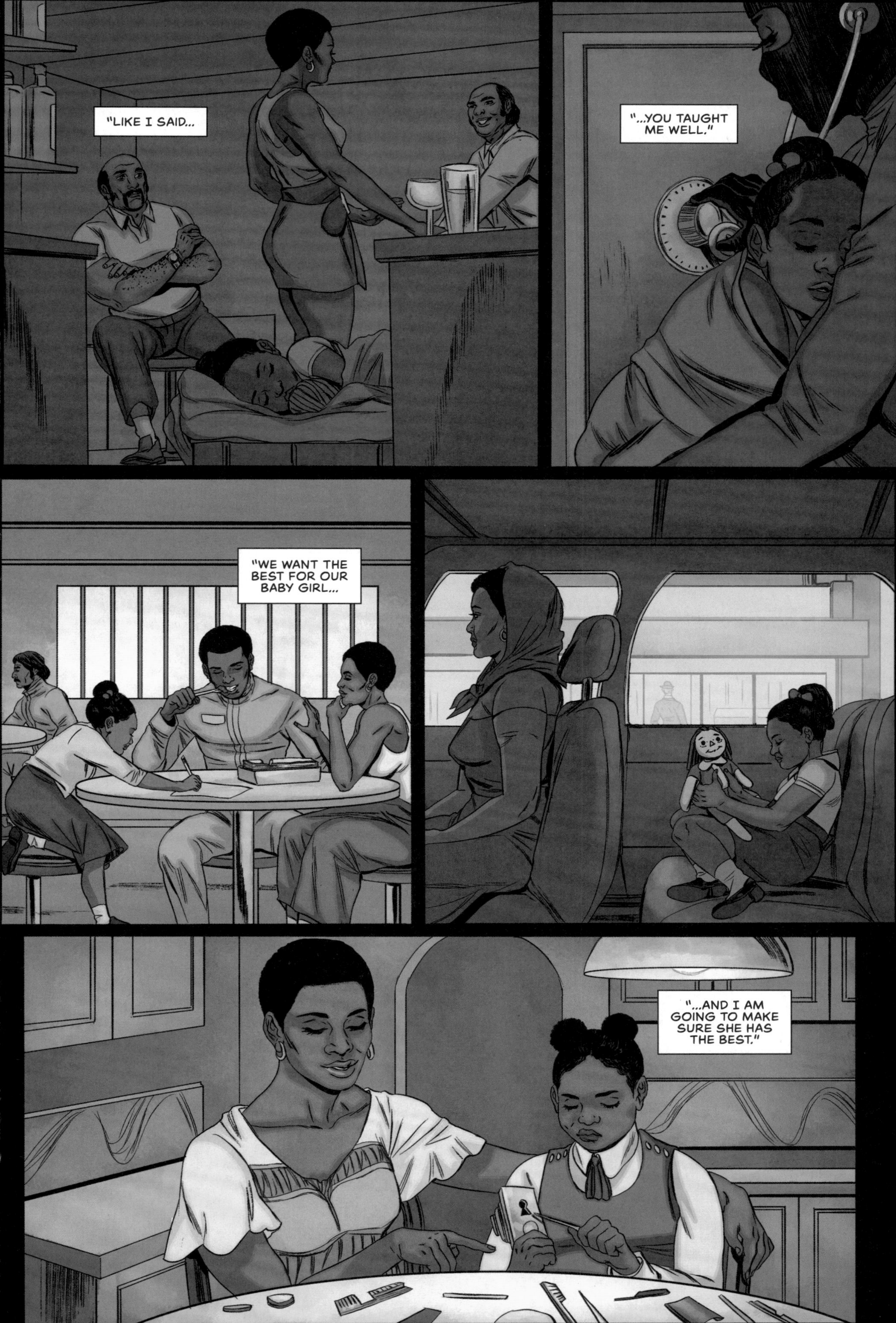
"LIKE I SAID...
"...YOU TAUGHT ME WELL."
"WE WANT THE BEST FOR OUR BABY GIRL...
"...AND I AM GOING TO MAKE SURE SHE HAS THE BEST."

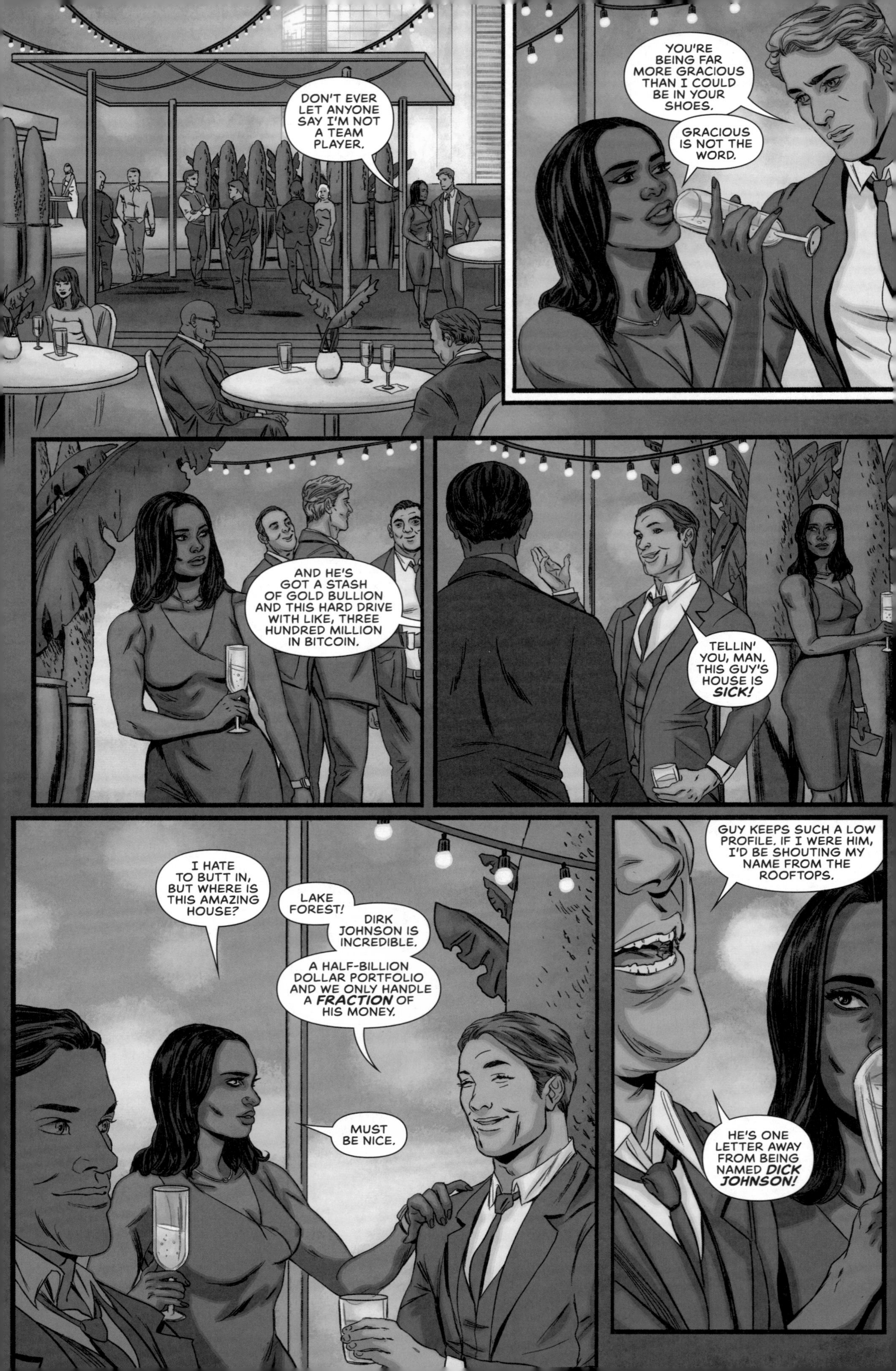
DON'T EVER LET ANYONE SAY I'M NOT A TEAM PLAYER.
YOU'RE BEING FAR MORE GRACIOUS THAN I COULD BE IN YOUR SHOES.
GRACIOUS IS NOT THE WORD.
AND HE'S GOT A STASH OF GOLD BULLION AND THIS HARD DRIVE WITH LIKE, THREE HUNDRED MILLION IN BITCOIN.
TELLIN' YOU, MAN. THIS GUY'S HOUSE IS SICK!
I HATE TO BUTT IN, BUT WHERE IS THIS AMAZING HOUSE?
LAKE FOREST!
DIRK JOHNSON IS INCREDIBLE.
A HALF-BILLION DOLLAR PORTFOLIO AND WE ONLY HANDLE A FRACTION OF HIS MONEY.
MUST BE NICE.
GUY KEEPS SUCH A LOW PROFILE. IF I WERE HIM, I'D BE SHOUTING MY NAME FROM THE ROOFTOPS.
HE'S ONE LETTER AWAY FROM BEING NAMED DICK JOHNSON!

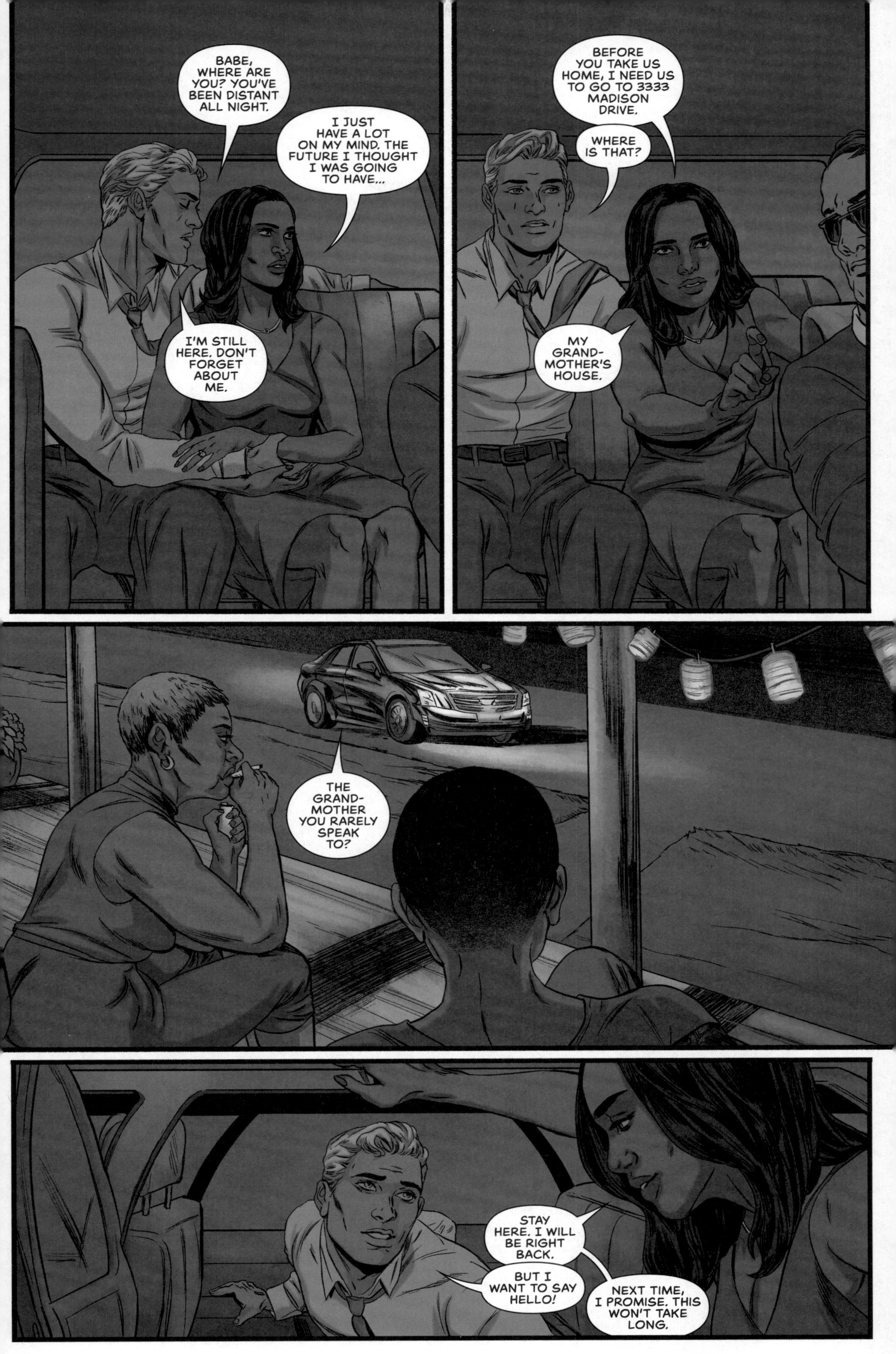
BABE, WHERE ARE YOU? YOU'VE BEEN DISTANT ALL NIGHT.
I JUST HAVE A LOT ON MY MIND. THE FUTURE I THOUGHT I WAS GOING TO HAVE...
I'M STILL HERE. DON'T FORGET ABOUT ME.
BEFORE YOU TAKE US HOME, I NEED US TO GO TO 3333 MADISON DRIVE.
WHERE IS THAT?
MY GRAND-MOTHER'S HOUSE.
THE GRAND-MOTHER YOU RARELY SPEAK TO?
STAY HERE. I WILL BE RIGHT BACK.
BUT I WANT TO SAY HELLO!
NEXT TIME, I PROMISE. THIS WON'T TAKE LONG.

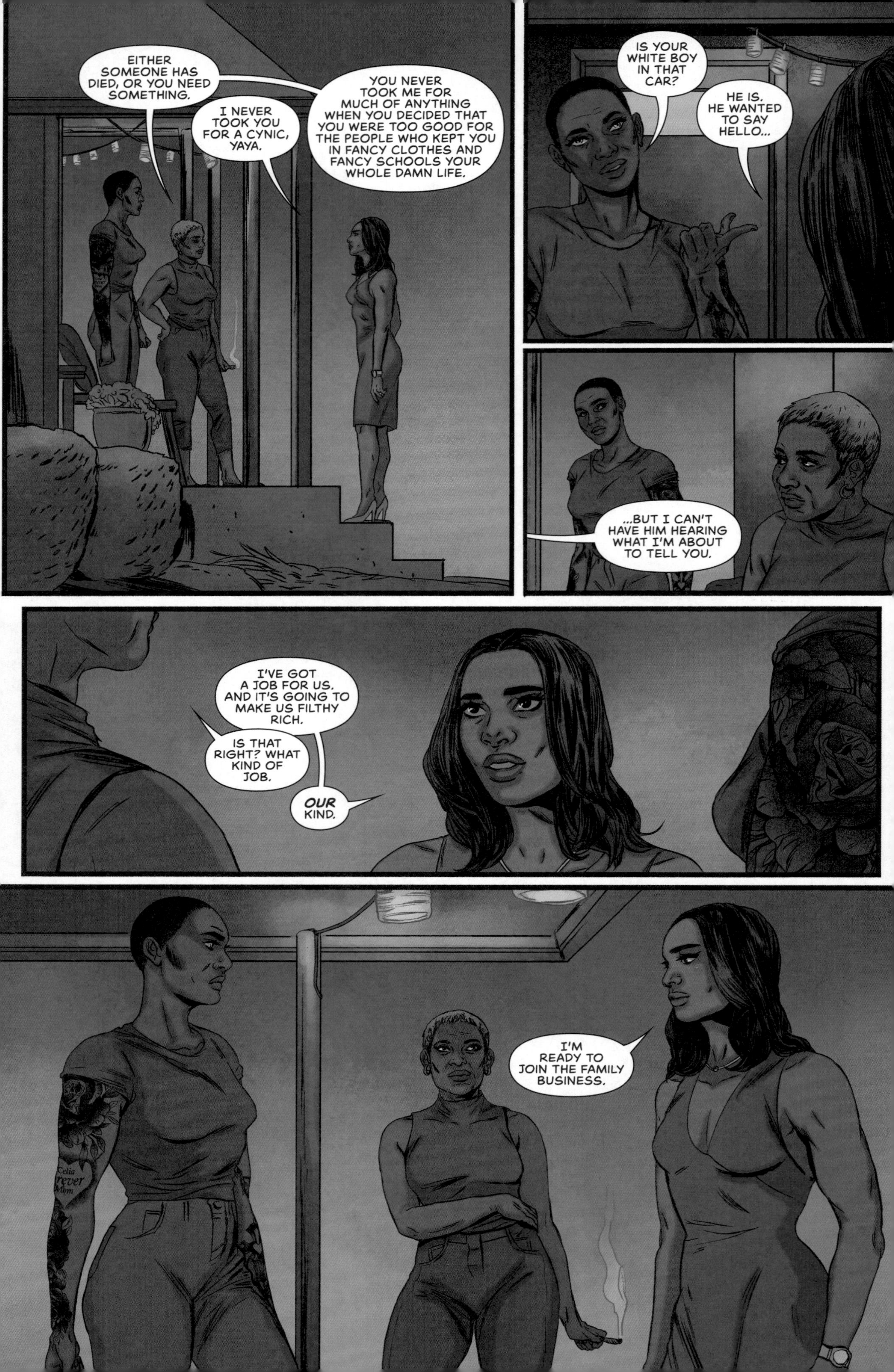
EITHER SOMEONE HAS DIED, OR YOU NEED SOMETHING.
I NEVER TOOK YOU FOR A CYNIC, YAYA.
YOU NEVER TOOK ME FOR MUCH OF ANYTHING WHEN YOU DECIDED THAT YOU WERE TOO GOOD FOR THE PEOPLE WHO KEPT YOU IN FANCY CLOTHES AND FANCY SCHOOLS YOUR WHOLE DAMN LIFE.
IS YOUR WHITE BOY IN THAT CAR?
HE IS. HE WANTED TO SAY HELLO...
...BUT I CAN'T HAVE HIM HEARING WHAT I'M ABOUT TO TELL YOU.
I'VE GOT A JOB FOR US. AND IT'S GOING TO MAKE US FILTHY RICH.
IS THAT RIGHT? WHAT KIND OF JOB.
OUR KIND.
I'M READY TO JOIN THE FAMILY BUSINESS.

CHAPTER 2

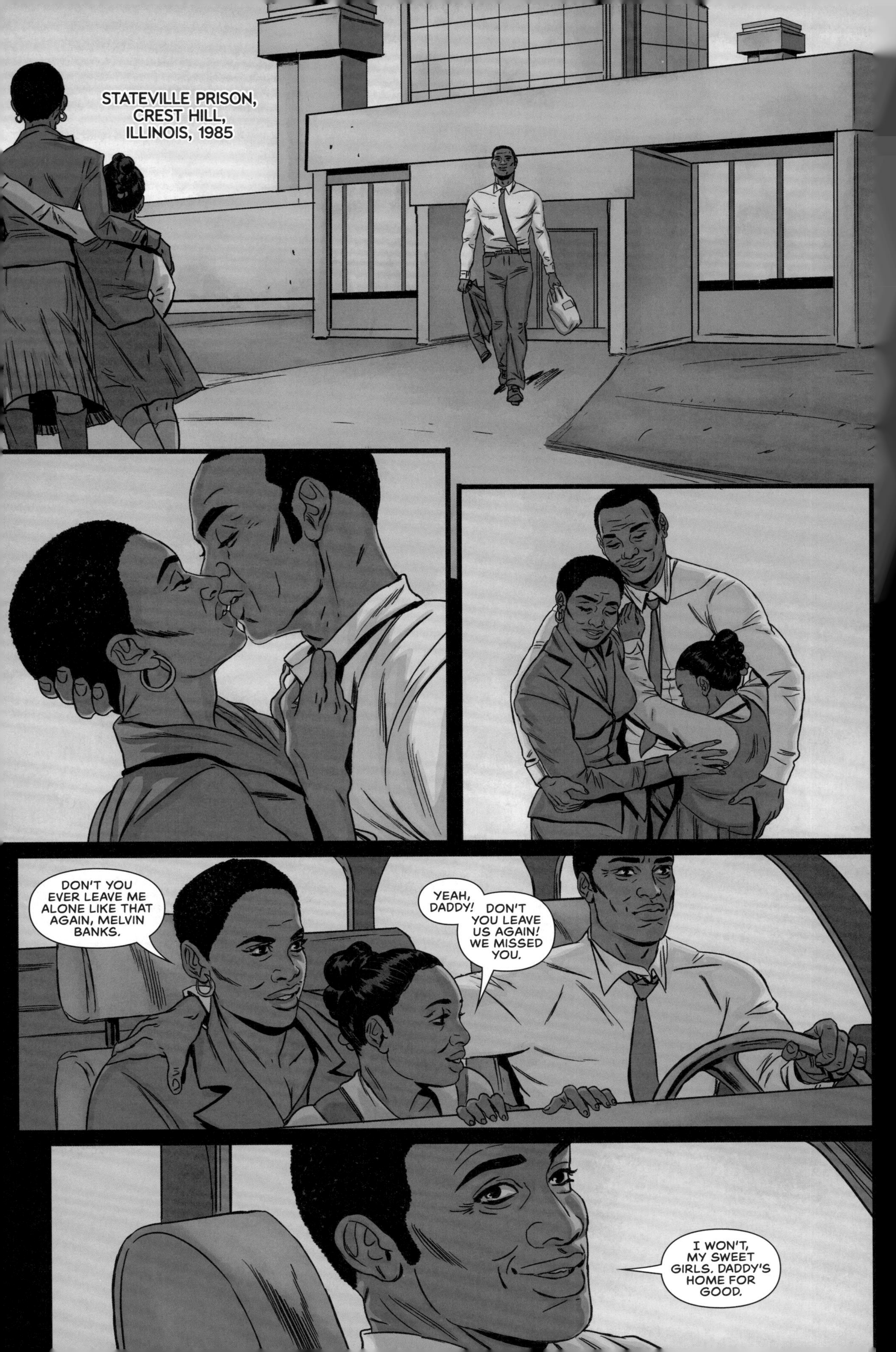
STATEVILLE PRISON, CREST HILL, ILLINOIS, 1985
DON'T YOU EVER LEAVE ME ALONE LIKE THAT AGAIN, MELVIN BANKS.
YEAH, DADDY!
DON'T YOU LEAVE US AGAIN! WE MISSED YOU.
I WON'T, MY SWEET GIRLS. DADDY'S HOME FOR GOOD.

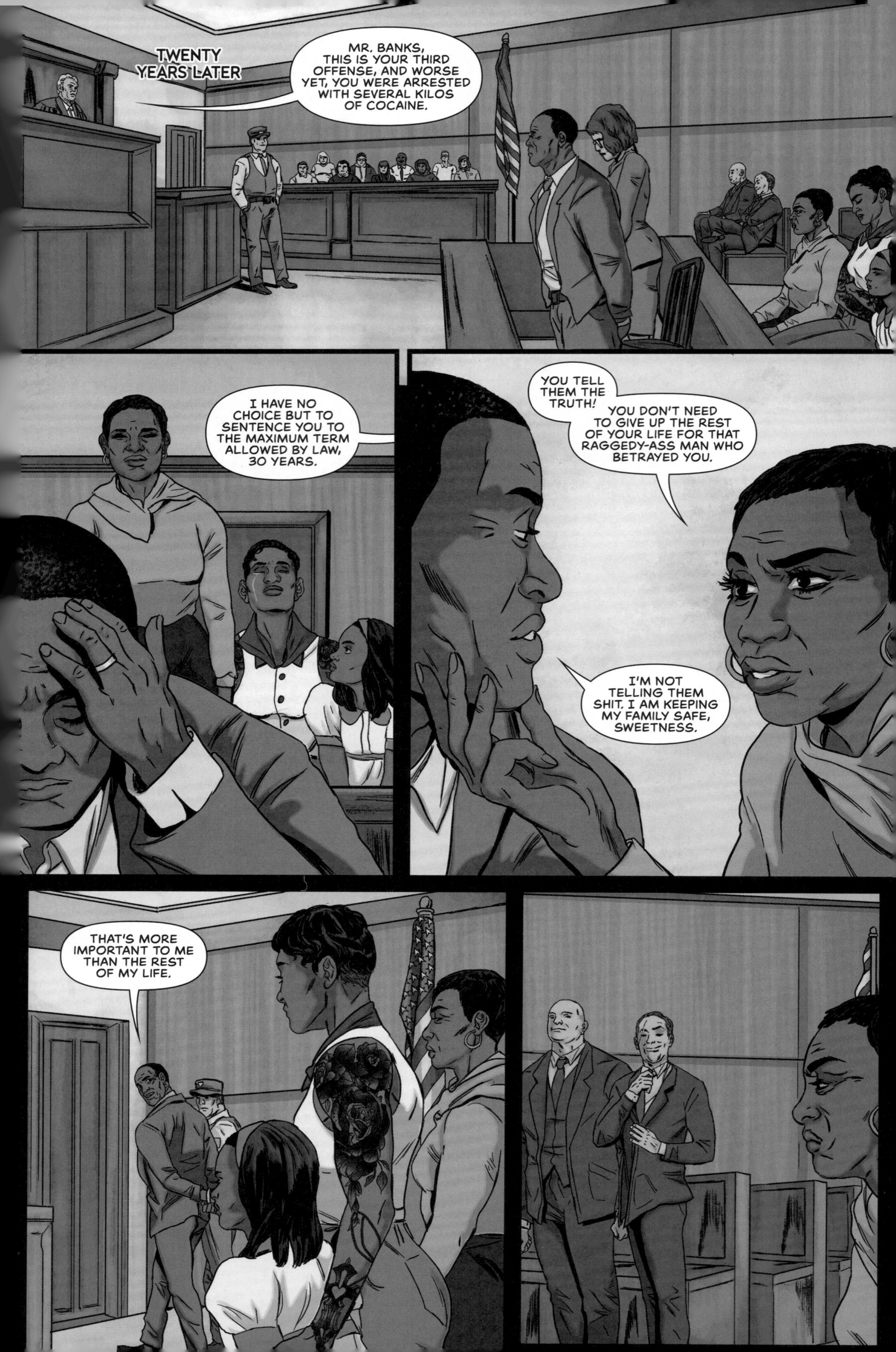
TWENTY YEARS LATER
MR. BANKS, THIS IS YOUR THIRD OFFENSE, AND WORSE YET, YOU WERE ARRESTED WITH SEVERAL KILOS OF COCAINE.
I HAVE NO CHOICE BUT TO SENTENCE YOU TO THE MAXIMUM TERM ALLOWED BY LAW, 30 YEARS.
YOU TELL THEM THE TRUTH!
YOU DON'T NEED TO GIVE UP THE REST OF YOUR LIFE FOR THAT RAGGEDY-ASS MAN WHO BETRAYED YOU.
I'M NOT TELLING THEM SHIT. I AM KEEPING MY FAMILY SAFE, SWEETNESS.
THAT'S MORE IMPORTANT TO ME THAN THE REST OF MY LIFE.

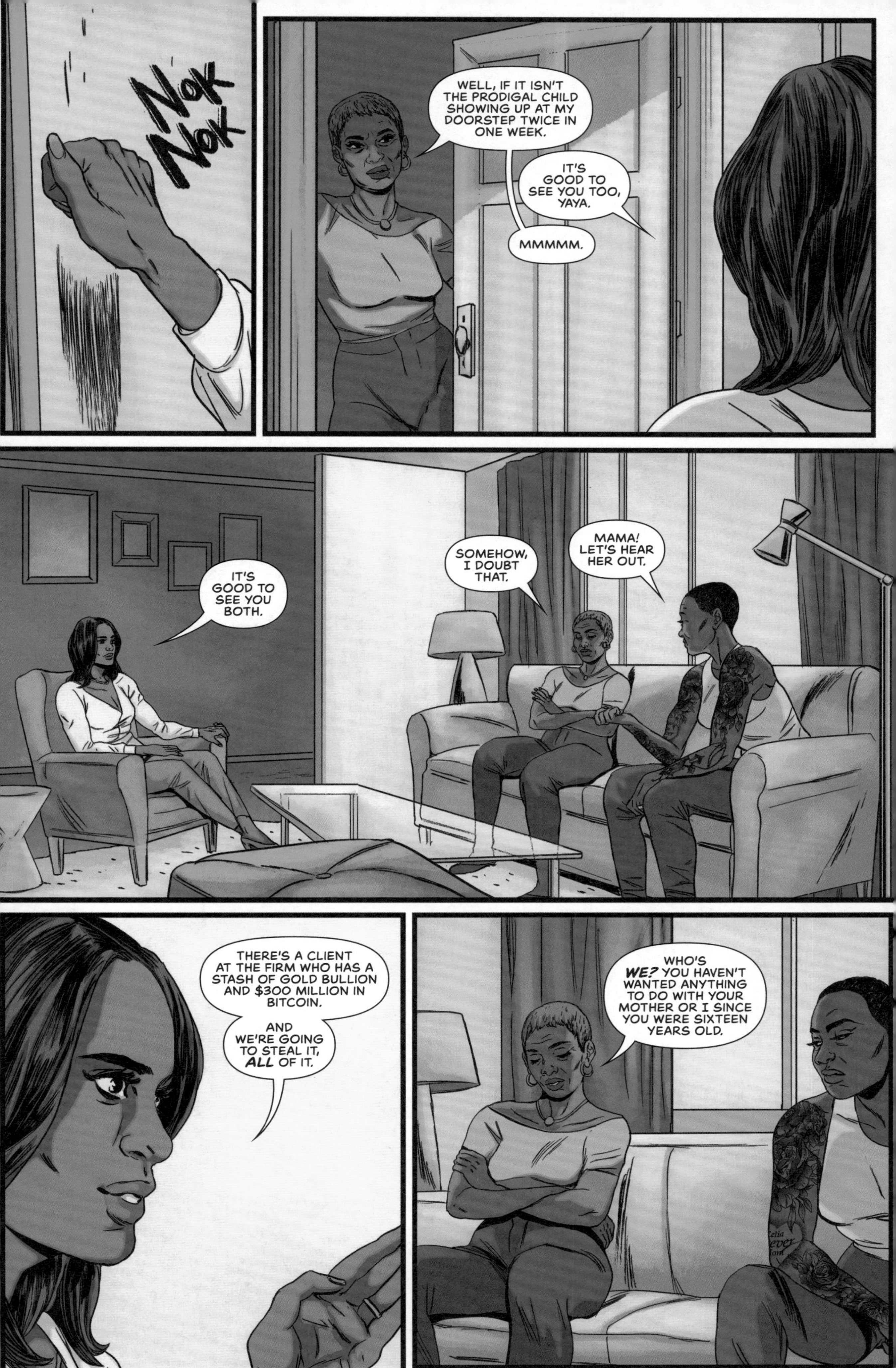
NOK NOK
WELL, IF IT ISN'T THE PRODIGAL CHILD SHOWING UP AT MY DOORSTEP TWICE IN ONE WEEK.
IT'S GOOD TO SEE YOU TOO, YAYA.
MMMMM.
IT'S GOOD TO SEE YOU BOTH.
SOMEHOW, I DOUBT THAT.
MAMA! LET'S HEAR HER OUT.
THERE'S A CLIENT AT THE FIRM WHO HAS A STASH OF GOLD BULLION AND $300 MILLION IN BITCOIN.
AND WE'RE GOING TO STEAL IT, ALL OF IT.
WHO'S WE? YOU HAVEN'T WANTED ANYTHING TO DO WITH YOUR MOTHER OR I SINCE YOU WERE SIXTEEN YEARS OLD.

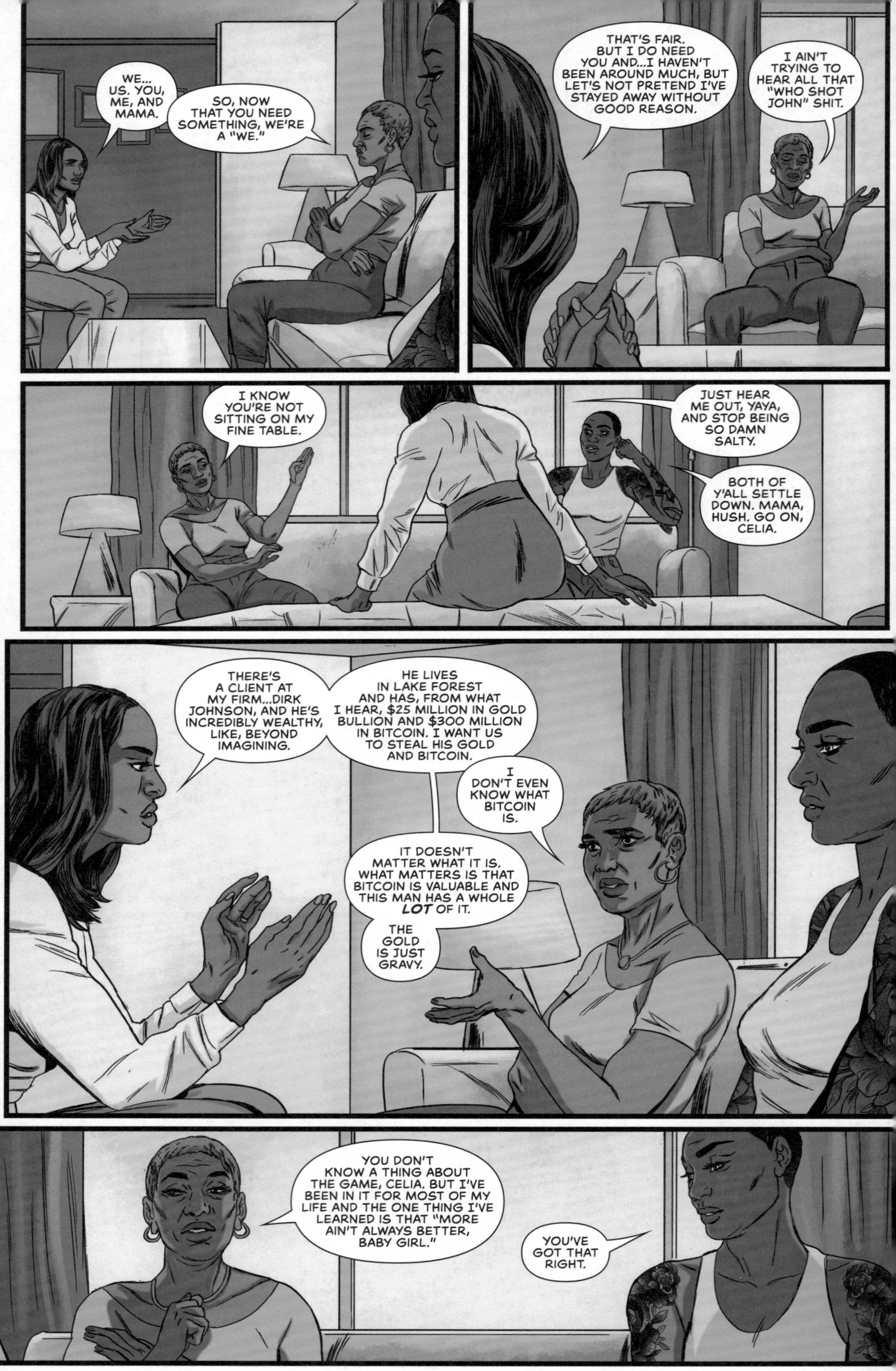
WE... US. YOU, ME, AND MAMA.
SO, NOW THAT YOU NEED SOMETHING, WE'RE A "WE."
THAT'S FAIR. BUT I DO NEED YOU AND...I HAVEN'T BEEN AROUND MUCH, BUT LET'S NOT PRETEND I'VE STAYED AWAY WITHOUT GOOD REASON.
I AIN'T TRYING TO HEAR ALL THAT "WHO SHOT JOHN" SHIT.
I KNOW YOU'RE NOT SITTING ON MY FINE TABLE.
JUST HEAR ME OUT, YAYA, AND STOP BEING SO DAMN SALTY.
BOTH OF Y'ALL SETTLE DOWN. MAMA, HUSH. GO ON, CELIA.
THERE'S A CLIENT AT MY FIRM...DIRK JOHNSON, AND HE'S INCREDIBLY WEALTHY, LIKE, BEYOND IMAGINING.
HE LIVES IN LAKE FOREST AND HAS, FROM WHAT I HEAR, $25 MILLION IN GOLD BULLION AND $300 MILLION IN BITCOIN. I WANT US TO STEAL HIS GOLD AND BITCOIN.
I DON'T EVEN KNOW WHAT BITCOIN IS.
IT DOESN'T MATTER WHAT IT IS. WHAT MATTERS IS THAT BITCOIN IS VALUABLE AND THIS MAN HAS A WHOLE LOT OF IT.
THE GOLD IS JUST GRAVY.
YOU DON'T KNOW A THING ABOUT THE GAME, CELIA, BUT I'VE BEEN IN IT FOR MOST OF MY LIFE AND THE ONE THING I'VE LEARNED IS THAT "MORE AIN'T ALWAYS BETTER, BABY GIRL."
YOU'VE GOT THAT RIGHT.

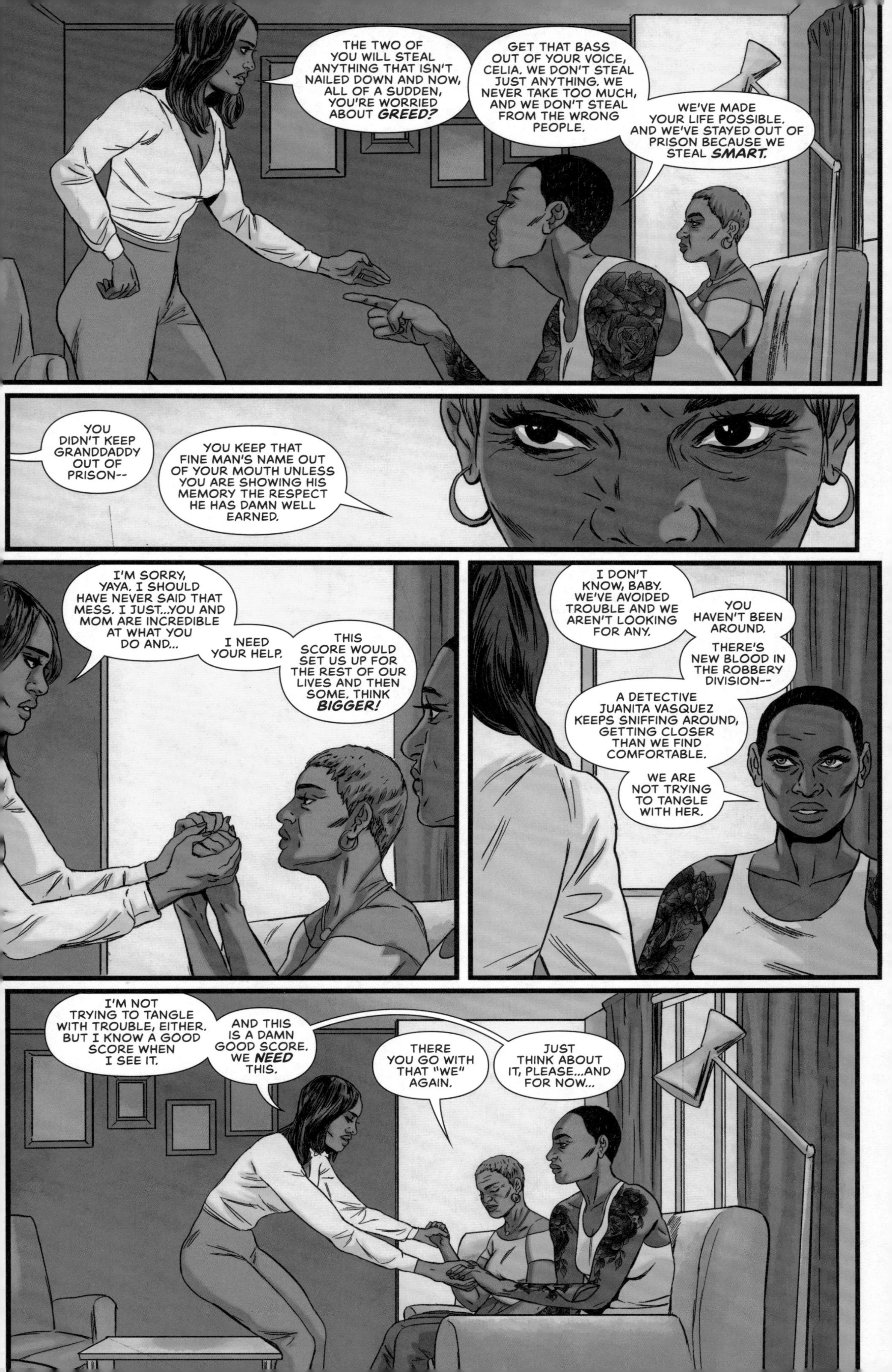
THE TWO OF YOU WILL STEAL ANYTHING THAT ISN'T NAILED DOWN AND NOW, ALL OF A SUDDEN, YOU'RE WORRIED ABOUT **GREED?**
GET THAT BASS OUT OF YOUR VOICE, CELIA. WE DON'T STEAL JUST ANYTHING. WE NEVER TAKE TOO MUCH, AND WE DON'T STEAL FROM THE WRONG PEOPLE.
WE'VE MADE YOUR LIFE POSSIBLE. AND WE'VE STAYED OUT OF PRISON BECAUSE WE STEAL **SMART.**
YOU DIDN'T KEEP GRANDDADDY OUT OF PRISON--
YOU KEEP THAT FINE MAN'S NAME OUT OF YOUR MOUTH UNLESS YOU ARE SHOWING HIS MEMORY THE RESPECT HE HAS DAMN WELL EARNED.
I'M SORRY, YAYA. I SHOULD HAVE NEVER SAID THAT MESS. I JUST...YOU AND MOM ARE INCREDIBLE AT WHAT YOU DO AND...
I NEED YOUR HELP.
THIS SCORE WOULD SET US UP FOR THE REST OF OUR LIVES AND THEN SOME. THINK **BIGGER!**
I DON'T KNOW, BABY. WE'VE AVOIDED TROUBLE AND WE AREN'T LOOKING FOR ANY.
YOU HAVEN'T BEEN AROUND.
THERE'S NEW BLOOD IN THE ROBBERY DIVISION--
A DETECTIVE JUANITA VASQUEZ KEEPS SNIFFING AROUND, GETTING CLOSER THAN WE FIND COMFORTABLE.
WE ARE NOT TRYING TO TANGLE WITH HER.
I'M NOT TRYING TO TANGLE WITH TROUBLE, EITHER. BUT I KNOW A GOOD SCORE WHEN I SEE IT.
AND THIS IS A DAMN GOOD SCORE. WE **NEED** THIS.
THERE YOU GO WITH THAT "WE" AGAIN.
JUST THINK ABOUT IT, PLEASE...AND FOR NOW...

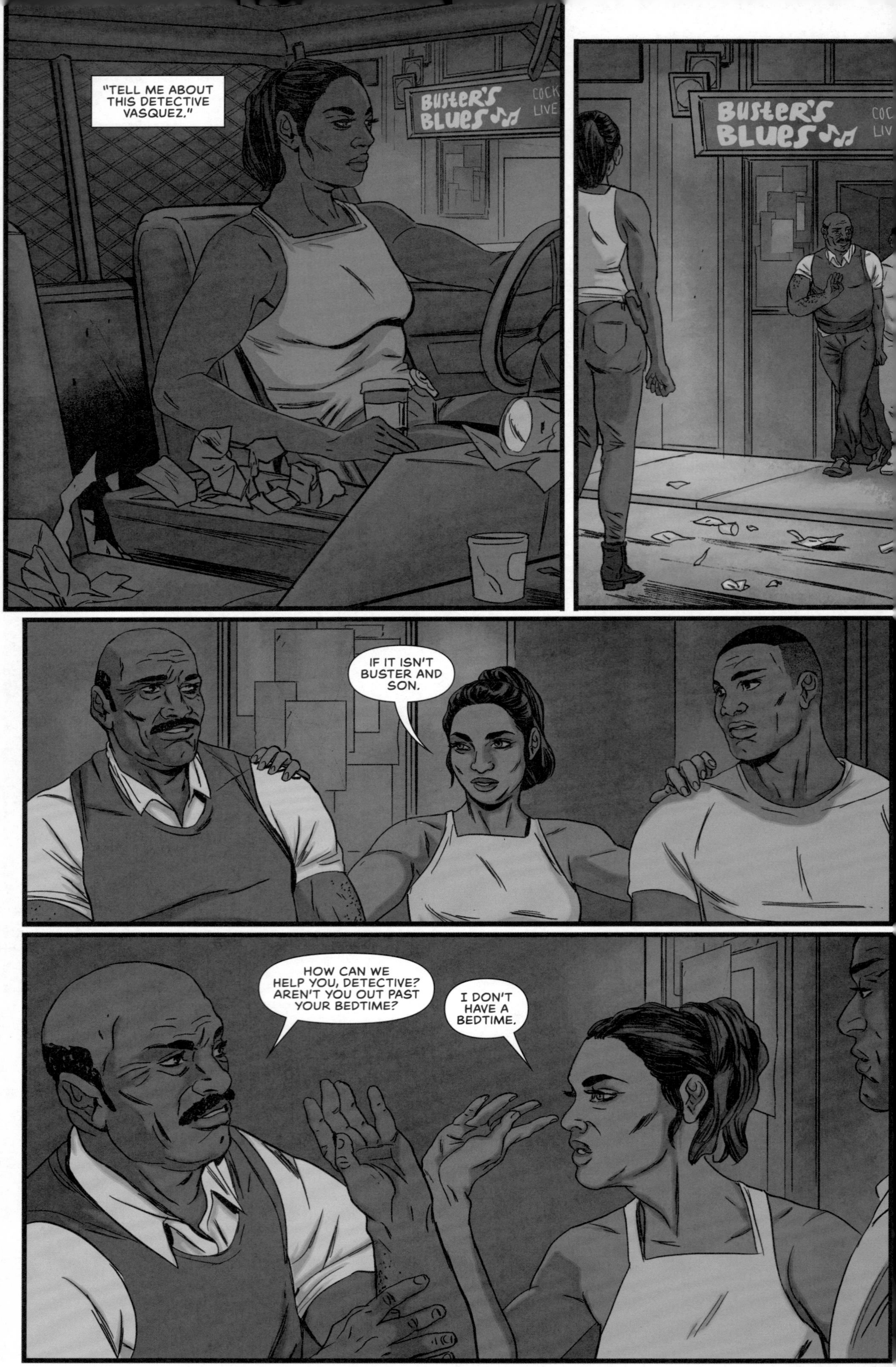
"TELL ME ABOUT THIS DETECTIVE VASQUEZ."
BUSTER'S BLUES
COCK
LIVE
BUSTER'S BLUES
COC
LIV
IF IT ISN'T BUSTER AND SON.
HOW CAN WE HELP YOU, DETECTIVE? AREN'T YOU OUT PAST YOUR BEDTIME?
I DON'T HAVE A BEDTIME.

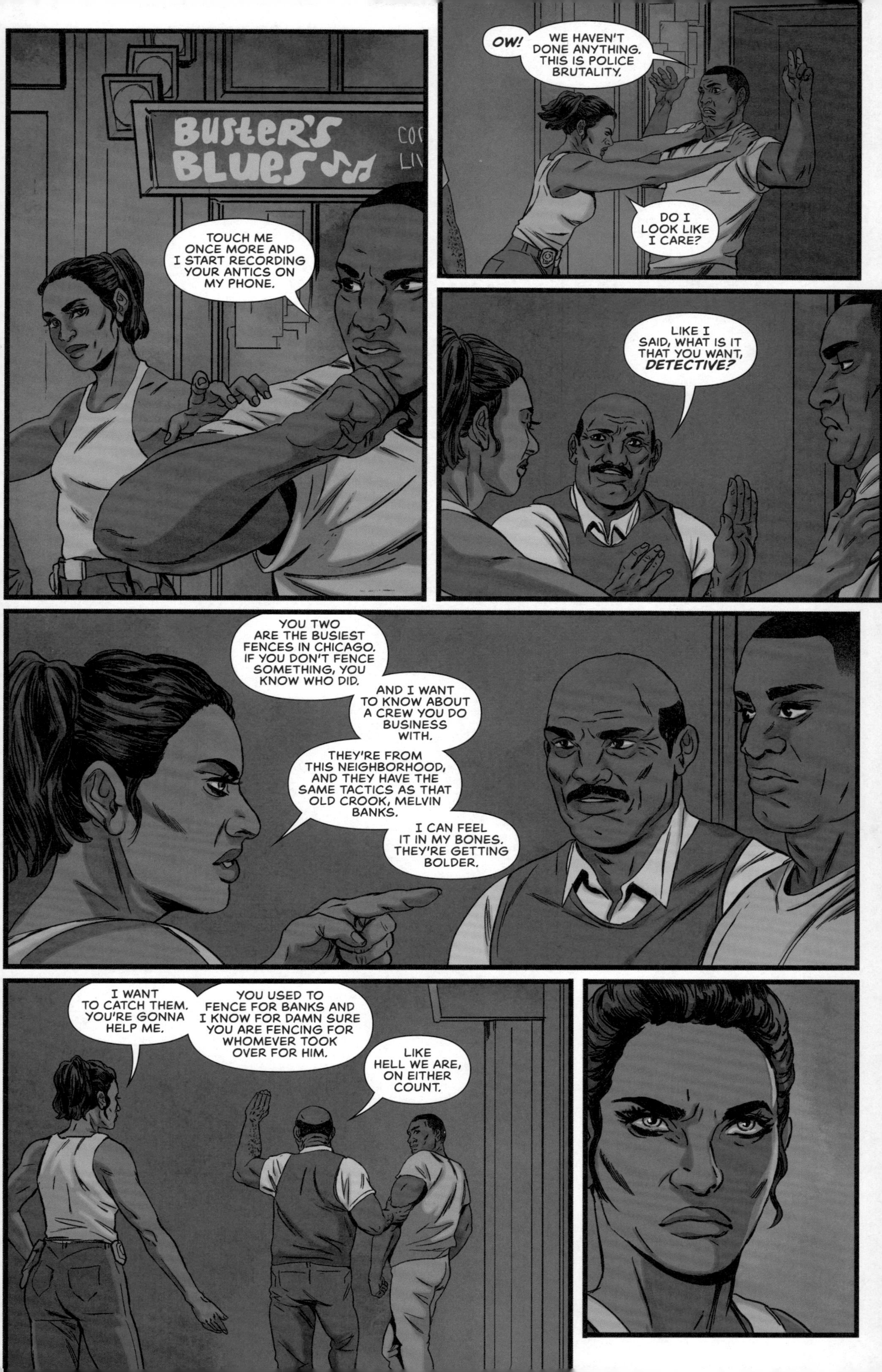
BUSTER'S BLUES
TOUCH ME ONCE MORE AND I START RECORDING YOUR ANTICS ON MY PHONE.
OW!
WE HAVEN'T DONE ANYTHING. THIS IS POLICE BRUTALITY.
DO I LOOK LIKE I CARE?
LIKE I SAID, WHAT IS IT THAT YOU WANT, *DETECTIVE?*
YOU TWO ARE THE BUSIEST FENCES IN CHICAGO. IF YOU DON'T FENCE SOMETHING, YOU KNOW WHO DID.
AND I WANT TO KNOW ABOUT A CREW YOU DO BUSINESS WITH.
THEY'RE FROM THIS NEIGHBORHOOD, AND THEY HAVE THE SAME TACTICS AS THAT OLD CROOK, MELVIN BANKS.
I CAN FEEL IT IN MY BONES. THEY'RE GETTING BOLDER.
I WANT TO CATCH THEM. YOU'RE GONNA HELP ME.
YOU USED TO FENCE FOR BANKS AND I KNOW FOR DAMN SURE YOU ARE FENCING FOR WHOMEVER TOOK OVER FOR HIM.
LIKE HELL WE ARE, ON EITHER COUNT.

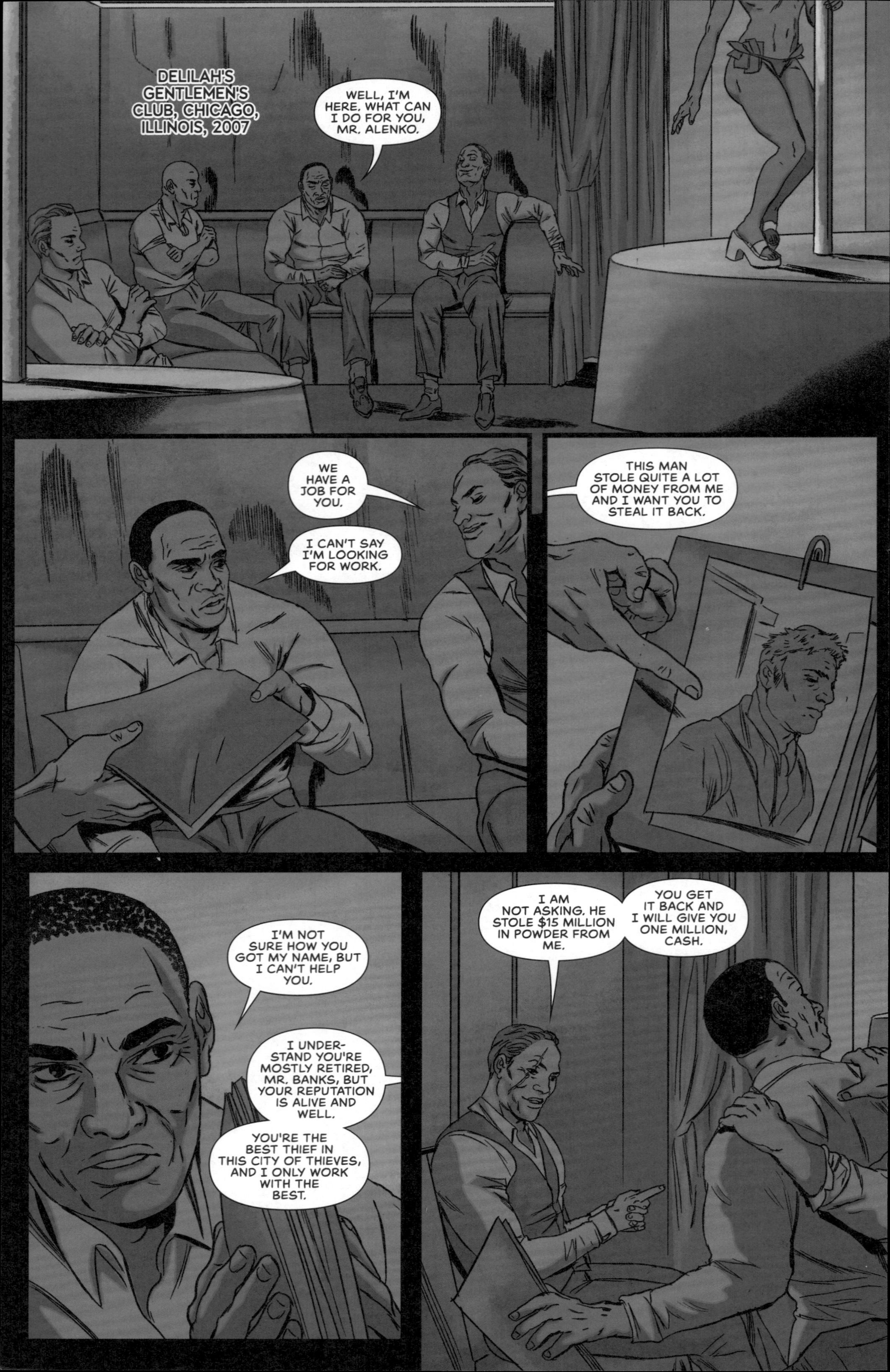
DELILAH'S GENTLEMEN'S CLUB, CHICAGO, ILLINOIS, 2007
WELL, I'M HERE. WHAT CAN I DO FOR YOU, MR. ALENKO.
WE HAVE A JOB FOR YOU.
I CAN'T SAY I'M LOOKING FOR WORK.
THIS MAN STOLE QUITE A LOT OF MONEY FROM ME AND I WANT YOU TO STEAL IT BACK.
I'M NOT SURE HOW YOU GOT MY NAME, BUT I CAN'T HELP YOU.
I UNDER-STAND YOU'RE MOSTLY RETIRED, MR. BANKS, BUT YOUR REPUTATION IS ALIVE AND WELL.
YOU'RE THE BEST THIEF IN THIS CITY OF THIEVES, AND I ONLY WORK WITH THE BEST.
I AM NOT ASKING. HE STOLE $15 MILLION IN POWDER FROM ME.
YOU GET IT BACK AND I WILL GIVE YOU ONE MILLION, CASH.

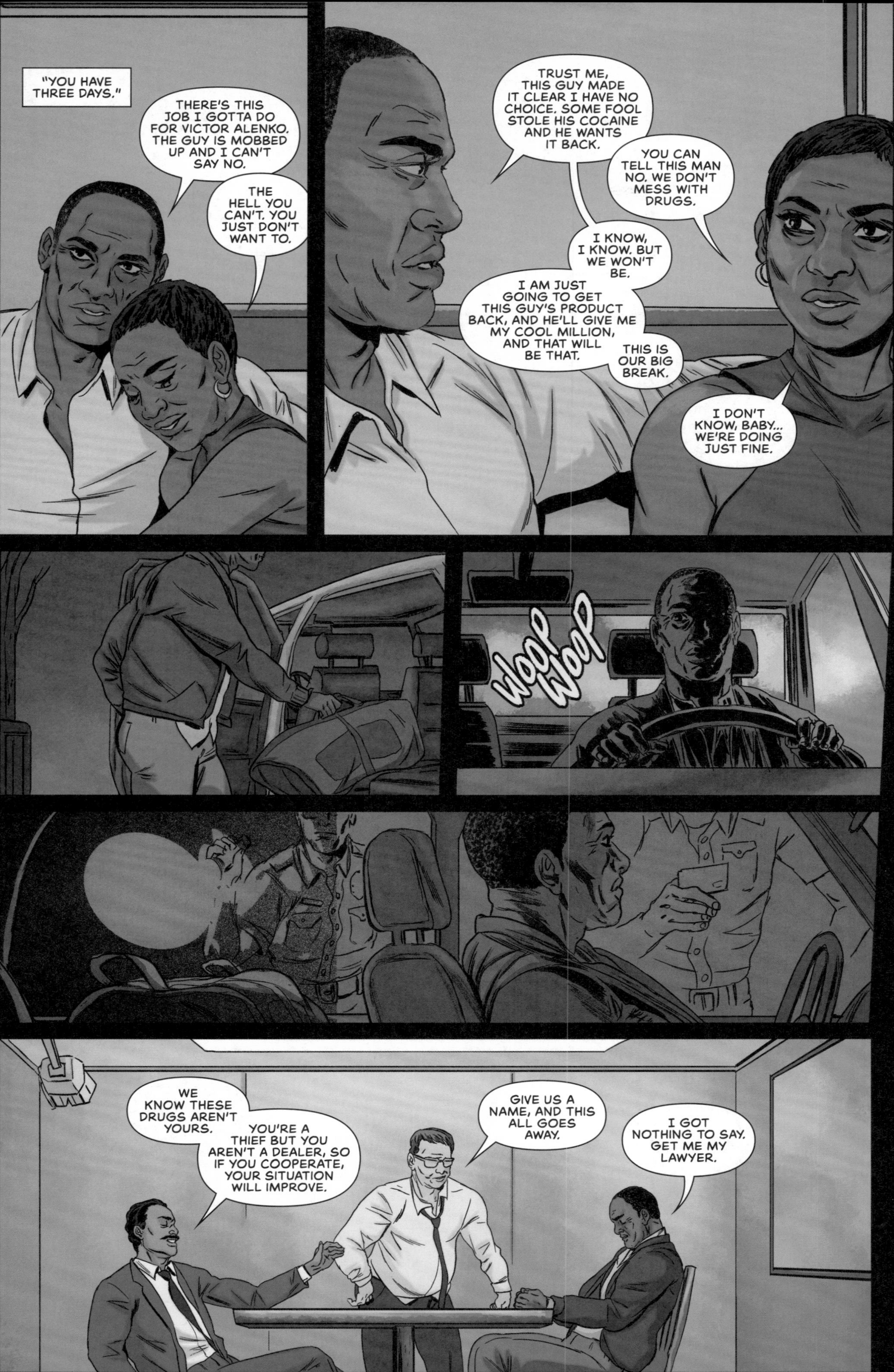
"YOU HAVE THREE DAYS."
THERE'S THIS JOB I GOTTA DO FOR VICTOR ALENKO. THE GUY IS MOBBED UP AND I CAN'T SAY NO.
THE HELL YOU CAN'T. YOU JUST DON'T WANT TO.
TRUST ME, THIS GUY MADE IT CLEAR I HAVE NO CHOICE. SOME FOOL STOLE HIS COCAINE AND HE WANTS IT BACK.
YOU CAN TELL THIS MAN NO. WE DON'T MESS WITH DRUGS.
I KNOW, I KNOW. BUT WE WON'T BE.
I AM JUST GOING TO GET THIS GUY'S PRODUCT BACK, AND HE'LL GIVE ME MY COOL MILLION, AND THAT WILL BE THAT.
THIS IS OUR BIG BREAK.
I DON'T KNOW, BABY... WE'RE DOING JUST FINE.
WOOP WOOP
WE KNOW THESE DRUGS AREN'T YOURS.
YOU'RE A THIEF BUT YOU AREN'T A DEALER, SO IF YOU COOPERATE, YOUR SITUATION WILL IMPROVE.
GIVE US A NAME, AND THIS ALL GOES AWAY.
I GOT NOTHING TO SAY. GET ME MY LAWYER.

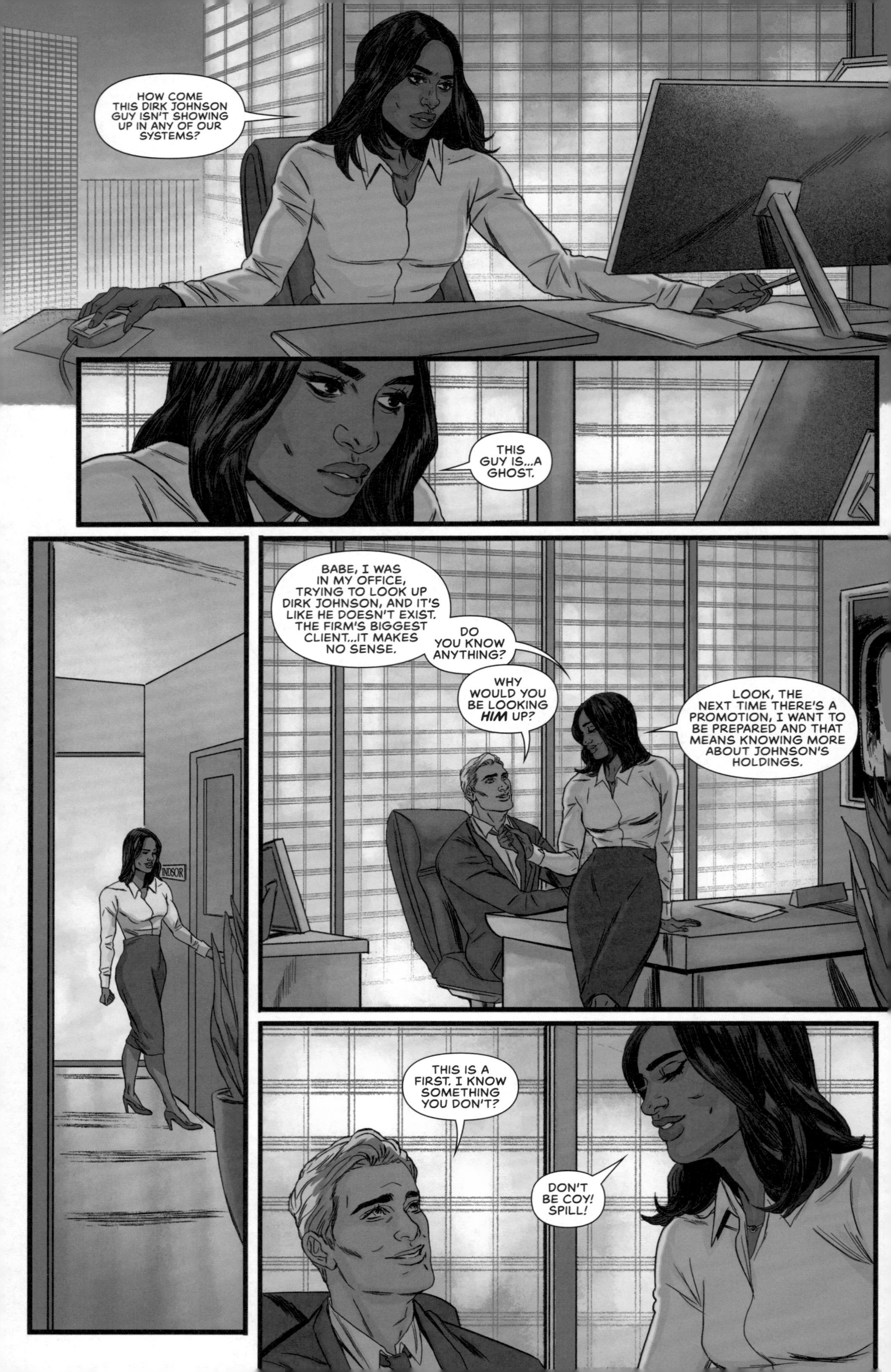
HOW COME THIS DIRK JOHNSON GUY ISN'T SHOWING UP IN ANY OF OUR SYSTEMS?
THIS GUY IS...A GHOST.
INDSOR
BABE, I WAS IN MY OFFICE, TRYING TO LOOK UP DIRK JOHNSON, AND IT'S LIKE HE DOESN'T EXIST. THE FIRM'S BIGGEST CLIENT...IT MAKES NO SENSE.
DO YOU KNOW ANYTHING?
WHY WOULD YOU BE LOOKING *HIM* UP?
LOOK, THE NEXT TIME THERE'S A PROMOTION, I WANT TO BE PREPARED AND THAT MEANS KNOWING MORE ABOUT JOHNSON'S HOLDINGS.
THIS IS A FIRST. I KNOW SOMETHING YOU DON'T?
DON'T BE COY! SPILL!

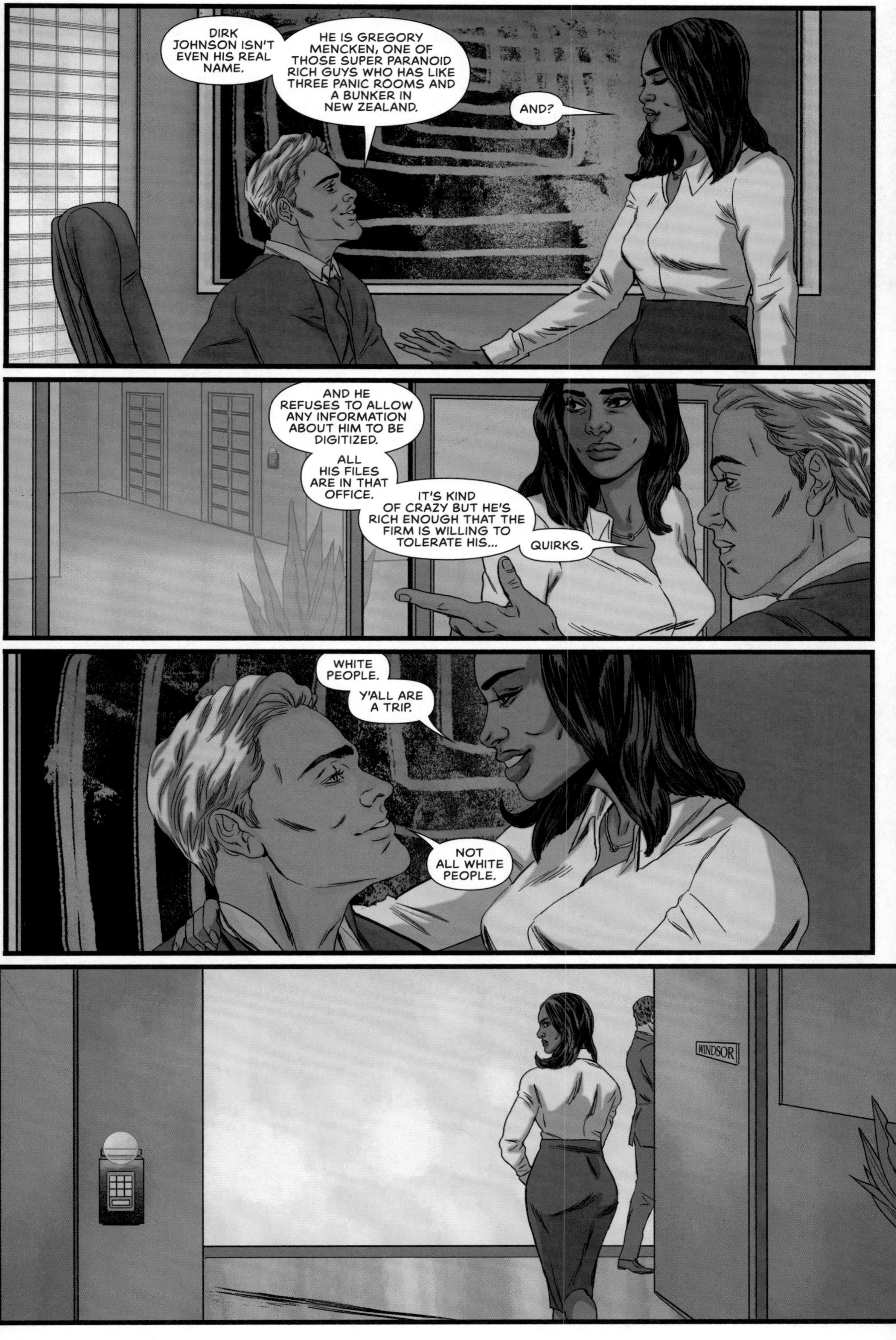
DIRK JOHNSON ISN'T EVEN HIS REAL NAME.
HE IS GREGORY MENCKEN, ONE OF THOSE SUPER PARANOID RICH GUYS WHO HAS LIKE THREE PANIC ROOMS AND A BUNKER IN NEW ZEALAND.
AND?
AND HE REFUSES TO ALLOW ANY INFORMATION ABOUT HIM TO BE DIGITIZED.
ALL HIS FILES ARE IN THAT OFFICE.
IT'S KIND OF CRAZY BUT HE'S RICH ENOUGH THAT THE FIRM IS WILLING TO TOLERATE HIS...
QUIRKS.
WHITE PEOPLE.
Y'ALL ARE A TRIP.
NOT ALL WHITE PEOPLE.
WINDSOR

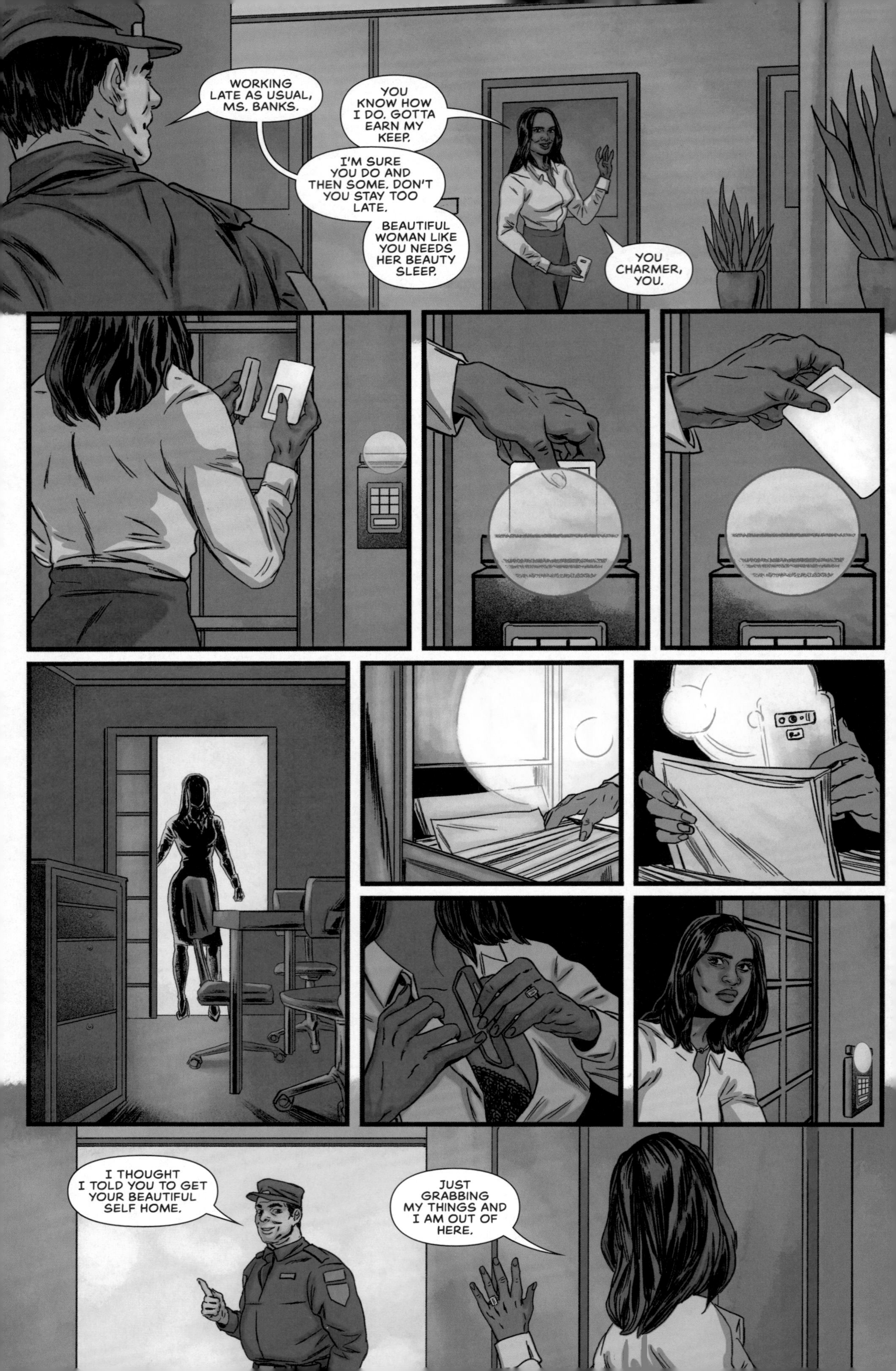
WORKING LATE AS USUAL, MS. BANKS.
YOU KNOW HOW I DO, GOTTA EARN MY KEEP.
I'M SURE YOU DO AND THEN SOME. DON'T YOU STAY TOO LATE.
BEAUTIFUL WOMAN LIKE YOU NEEDS HER BEAUTY SLEEP.
YOU CHARMER, YOU.
I THOUGHT I TOLD YOU TO GET YOUR BEAUTIFUL SELF HOME.
JUST GRABBING MY THINGS AND I AM OUT OF HERE.

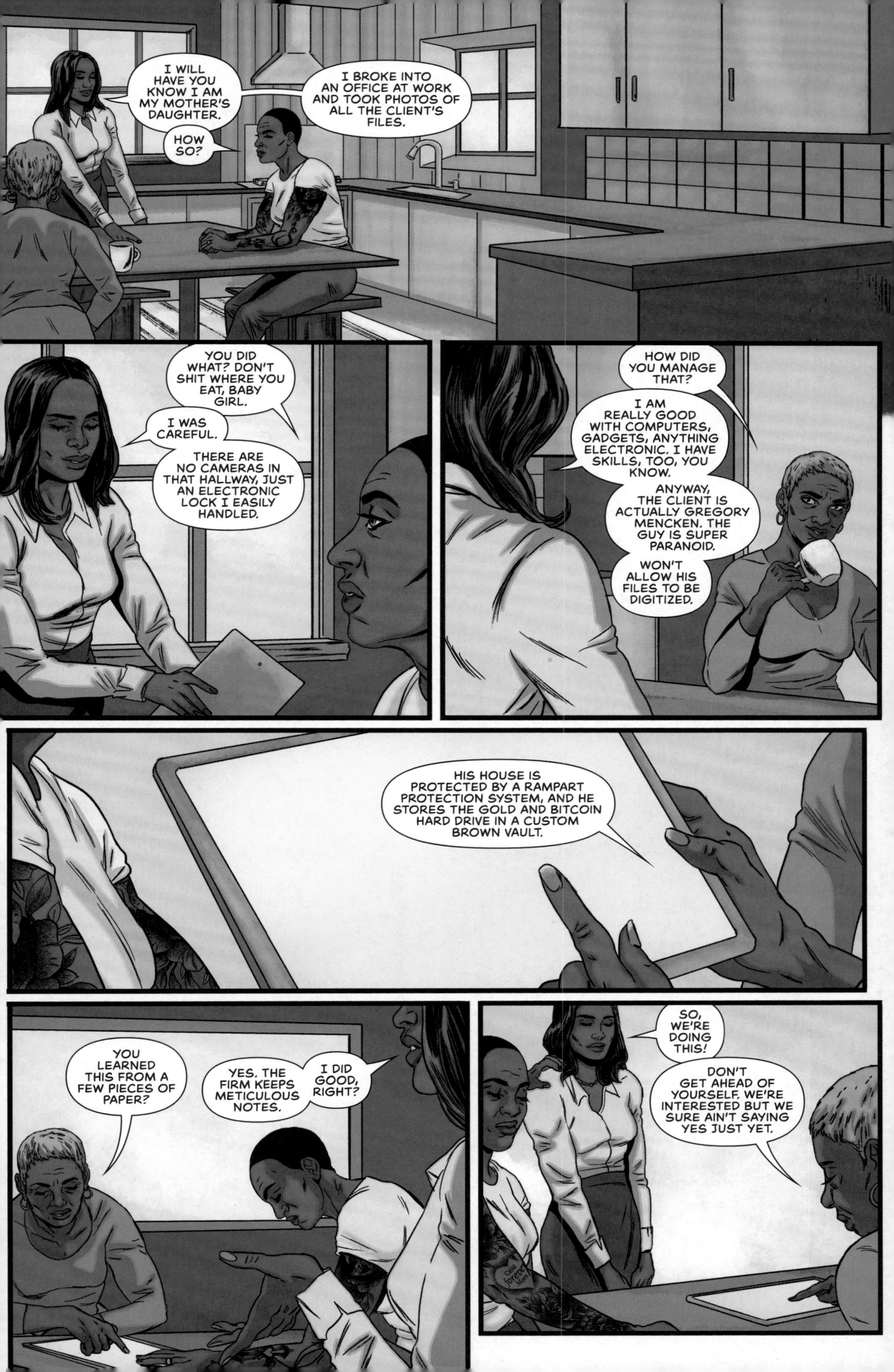
I WILL HAVE YOU KNOW I AM MY MOTHER'S DAUGHTER.
HOW SO?
I BROKE INTO AN OFFICE AT WORK AND TOOK PHOTOS OF ALL THE CLIENT'S FILES.
YOU DID WHAT? DON'T SHIT WHERE YOU EAT, BABY GIRL.
I WAS CAREFUL.
THERE ARE NO CAMERAS IN THAT HALLWAY, JUST AN ELECTRONIC LOCK I EASILY HANDLED.
HOW DID YOU MANAGE THAT?
I AM REALLY GOOD WITH COMPUTERS, GADGETS, ANYTHING ELECTRONIC. I HAVE SKILLS, TOO, YOU KNOW.
ANYWAY, THE CLIENT IS ACTUALLY GREGORY MENCKEN. THE GUY IS SUPER PARANOID.
WON'T ALLOW HIS FILES TO BE DIGITIZED.
HIS HOUSE IS PROTECTED BY A RAMPART PROTECTION SYSTEM, AND HE STORES THE GOLD AND BITCOIN HARD DRIVE IN A CUSTOM BROWN VAULT.
YOU LEARNED THIS FROM A FEW PIECES OF PAPER?
YES. THE FIRM KEEPS METICULOUS NOTES.
I DID GOOD, RIGHT?
SO, WE'RE DOING THIS!
DON'T GET AHEAD OF YOURSELF. WE'RE INTERESTED BUT WE SURE AIN'T SAYING YES JUST YET.

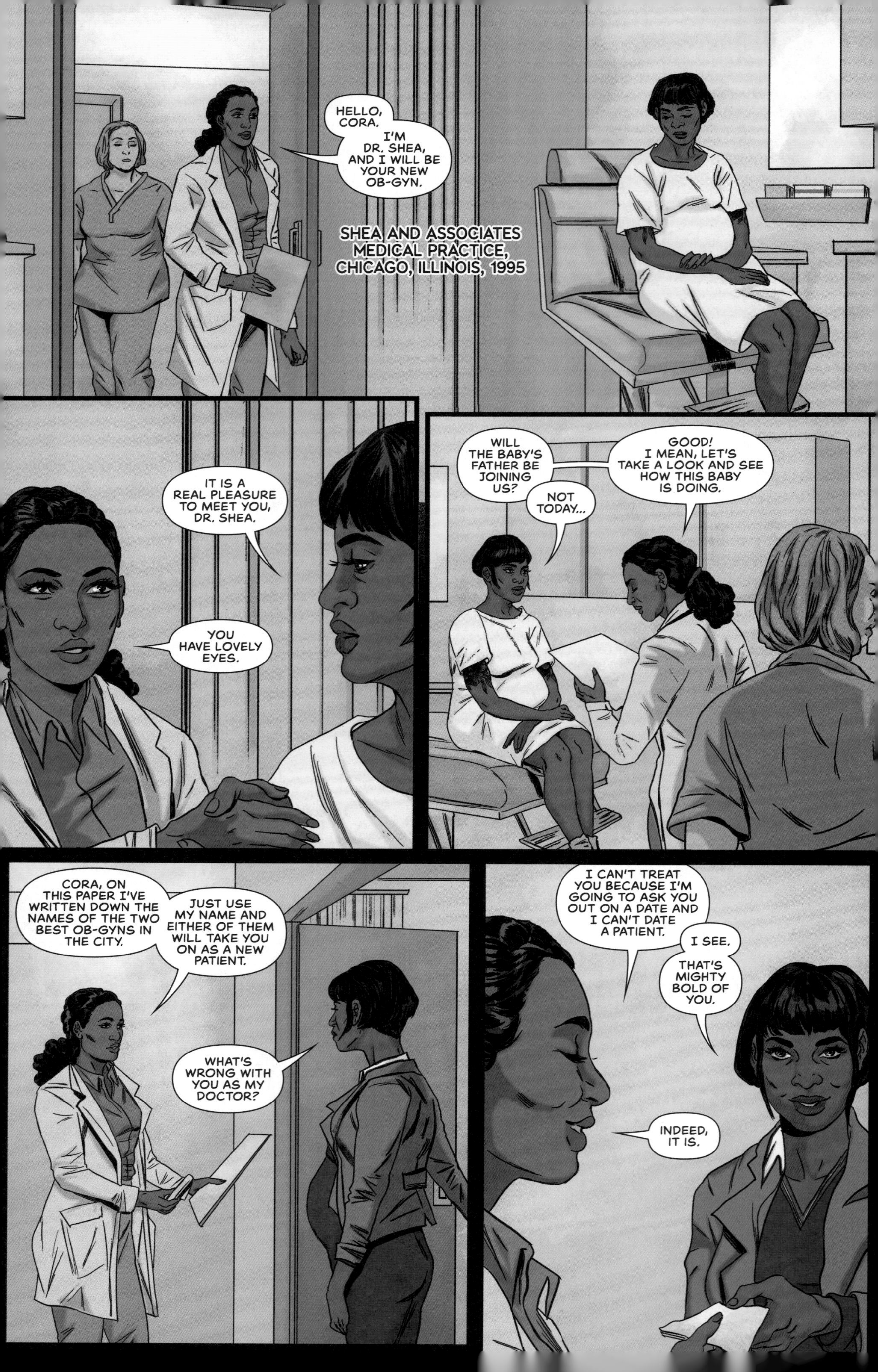
HELLO, CORA.
I'M DR. SHEA, AND I WILL BE YOUR NEW OB-GYN.
SHEA AND ASSOCIATES MEDICAL PRACTICE, CHICAGO, ILLINOIS, 1995
IT IS A REAL PLEASURE TO MEET YOU, DR. SHEA.
YOU HAVE LOVELY EYES.
WILL THE BABY'S FATHER BE JOINING US?
NOT TODAY...
GOOD! I MEAN, LET'S TAKE A LOOK AND SEE HOW THIS BABY IS DOING.
CORA, ON THIS PAPER I'VE WRITTEN DOWN THE NAMES OF THE TWO BEST OB-GYNS IN THE CITY.
JUST USE MY NAME AND EITHER OF THEM WILL TAKE YOU ON AS A NEW PATIENT.
WHAT'S WRONG WITH YOU AS MY DOCTOR?
I CAN'T TREAT YOU BECAUSE I'M GOING TO ASK YOU OUT ON A DATE AND I CAN'T DATE A PATIENT.
I SEE.
THAT'S MIGHTY BOLD OF YOU.
INDEED, IT IS.

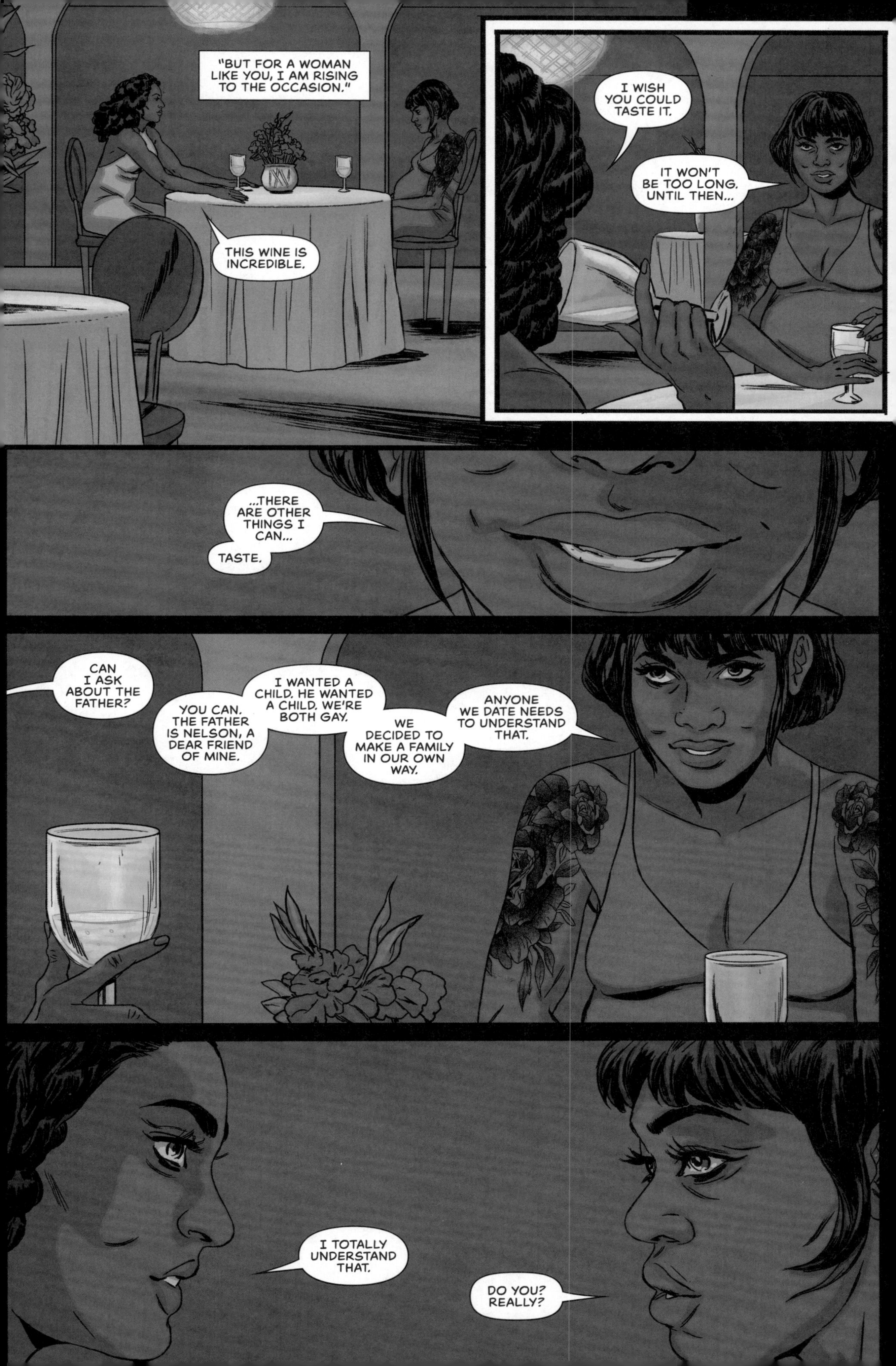
"BUT FOR A WOMAN LIKE YOU, I AM RISING TO THE OCCASION."
THIS WINE IS INCREDIBLE.
I WISH YOU COULD TASTE IT.
IT WON'T BE TOO LONG. UNTIL THEN...
...THERE ARE OTHER THINGS I CAN...
TASTE.
CAN I ASK ABOUT THE FATHER?
YOU CAN. THE FATHER IS NELSON, A DEAR FRIEND OF MINE.
I WANTED A CHILD. HE WANTED A CHILD. WE'RE BOTH GAY.
WE DECIDED TO MAKE A FAMILY IN OUR OWN WAY.
ANYONE WE DATE NEEDS TO UNDERSTAND THAT.
I TOTALLY UNDERSTAND THAT.
DO YOU? REALLY?

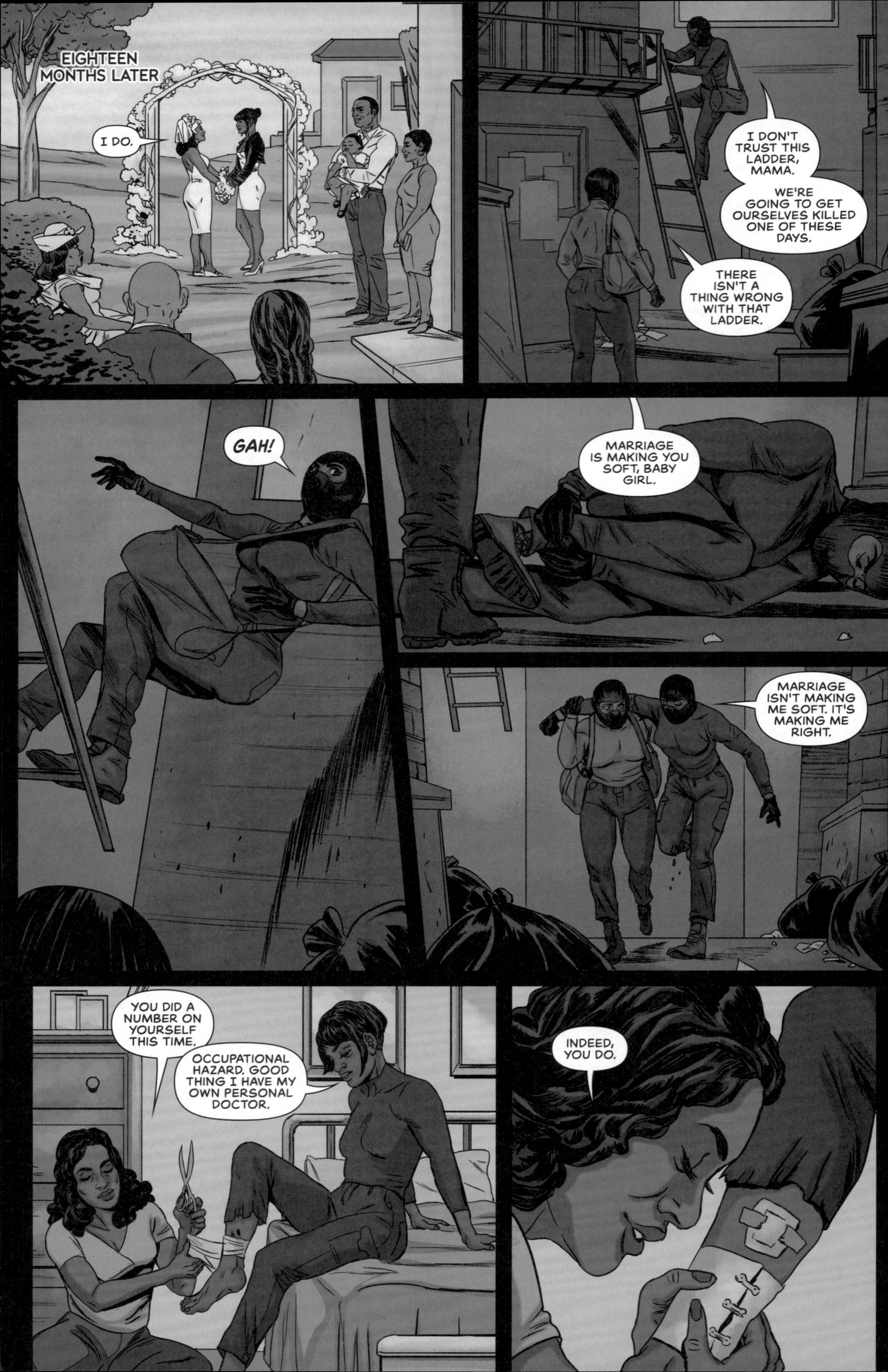
EIGHTEEN MONTHS LATER
I DO.
I DON'T TRUST THIS LADDER, MAMA.
WE'RE GOING TO GET OURSELVES KILLED ONE OF THESE DAYS.
THERE ISN'T A THING WRONG WITH THAT LADDER.
GAH!
MARRIAGE IS MAKING YOU SOFT, BABY GIRL.
MARRIAGE ISN'T MAKING ME SOFT. IT'S MAKING ME RIGHT.
YOU DID A NUMBER ON YOURSELF THIS TIME.
OCCUPATIONAL HAZARD. GOOD THING I HAVE MY OWN PERSONAL DOCTOR.
INDEED, YOU DO.

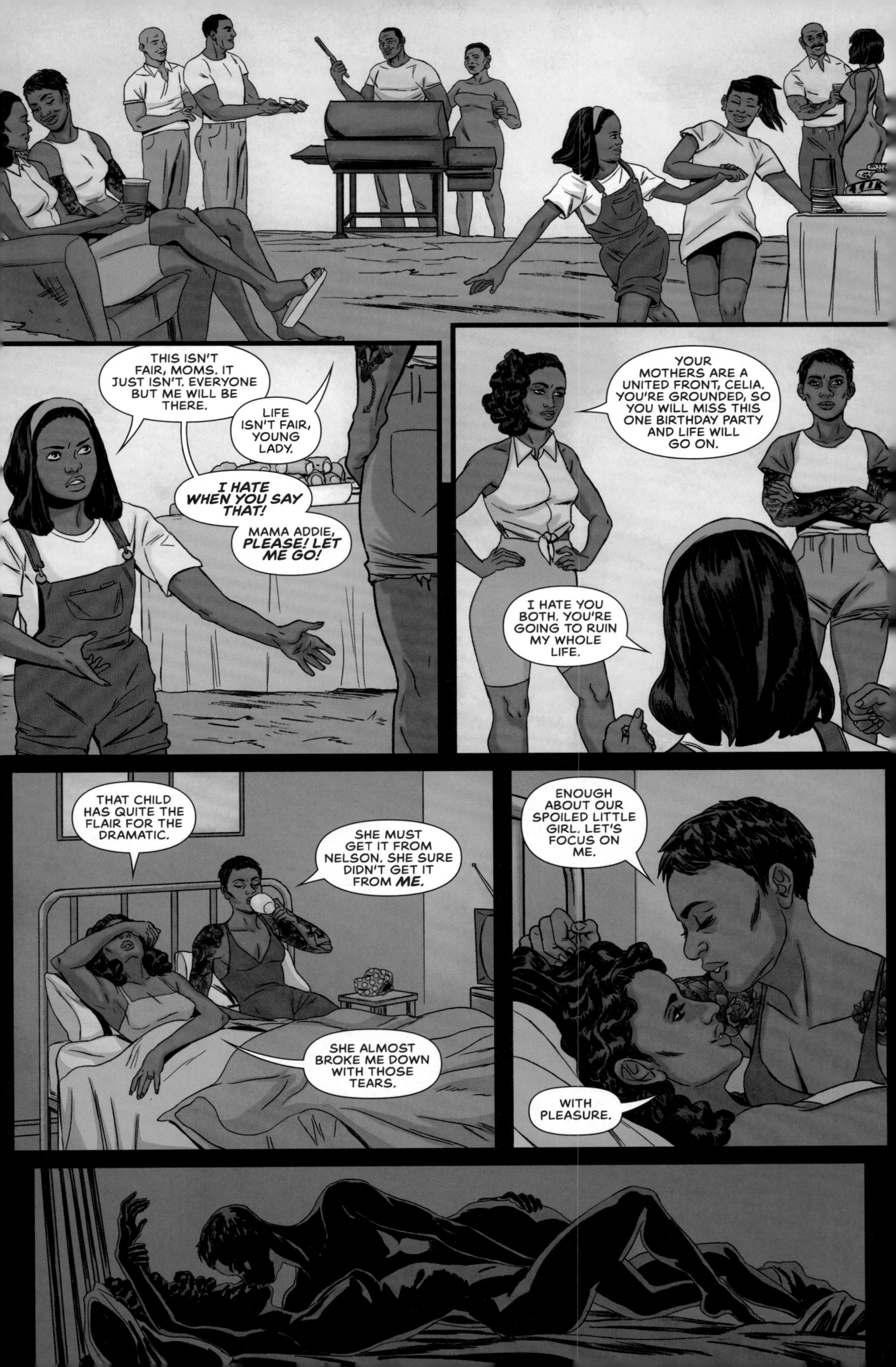
THIS ISN'T FAIR, MOMS. IT JUST ISN'T. EVERYONE BUT ME WILL BE THERE.
LIFE ISN'T FAIR, YOUNG LADY.
I HATE WHEN YOU SAY THAT!
MAMA ADDIE, PLEASE! LET ME GO!
YOUR MOTHERS ARE A UNITED FRONT, CELIA. YOU'RE GROUNDED, SO YOU WILL MISS THIS ONE BIRTHDAY PARTY AND LIFE WILL GO ON.
I HATE YOU BOTH. YOU'RE GOING TO RUIN MY WHOLE LIFE.
THAT CHILD HAS QUITE THE FLAIR FOR THE DRAMATIC.
SHE MUST GET IT FROM NELSON. SHE SURE DIDN'T GET IT FROM ME.
SHE ALMOST BROKE ME DOWN WITH THOSE TEARS.
ENOUGH ABOUT OUR SPOILED LITTLE GIRL. LET'S FOCUS ON ME.
WITH PLEASURE.

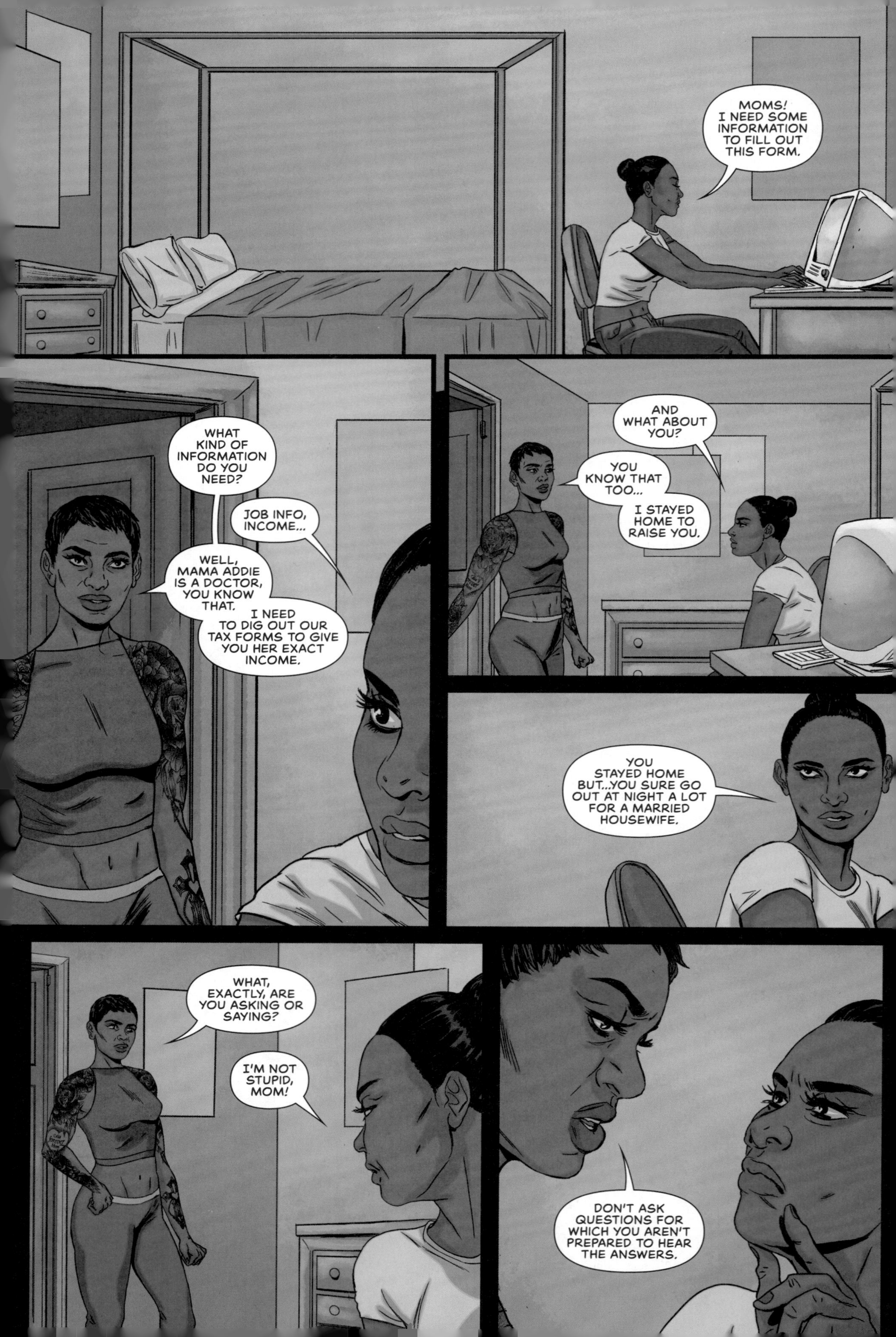
MOMS! I NEED SOME INFORMATION TO FILL OUT THIS FORM.
WHAT KIND OF INFORMATION DO YOU NEED?
JOB INFO, INCOME...
WELL, MAMA ADDIE IS A DOCTOR, YOU KNOW THAT.
I NEED TO DIG OUT OUR TAX FORMS TO GIVE YOU HER EXACT INCOME.
AND WHAT ABOUT YOU?
YOU KNOW THAT TOO...
I STAYED HOME TO RAISE YOU.
YOU STAYED HOME BUT...YOU SURE GO OUT AT NIGHT A LOT FOR A MARRIED HOUSEWIFE.
WHAT, EXACTLY, ARE YOU ASKING OR SAYING?
I'M NOT STUPID, MOM!
DON'T ASK QUESTIONS FOR WHICH YOU AREN'T PREPARED TO HEAR THE ANSWERS.

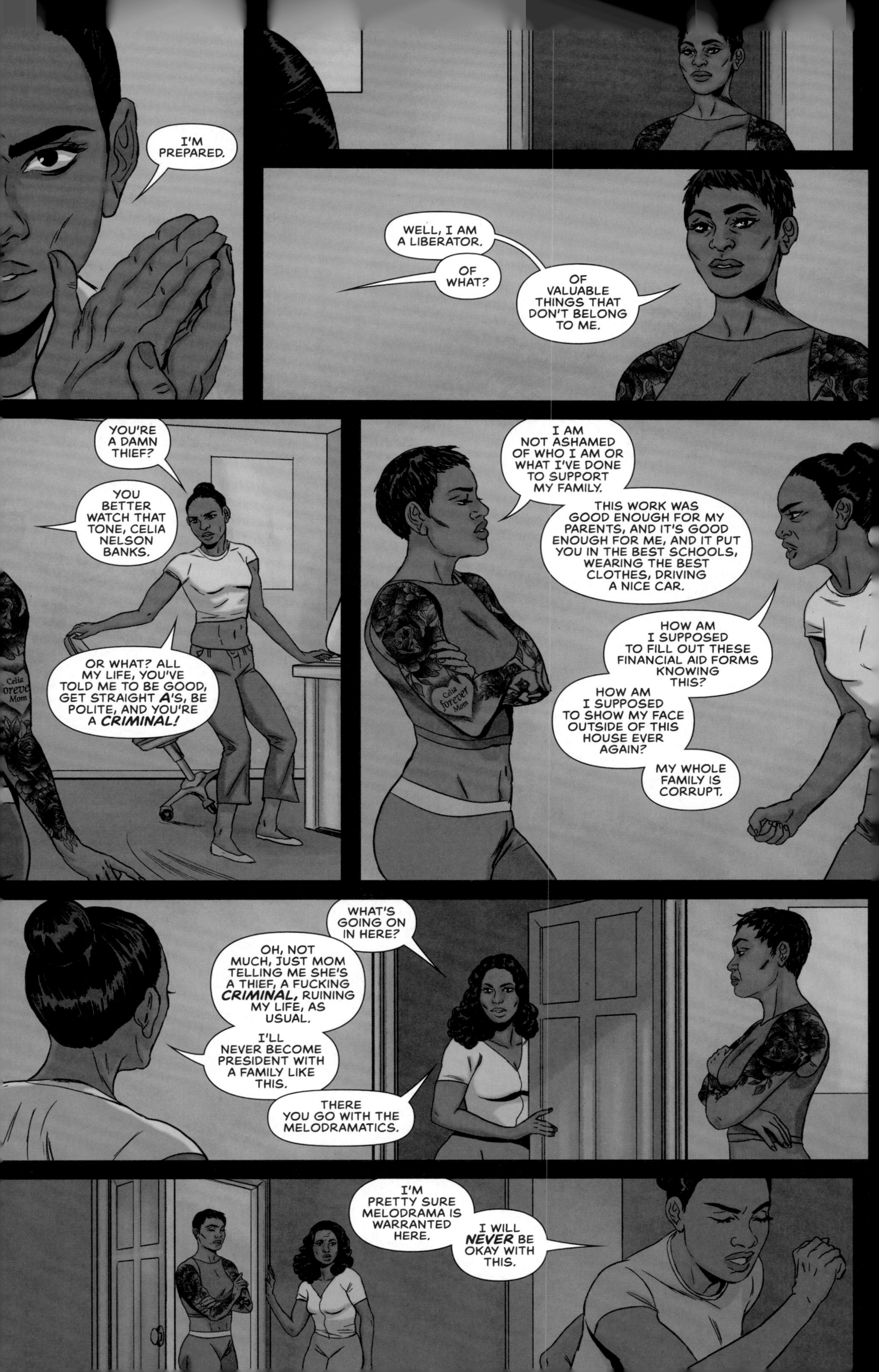
I'M PREPARED.
WELL, I AM A LIBERATOR.
OF WHAT?
OF VALUABLE THINGS THAT DON'T BELONG TO ME.
YOU'RE A DAMN THIEF?
YOU BETTER WATCH THAT TONE, CELIA NELSON BANKS.
OR WHAT? ALL MY LIFE, YOU'VE TOLD ME TO BE GOOD, GET STRAIGHT A'S, BE POLITE, AND YOU'RE A CRIMINAL!
Celia forever Mom
I AM NOT ASHAMED OF WHO I AM OR WHAT I'VE DONE TO SUPPORT MY FAMILY.
THIS WORK WAS GOOD ENOUGH FOR MY PARENTS, AND IT'S GOOD ENOUGH FOR ME, AND IT PUT YOU IN THE BEST SCHOOLS, WEARING THE BEST CLOTHES, DRIVING A NICE CAR.
HOW AM I SUPPOSED TO FILL OUT THESE FINANCIAL AID FORMS KNOWING THIS?
HOW AM I SUPPOSED TO SHOW MY FACE OUTSIDE OF THIS HOUSE EVER AGAIN?
MY WHOLE FAMILY IS CORRUPT.
WHAT'S GOING ON IN HERE?
OH, NOT MUCH, JUST MOM TELLING ME SHE'S A THIEF, A FUCKING CRIMINAL, RUINING MY LIFE, AS USUAL.
I'LL NEVER BECOME PRESIDENT WITH A FAMILY LIKE THIS.
THERE YOU GO WITH THE MELODRAMATICS.
I'M PRETTY SURE MELODRAMA IS WARRANTED HERE.
I WILL NEVER BE OKAY WITH THIS.

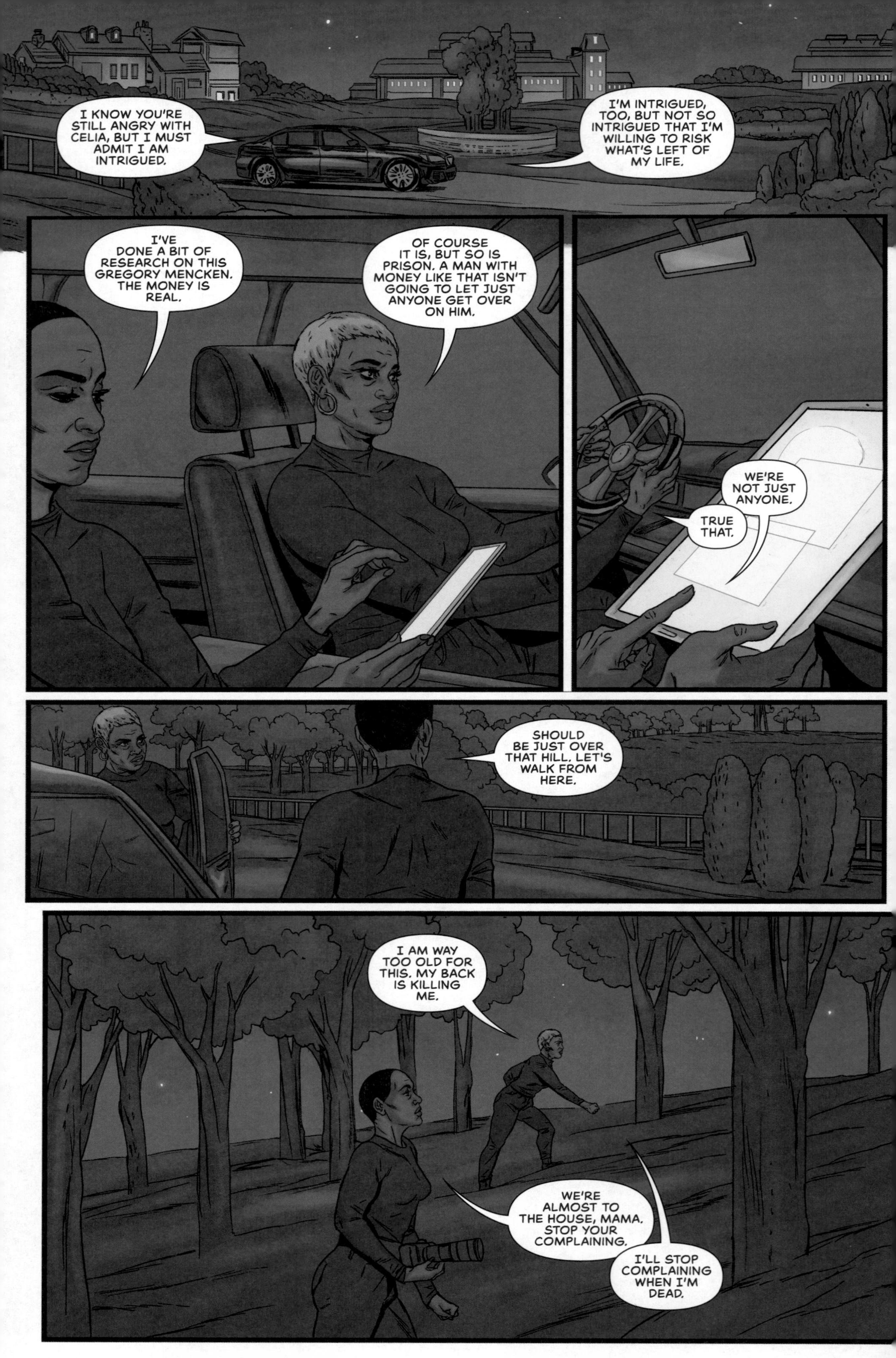

I KNOW YOU'RE STILL ANGRY WITH CELIA, BUT I MUST ADMIT I AM INTRIGUED.
I'M INTRIGUED, TOO, BUT NOT SO INTRIGUED THAT I'M WILLING TO RISK WHAT'S LEFT OF MY LIFE.
I'VE DONE A BIT OF RESEARCH ON THIS GREGORY MENCKEN. THE MONEY IS REAL.
OF COURSE IT IS, BUT SO IS PRISON. A MAN WITH MONEY LIKE THAT ISN'T GOING TO LET JUST ANYONE GET OVER ON HIM.
WE'RE NOT JUST ANYONE.
TRUE THAT.
SHOULD BE JUST OVER THAT HILL. LET'S WALK FROM HERE.
I AM WAY TOO OLD FOR THIS. MY BACK IS KILLING ME.
WE'RE ALMOST TO THE HOUSE, MAMA. STOP YOUR COMPLAINING.
I'LL STOP COMPLAINING WHEN I'M DEAD.

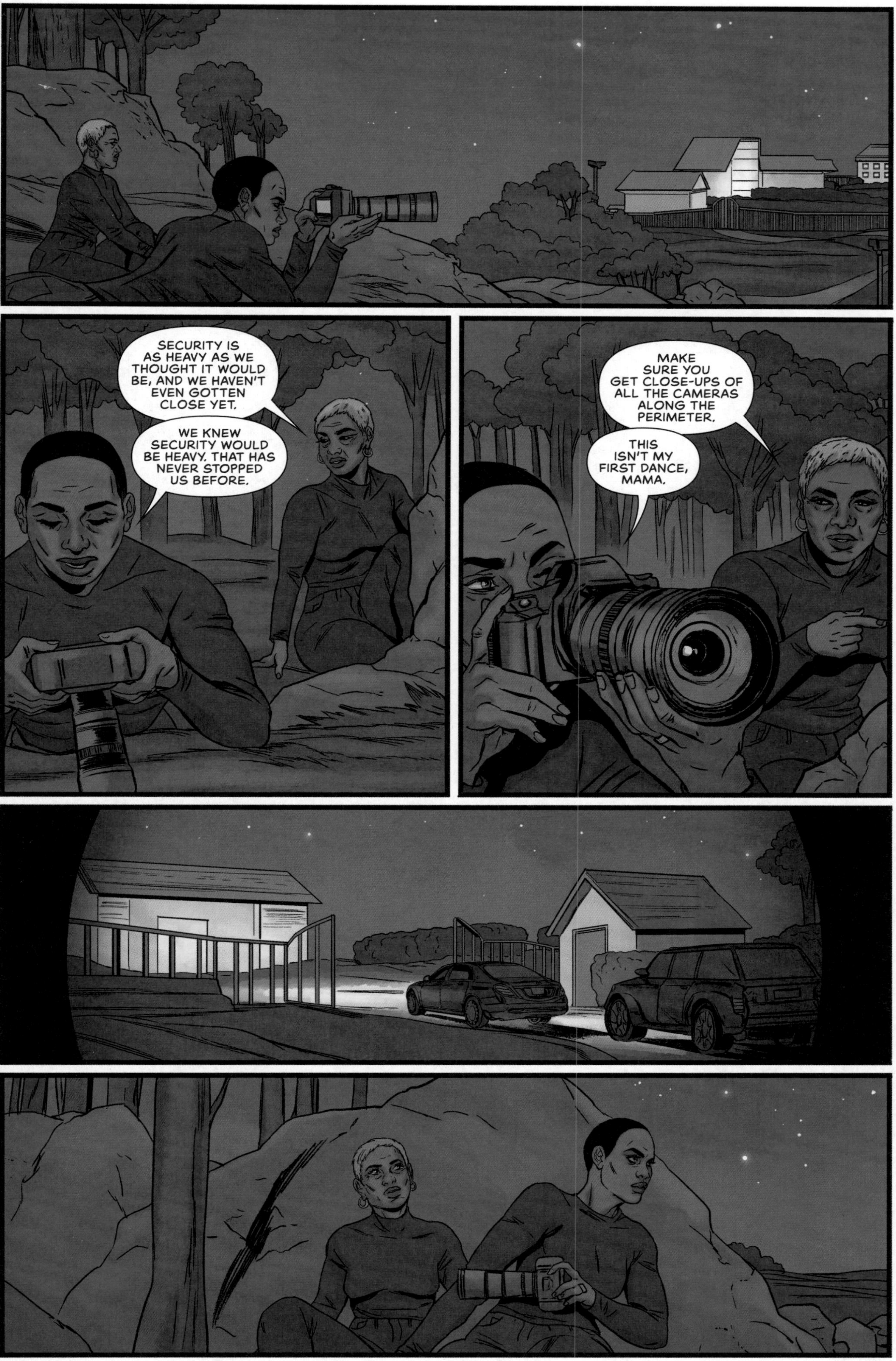
SECURITY IS AS HEAVY AS WE THOUGHT IT WOULD BE, AND WE HAVEN'T EVEN GOTTEN CLOSE YET.
WE KNEW SECURITY WOULD BE HEAVY. THAT HAS NEVER STOPPED US BEFORE.
MAKE SURE YOU GET CLOSE-UPS OF ALL THE CAMERAS ALONG THE PERIMETER.
THIS ISN'T MY FIRST DANCE, MAMA.

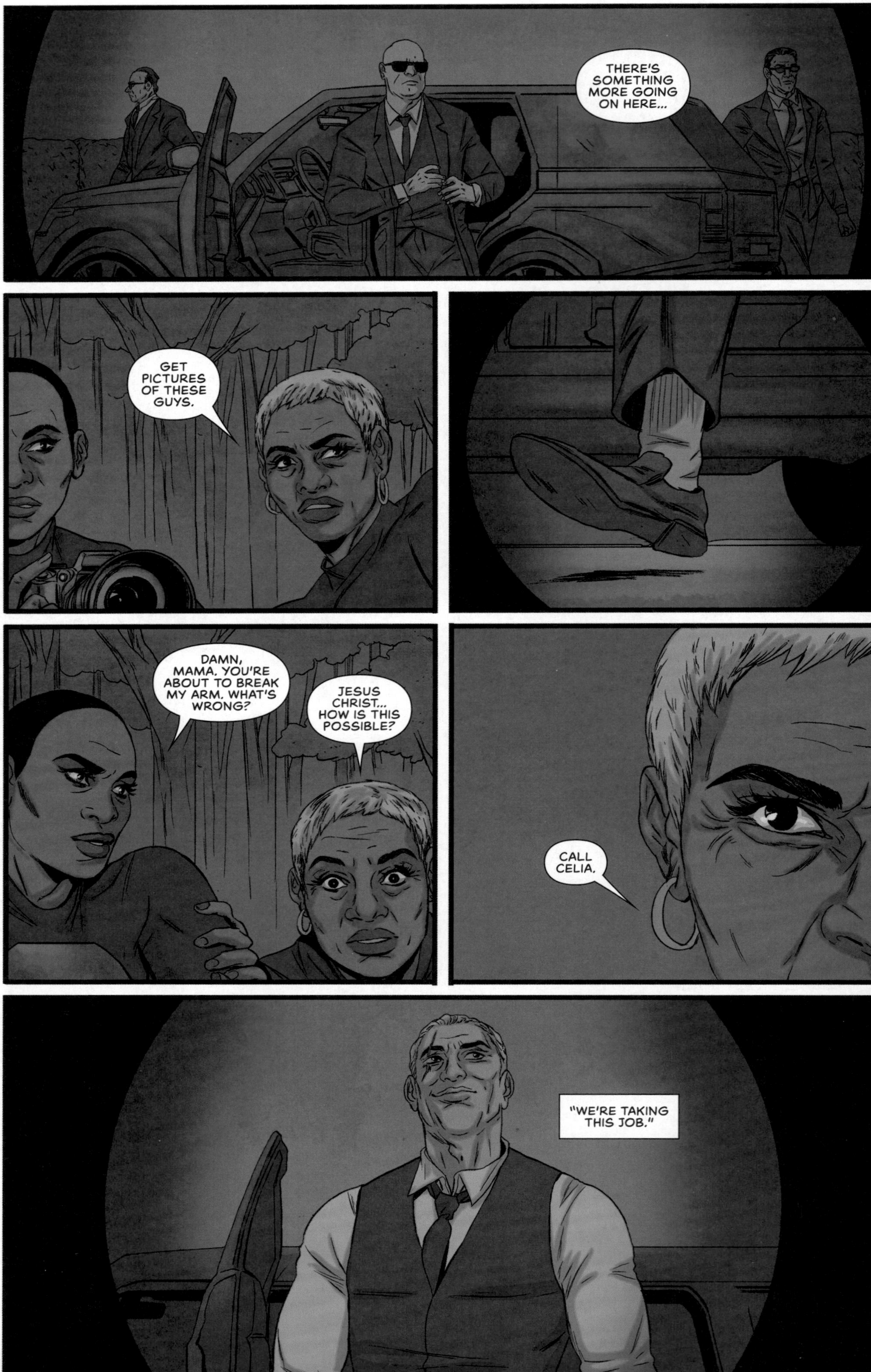
THERE'S SOMETHING MORE GOING ON HERE...
GET PICTURES OF THESE GUYS.
DAMN, MAMA. YOU'RE ABOUT TO BREAK MY ARM. WHAT'S WRONG?
JESUS CHRIST... HOW IS THIS POSSIBLE?
CALL CELIA.
"WE'RE TAKING THIS JOB."

CHAPTER 3

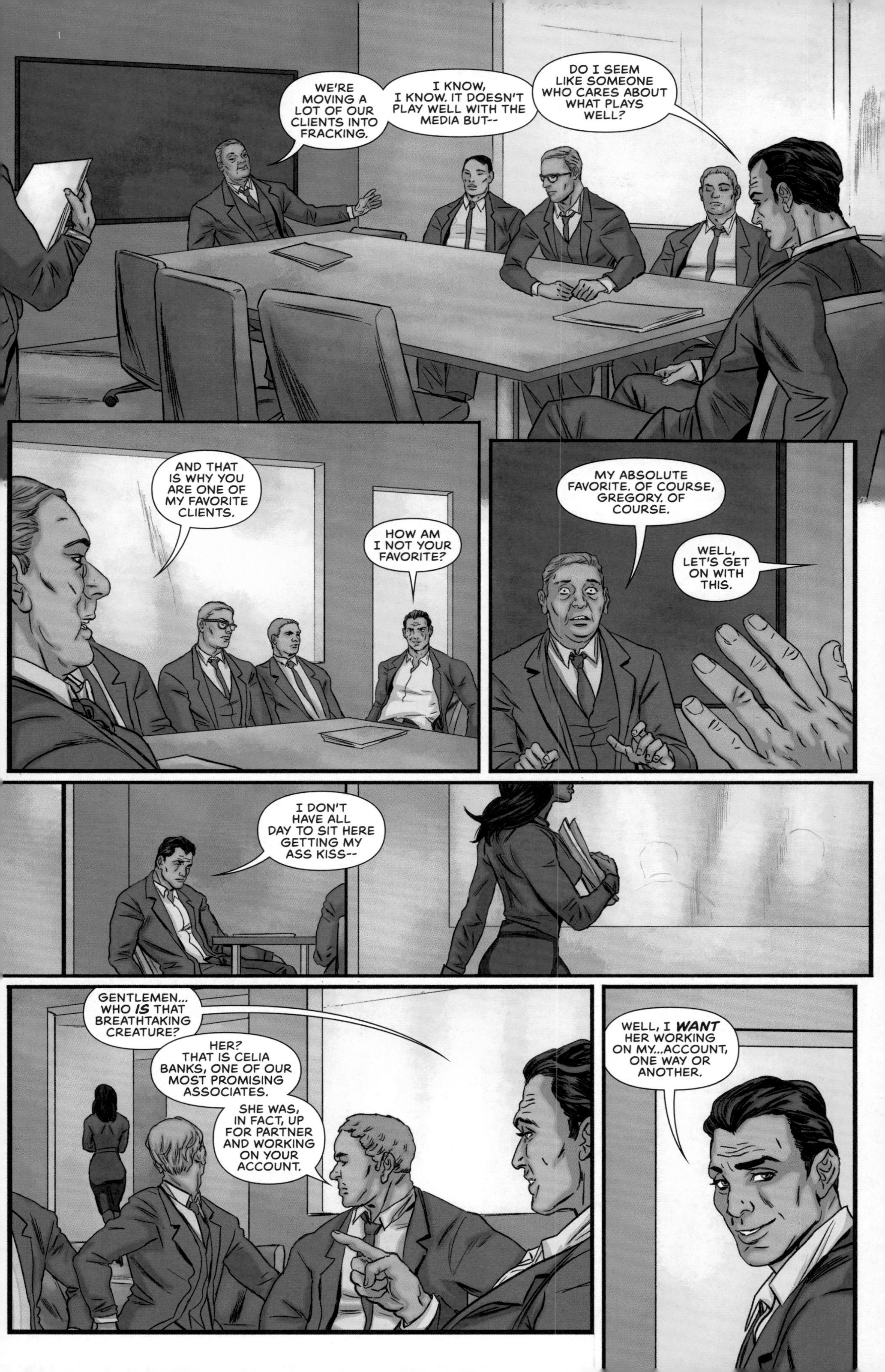
WE'RE MOVING A LOT OF OUR CLIENTS INTO FRACKING.
I KNOW, I KNOW. IT DOESN'T PLAY WELL WITH THE MEDIA BUT--
DO I SEEM LIKE SOMEONE WHO CARES ABOUT WHAT PLAYS WELL?
AND THAT IS WHY YOU ARE ONE OF MY FAVORITE CLIENTS.
HOW AM I NOT YOUR FAVORITE?
MY ABSOLUTE FAVORITE. OF COURSE, GREGORY. OF COURSE.
WELL, LET'S GET ON WITH THIS.
I DON'T HAVE ALL DAY TO SIT HERE GETTING MY ASS KISS--
GENTLEMEN... WHO *IS* THAT BREATHTAKING CREATURE?
HER? THAT IS CELIA BANKS, ONE OF OUR MOST PROMISING ASSOCIATES.
SHE WAS, IN FACT, UP FOR PARTNER AND WORKING ON YOUR ACCOUNT.
WELL, I ***WANT*** HER WORKING ON MY...ACCOUNT, ONE WAY OR ANOTHER.

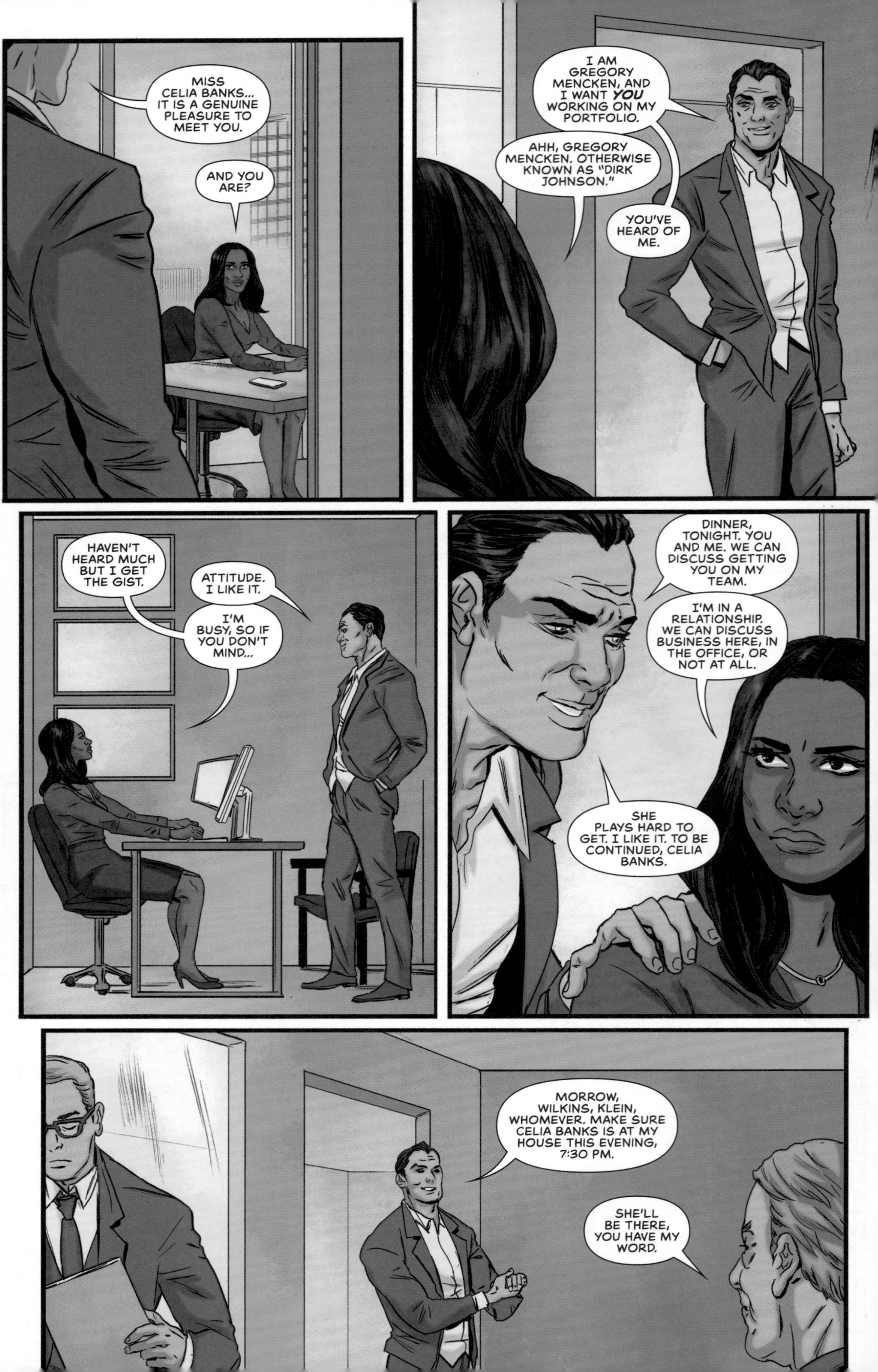
MISS CELIA BANKS... IT IS A GENUINE PLEASURE TO MEET YOU.
AND YOU ARE?
I AM GREGORY MENCKEN, AND I WANT *YOU* WORKING ON MY PORTFOLIO.
AHH, GREGORY MENCKEN. OTHERWISE KNOWN AS "DIRK JOHNSON."
YOU'VE HEARD OF ME.
HAVEN'T HEARD MUCH BUT I GET THE GIST.
ATTITUDE. I LIKE IT.
I'M BUSY, SO IF YOU DON'T MIND...
DINNER, TONIGHT. YOU AND ME. WE CAN DISCUSS GETTING YOU ON MY TEAM.
I'M IN A RELATIONSHIP. WE CAN DISCUSS BUSINESS HERE, IN THE OFFICE, OR NOT AT ALL.
SHE PLAYS HARD TO GET. I LIKE IT. TO BE CONTINUED, CELIA BANKS.
MORROW, WILKINS, KLEIN, WHOMEVER. MAKE SURE CELIA BANKS IS AT MY HOUSE THIS EVENING, 7:30 PM.
SHE'LL BE THERE, YOU HAVE MY WORD.

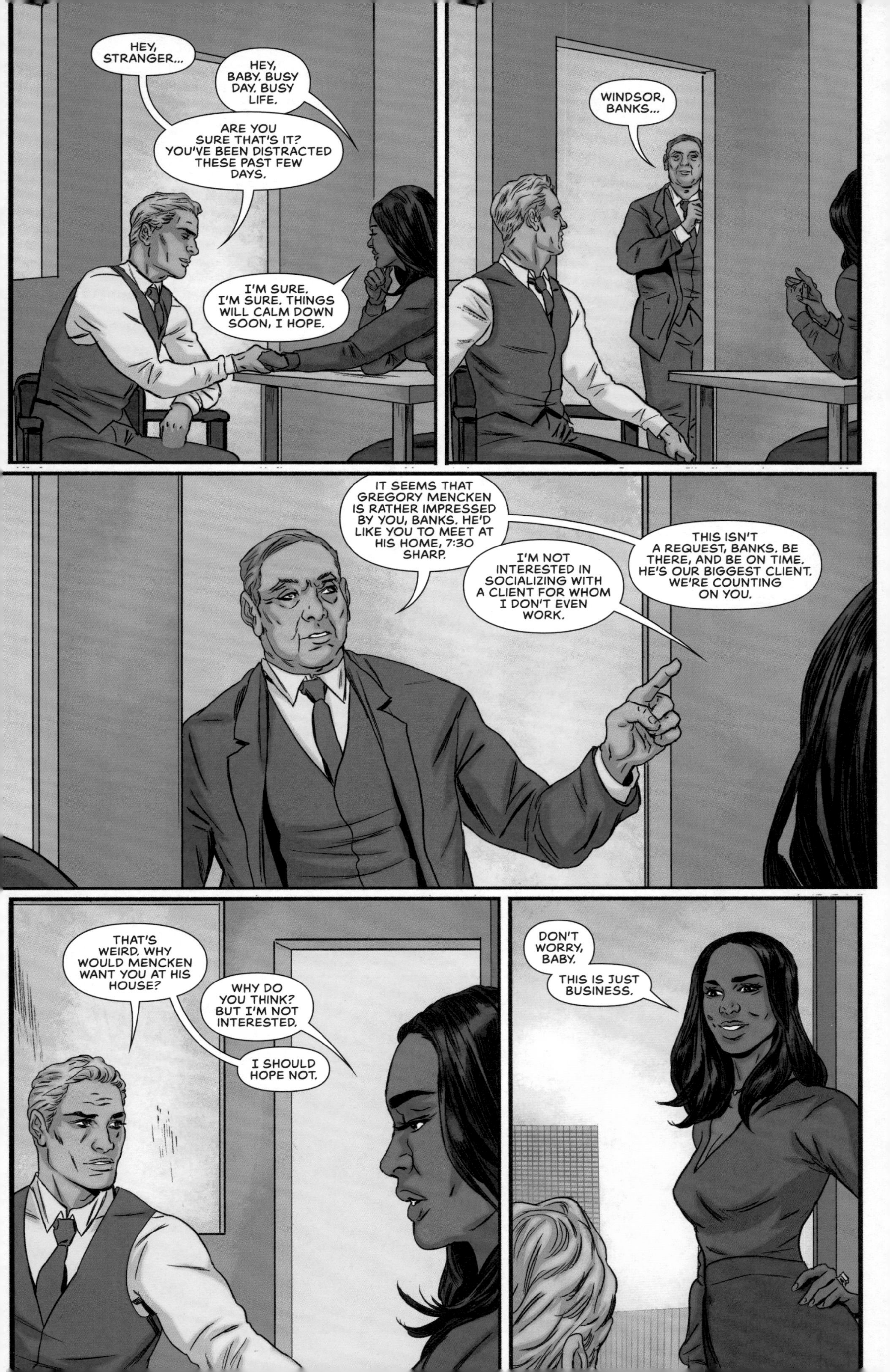
HEY, STRANGER...
HEY, BABY. BUSY DAY, BUSY LIFE.
ARE YOU SURE THAT'S IT? YOU'VE BEEN DISTRACTED THESE PAST FEW DAYS.
I'M SURE, I'M SURE. THINGS WILL CALM DOWN SOON, I HOPE.
WINDSOR, BANKS...
IT SEEMS THAT GREGORY MENCKEN IS RATHER IMPRESSED BY YOU, BANKS. HE'D LIKE YOU TO MEET AT HIS HOME, 7:30 SHARP.
I'M NOT INTERESTED IN SOCIALIZING WITH A CLIENT FOR WHOM I DON'T EVEN WORK.
THIS ISN'T A REQUEST, BANKS. BE THERE, AND BE ON TIME. HE'S OUR BIGGEST CLIENT. WE'RE COUNTING ON YOU.
THAT'S WEIRD. WHY WOULD MENCKEN WANT YOU AT HIS HOUSE?
WHY DO YOU THINK? BUT I'M NOT INTERESTED.
I SHOULD HOPE NOT.
DON'T WORRY, BABY.
THIS IS JUST BUSINESS.

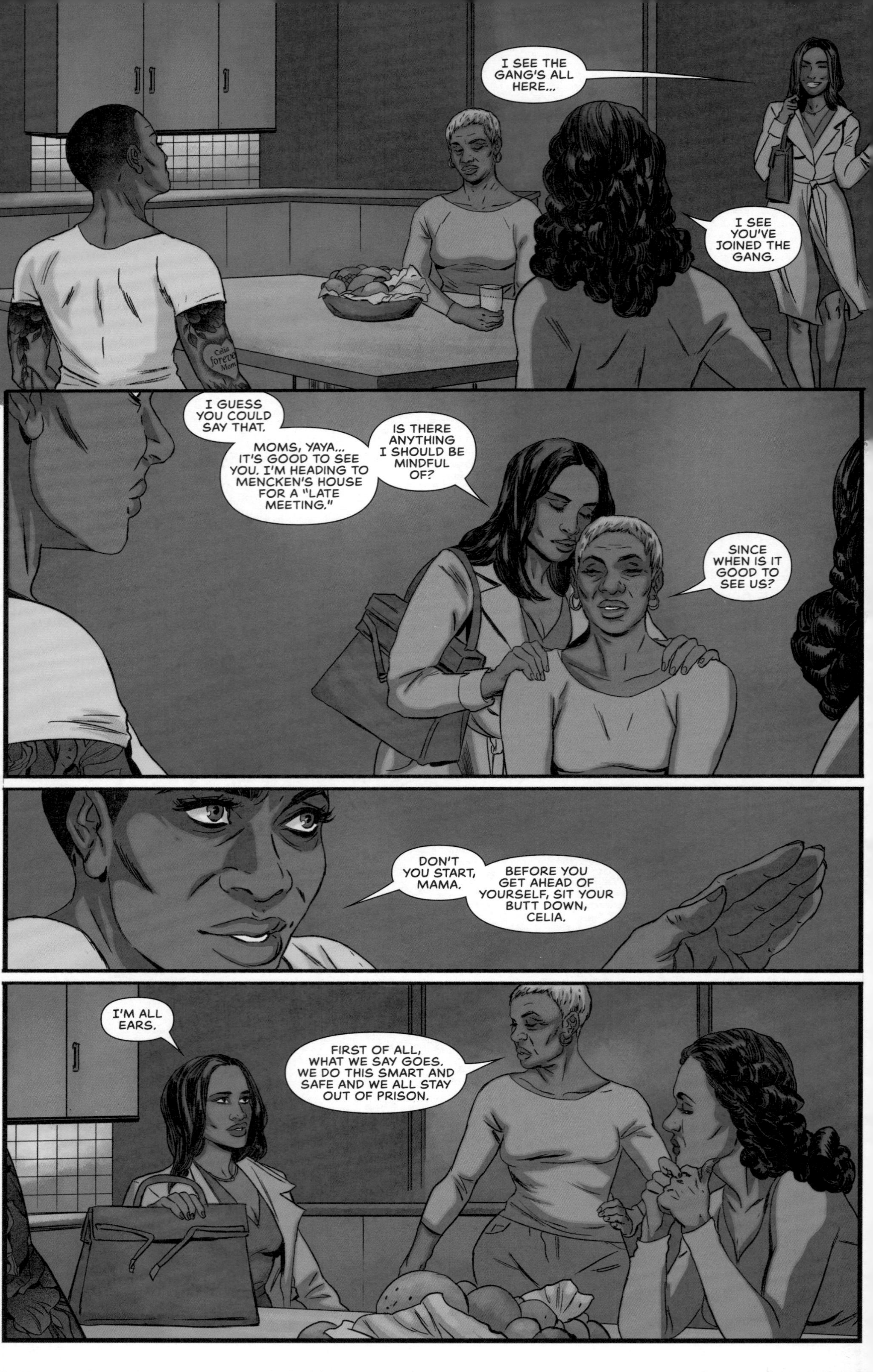
I SEE THE GANG'S ALL HERE...
I SEE YOU'VE JOINED THE GANG.
Celia forever Mom
I GUESS YOU COULD SAY THAT.
MOMS, YAYA... IT'S GOOD TO SEE YOU. I'M HEADING TO MENCKEN'S HOUSE FOR A "LATE MEETING."
IS THERE ANYTHING I SHOULD BE MINDFUL OF?
SINCE WHEN IS IT GOOD TO SEE US?
DON'T YOU START, MAMA.
BEFORE YOU GET AHEAD OF YOURSELF, SIT YOUR BUTT DOWN, CELIA.
I'M ALL EARS.
FIRST OF ALL, WHAT WE SAY GOES. WE DO THIS SMART AND SAFE AND WE ALL STAY OUT OF PRISON.

DONE!

I'M NOT PLAYING, YOUNG LADY, WHAT WE SAY GOES.

ASK YOUR MOM WHAT HAPPENED THE ONE TIME SHE DIDN'T LISTEN TO ME ON A JOB.

WHAT'S SHE TALKING ABOUT, MOM?

YOU AND YOUR MOM ARE EXACTLY ALIKE. SOMETIMES, Y'ALL REFUSE TO LISTEN.

WHEN I WAS MUCH YOUNGER I THOUGHT I KNEW IT ALL, AND DID A JOB BOTH YOUR GRANDMA AND ADDIE TOLD ME NOT TO TAKE.

CLOSEST I'VE EVER COME TO JOINING DADDY IN PRISON.

THERE HAS TO BE MORE TO THE STORY.

WE CAN GET INTO ALL THAT LATER. FOR NOW, JUST KNOW WHAT WE SAY GOES.

WE DON'T TAKE UNNECESSARY RISKS, WE PLAN THIS JOB EVERY DAMN STEP OF THE WAY.

AND WE DON'T GET GREEDY. AS FOR TONIGHT, YOU DON'T DO ANYTHING UNNECESSARY.

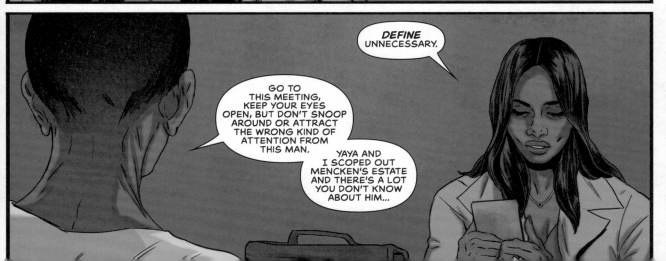

DEFINE UNNECESSARY.

GO TO THIS MEETING, KEEP YOUR EYES OPEN, BUT DON'T SNOOP AROUND OR ATTRACT THE WRONG KIND OF ATTENTION FROM THIS MAN.

YAYA AND I SCOPED OUT MENCKEN'S ESTATE AND THERE'S A LOT YOU DON'T KNOW ABOUT HIM...

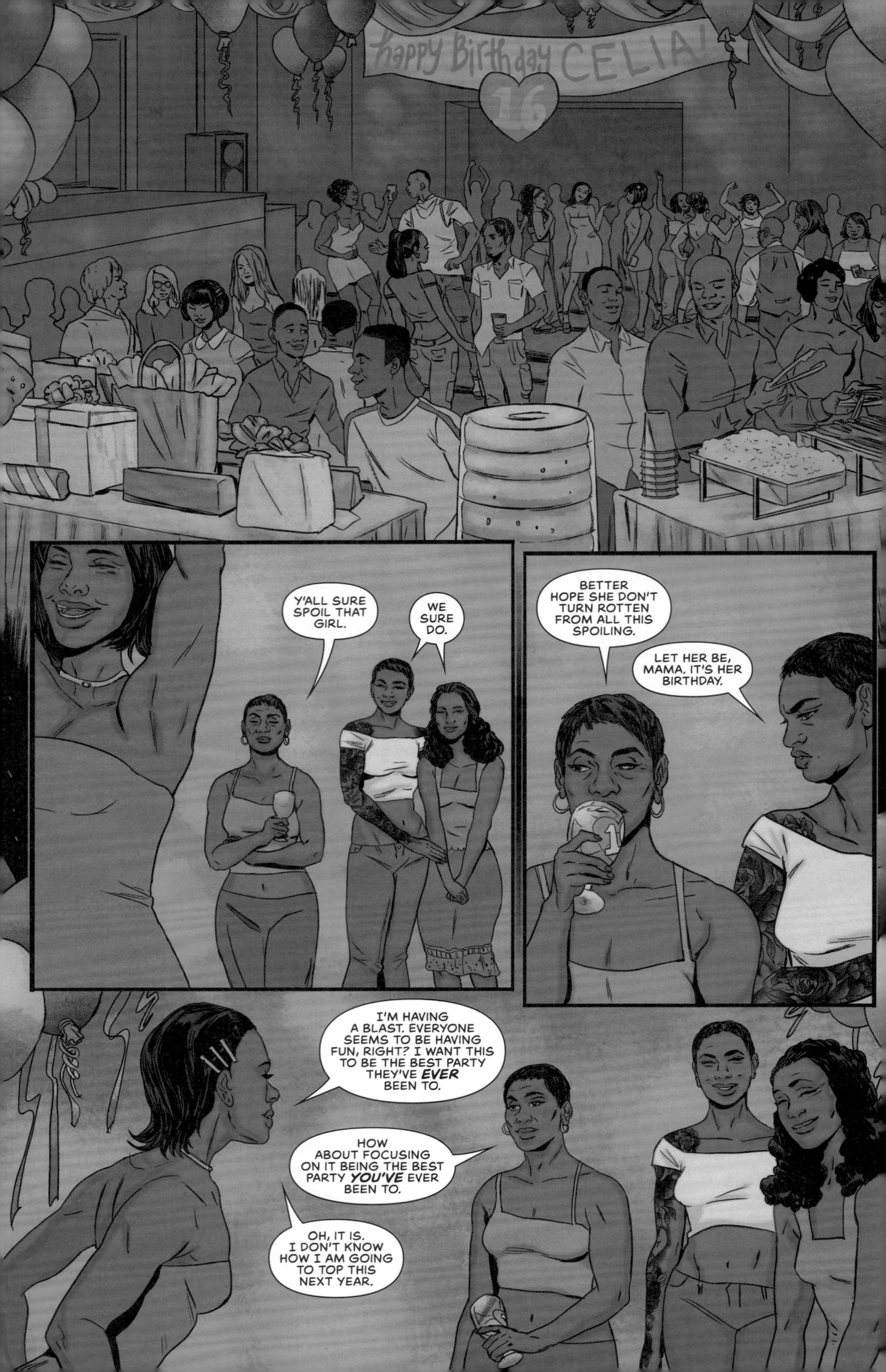
happy Birthday CELIA!
16
Y'ALL SURE SPOIL THAT GIRL.
WE SURE DO.
BETTER HOPE SHE DON'T TURN ROTTEN FROM ALL THIS SPOILING.
LET HER BE, MAMA. IT'S HER BIRTHDAY.
I'M HAVING A BLAST. EVERYONE SEEMS TO BE HAVING FUN, RIGHT? I WANT THIS TO BE THE BEST PARTY THEY'VE *EVER* BEEN TO.
HOW ABOUT FOCUSING ON IT BEING THE BEST PARTY *YOU'VE* EVER BEEN TO.
OH, IT IS. I DON'T KNOW HOW I AM GOING TO TOP THIS NEXT YEAR.

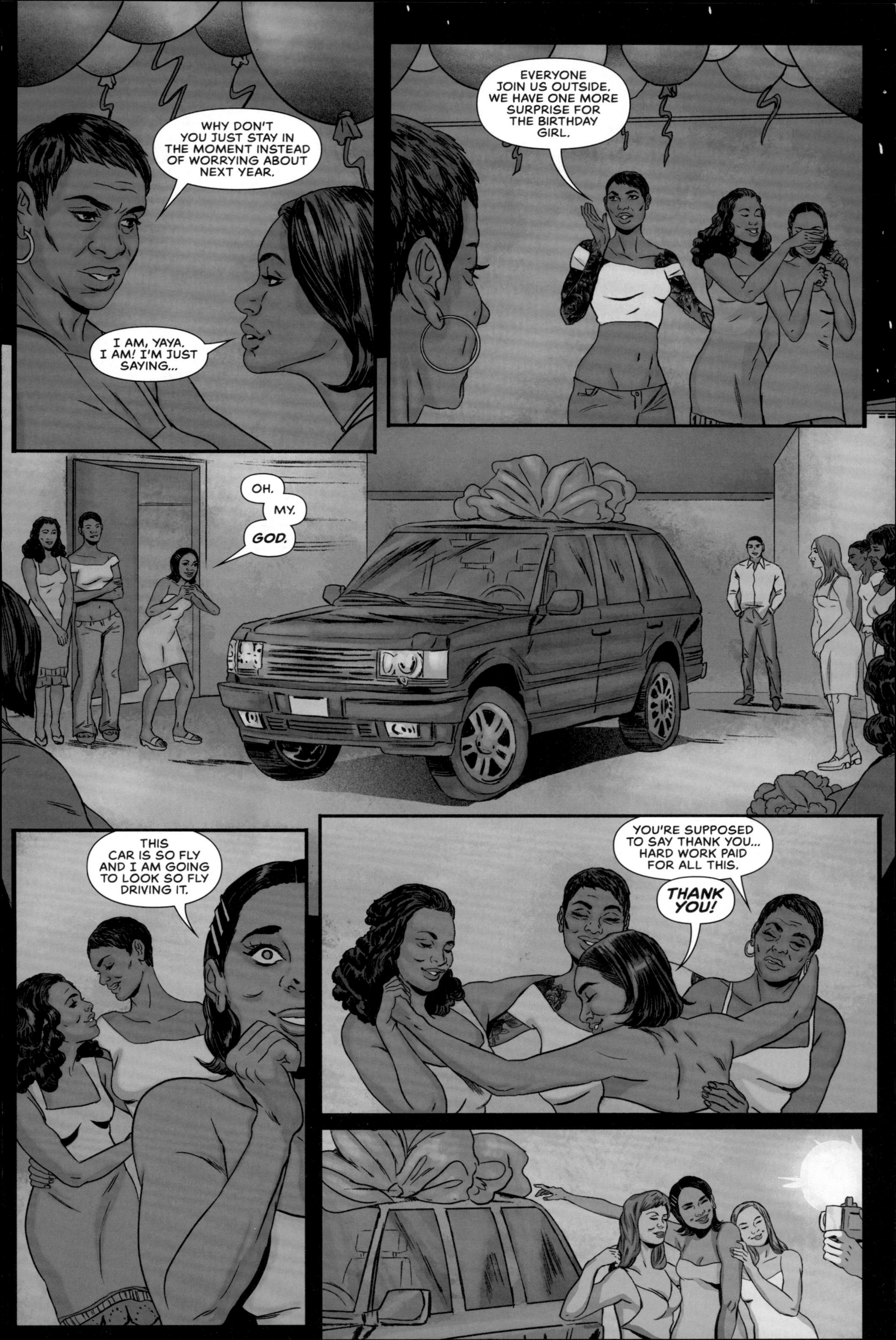
WHY DON'T YOU JUST STAY IN THE MOMENT INSTEAD OF WORRYING ABOUT NEXT YEAR.
I AM, YAYA. I AM! I'M JUST SAYING...
EVERYONE JOIN US OUTSIDE. WE HAVE ONE MORE SURPRISE FOR THE BIRTHDAY GIRL.
OH.
MY.
GOD.
THIS CAR IS SO FLY AND I AM GOING TO LOOK SO FLY DRIVING IT.
YOU'RE SUPPOSED TO SAY THANK YOU... HARD WORK PAID FOR ALL THIS.
THANK YOU!

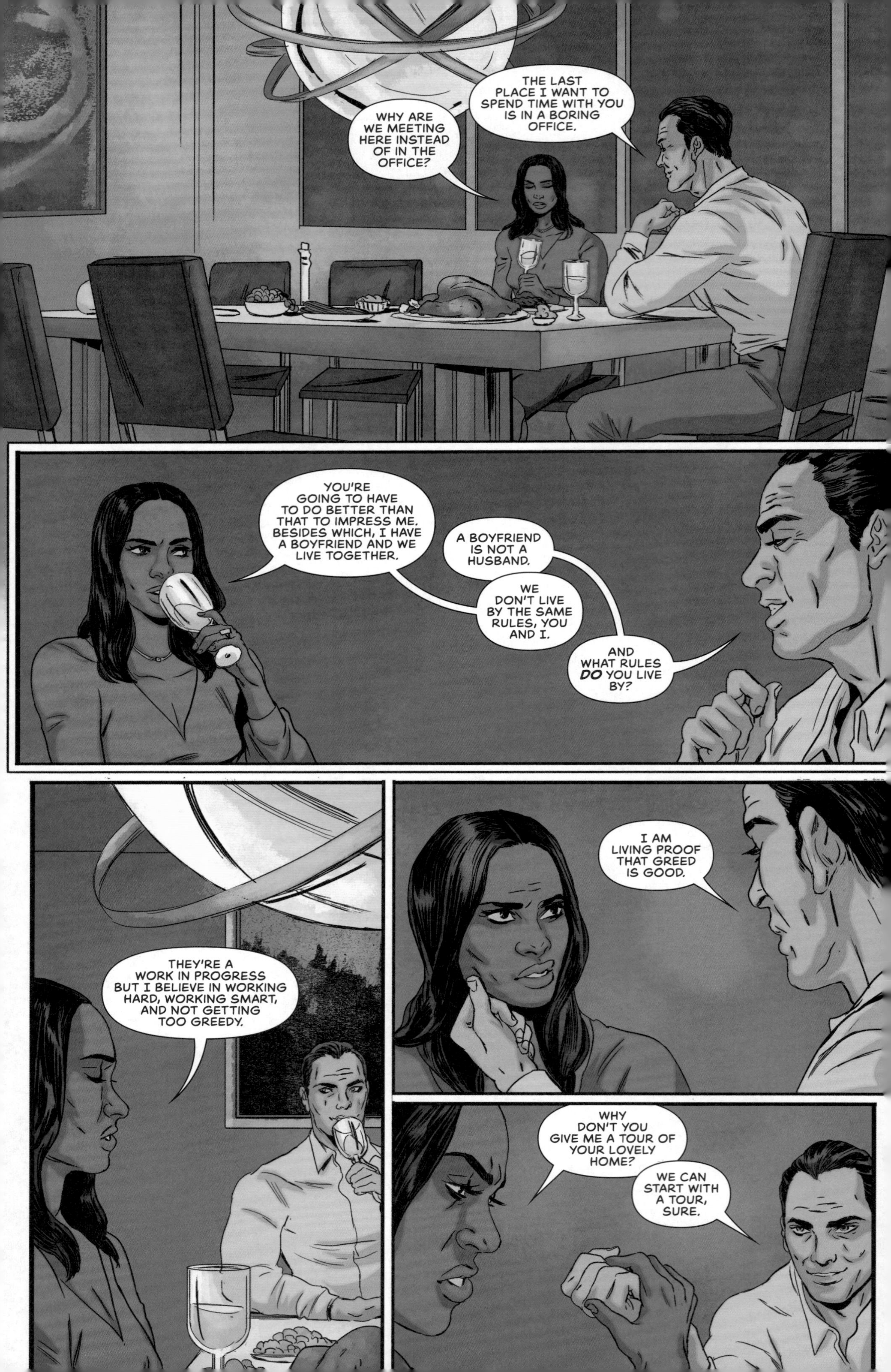
WHY ARE WE MEETING HERE INSTEAD OF IN THE OFFICE?
THE LAST PLACE I WANT TO SPEND TIME WITH YOU IS IN A BORING OFFICE.
YOU'RE GOING TO HAVE TO DO BETTER THAN THAT TO IMPRESS ME. BESIDES WHICH, I HAVE A BOYFRIEND AND WE LIVE TOGETHER.
A BOYFRIEND IS NOT A HUSBAND.
WE DON'T LIVE BY THE SAME RULES, YOU AND I.
AND WHAT RULES *DO* YOU LIVE BY?
THEY'RE A WORK IN PROGRESS BUT I BELIEVE IN WORKING HARD, WORKING SMART, AND NOT GETTING TOO GREEDY.
I AM LIVING PROOF THAT GREED IS GOOD.
WHY DON'T YOU GIVE ME A TOUR OF YOUR LOVELY HOME?
WE CAN START WITH A TOUR, SURE.

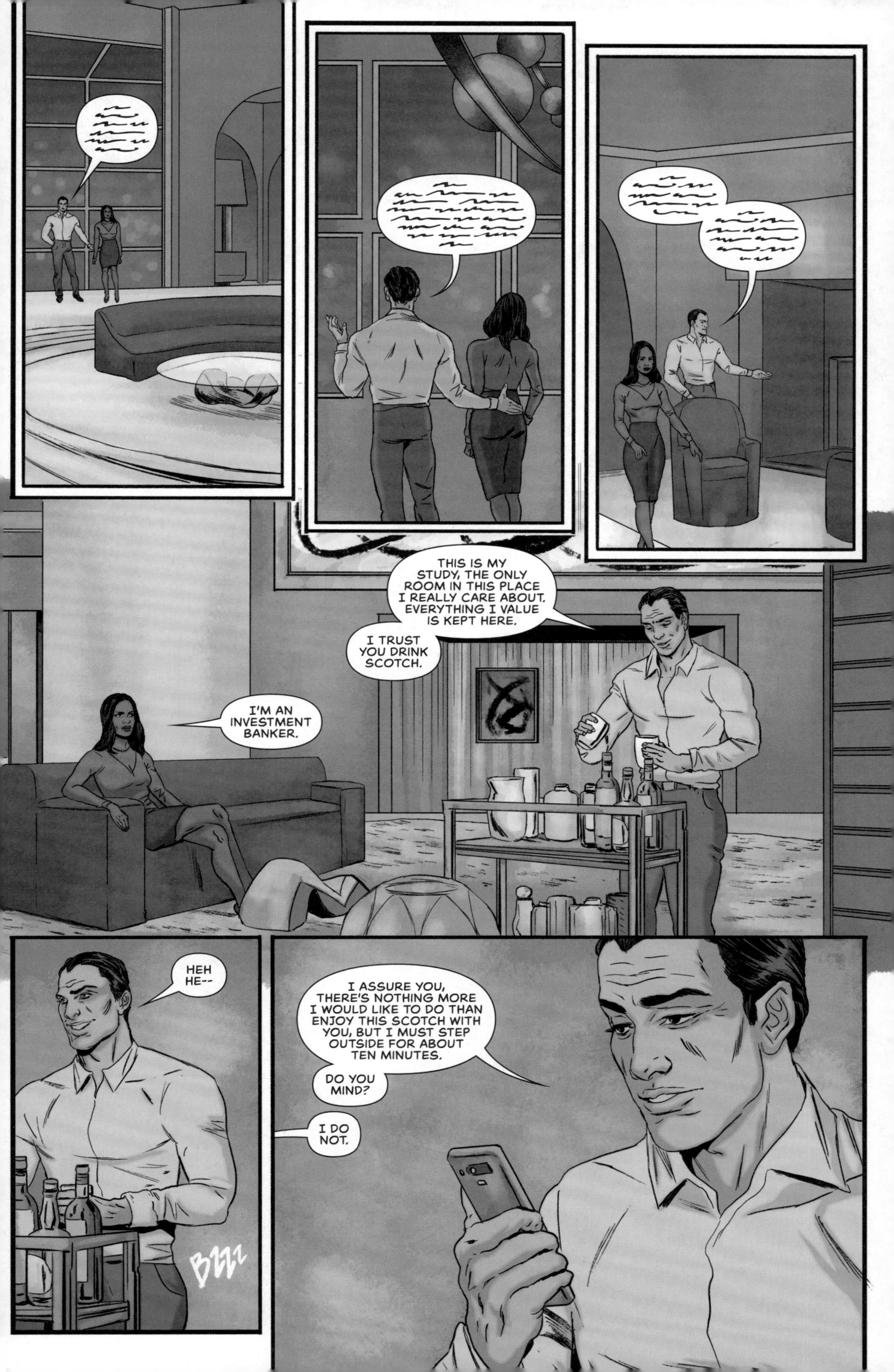
THIS IS MY STUDY, THE ONLY ROOM IN THIS PLACE I REALLY CARE ABOUT. EVERYTHING I VALUE IS KEPT HERE.
I TRUST YOU DRINK SCOTCH.
I'M AN INVESTMENT BANKER.
HEH HE--
BZZZ
I ASSURE YOU, THERE'S NOTHING MORE I WOULD LIKE TO DO THAN ENJOY THIS SCOTCH WITH YOU, BUT I MUST STEP OUTSIDE FOR ABOUT TEN MINUTES.
DO YOU MIND?
I DO NOT.

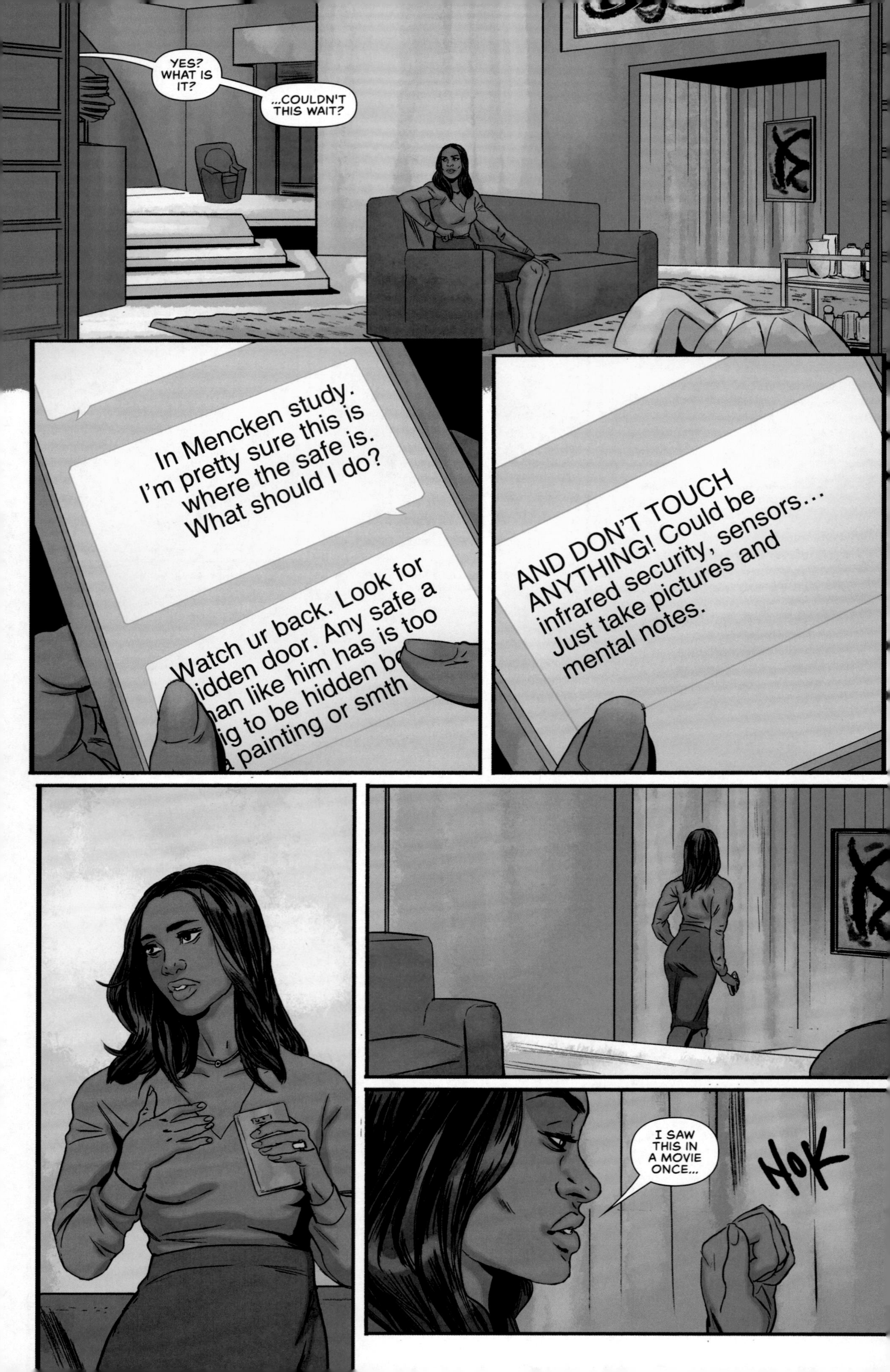
YES? WHAT IS IT?
...COULDN'T THIS WAIT?
In Mencken study. I'm pretty sure this is where the safe is. What should I do?
Watch ur back. Look for hidden door. Any safe a man like him has is too big to be hidden be a painting or smth
AND DON'T TOUCH ANYTHING! Could be infrared security, sensors... Just take pictures and mental notes.
I SAW THIS IN A MOVIE ONCE...
NOK

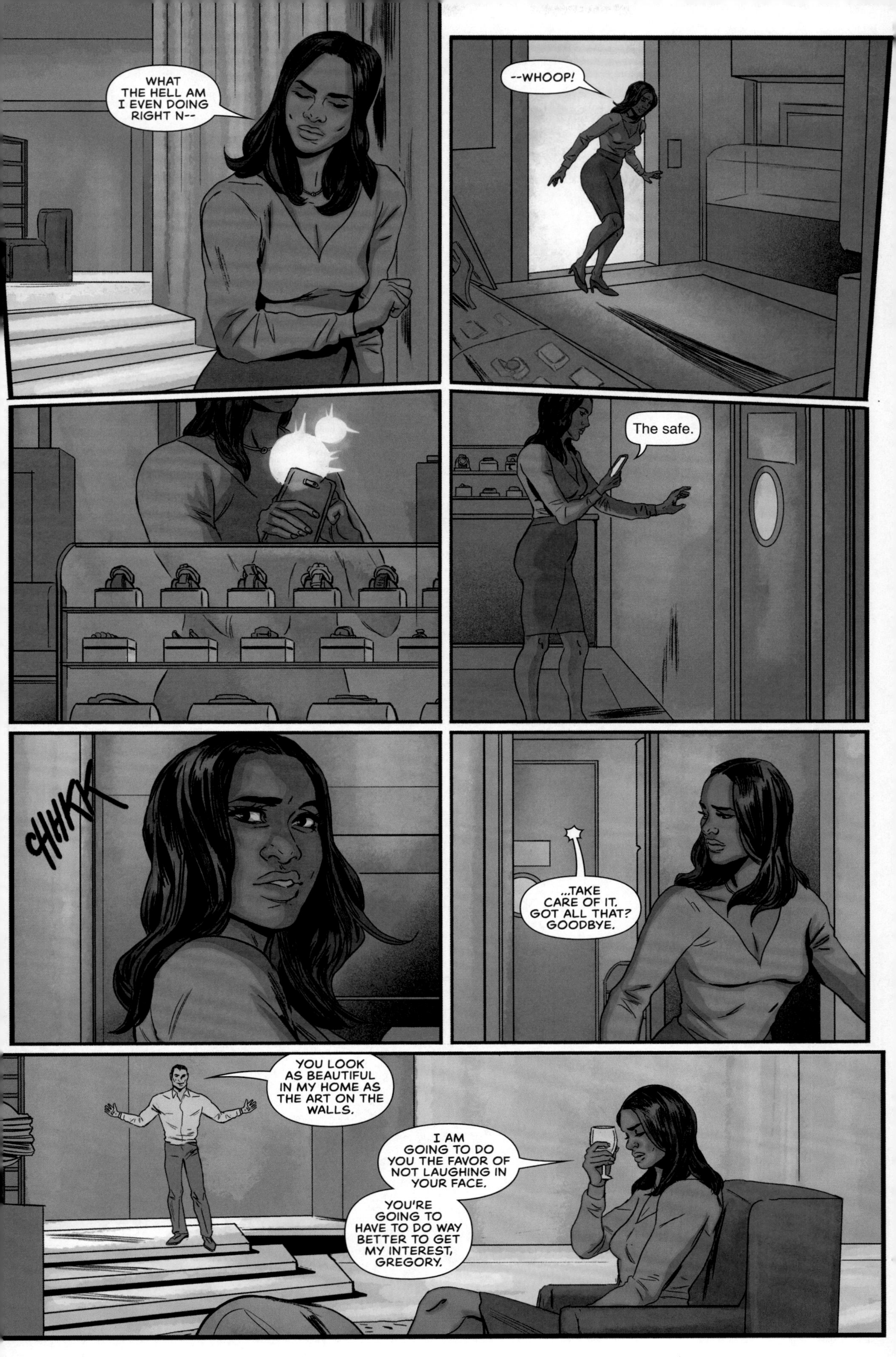
WHAT THE HELL AM I EVEN DOING RIGHT N--
--WHOOP!
The safe.
CHHKK
...TAKE CARE OF IT. GOT ALL THAT? GOODBYE.
YOU LOOK AS BEAUTIFUL IN MY HOME AS THE ART ON THE WALLS.
I AM GOING TO DO YOU THE FAVOR OF NOT LAUGHING IN YOUR FACE.
YOU'RE GOING TO HAVE TO DO WAY BETTER TO GET MY INTEREST, GREGORY.

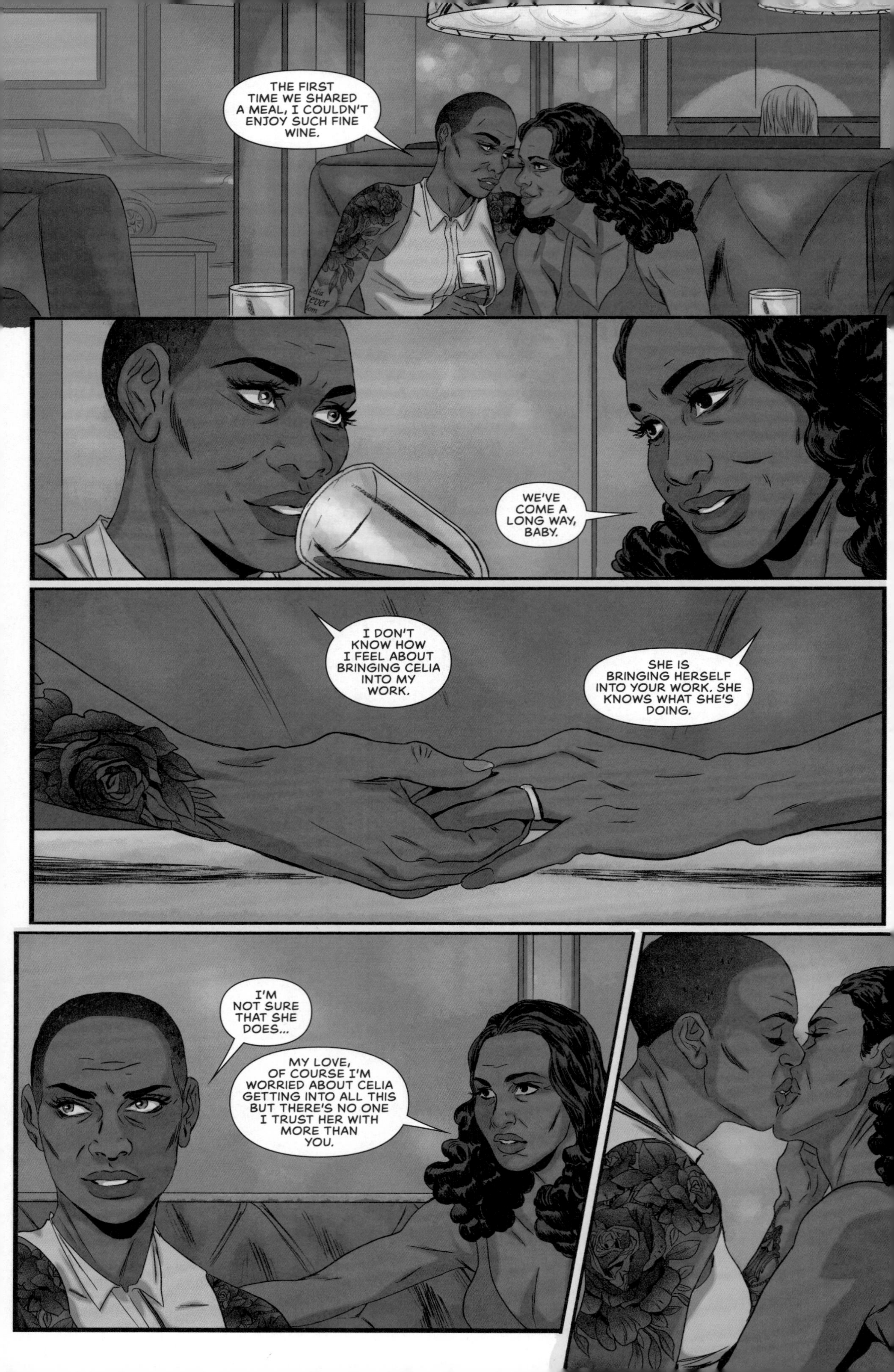
THE FIRST TIME WE SHARED A MEAL, I COULDN'T ENJOY SUCH FINE WINE.
WE'VE COME A LONG WAY, BABY.
I DON'T KNOW HOW I FEEL ABOUT BRINGING CELIA INTO MY WORK.
SHE IS BRINGING HERSELF INTO YOUR WORK. SHE KNOWS WHAT SHE'S DOING.
I'M NOT SURE THAT SHE DOES...
MY LOVE, OF COURSE I'M WORRIED ABOUT CELIA GETTING INTO ALL THIS BUT THERE'S NO ONE I TRUST HER WITH MORE THAN YOU.

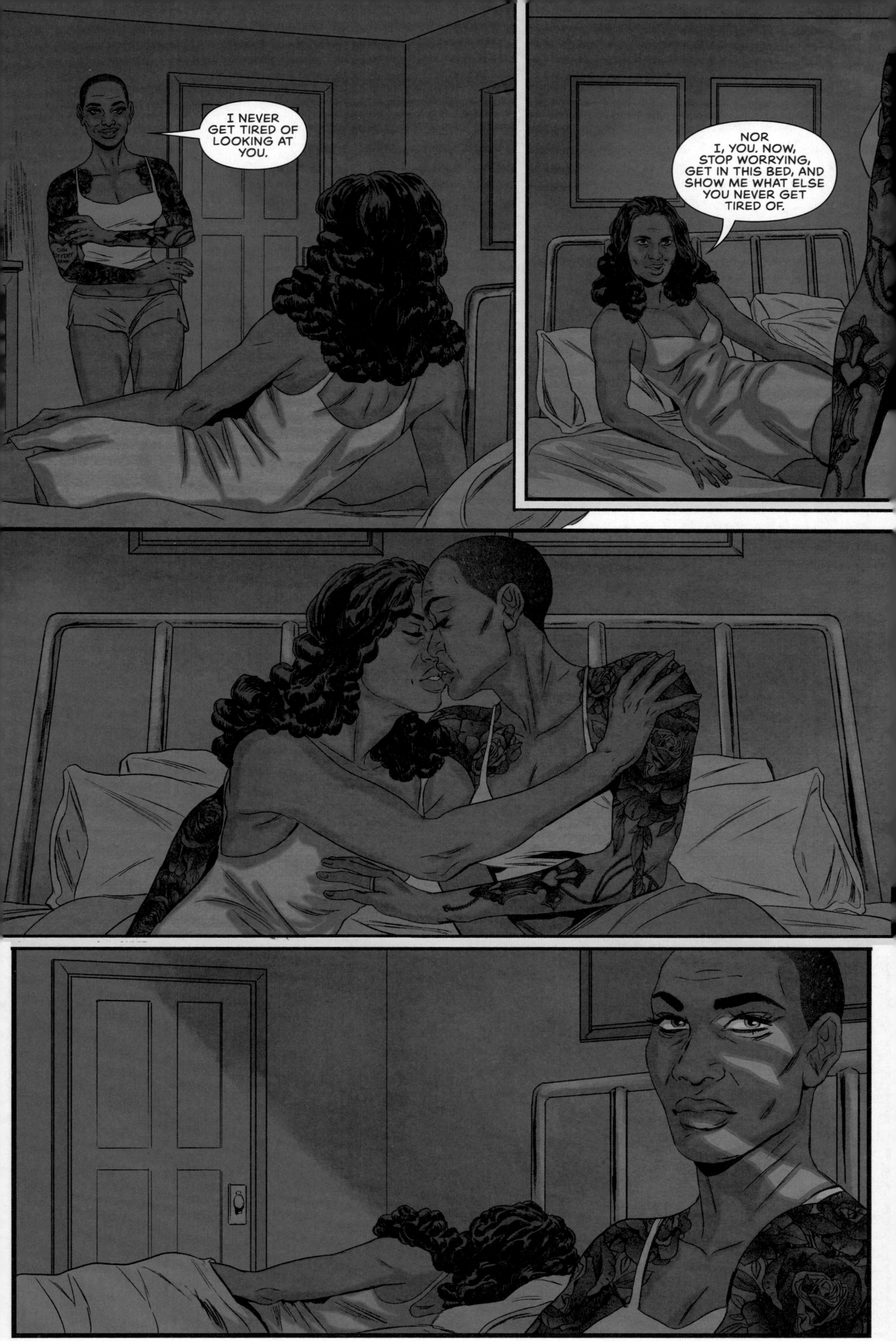
I NEVER GET TIRED OF LOOKING AT YOU.
NOR I, YOU. NOW, STOP WORRYING, GET IN THIS BED, AND SHOW ME WHAT ELSE YOU NEVER GET TIRED OF.

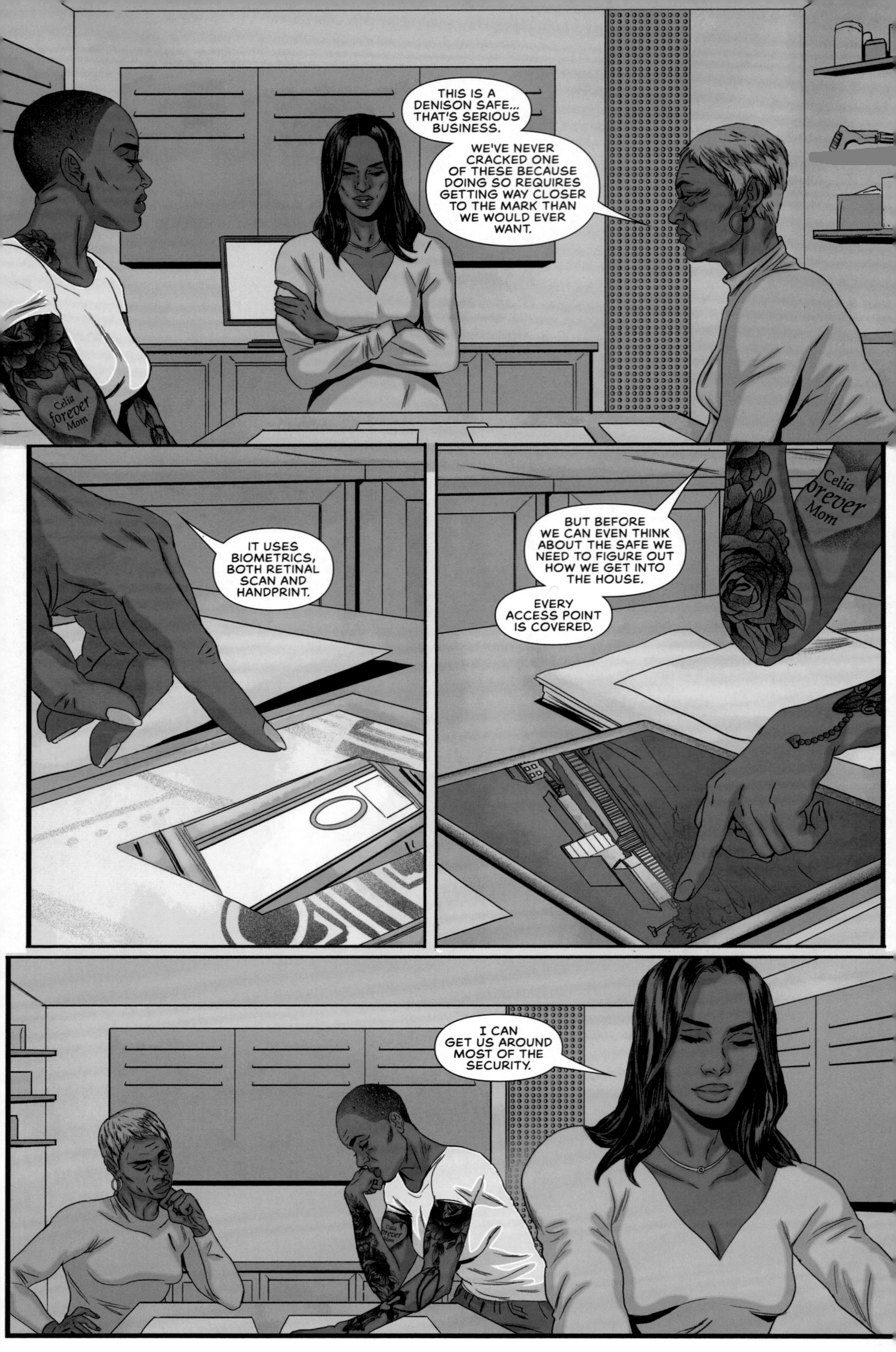
THIS IS A DENISON SAFE... THAT'S SERIOUS BUSINESS.
WE'VE NEVER CRACKED ONE OF THESE BECAUSE DOING SO REQUIRES GETTING WAY CLOSER TO THE MARK THAN WE WOULD EVER WANT.
Celia forever Mom
IT USES BIOMETRICS, BOTH RETINAL SCAN AND HANDPRINT.
BUT BEFORE WE CAN EVEN THINK ABOUT THE SAFE WE NEED TO FIGURE OUT HOW WE GET INTO THE HOUSE.
EVERY ACCESS POINT IS COVERED.
Celia forever Mom
I CAN GET US AROUND MOST OF THE SECURITY.

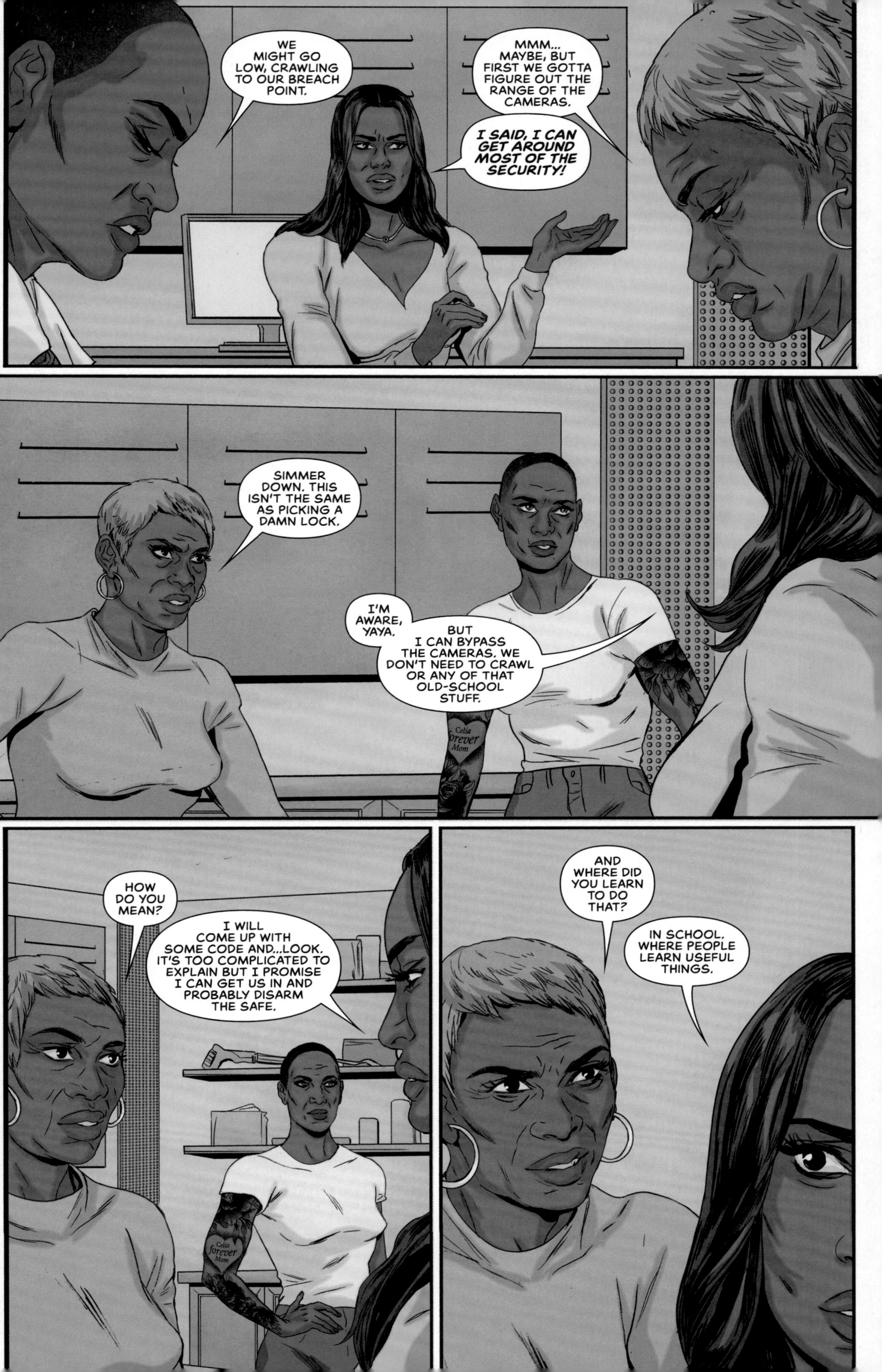
WE MIGHT GO LOW, CRAWLING TO OUR BREACH POINT.
MMM... MAYBE, BUT FIRST WE GOTTA FIGURE OUT THE RANGE OF THE CAMERAS.
I SAID, I CAN GET AROUND MOST OF THE SECURITY!
SIMMER DOWN. THIS ISN'T THE SAME AS PICKING A DAMN LOCK.
I'M AWARE, YAYA.
BUT I CAN BYPASS THE CAMERAS. WE DON'T NEED TO CRAWL OR ANY OF THAT OLD-SCHOOL STUFF.
Celia forever Mom
HOW DO YOU MEAN?
I WILL COME UP WITH SOME CODE AND...LOOK. IT'S TOO COMPLICATED TO EXPLAIN BUT I PROMISE I CAN GET US IN AND PROBABLY DISARM THE SAFE.
Celia forever Mom
AND WHERE DID YOU LEARN TO DO THAT?
IN SCHOOL. WHERE PEOPLE LEARN USEFUL THINGS.

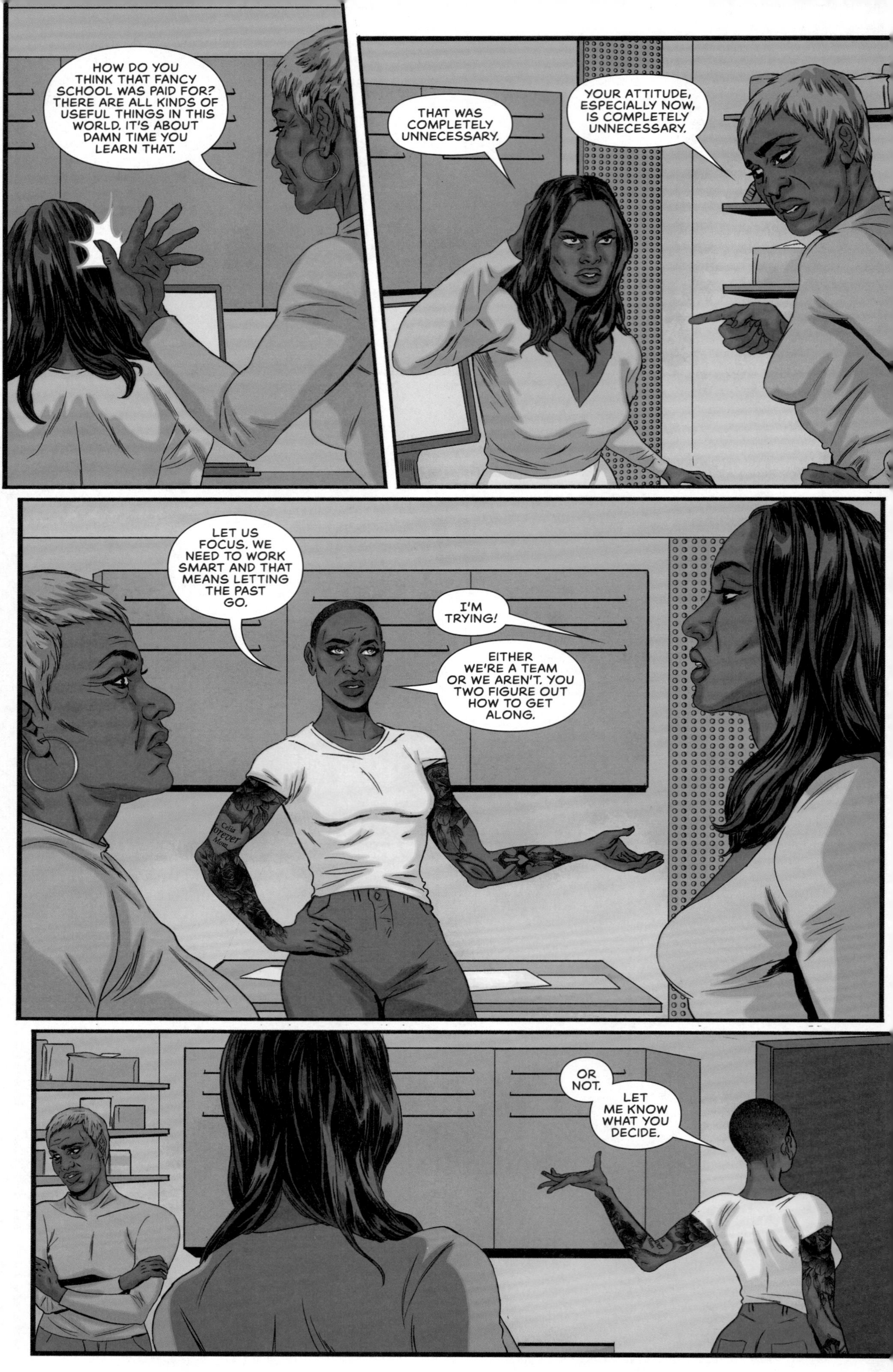
HOW DO YOU THINK THAT FANCY SCHOOL WAS PAID FOR? THERE ARE ALL KINDS OF USEFUL THINGS IN THIS WORLD, IT'S ABOUT DAMN TIME YOU LEARN THAT.
THAT WAS COMPLETELY UNNECESSARY.
YOUR ATTITUDE, ESPECIALLY NOW, IS COMPLETELY UNNECESSARY.
LET US FOCUS. WE NEED TO WORK SMART AND THAT MEANS LETTING THE PAST GO.
I'M TRYING!
EITHER WE'RE A TEAM OR WE AREN'T. YOU TWO FIGURE OUT HOW TO GET ALONG.
OR NOT.
LET ME KNOW WHAT YOU DECIDE.

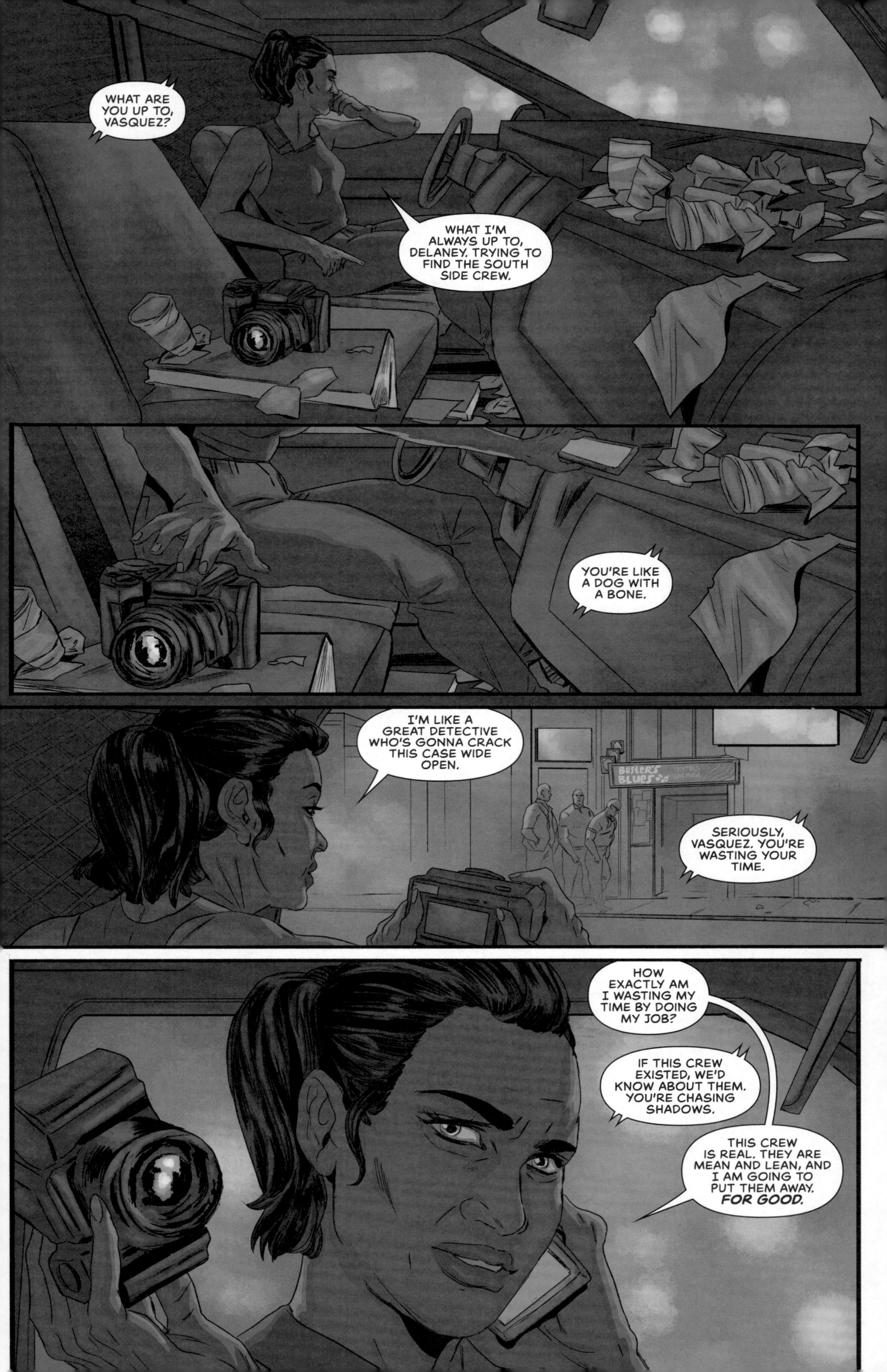
WHAT ARE YOU UP TO, VASQUEZ?
WHAT I'M ALWAYS UP TO, DELANEY. TRYING TO FIND THE SOUTH SIDE CREW.
YOU'RE LIKE A DOG WITH A BONE.
I'M LIKE A GREAT DETECTIVE WHO'S GONNA CRACK THIS CASE WIDE OPEN.
BUSTER'S BLUES
SERIOUSLY, VASQUEZ, YOU'RE WASTING YOUR TIME.
HOW EXACTLY AM I WASTING MY TIME BY DOING MY JOB?
IF THIS CREW EXISTED, WE'D KNOW ABOUT THEM. YOU'RE CHASING SHADOWS.
THIS CREW IS REAL. THEY ARE MEAN AND LEAN, AND I AM GOING TO PUT THEM AWAY. ***FOR GOOD.***

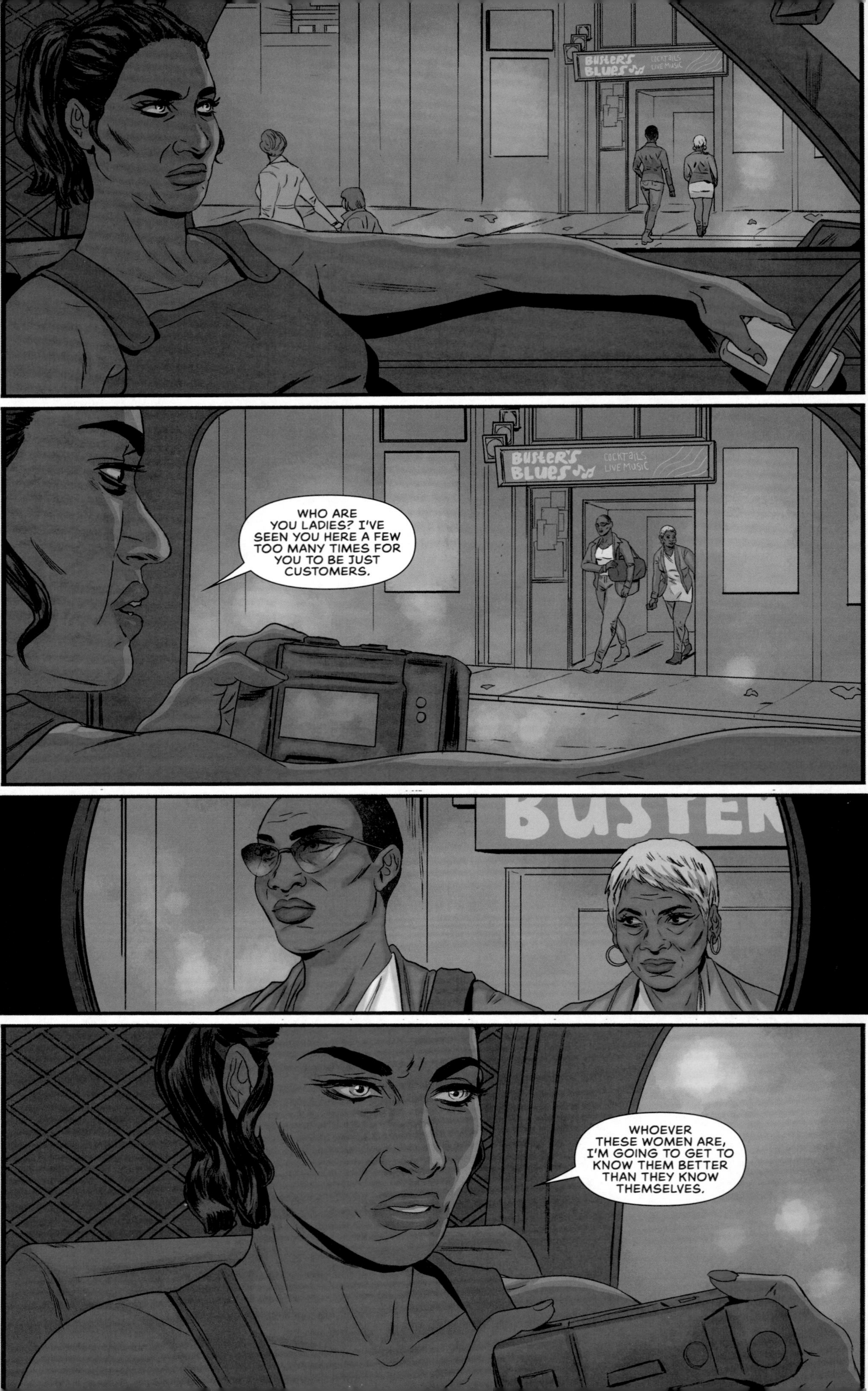
BUSTER'S BLUES
COCKTAILS LIVE MUSIC
BUSTER'S BLUES
COCKTAILS LIVE MUSIC
WHO ARE YOU LADIES? I'VE SEEN YOU HERE A FEW TOO MANY TIMES FOR YOU TO BE JUST CUSTOMERS.
BUSTER
WHOEVER THESE WOMEN ARE, I'M GOING TO GET TO KNOW THEM BETTER THAN THEY KNOW THEMSELVES.

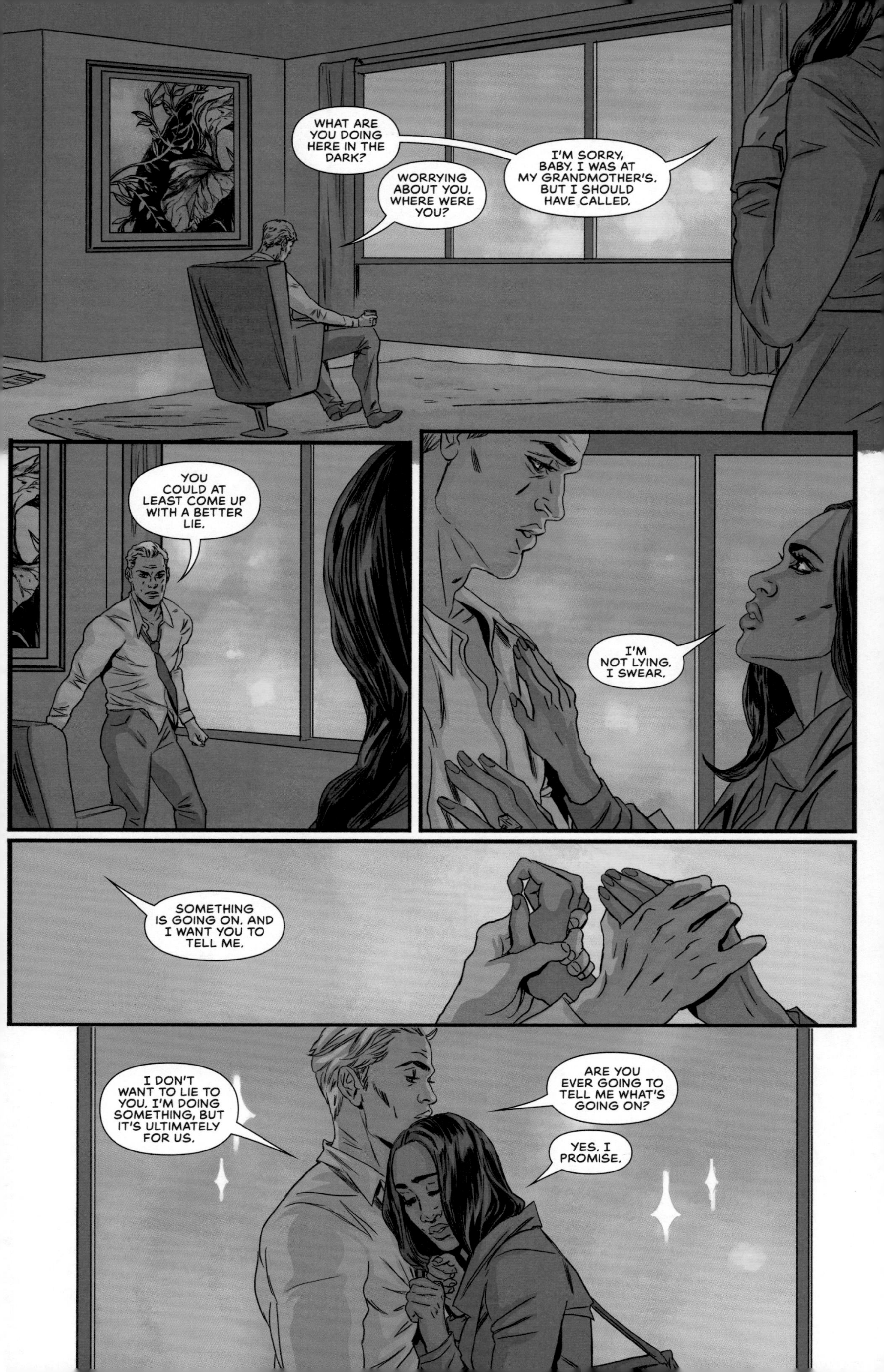
WHAT ARE YOU DOING HERE IN THE DARK?
WORRYING ABOUT YOU. WHERE WERE YOU?
I'M SORRY, BABY. I WAS AT MY GRANDMOTHER'S. BUT I SHOULD HAVE CALLED.
YOU COULD AT LEAST COME UP WITH A BETTER LIE.
I'M NOT LYING. I SWEAR.
SOMETHING IS GOING ON, AND I WANT YOU TO TELL ME.
I DON'T WANT TO LIE TO YOU. I'M DOING SOMETHING, BUT IT'S ULTIMATELY FOR US.
ARE YOU EVER GOING TO TELL ME WHAT'S GOING ON?
YES. I PROMISE.

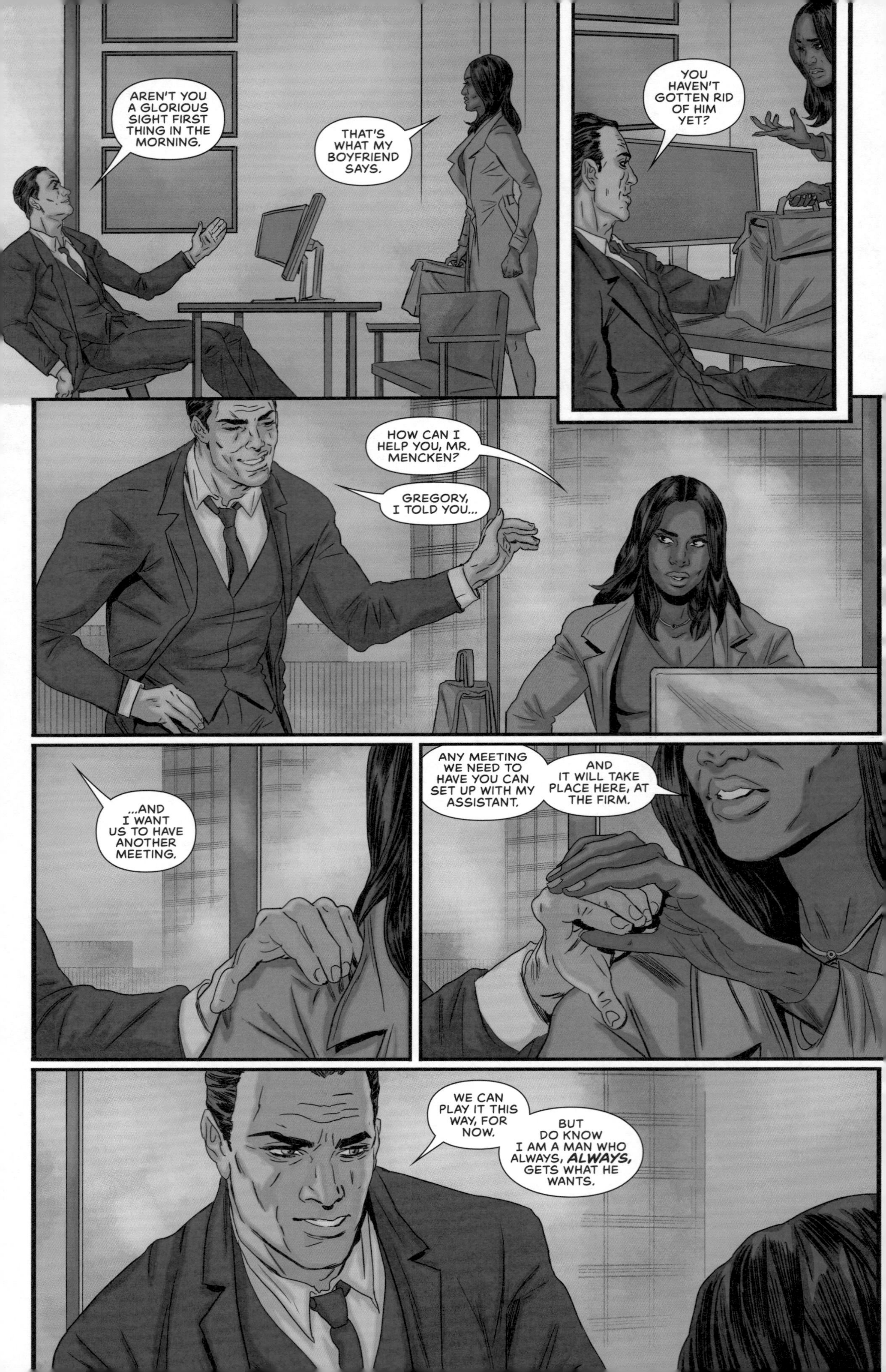
AREN'T YOU A GLORIOUS SIGHT FIRST THING IN THE MORNING.
THAT'S WHAT MY BOYFRIEND SAYS.
YOU HAVEN'T GOTTEN RID OF HIM YET?
HOW CAN I HELP YOU, MR. MENCKEN?
GREGORY, I TOLD YOU...
...AND I WANT US TO HAVE ANOTHER MEETING.
ANY MEETING WE NEED TO HAVE YOU CAN SET UP WITH MY ASSISTANT.
AND IT WILL TAKE PLACE HERE, AT THE FIRM.
WE CAN PLAY IT THIS WAY, FOR NOW.
BUT DO KNOW I AM A MAN WHO ALWAYS, ***ALWAYS,*** GETS WHAT HE WANTS.

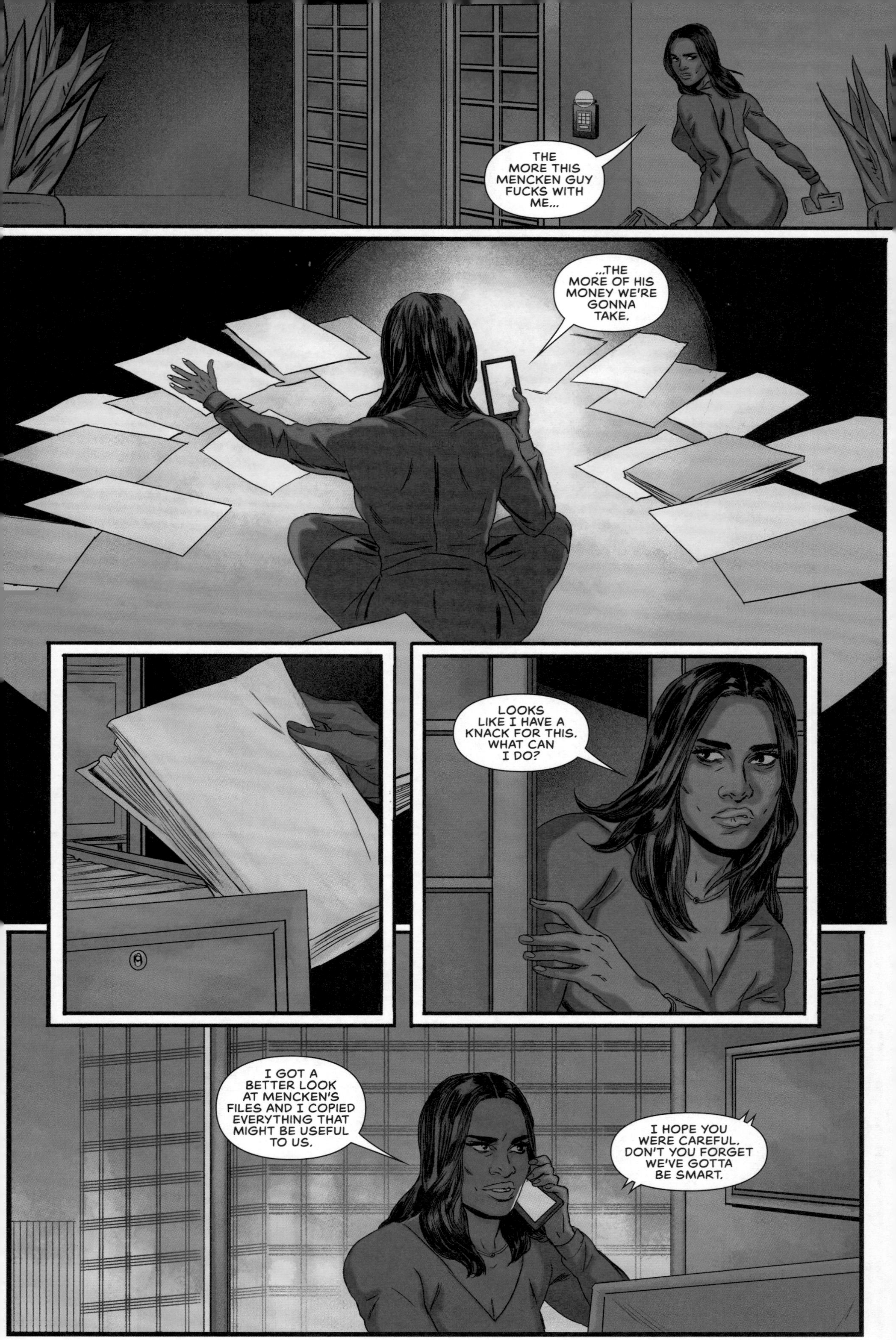
THE MORE THIS MENCKEN GUY FUCKS WITH ME...
...THE MORE OF HIS MONEY WE'RE GONNA TAKE.
LOOKS LIKE I HAVE A KNACK FOR THIS. WHAT CAN I DO?
I GOT A BETTER LOOK AT MENCKEN'S FILES AND I COPIED EVERYTHING THAT MIGHT BE USEFUL TO US.
I HOPE YOU WERE CAREFUL. DON'T YOU FORGET WE'VE GOTTA BE SMART.

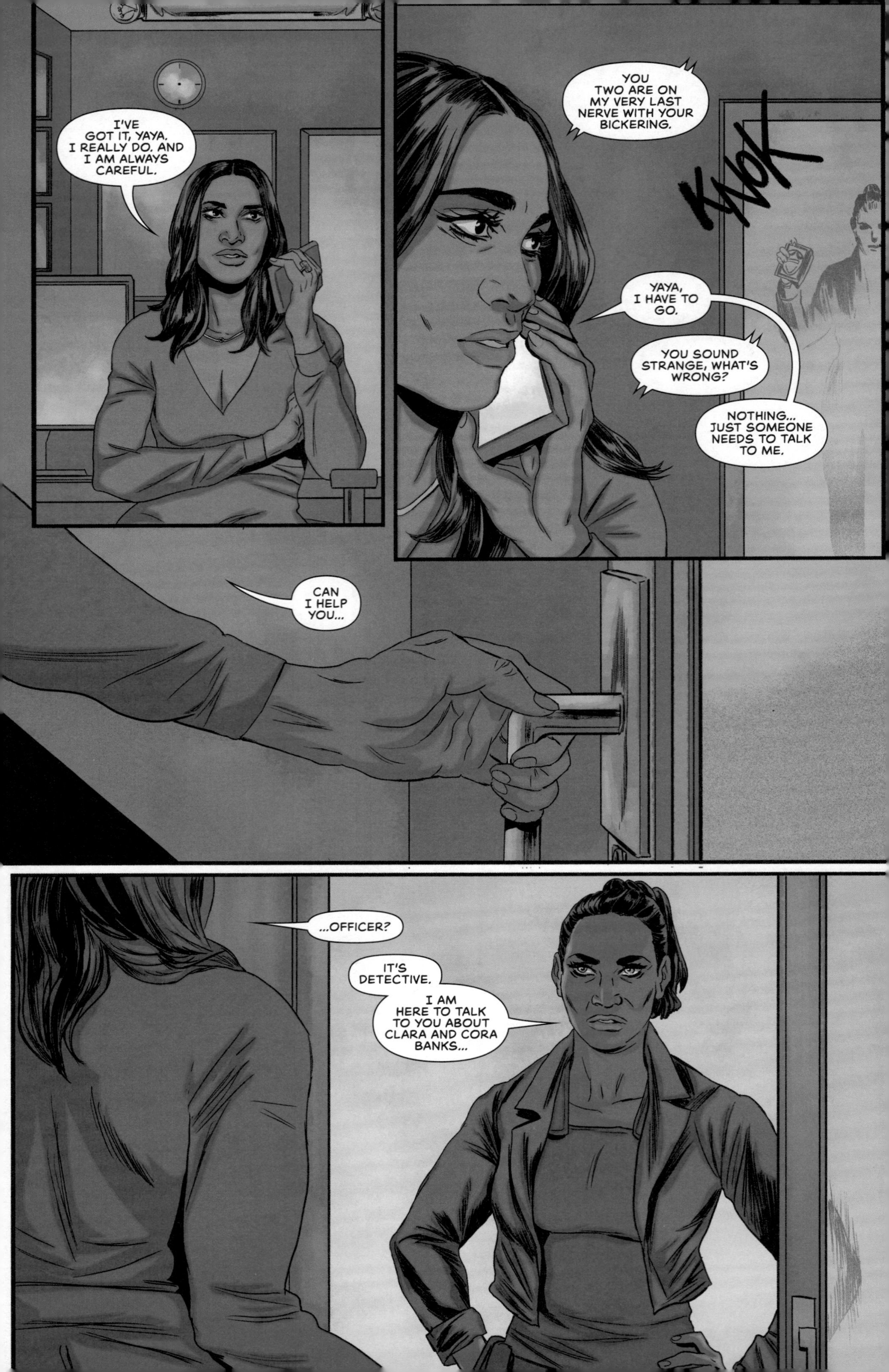
I'VE GOT IT, YAYA. I REALLY DO. AND I AM ALWAYS CAREFUL.
YOU TWO ARE ON MY VERY LAST NERVE WITH YOUR BICKERING.
KNOK
YAYA, I HAVE TO GO.
YOU SOUND STRANGE, WHAT'S WRONG?
NOTHING... JUST SOMEONE NEEDS TO TALK TO ME.
CAN I HELP YOU...
...OFFICER?
IT'S DETECTIVE.
I AM HERE TO TALK TO YOU ABOUT CLARA AND CORA BANKS...

CHAPTER 4

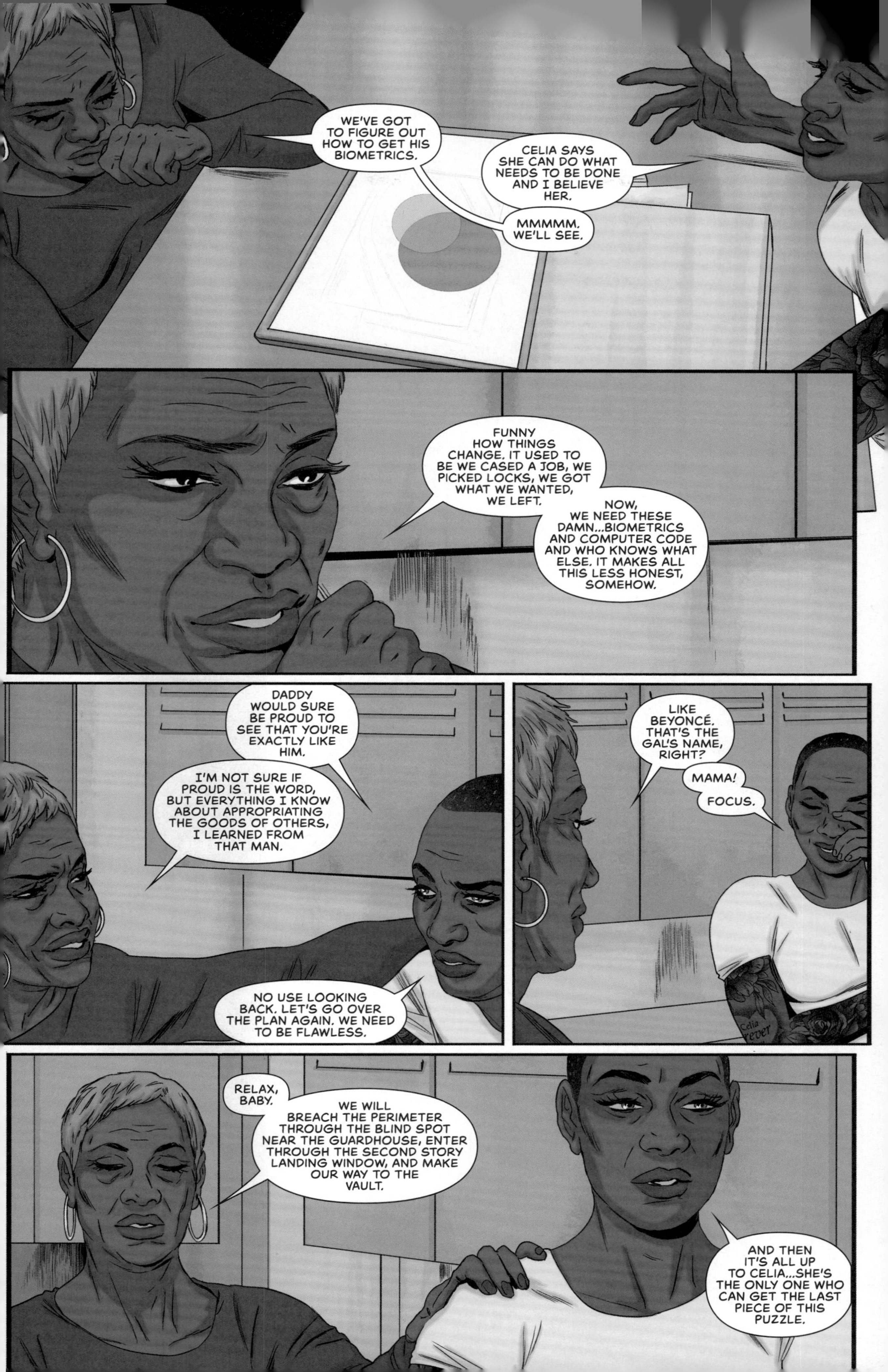
WE'VE GOT TO FIGURE OUT HOW TO GET HIS BIOMETRICS.
CELIA SAYS SHE CAN DO WHAT NEEDS TO BE DONE AND I BELIEVE HER.
MMMMM. WE'LL SEE.
FUNNY HOW THINGS CHANGE. IT USED TO BE WE CASED A JOB, WE PICKED LOCKS, WE GOT WHAT WE WANTED, WE LEFT.
NOW, WE NEED THESE DAMN...BIOMETRICS AND COMPUTER CODE AND WHO KNOWS WHAT ELSE. IT MAKES ALL THIS LESS HONEST, SOMEHOW.
DADDY WOULD SURE BE PROUD TO SEE THAT YOU'RE EXACTLY LIKE HIM.
I'M NOT SURE IF PROUD IS THE WORD, BUT EVERYTHING I KNOW ABOUT APPROPRIATING THE GOODS OF OTHERS, I LEARNED FROM THAT MAN.
NO USE LOOKING BACK. LET'S GO OVER THE PLAN AGAIN. WE NEED TO BE FLAWLESS.
LIKE BEYONCÉ. THAT'S THE GAL'S NAME, RIGHT?
MAMA!
FOCUS.
Celia
RELAX, BABY.
WE WILL BREACH THE PERIMETER THROUGH THE BLIND SPOT NEAR THE GUARDHOUSE, ENTER THROUGH THE SECOND STORY LANDING WINDOW, AND MAKE OUR WAY TO THE VAULT.
AND THEN IT'S ALL UP TO CELIA...SHE'S THE ONLY ONE WHO CAN GET THE LAST PIECE OF THIS PUZZLE.

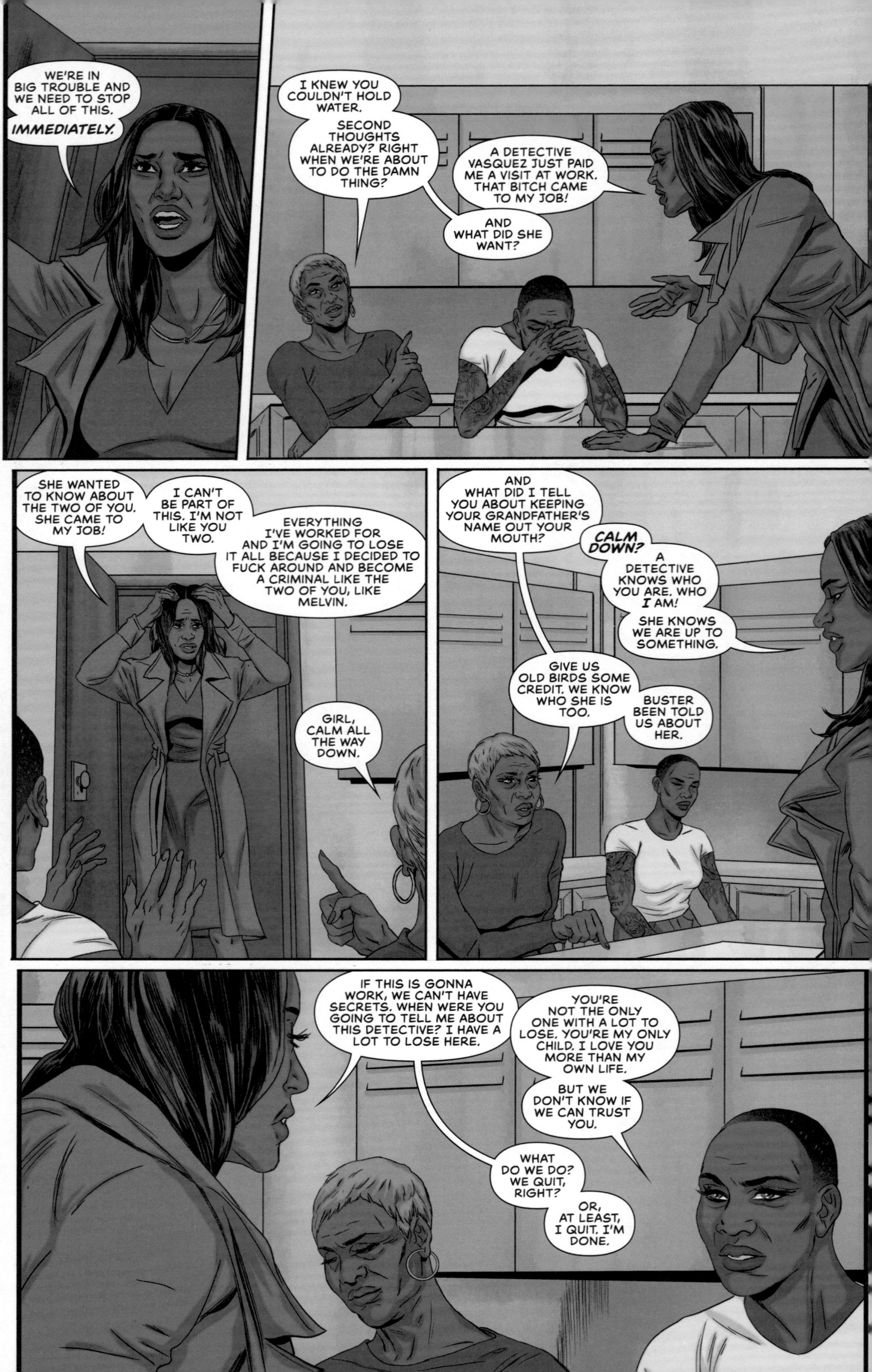
WE'RE IN BIG TROUBLE AND WE NEED TO STOP ALL OF THIS. IMMEDIATELY.
I KNEW YOU COULDN'T HOLD WATER.
SECOND THOUGHTS ALREADY? RIGHT WHEN WE'RE ABOUT TO DO THE DAMN THING?
A DETECTIVE VASQUEZ JUST PAID ME A VISIT AT WORK. THAT BITCH CAME TO MY JOB!
AND WHAT DID SHE WANT?
SHE WANTED TO KNOW ABOUT THE TWO OF YOU. SHE CAME TO MY JOB!
I CAN'T BE PART OF THIS. I'M NOT LIKE YOU TWO.
EVERYTHING I'VE WORKED FOR AND I'M GOING TO LOSE IT ALL BECAUSE I DECIDED TO FUCK AROUND AND BECOME A CRIMINAL LIKE THE TWO OF YOU, LIKE MELVIN.
GIRL, CALM ALL THE WAY DOWN.
AND WHAT DID I TELL YOU ABOUT KEEPING YOUR GRANDFATHER'S NAME OUT YOUR MOUTH?
CALM DOWN?
A DETECTIVE KNOWS WHO YOU ARE, WHO I AM!
SHE KNOWS WE ARE UP TO SOMETHING.
GIVE US OLD BIRDS SOME CREDIT. WE KNOW WHO SHE IS TOO.
BUSTER BEEN TOLD US ABOUT HER.
IF THIS IS GONNA WORK, WE CAN'T HAVE SECRETS. WHEN WERE YOU GOING TO TELL ME ABOUT THIS DETECTIVE? I HAVE A LOT TO LOSE HERE.
YOU'RE NOT THE ONLY ONE WITH A LOT TO LOSE. YOU'RE MY ONLY CHILD. I LOVE YOU MORE THAN MY OWN LIFE.
BUT WE DON'T KNOW IF WE CAN TRUST YOU.
WHAT DO WE DO? WE QUIT, RIGHT?
OR, AT LEAST, I QUIT. I'M DONE.

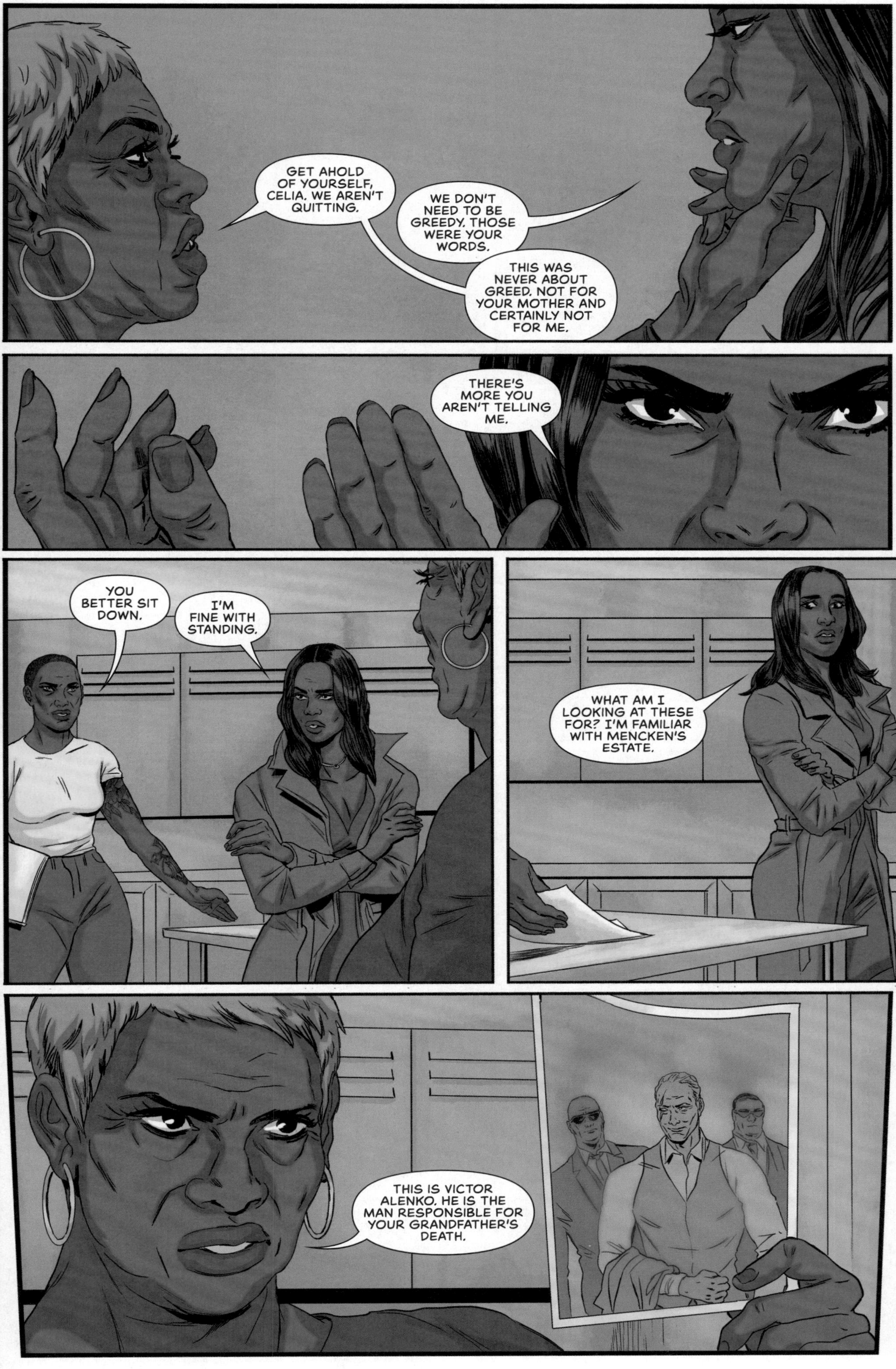
GET AHOLD OF YOURSELF, CELIA. WE AREN'T QUITTING.
WE DON'T NEED TO BE GREEDY. THOSE WERE YOUR WORDS.
THIS WAS NEVER ABOUT GREED. NOT FOR YOUR MOTHER AND CERTAINLY NOT FOR ME.
THERE'S MORE YOU AREN'T TELLING ME.
YOU BETTER SIT DOWN.
I'M FINE WITH STANDING.
WHAT AM I LOOKING AT THESE FOR? I'M FAMILIAR WITH MENCKEN'S ESTATE.
THIS IS VICTOR ALENKO. HE IS THE MAN RESPONSIBLE FOR YOUR GRANDFATHER'S DEATH.

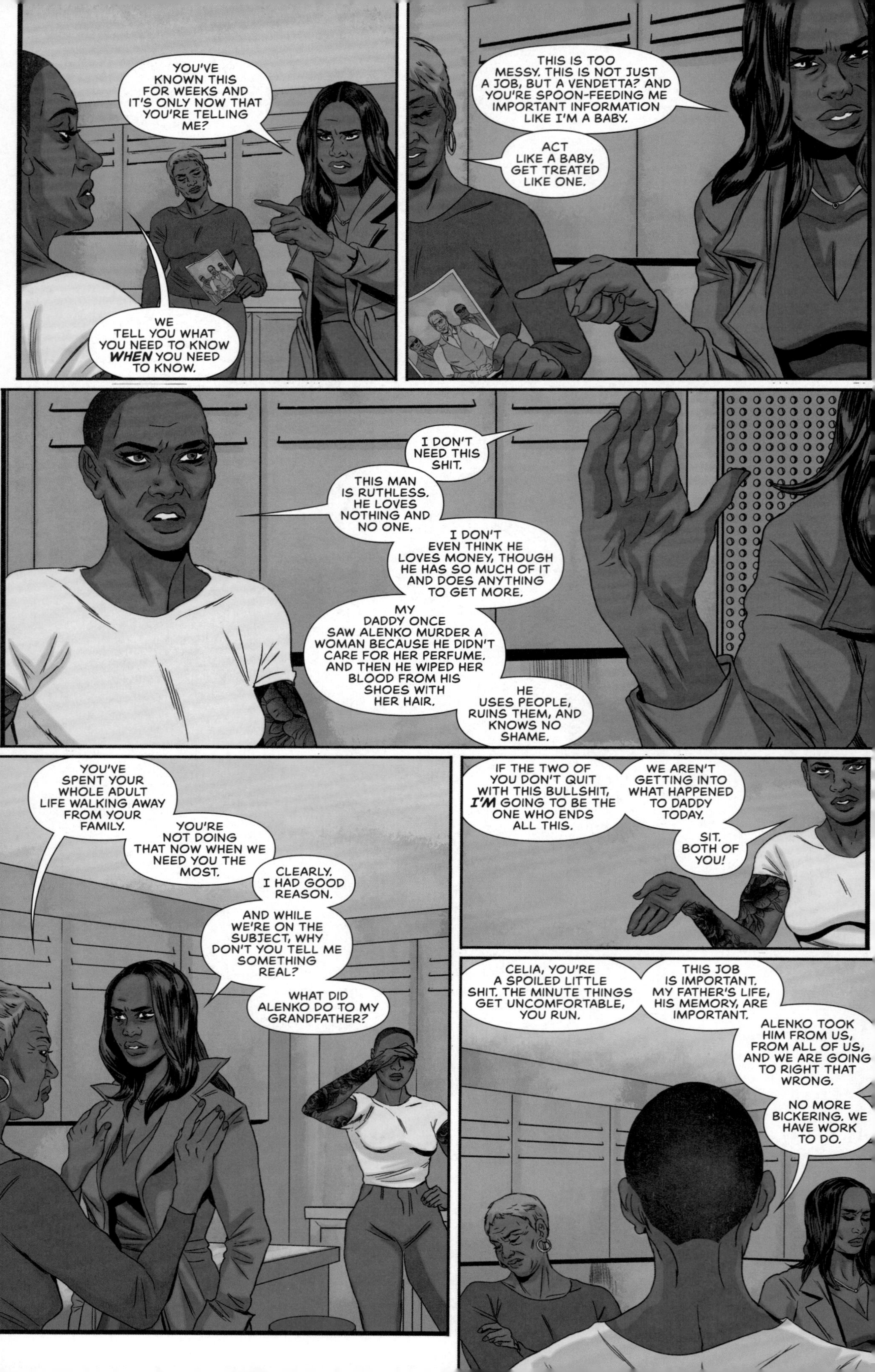
YOU'VE KNOWN THIS FOR WEEKS AND IT'S ONLY NOW THAT YOU'RE TELLING ME?
WE TELL YOU WHAT YOU NEED TO KNOW **WHEN** YOU NEED TO KNOW.
THIS IS TOO MESSY. THIS IS NOT JUST A JOB, BUT A VENDETTA? AND YOU'RE SPOON-FEEDING ME IMPORTANT INFORMATION LIKE I'M A BABY.
ACT LIKE A BABY, GET TREATED LIKE ONE.
I DON'T NEED THIS SHIT.
THIS MAN IS RUTHLESS. HE LOVES NOTHING AND NO ONE.
I DON'T EVEN THINK HE LOVES MONEY, THOUGH HE HAS SO MUCH OF IT AND DOES ANYTHING TO GET MORE.
MY DADDY ONCE SAW ALENKO MURDER A WOMAN BECAUSE HE DIDN'T CARE FOR HER PERFUME. AND THEN HE WIPED HER BLOOD FROM HIS SHOES WITH HER HAIR.
HE USES PEOPLE, RUINS THEM, AND KNOWS NO SHAME.
YOU'VE SPENT YOUR WHOLE ADULT LIFE WALKING AWAY FROM YOUR FAMILY.
YOU'RE NOT DOING THAT NOW WHEN WE NEED YOU THE MOST.
CLEARLY. I HAD GOOD REASON.
AND WHILE WE'RE ON THE SUBJECT, WHY DON'T YOU TELL ME SOMETHING REAL?
WHAT DID ALENKO DO TO MY GRANDFATHER?
IF THE TWO OF YOU DON'T QUIT WITH THIS BULLSHIT, ***I'M*** GOING TO BE THE ONE WHO ENDS ALL THIS.
WE AREN'T GETTING INTO WHAT HAPPENED TO DADDY TODAY.
SIT. BOTH OF YOU!
CELIA, YOU'RE A SPOILED LITTLE SHIT. THE MINUTE THINGS GET UNCOMFORTABLE, YOU RUN.
THIS JOB IS IMPORTANT. MY FATHER'S LIFE, HIS MEMORY, ARE IMPORTANT.
ALENKO TOOK HIM FROM US, FROM ALL OF US, AND WE ARE GOING TO RIGHT THAT WRONG.
NO MORE BICKERING. WE HAVE WORK TO DO.

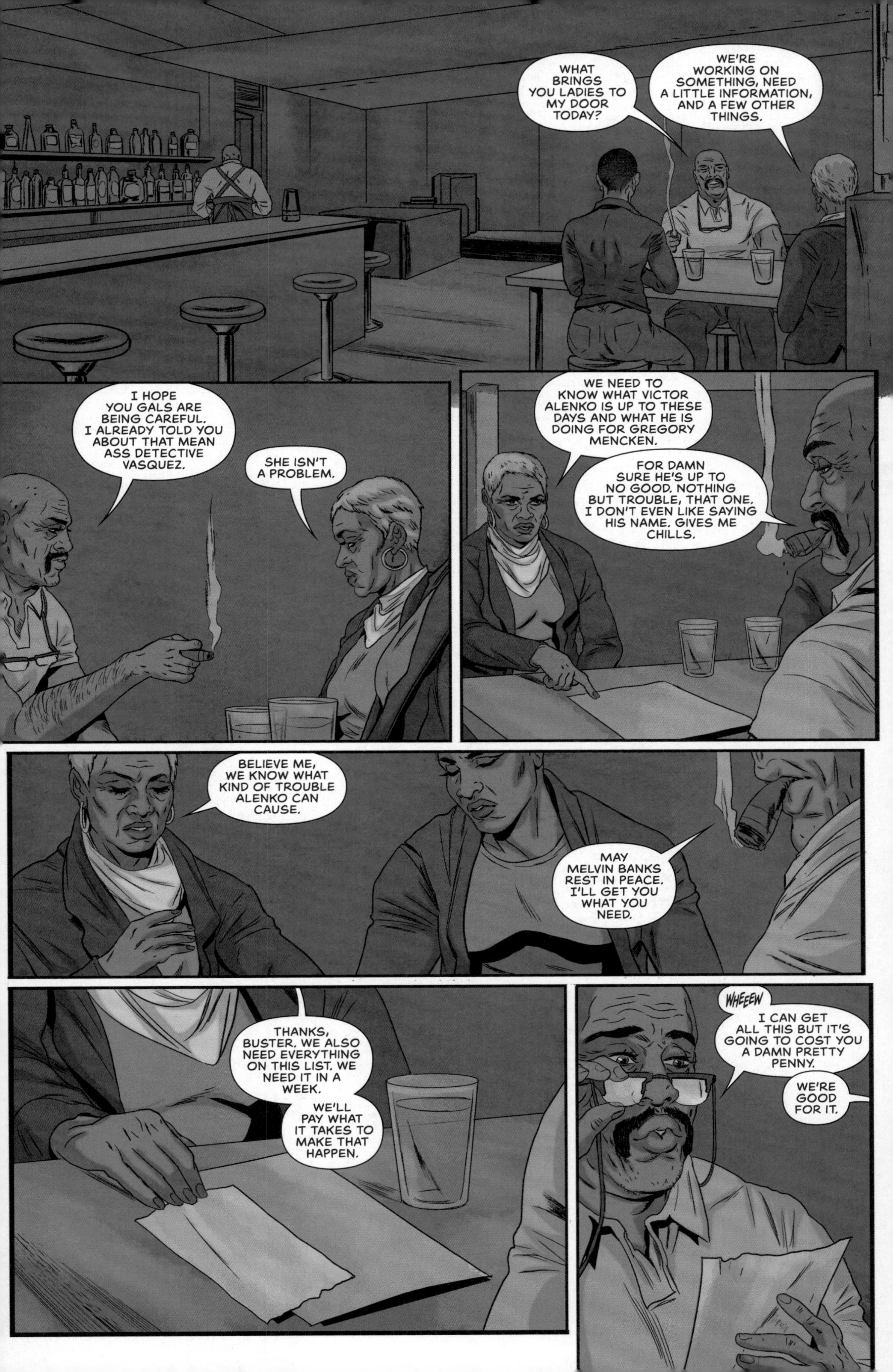
WHAT BRINGS YOU LADIES TO MY DOOR TODAY?
WE'RE WORKING ON SOMETHING, NEED A LITTLE INFORMATION, AND A FEW OTHER THINGS.
I HOPE YOU GALS ARE BEING CAREFUL. I ALREADY TOLD YOU ABOUT THAT MEAN ASS DETECTIVE VASQUEZ.
SHE ISN'T A PROBLEM.
WE NEED TO KNOW WHAT VICTOR ALENKO IS UP TO THESE DAYS AND WHAT HE IS DOING FOR GREGORY MENCKEN.
FOR DAMN SURE HE'S UP TO NO GOOD. NOTHING BUT TROUBLE, THAT ONE. I DON'T EVEN LIKE SAYING HIS NAME. GIVES ME CHILLS.
BELIEVE ME, WE KNOW WHAT KIND OF TROUBLE ALENKO CAN CAUSE.
MAY MELVIN BANKS REST IN PEACE. I'LL GET YOU WHAT YOU NEED.
THANKS, BUSTER. WE ALSO NEED EVERYTHING ON THIS LIST. WE NEED IT IN A WEEK.
WE'LL PAY WHAT IT TAKES TO MAKE THAT HAPPEN.
WHEEEW
I CAN GET ALL THIS BUT IT'S GOING TO COST YOU A DAMN PRETTY PENNY.
WE'RE GOOD FOR IT.

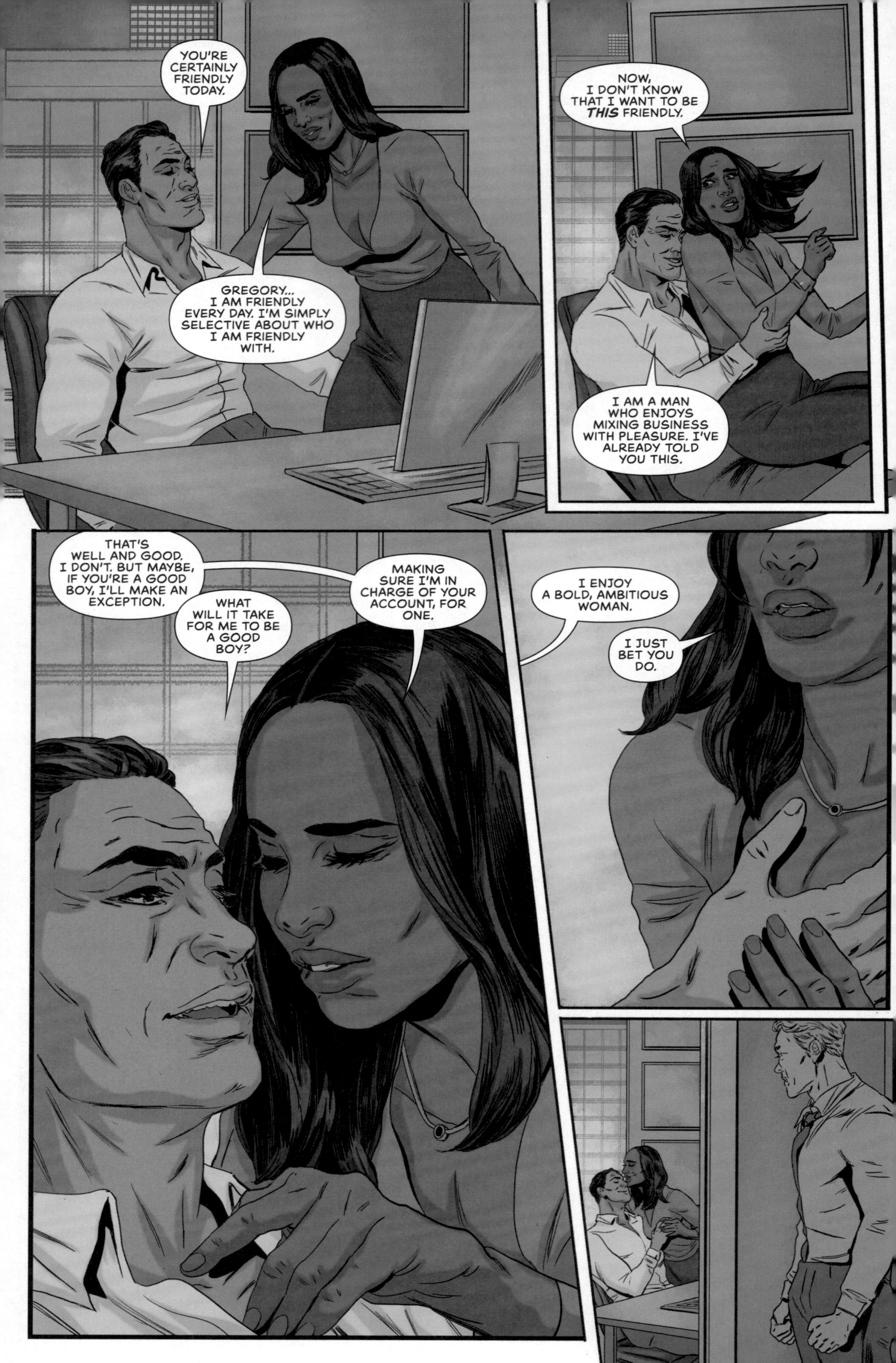
YOU'RE CERTAINLY FRIENDLY TODAY.
GREGORY... I AM FRIENDLY EVERY DAY. I'M SIMPLY SELECTIVE ABOUT WHO I AM FRIENDLY WITH.
NOW, I DON'T KNOW THAT I WANT TO BE THIS FRIENDLY.
I AM A MAN WHO ENJOYS MIXING BUSINESS WITH PLEASURE. I'VE ALREADY TOLD YOU THIS.
THAT'S WELL AND GOOD. I DON'T. BUT MAYBE, IF YOU'RE A GOOD BOY, I'LL MAKE AN EXCEPTION.
WHAT WILL IT TAKE FOR ME TO BE A GOOD BOY?
MAKING SURE I'M IN CHARGE OF YOUR ACCOUNT, FOR ONE.
I ENJOY A BOLD, AMBITIOUS WOMAN.
I JUST BET YOU DO.

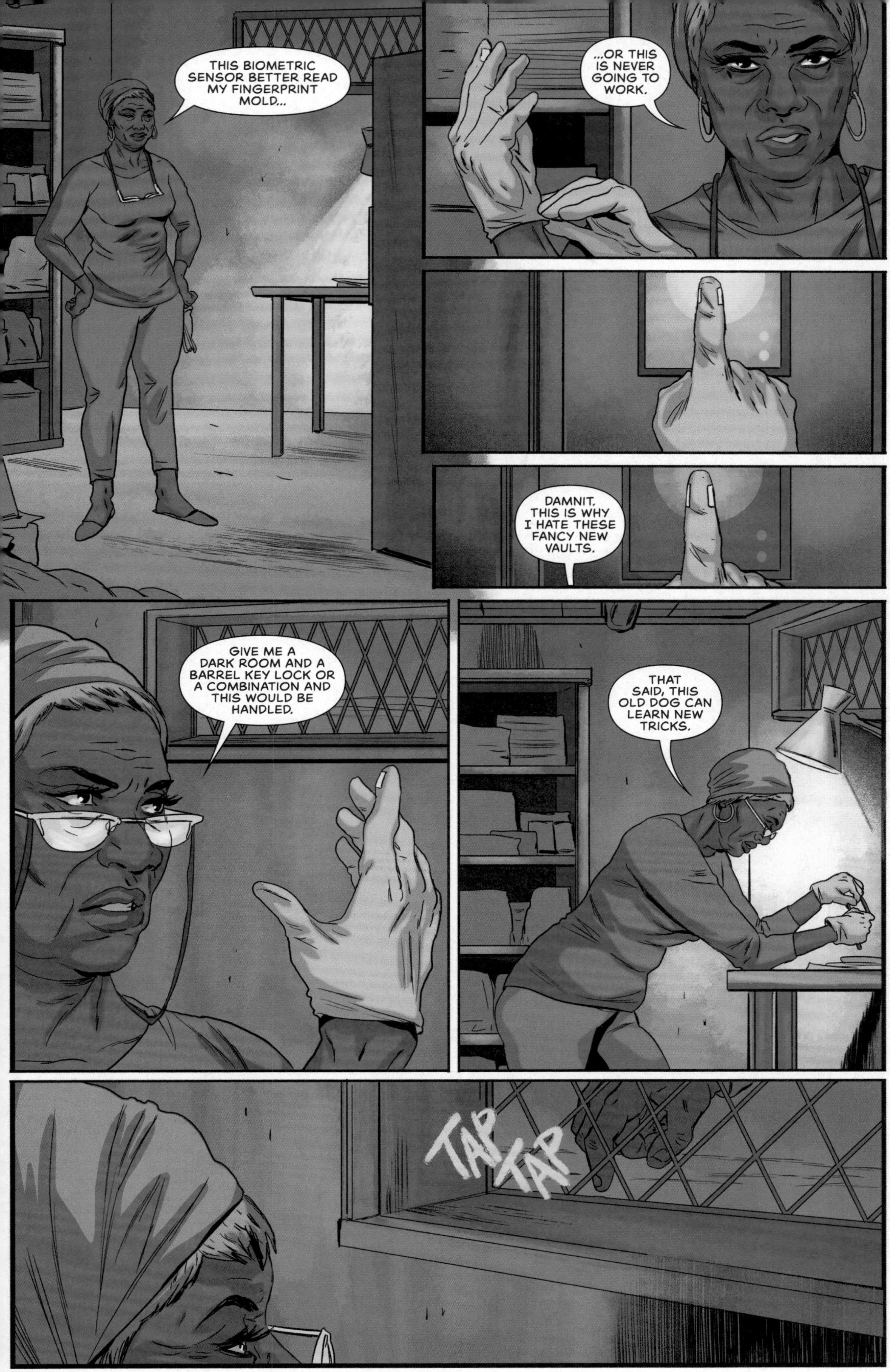

THIS BIOMETRIC SENSOR BETTER READ MY FINGERPRINT MOLD...
...OR THIS IS NEVER GOING TO WORK.
DAMNIT. THIS IS WHY I HATE THESE FANCY NEW VAULTS.
GIVE ME A DARK ROOM AND A BARREL KEY LOCK OR A COMBINATION AND THIS WOULD BE HANDLED.
THAT SAID, THIS OLD DOG CAN LEARN NEW TRICKS.
TAP TAP

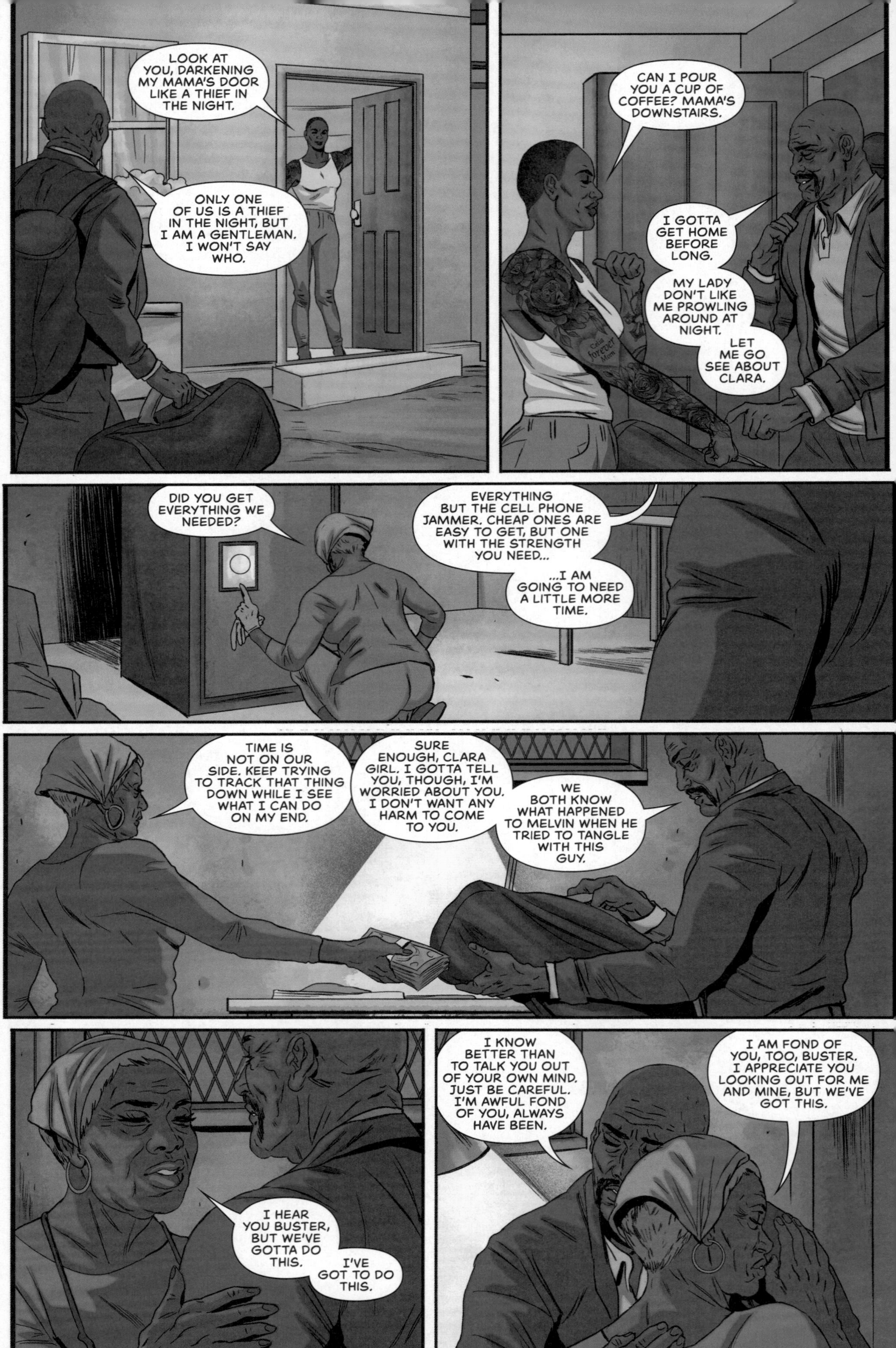

LOOK AT YOU, DARKENING MY MAMA'S DOOR LIKE A THIEF IN THE NIGHT.
ONLY ONE OF US IS A THIEF IN THE NIGHT, BUT I AM A GENTLEMAN. I WON'T SAY WHO.
CAN I POUR YOU A CUP OF COFFEE? MAMA'S DOWNSTAIRS.
I GOTTA GET HOME BEFORE LONG.
MY LADY DON'T LIKE ME PROWLING AROUND AT NIGHT.
LET ME GO SEE ABOUT CLARA.
DID YOU GET EVERYTHING WE NEEDED?
EVERYTHING BUT THE CELL PHONE JAMMER. CHEAP ONES ARE EASY TO GET, BUT ONE WITH THE STRENGTH YOU NEED...
...I AM GOING TO NEED A LITTLE MORE TIME.
TIME IS NOT ON OUR SIDE. KEEP TRYING TO TRACK THAT THING DOWN WHILE I SEE WHAT I CAN DO ON MY END.
SURE ENOUGH, CLARA GIRL. I GOTTA TELL YOU, THOUGH, I'M WORRIED ABOUT YOU. I DON'T WANT ANY HARM TO COME TO YOU.
WE BOTH KNOW WHAT HAPPENED TO MELVIN WHEN HE TRIED TO TANGLE WITH THIS GUY.
I HEAR YOU BUSTER, BUT WE'VE GOTTA DO THIS.
I'VE GOT TO DO THIS.
I KNOW BETTER THAN TO TALK YOU OUT OF YOUR OWN MIND. JUST BE CAREFUL. I'M AWFUL FOND OF YOU, ALWAYS HAVE BEEN.
I AM FOND OF YOU, TOO, BUSTER. I APPRECIATE YOU LOOKING OUT FOR ME AND MINE, BUT WE'VE GOT THIS.

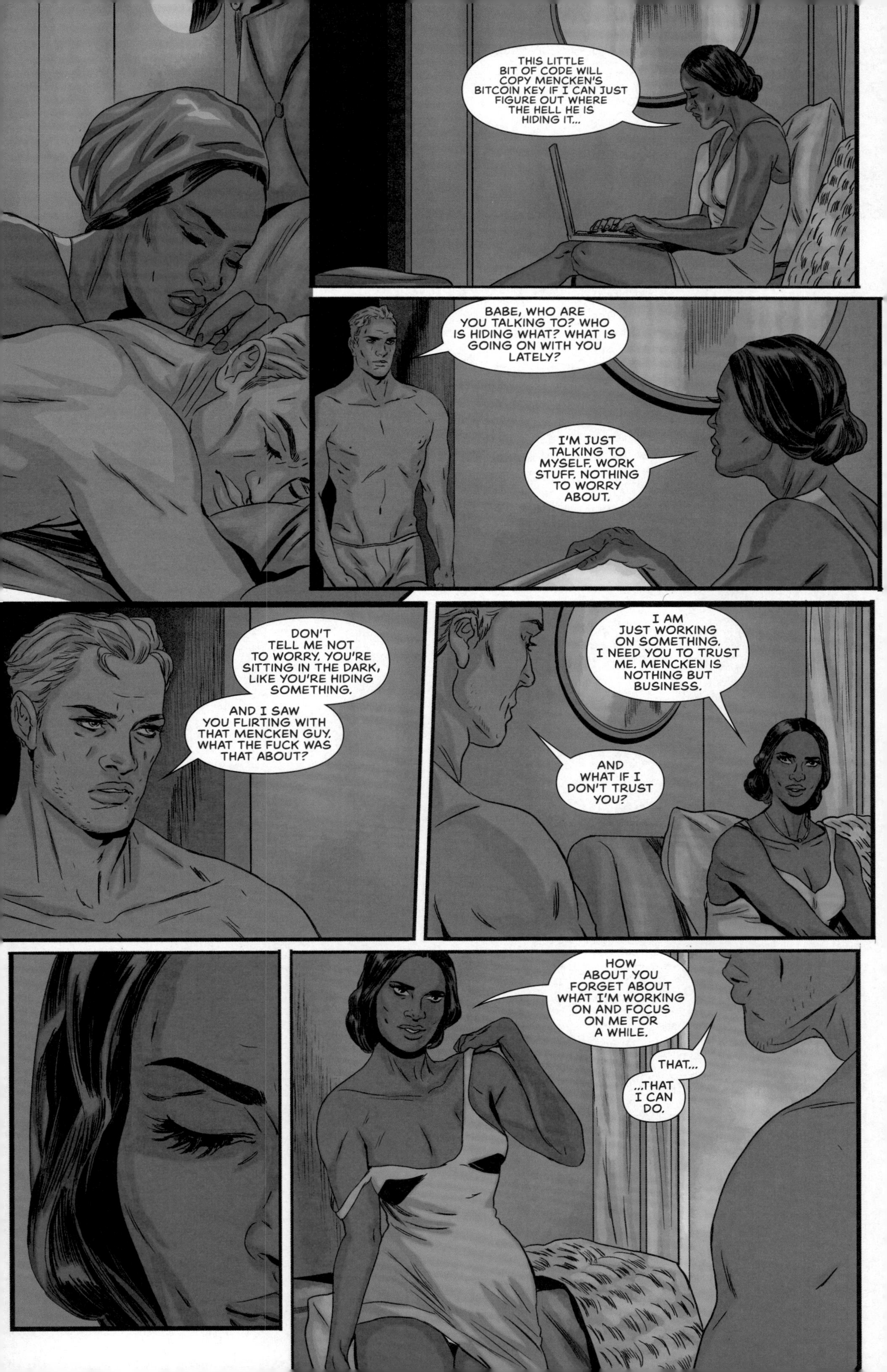

THIS LITTLE BIT OF CODE WILL COPY MENCKEN'S BITCOIN KEY IF I CAN JUST FIGURE OUT WHERE THE HELL HE IS HIDING IT...
BABE, WHO ARE YOU TALKING TO? WHO IS HIDING WHAT? WHAT IS GOING ON WITH YOU LATELY?
I'M JUST TALKING TO MYSELF. WORK STUFF. NOTHING TO WORRY ABOUT.
DON'T TELL ME NOT TO WORRY. YOU'RE SITTING IN THE DARK, LIKE YOU'RE HIDING SOMETHING.
AND I SAW YOU FLIRTING WITH THAT MENCKEN GUY. WHAT THE FUCK WAS THAT ABOUT?
I AM JUST WORKING ON SOMETHING. I NEED YOU TO TRUST ME. MENCKEN IS NOTHING BUT BUSINESS.
AND WHAT IF I DON'T TRUST YOU?
HOW ABOUT YOU FORGET ABOUT WHAT I'M WORKING ON AND FOCUS ON ME FOR A WHILE.
THAT...
...THAT I CAN DO.

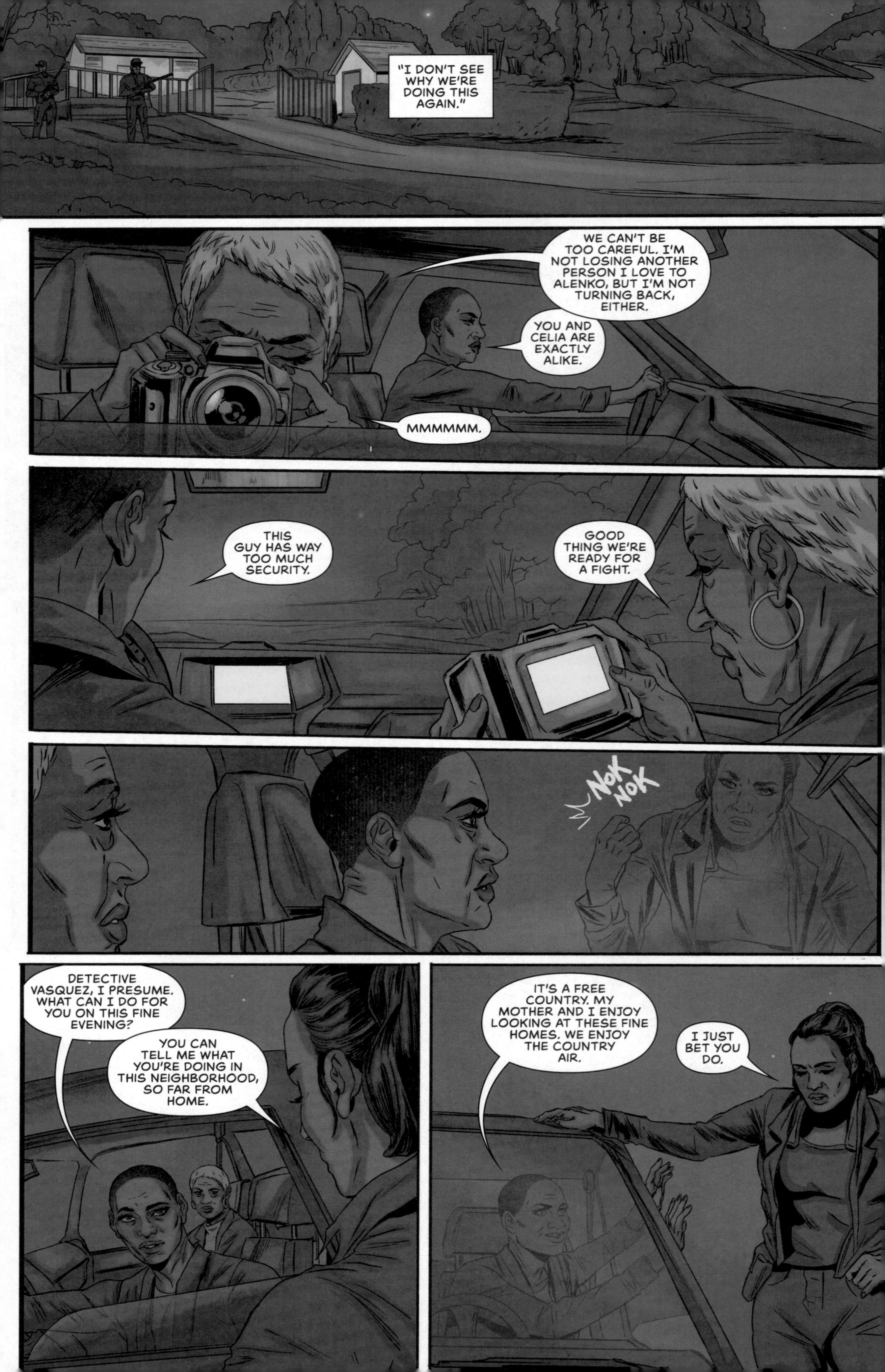
"I DON'T SEE WHY WE'RE DOING THIS AGAIN."
WE CAN'T BE TOO CAREFUL. I'M NOT LOSING ANOTHER PERSON I LOVE TO ALENKO, BUT I'M NOT TURNING BACK, EITHER.
YOU AND CELIA ARE EXACTLY ALIKE.
MMMMMM.
THIS GUY HAS WAY TOO MUCH SECURITY.
GOOD THING WE'RE READY FOR A FIGHT.
NOK NOK
DETECTIVE VASQUEZ, I PRESUME. WHAT CAN I DO FOR YOU ON THIS FINE EVENING?
YOU CAN TELL ME WHAT YOU'RE DOING IN THIS NEIGHBORHOOD, SO FAR FROM HOME.
IT'S A FREE COUNTRY. MY MOTHER AND I ENJOY LOOKING AT THESE FINE HOMES. WE ENJOY THE COUNTRY AIR.
I JUST BET YOU DO.

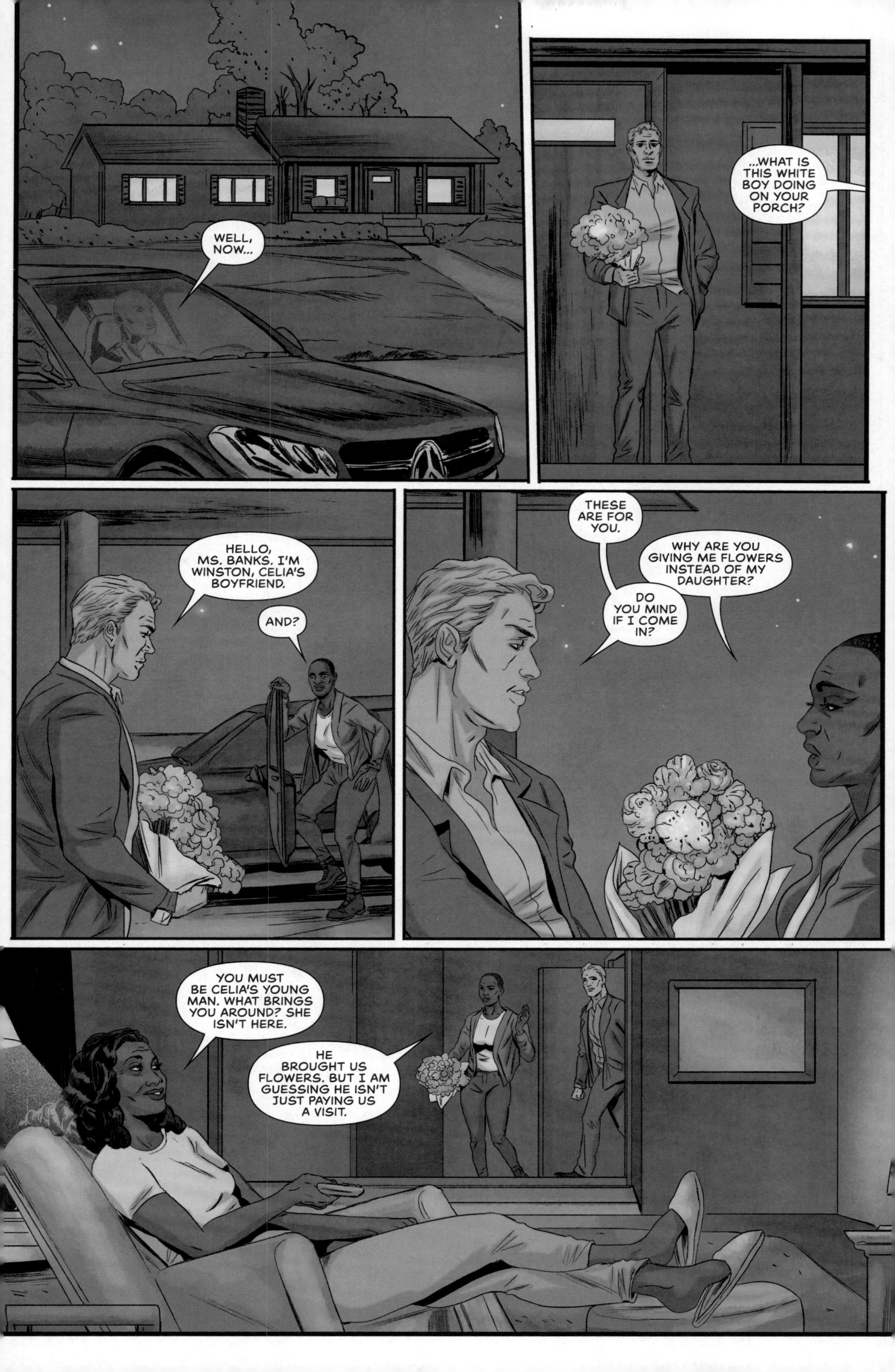
WELL, NOW...
...WHAT IS THIS WHITE BOY DOING ON YOUR PORCH?
HELLO, MS. BANKS. I'M WINSTON, CELIA'S BOYFRIEND.
AND?
THESE ARE FOR YOU.
WHY ARE YOU GIVING ME FLOWERS INSTEAD OF MY DAUGHTER?
DO YOU MIND IF I COME IN?
YOU MUST BE CELIA'S YOUNG MAN. WHAT BRINGS YOU AROUND? SHE ISN'T HERE.
HE BROUGHT US FLOWERS. BUT I AM GUESSING HE ISN'T JUST PAYING US A VISIT.

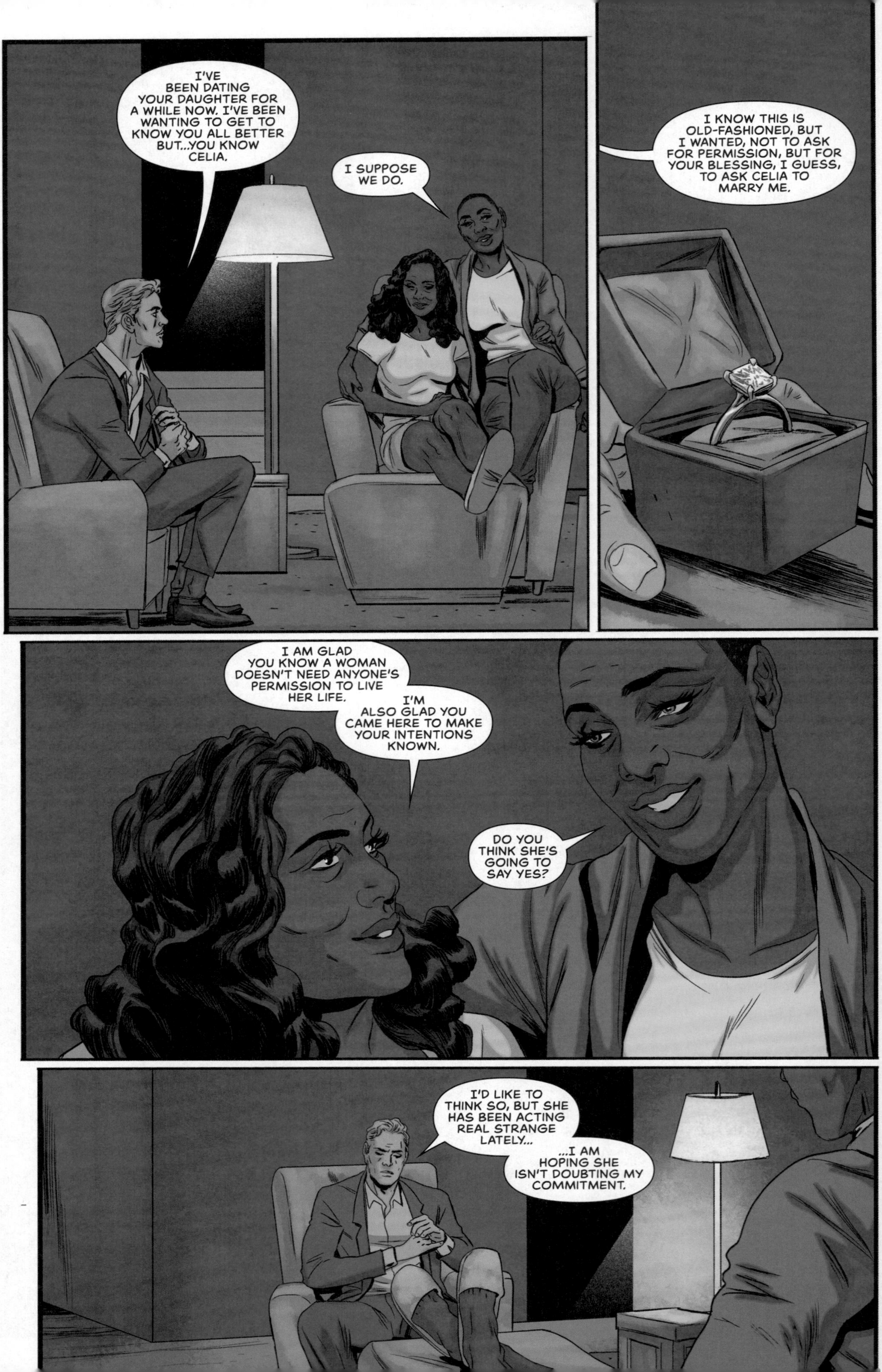
I'VE BEEN DATING YOUR DAUGHTER FOR A WHILE NOW. I'VE BEEN WANTING TO GET TO KNOW YOU ALL BETTER BUT...YOU KNOW CELIA.
I SUPPOSE WE DO.
I KNOW THIS IS OLD-FASHIONED, BUT I WANTED, NOT TO ASK FOR PERMISSION, BUT FOR YOUR BLESSING, I GUESS, TO ASK CELIA TO MARRY ME.
I AM GLAD YOU KNOW A WOMAN DOESN'T NEED ANYONE'S PERMISSION TO LIVE HER LIFE.
I'M ALSO GLAD YOU CAME HERE TO MAKE YOUR INTENTIONS KNOWN.
DO YOU THINK SHE'S GOING TO SAY YES?
I'D LIKE TO THINK SO, BUT SHE HAS BEEN ACTING REAL STRANGE LATELY...
...I AM HOPING SHE ISN'T DOUBTING MY COMMITMENT.

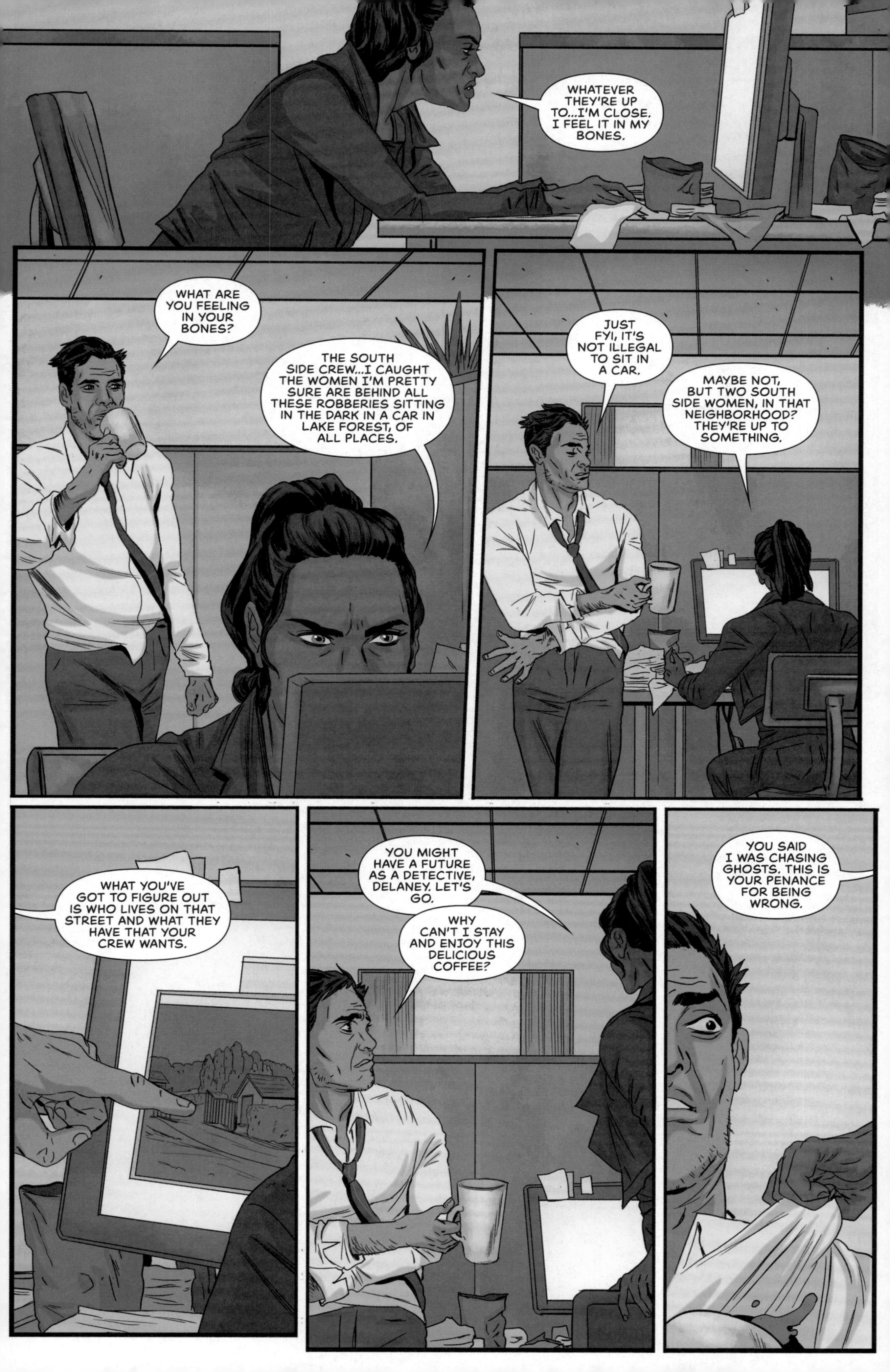
WHATEVER THEY'RE UP TO...I'M CLOSE. I FEEL IT IN MY BONES.
WHAT ARE YOU FEELING IN YOUR BONES?
THE SOUTH SIDE CREW...I CAUGHT THE WOMEN I'M PRETTY SURE ARE BEHIND ALL THESE ROBBERIES SITTING IN THE DARK IN A CAR IN LAKE FOREST, OF ALL PLACES.
JUST FYI, IT'S NOT ILLEGAL TO SIT IN A CAR.
MAYBE NOT, BUT TWO SOUTH SIDE WOMEN, IN THAT NEIGHBORHOOD? THEY'RE UP TO SOMETHING.
WHAT YOU'VE GOT TO FIGURE OUT IS WHO LIVES ON THAT STREET AND WHAT THEY HAVE THAT YOUR CREW WANTS.
YOU MIGHT HAVE A FUTURE AS A DETECTIVE, DELANEY. LET'S GO.
WHY CAN'T I STAY AND ENJOY THIS DELICIOUS COFFEE?
YOU SAID I WAS CHASING GHOSTS. THIS IS YOUR PENANCE FOR BEING WRONG.

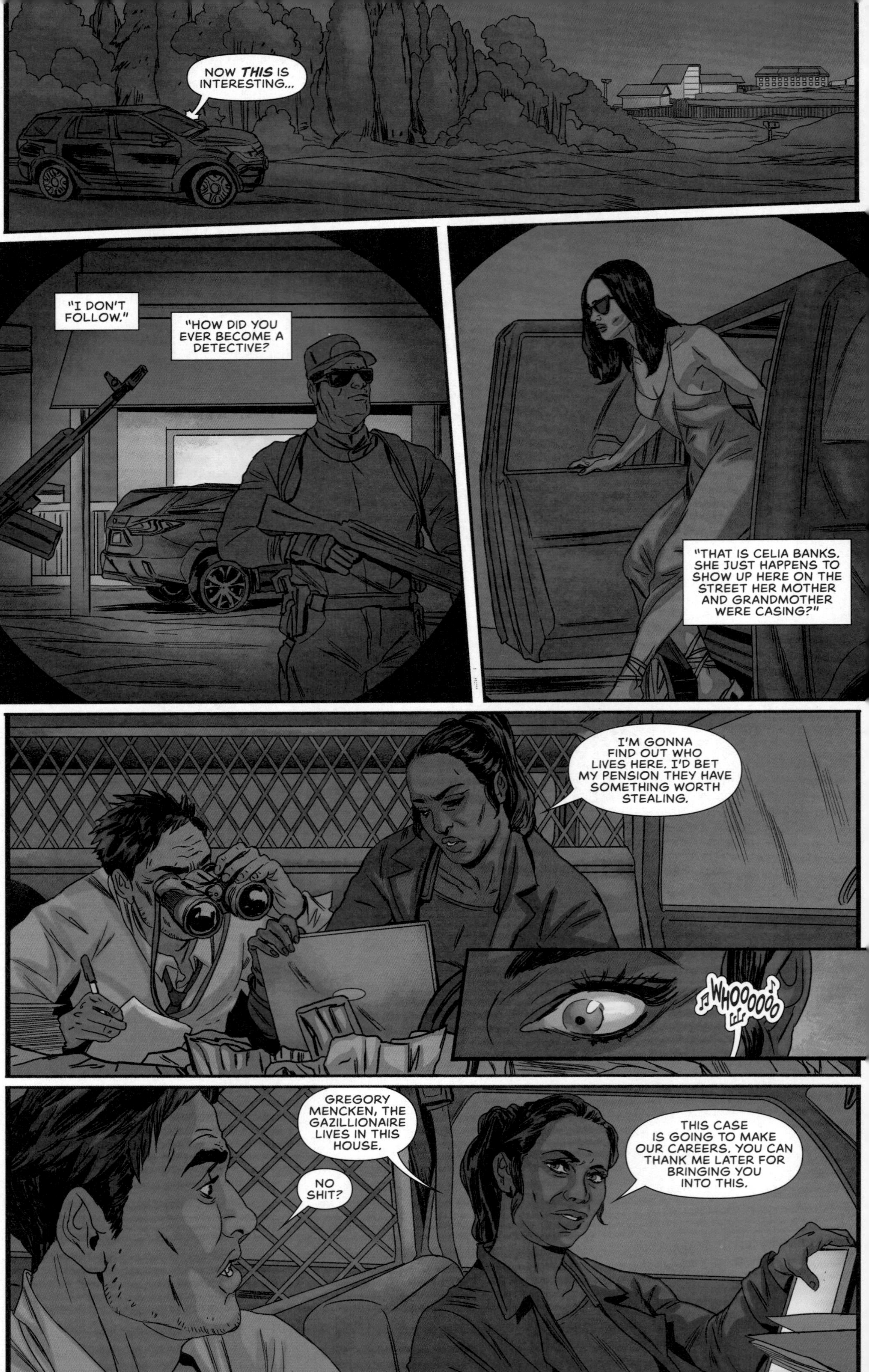
NOW *THIS* IS INTERESTING...
"I DON'T FOLLOW."
"HOW DID YOU EVER BECOME A DETECTIVE?
"THAT IS CELIA BANKS. SHE JUST HAPPENS TO SHOW UP HERE ON THE STREET HER MOTHER AND GRANDMOTHER WERE CASING?"
I'M GONNA FIND OUT WHO LIVES HERE. I'D BET MY PENSION THEY HAVE SOMETHING WORTH STEALING.
WHOOOOOO
GREGORY MENCKEN, THE GAZILLIONAIRE LIVES IN THIS HOUSE.
NO SHIT?
THIS CASE IS GOING TO MAKE OUR CAREERS. YOU CAN THANK ME LATER FOR BRINGING YOU INTO THIS.

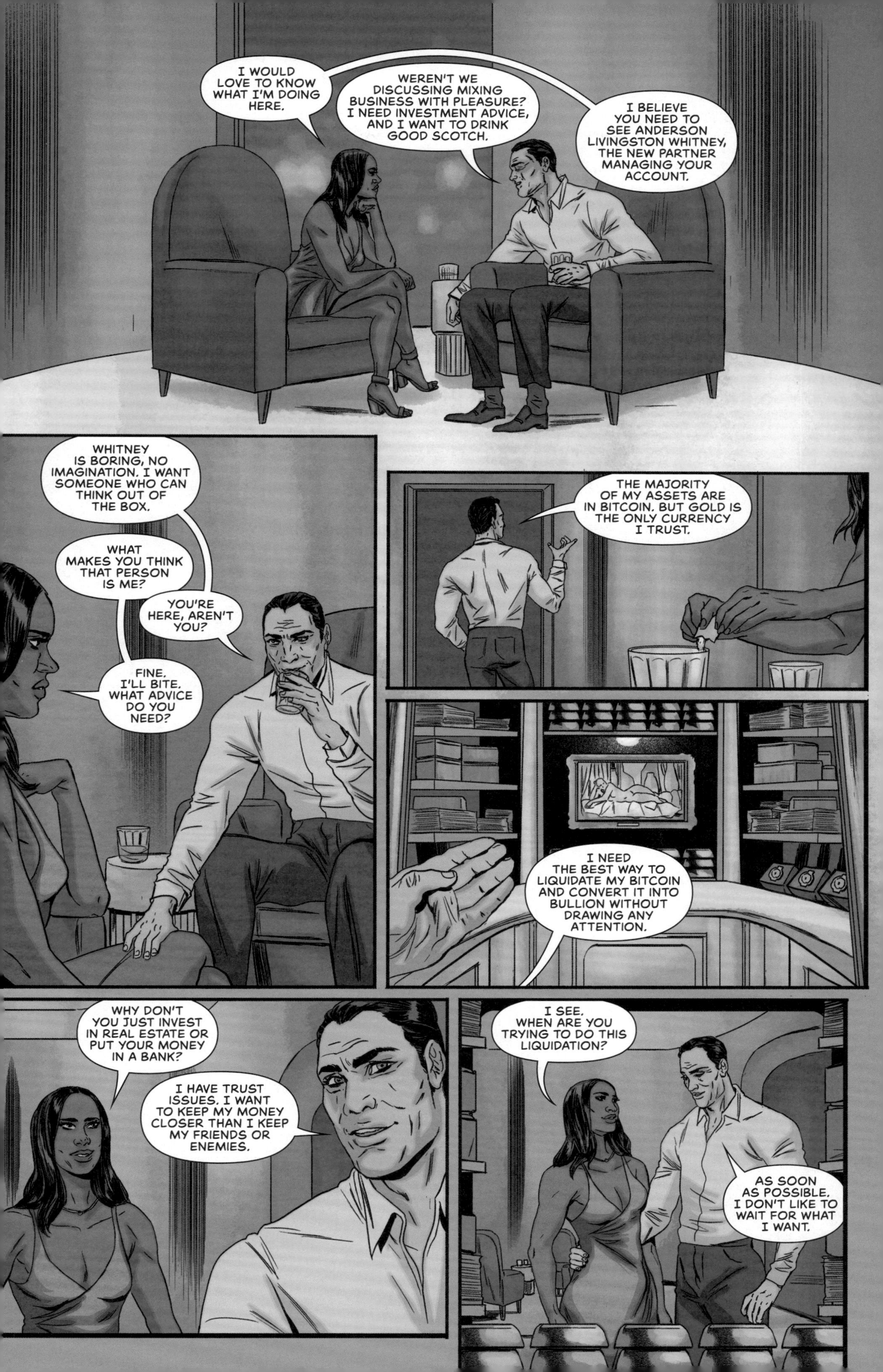
I WOULD LOVE TO KNOW WHAT I'M DOING HERE.
WEREN'T WE DISCUSSING MIXING BUSINESS WITH PLEASURE? I NEED INVESTMENT ADVICE, AND I WANT TO DRINK GOOD SCOTCH.
I BELIEVE YOU NEED TO SEE ANDERSON LIVINGSTON WHITNEY, THE NEW PARTNER MANAGING YOUR ACCOUNT.
WHITNEY IS BORING, NO IMAGINATION. I WANT SOMEONE WHO CAN THINK OUT OF THE BOX.
WHAT MAKES YOU THINK THAT PERSON IS ME?
YOU'RE HERE, AREN'T YOU?
FINE. I'LL BITE. WHAT ADVICE DO YOU NEED?
THE MAJORITY OF MY ASSETS ARE IN BITCOIN. BUT GOLD IS THE ONLY CURRENCY I TRUST.
I NEED THE BEST WAY TO LIQUIDATE MY BITCOIN AND CONVERT IT INTO BULLION WITHOUT DRAWING ANY ATTENTION.
WHY DON'T YOU JUST INVEST IN REAL ESTATE OR PUT YOUR MONEY IN A BANK?
I HAVE TRUST ISSUES. I WANT TO KEEP MY MONEY CLOSER THAN I KEEP MY FRIENDS OR ENEMIES.
I SEE. WHEN ARE YOU TRYING TO DO THIS LIQUIDATION?
AS SOON AS POSSIBLE. I DON'T LIKE TO WAIT FOR WHAT I WANT.

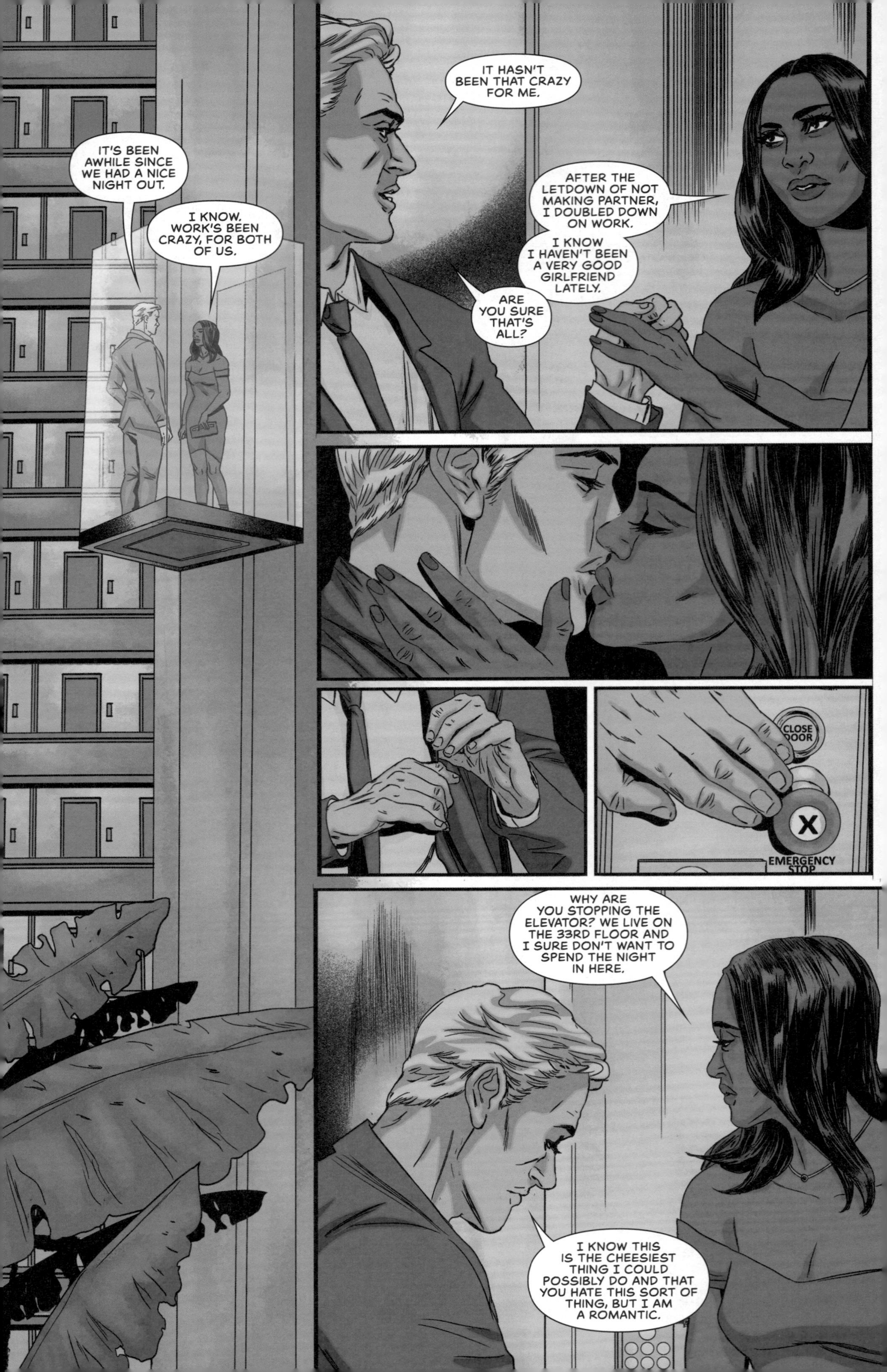
IT'S BEEN AWHILE SINCE WE HAD A NICE NIGHT OUT.
I KNOW. WORK'S BEEN CRAZY, FOR BOTH OF US.
IT HASN'T BEEN THAT CRAZY FOR ME.
AFTER THE LETDOWN OF NOT MAKING PARTNER, I DOUBLED DOWN ON WORK.
I KNOW I HAVEN'T BEEN A VERY GOOD GIRLFRIEND LATELY.
ARE YOU SURE THAT'S ALL?
CLOSE DOOR
EMERGENCY STOP
WHY ARE YOU STOPPING THE ELEVATOR? WE LIVE ON THE 33RD FLOOR AND I SURE DON'T WANT TO SPEND THE NIGHT IN HERE.
I KNOW THIS IS THE CHEESIEST THING I COULD POSSIBLY DO AND THAT YOU HATE THIS SORT OF THING, BUT I AM A ROMANTIC.

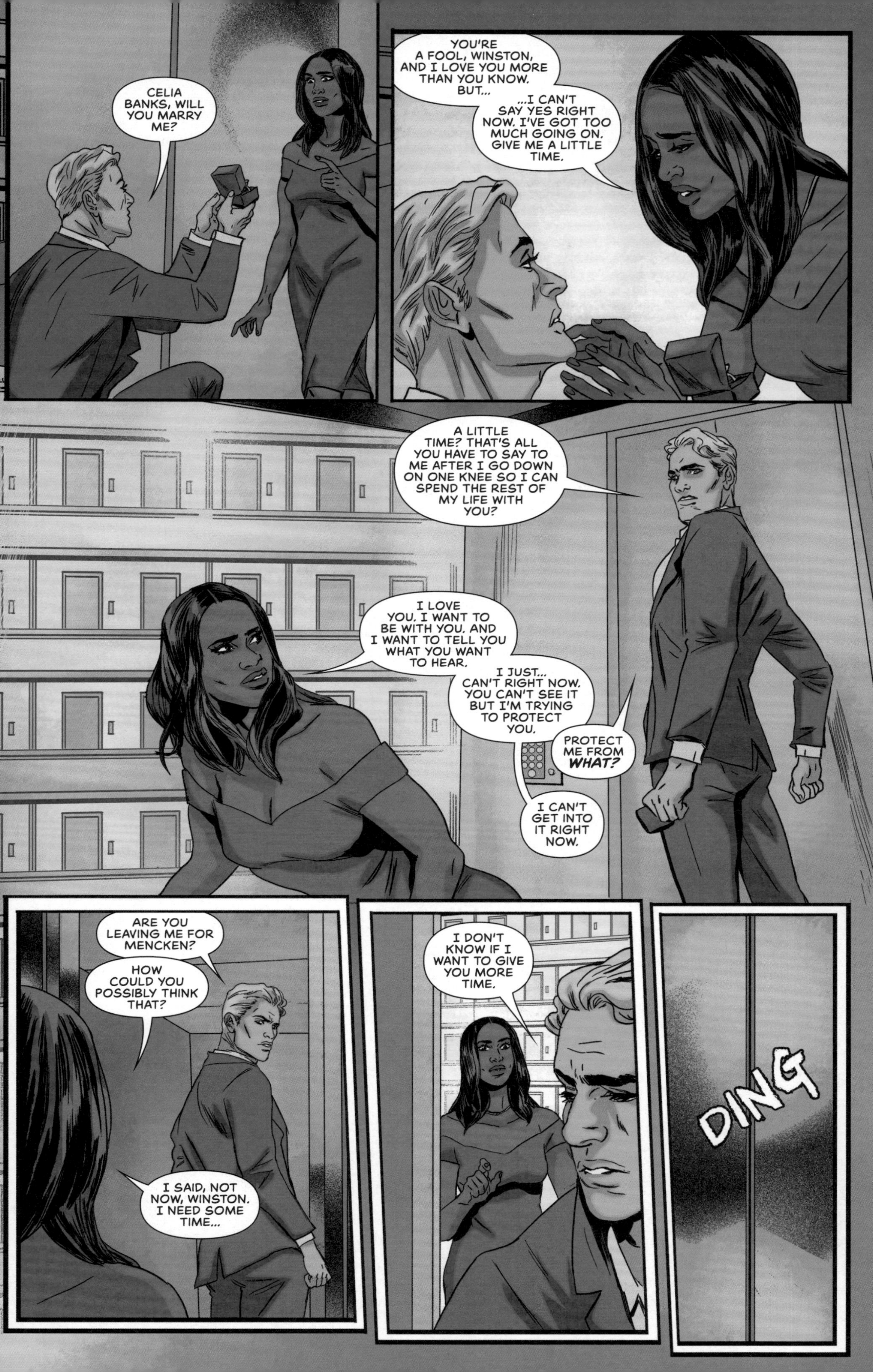
CELIA BANKS, WILL YOU MARRY ME?
YOU'RE A FOOL, WINSTON, AND I LOVE YOU MORE THAN YOU KNOW. BUT...
...I CAN'T SAY YES RIGHT NOW. I'VE GOT TOO MUCH GOING ON. GIVE ME A LITTLE TIME.
A LITTLE TIME? THAT'S ALL YOU HAVE TO SAY TO ME AFTER I GO DOWN ON ONE KNEE SO I CAN SPEND THE REST OF MY LIFE WITH YOU?
I LOVE YOU. I WANT TO BE WITH YOU. AND I WANT TO TELL YOU WHAT YOU WANT TO HEAR.
I JUST... CAN'T RIGHT NOW. YOU CAN'T SEE IT BUT I'M TRYING TO PROTECT YOU.
PROTECT ME FROM *WHAT?*
I CAN'T GET INTO IT RIGHT NOW.
ARE YOU LEAVING ME FOR MENCKEN?
HOW COULD YOU POSSIBLY THINK THAT?
I SAID, NOT NOW, WINSTON. I NEED SOME TIME...
I DON'T KNOW IF I WANT TO GIVE YOU MORE TIME.
DING

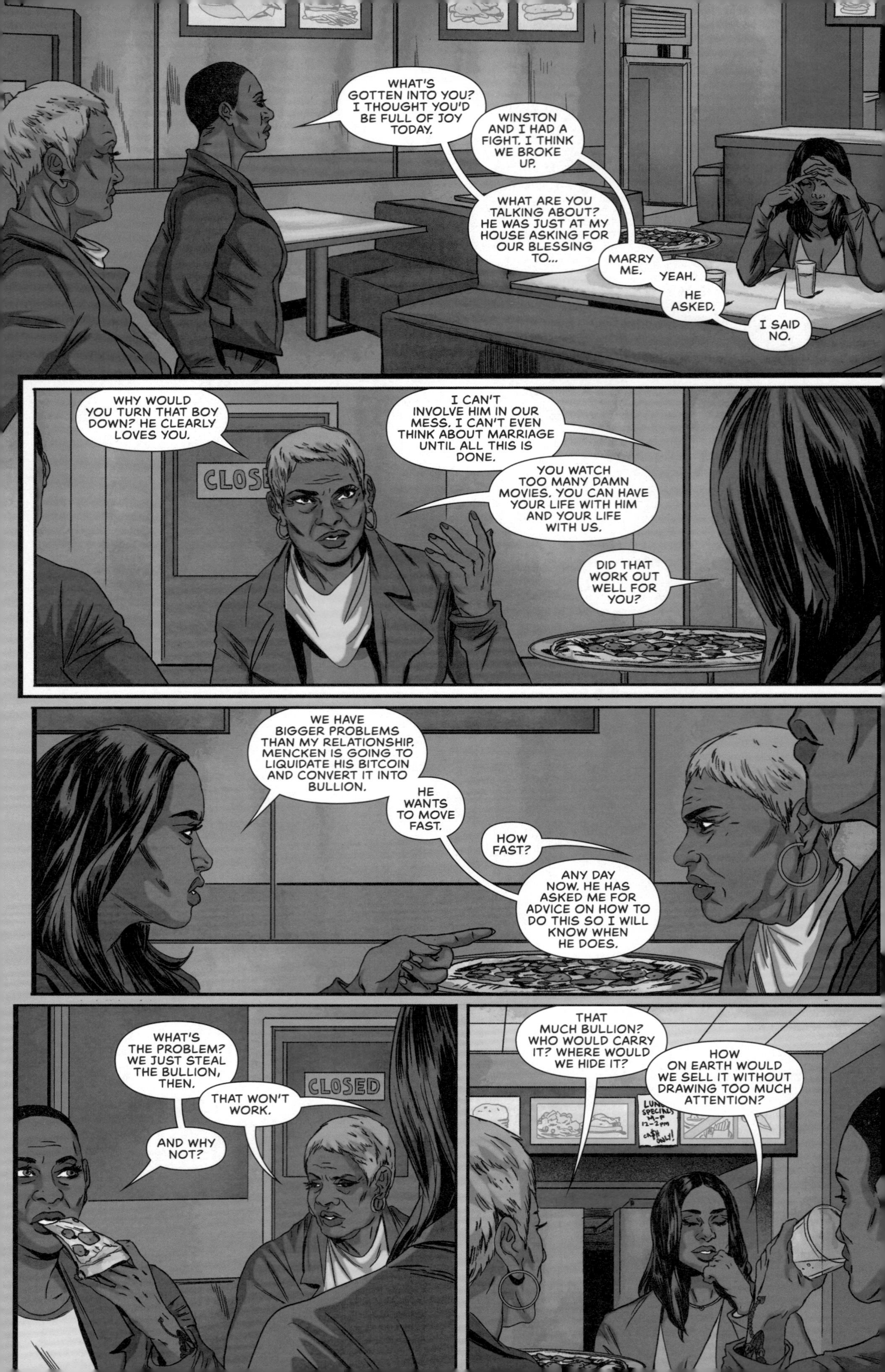
WHAT'S GOTTEN INTO YOU? I THOUGHT YOU'D BE FULL OF JOY TODAY.
WINSTON AND I HAD A FIGHT. I THINK WE BROKE UP.
WHAT ARE YOU TALKING ABOUT? HE WAS JUST AT MY HOUSE ASKING FOR OUR BLESSING TO...
MARRY ME.
YEAH.
HE ASKED.
I SAID NO.
WHY WOULD YOU TURN THAT BOY DOWN? HE CLEARLY LOVES YOU.
CLOSED
I CAN'T INVOLVE HIM IN OUR MESS. I CAN'T EVEN THINK ABOUT MARRIAGE UNTIL ALL THIS IS DONE.
YOU WATCH TOO MANY DAMN MOVIES. YOU CAN HAVE YOUR LIFE WITH HIM AND YOUR LIFE WITH US.
DID THAT WORK OUT WELL FOR YOU?
WE HAVE BIGGER PROBLEMS THAN MY RELATIONSHIP. MENCKEN IS GOING TO LIQUIDATE HIS BITCOIN AND CONVERT IT INTO BULLION.
HE WANTS TO MOVE FAST.
HOW FAST?
ANY DAY NOW. HE HAS ASKED ME FOR ADVICE ON HOW TO DO THIS SO I WILL KNOW WHEN HE DOES.
WHAT'S THE PROBLEM? WE JUST STEAL THE BULLION, THEN.
CLOSED
THAT WON'T WORK.
AND WHY NOT?
THAT MUCH BULLION? WHO WOULD CARRY IT? WHERE WOULD WE HIDE IT?
HOW ON EARTH WOULD WE SELL IT WITHOUT DRAWING TOO MUCH ATTENTION?

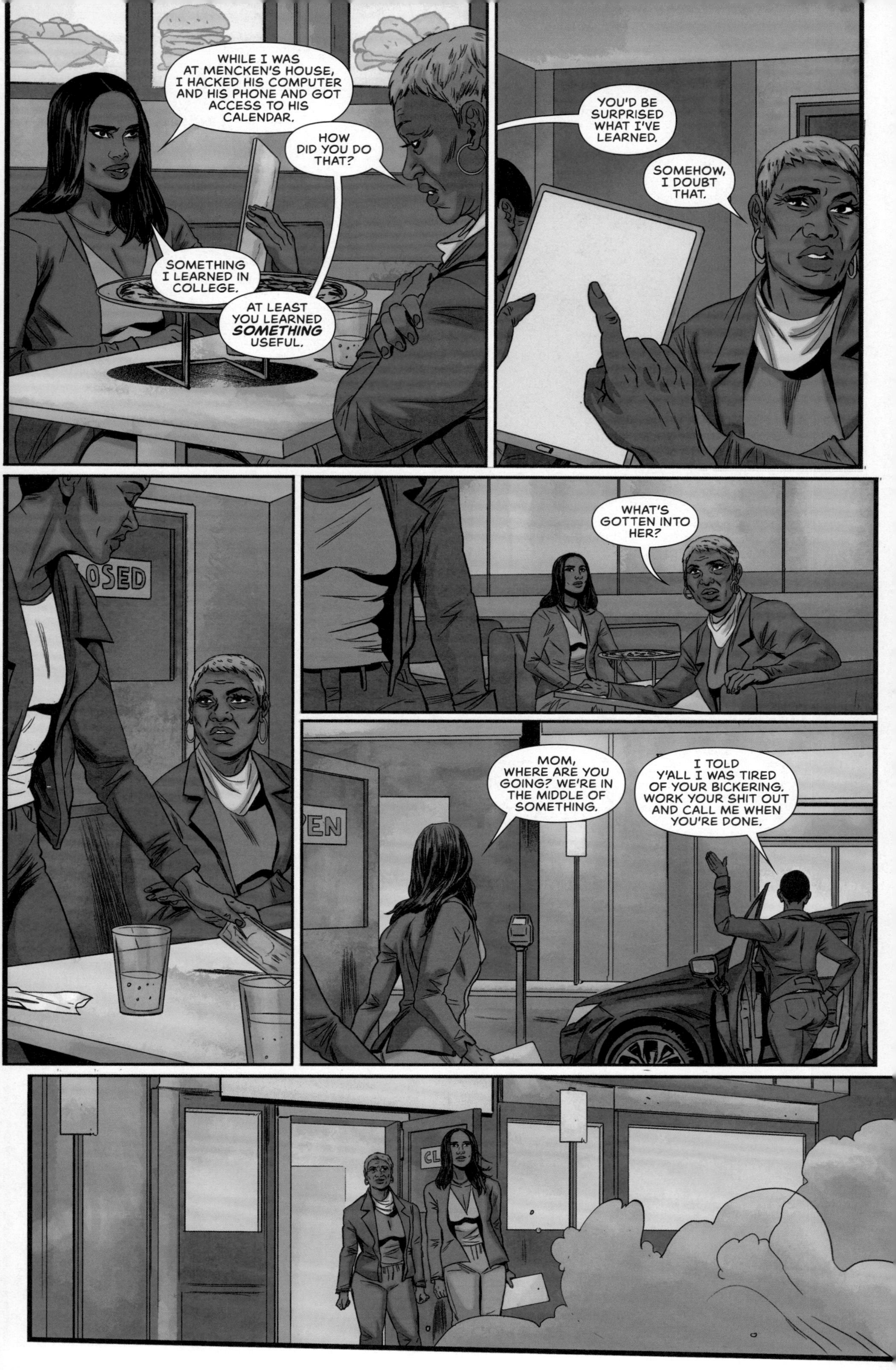
WHILE I WAS AT MENCKEN'S HOUSE, I HACKED HIS COMPUTER AND HIS PHONE AND GOT ACCESS TO HIS CALENDAR.
HOW DID YOU DO THAT?
SOMETHING I LEARNED IN COLLEGE.
AT LEAST YOU LEARNED **SOMETHING** USEFUL.
YOU'D BE SURPRISED WHAT I'VE LEARNED.
SOMEHOW, I DOUBT THAT.
LOSED
WHAT'S GOTTEN INTO HER?
PEN
MOM, WHERE ARE YOU GOING? WE'RE IN THE MIDDLE OF SOMETHING.
I TOLD Y'ALL I WAS TIRED OF YOUR BICKERING. WORK YOUR SHIT OUT AND CALL ME WHEN YOU'RE DONE.
CL

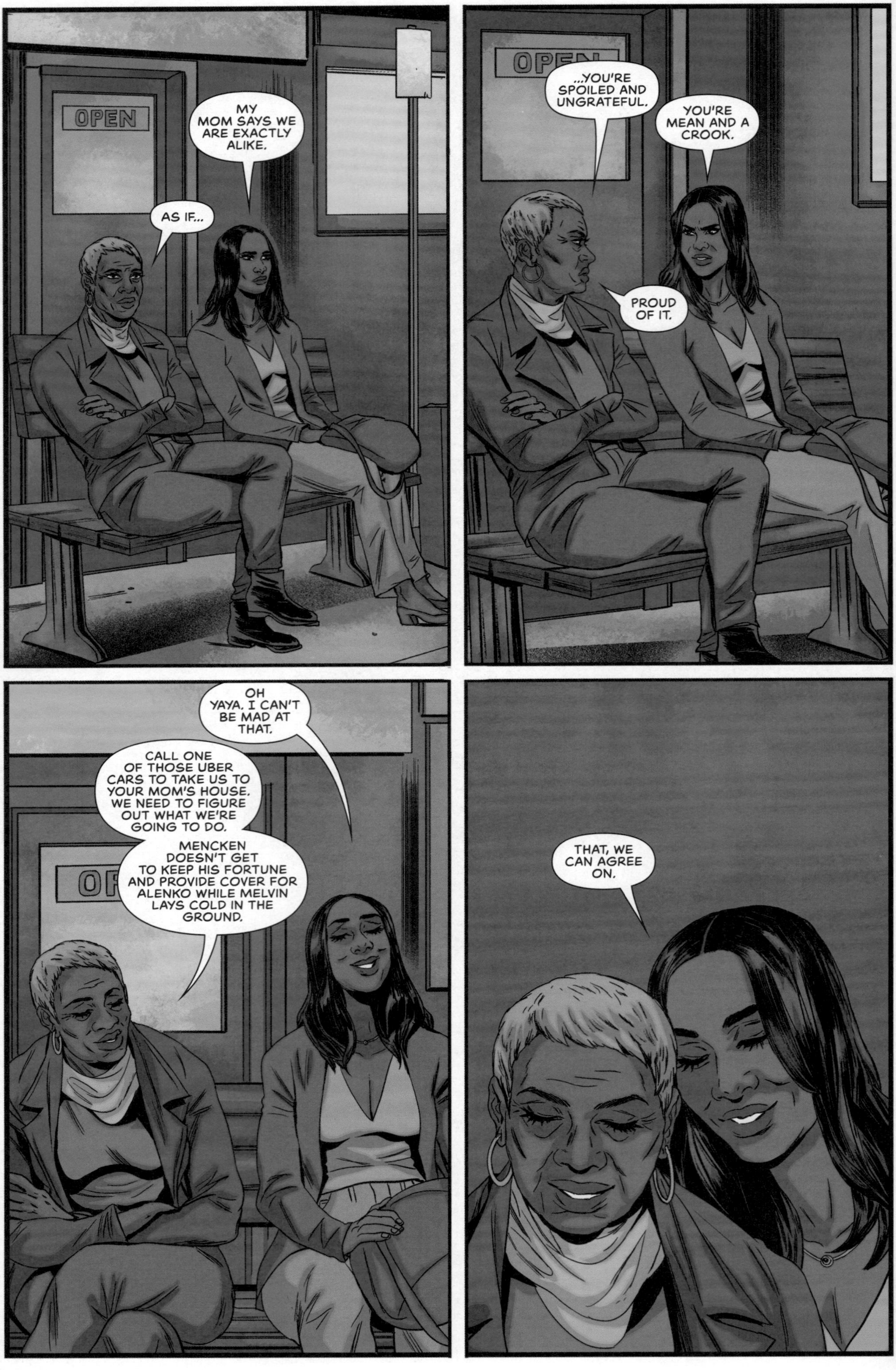

MY MOM SAYS WE ARE EXACTLY ALIKE.
AS IF...
...YOU'RE SPOILED AND UNGRATEFUL.
YOU'RE MEAN AND A CROOK.
PROUD OF IT.
OH YAYA. I CAN'T BE MAD AT THAT.
CALL ONE OF THOSE UBER CARS TO TAKE US TO YOUR MOM'S HOUSE. WE NEED TO FIGURE OUT WHAT WE'RE GOING TO DO.
MENCKEN DOESN'T GET TO KEEP HIS FORTUNE AND PROVIDE COVER FOR ALENKO WHILE MELVIN LAYS COLD IN THE GROUND.
THAT, WE CAN AGREE ON.

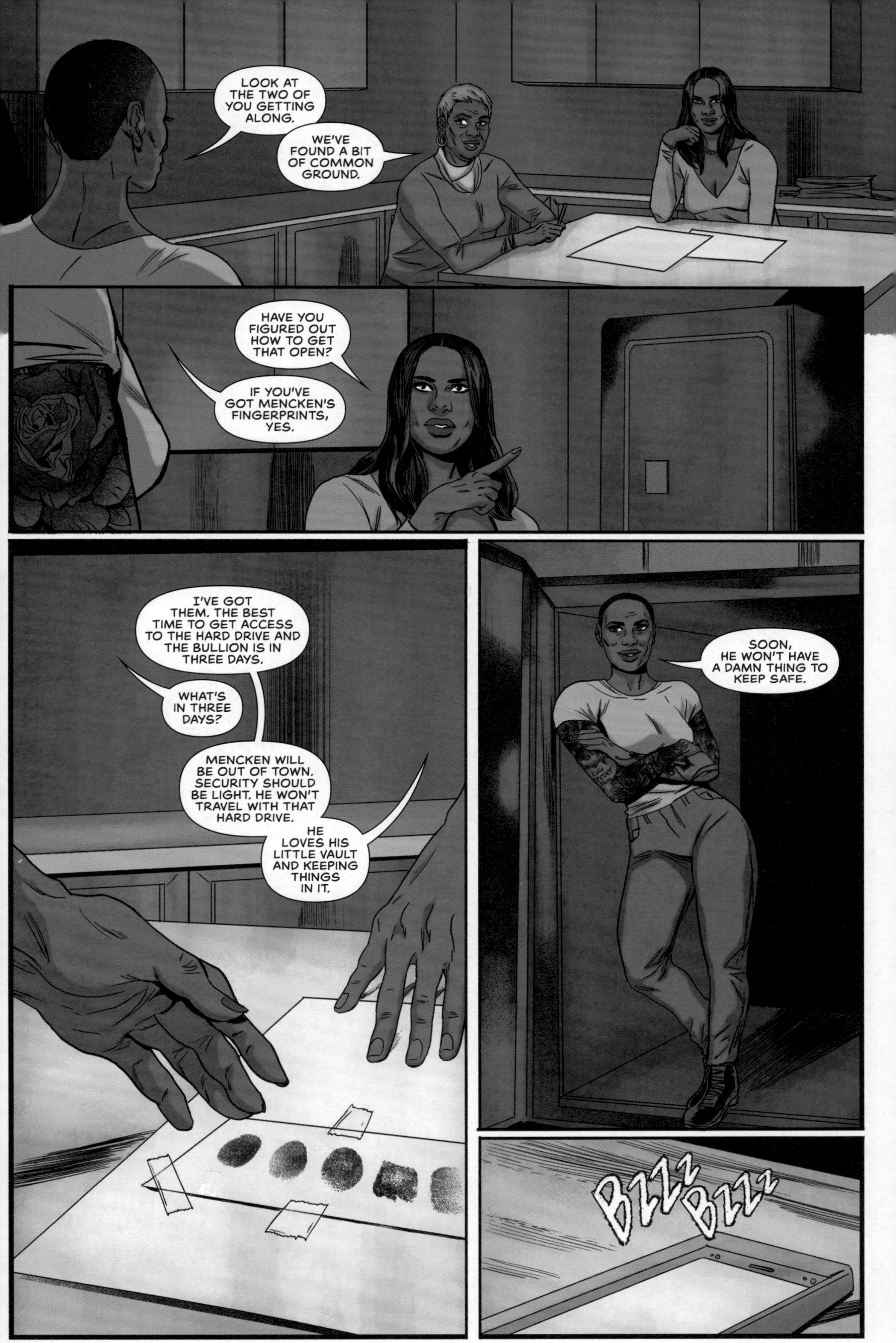
LOOK AT THE TWO OF YOU GETTING ALONG.
WE'VE FOUND A BIT OF COMMON GROUND.
HAVE YOU FIGURED OUT HOW TO GET THAT OPEN?
IF YOU'VE GOT MENCKEN'S FINGERPRINTS, YES.
I'VE GOT THEM. THE BEST TIME TO GET ACCESS TO THE HARD DRIVE AND THE BULLION IS IN THREE DAYS.
WHAT'S IN THREE DAYS?
MENCKEN WILL BE OUT OF TOWN. SECURITY SHOULD BE LIGHT. HE WON'T TRAVEL WITH THAT HARD DRIVE.
HE LOVES HIS LITTLE VAULT AND KEEPING THINGS IN IT.
SOON, HE WON'T HAVE A DAMN THING TO KEEP SAFE.
BZZZ BZZZ

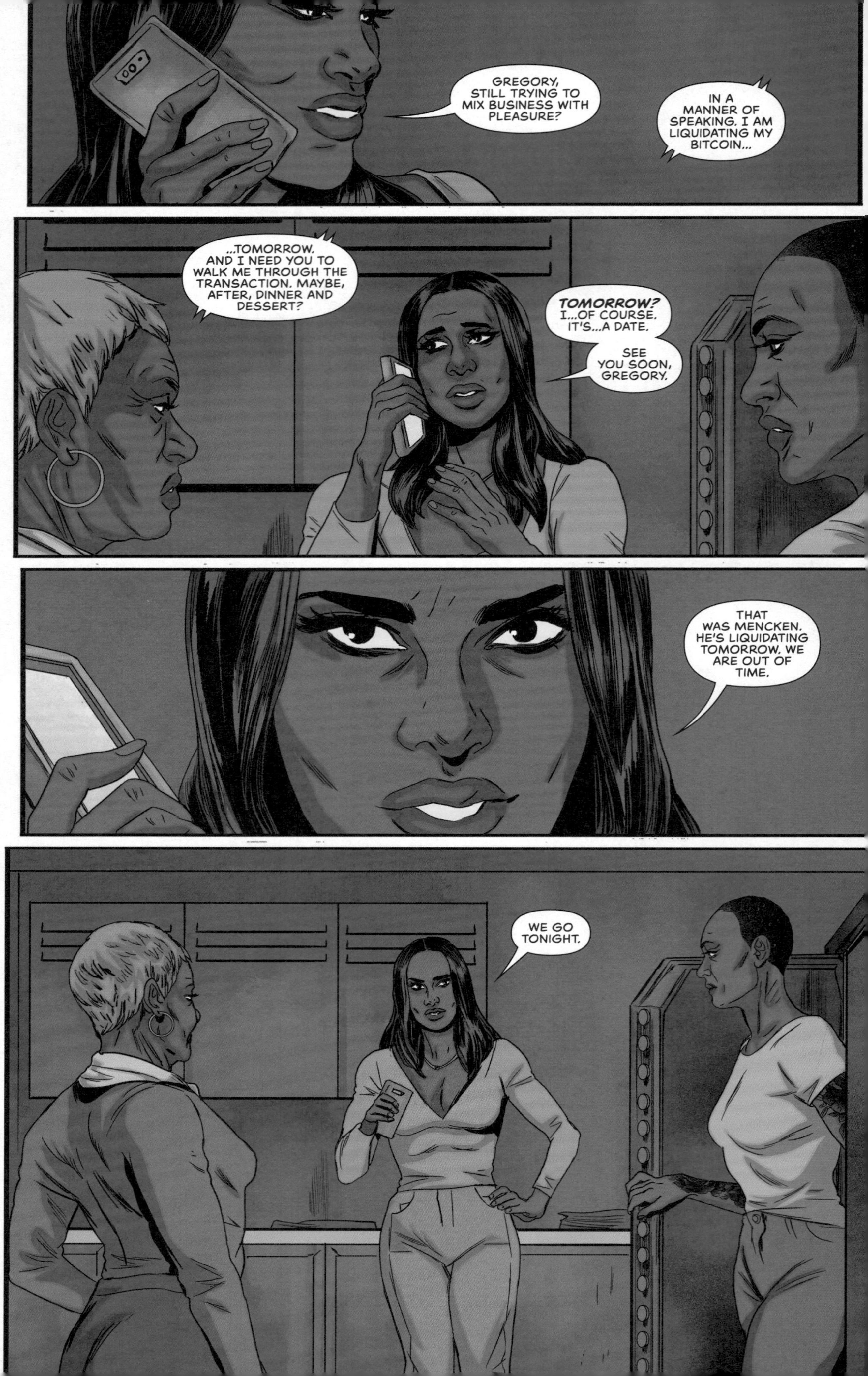
GREGORY, STILL TRYING TO MIX BUSINESS WITH PLEASURE?
IN A MANNER OF SPEAKING. I AM LIQUIDATING MY BITCOIN...
...TOMORROW. AND I NEED YOU TO WALK ME THROUGH THE TRANSACTION. MAYBE, AFTER, DINNER AND DESSERT?
TOMORROW? I...OF COURSE. IT'S...A DATE.
SEE YOU SOON, GREGORY.
THAT WAS MENCKEN. HE'S LIQUIDATING TOMORROW. WE ARE OUT OF TIME.
WE GO TONIGHT.

CHAPTER 5

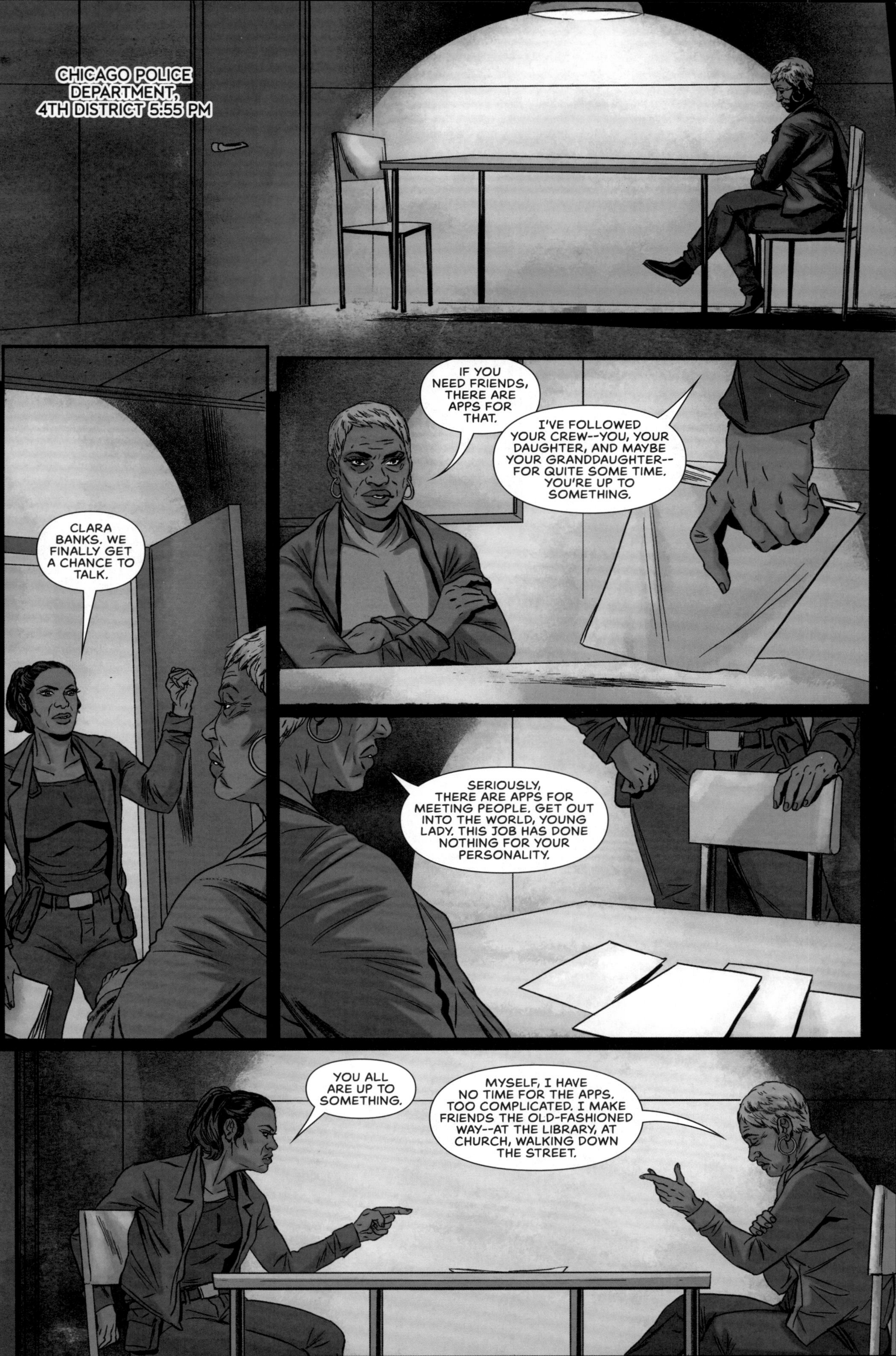
CHICAGO POLICE DEPARTMENT, 4TH DISTRICT 5:55 PM
CLARA BANKS. WE FINALLY GET A CHANCE TO TALK.
IF YOU NEED FRIENDS, THERE ARE APPS FOR THAT.
I'VE FOLLOWED YOUR CREW--YOU, YOUR DAUGHTER, AND MAYBE YOUR GRANDDAUGHTER-- FOR QUITE SOME TIME. YOU'RE UP TO SOMETHING.
SERIOUSLY, THERE ARE APPS FOR MEETING PEOPLE. GET OUT INTO THE WORLD, YOUNG LADY. THIS JOB HAS DONE NOTHING FOR YOUR PERSONALITY.
YOU ALL ARE UP TO SOMETHING.
MYSELF, I HAVE NO TIME FOR THE APPS. TOO COMPLICATED. I MAKE FRIENDS THE OLD-FASHIONED WAY--AT THE LIBRARY, AT CHURCH, WALKING DOWN THE STREET.

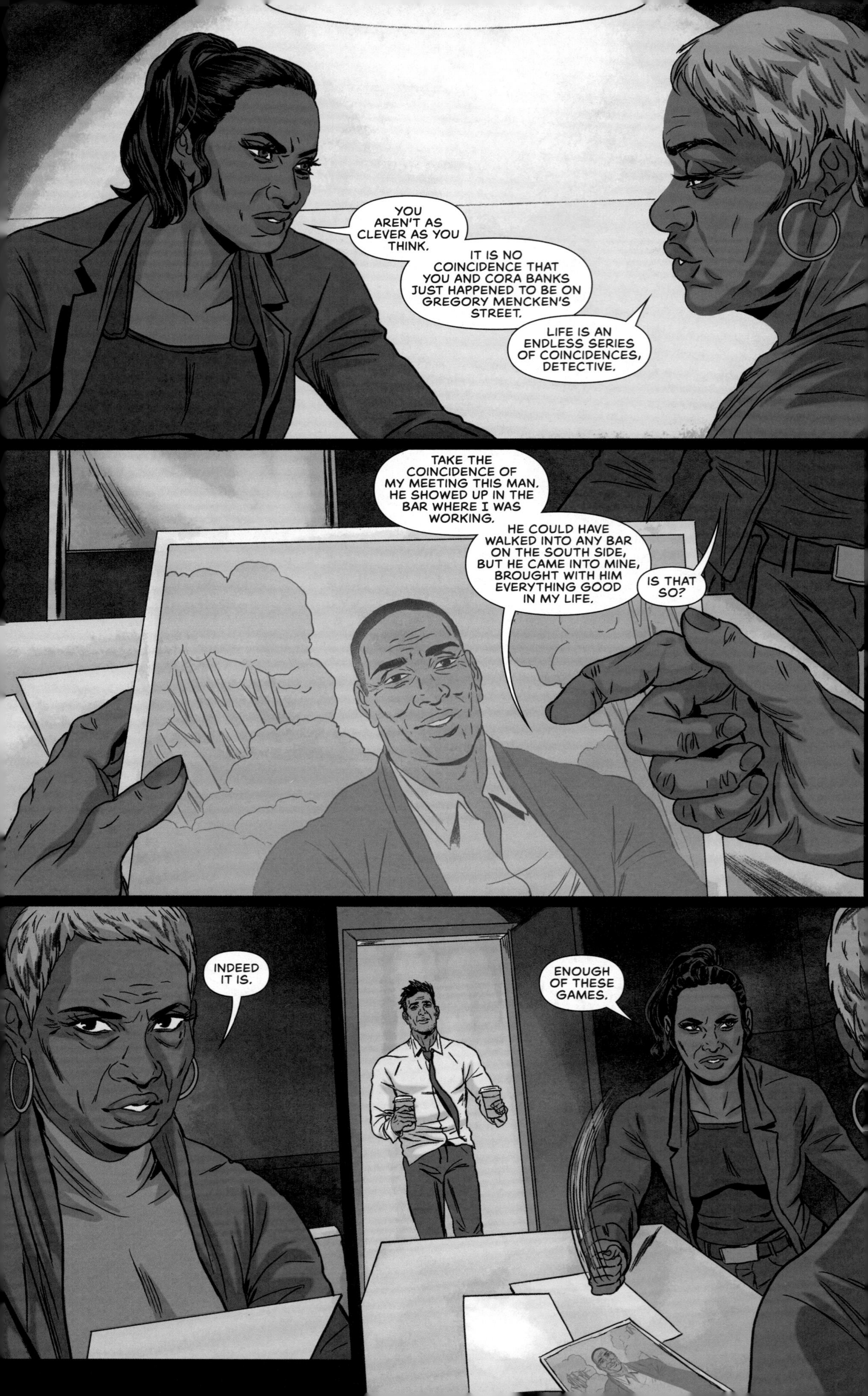
YOU AREN'T AS CLEVER AS YOU THINK.
IT IS NO COINCIDENCE THAT YOU AND CORA BANKS JUST HAPPENED TO BE ON GREGORY MENCKEN'S STREET.
LIFE IS AN ENDLESS SERIES OF COINCIDENCES, DETECTIVE.
TAKE THE COINCIDENCE OF MY MEETING THIS MAN. HE SHOWED UP IN THE BAR WHERE I WAS WORKING.
HE COULD HAVE WALKED INTO ANY BAR ON THE SOUTH SIDE, BUT HE CAME INTO MINE, BROUGHT WITH HIM EVERYTHING GOOD IN MY LIFE.
IS THAT SO?
INDEED IT IS.
ENOUGH OF THESE GAMES.

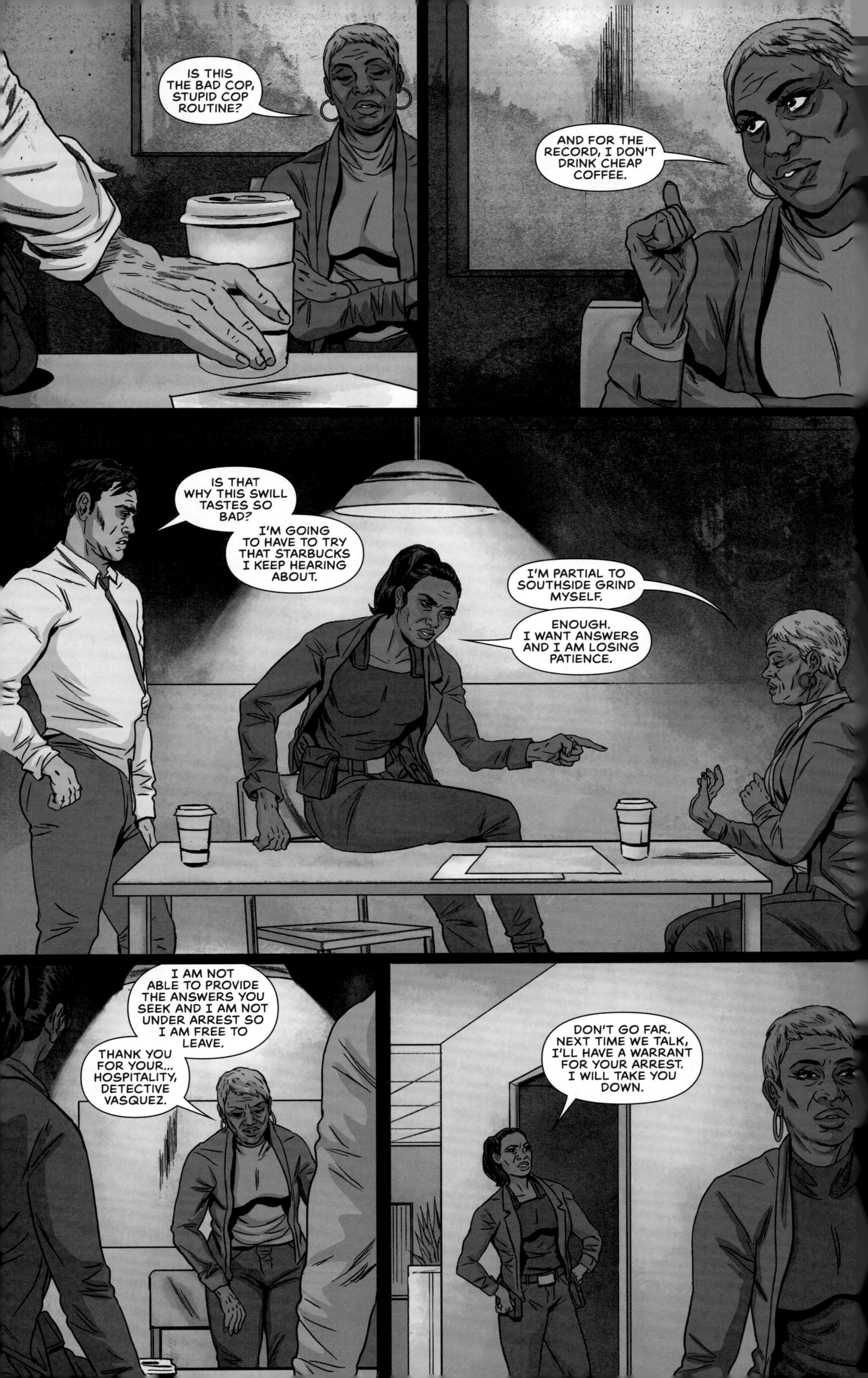
IS THIS THE BAD COP, STUPID COP ROUTINE?
AND FOR THE RECORD, I DON'T DRINK CHEAP COFFEE.
IS THAT WHY THIS SWILL TASTES SO BAD?
I'M GOING TO HAVE TO TRY THAT STARBUCKS I KEEP HEARING ABOUT.
I'M PARTIAL TO SOUTHSIDE GRIND MYSELF.
ENOUGH. I WANT ANSWERS AND I AM LOSING PATIENCE.
I AM NOT ABLE TO PROVIDE THE ANSWERS YOU SEEK AND I AM NOT UNDER ARREST SO I AM FREE TO LEAVE.
THANK YOU FOR YOUR... HOSPITALITY, DETECTIVE VASQUEZ.
DON'T GO FAR. NEXT TIME WE TALK, I'LL HAVE A WARRANT FOR YOUR ARREST. I WILL TAKE YOU DOWN.

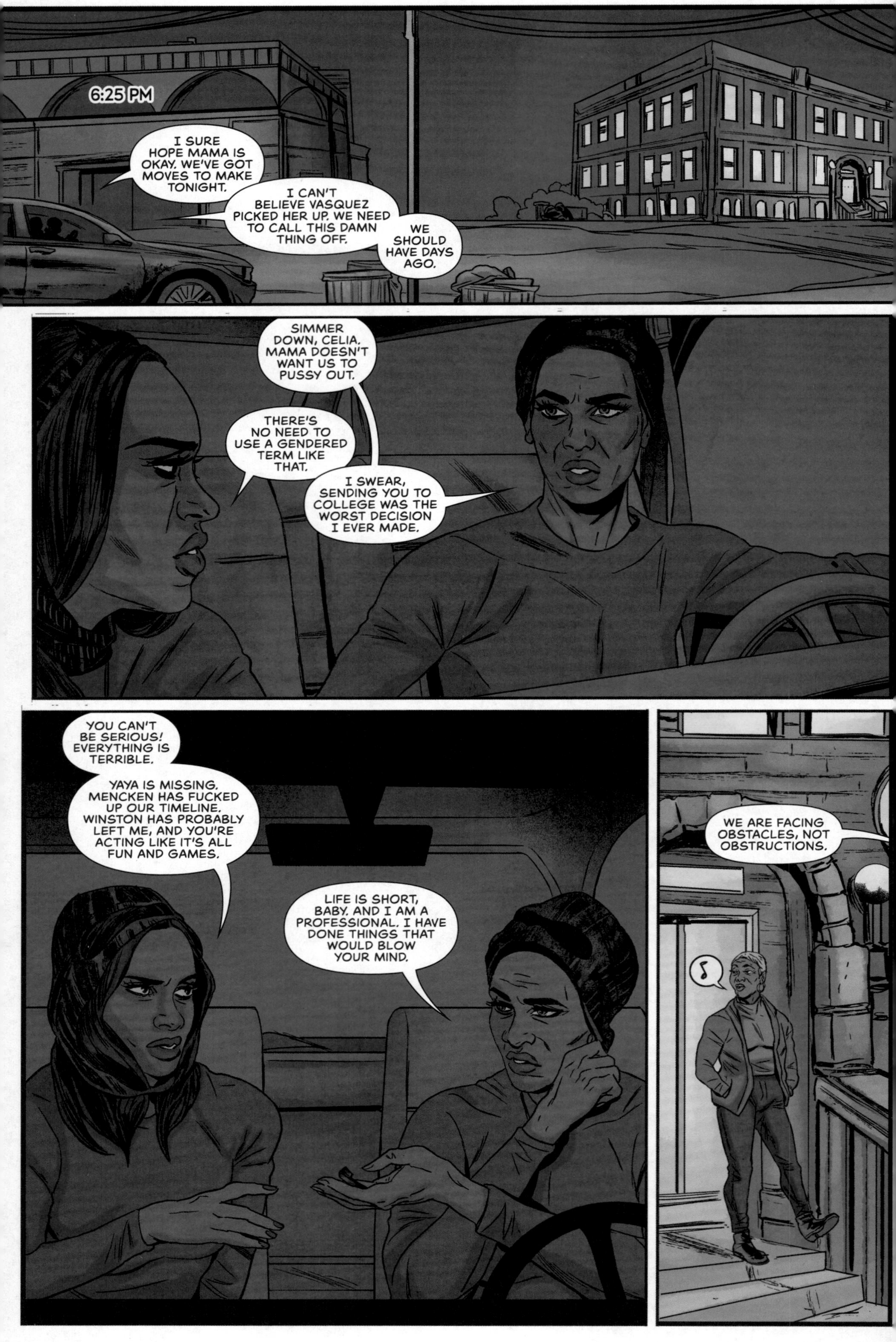
6:25 PM
I SURE HOPE MAMA IS OKAY. WE'VE GOT MOVES TO MAKE TONIGHT.
I CAN'T BELIEVE VASQUEZ PICKED HER UP. WE NEED TO CALL THIS DAMN THING OFF.
WE SHOULD HAVE DAYS AGO.
SIMMER DOWN, CELIA. MAMA DOESN'T WANT US TO PUSSY OUT.
THERE'S NO NEED TO USE A GENDERED TERM LIKE THAT.
I SWEAR, SENDING YOU TO COLLEGE WAS THE WORST DECISION I EVER MADE.
YOU CAN'T BE SERIOUS! EVERYTHING IS TERRIBLE.
YAYA IS MISSING. MENCKEN HAS FUCKED UP OUR TIMELINE. WINSTON HAS PROBABLY LEFT ME, AND YOU'RE ACTING LIKE IT'S ALL FUN AND GAMES.
LIFE IS SHORT, BABY. AND I AM A PROFESSIONAL. I HAVE DONE THINGS THAT WOULD BLOW YOUR MIND.
WE ARE FACING OBSTACLES, NOT OBSTRUCTIONS.

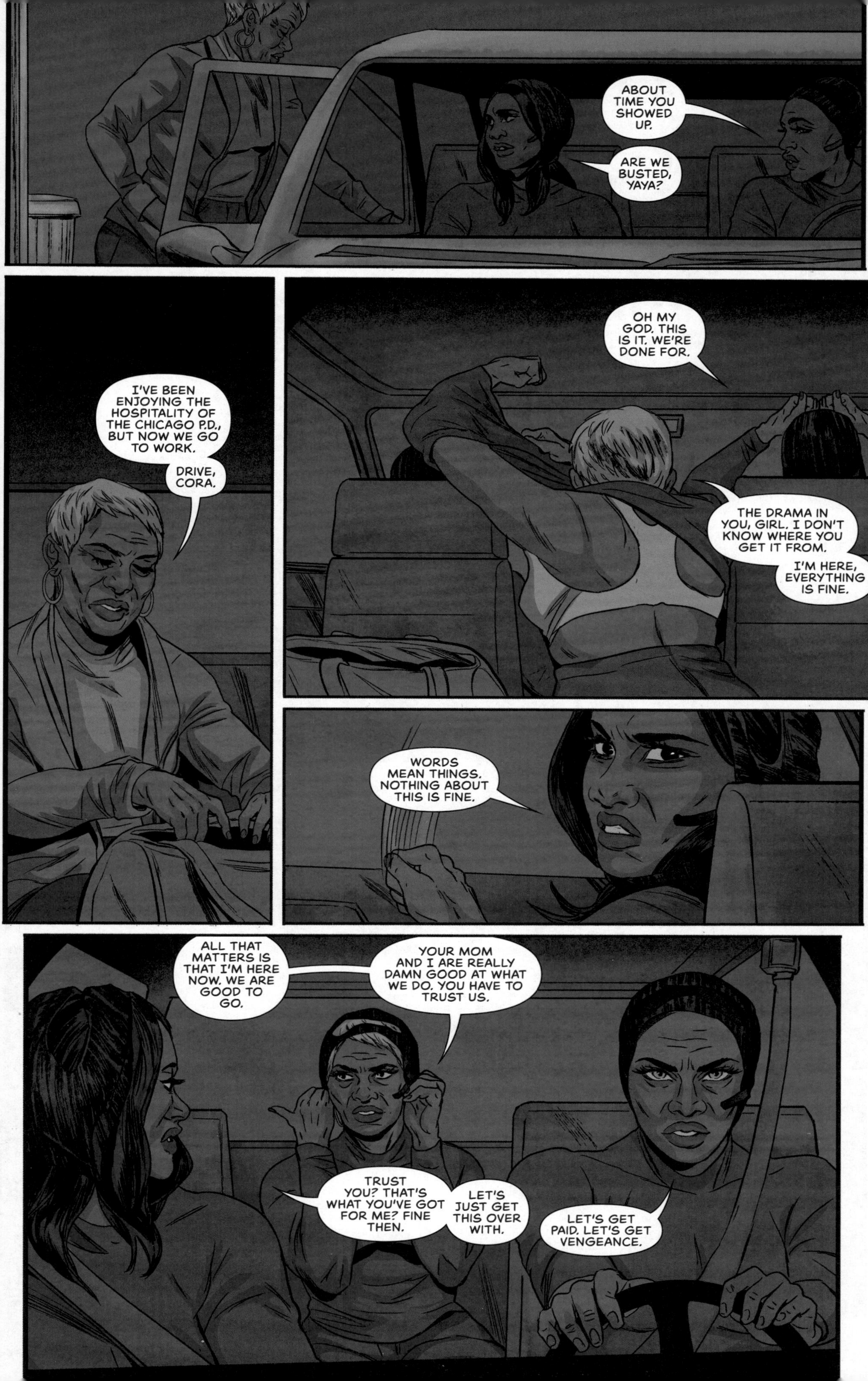
ABOUT TIME YOU SHOWED UP.
ARE WE BUSTED, YAYA?
I'VE BEEN ENJOYING THE HOSPITALITY OF THE CHICAGO P.D., BUT NOW WE GO TO WORK.
DRIVE, CORA.
OH MY GOD. THIS IS IT. WE'RE DONE FOR.
THE DRAMA IN YOU, GIRL. I DON'T KNOW WHERE YOU GET IT FROM.
I'M HERE, EVERYTHING IS FINE.
WORDS MEAN THINGS. NOTHING ABOUT THIS IS FINE.
ALL THAT MATTERS IS THAT I'M HERE NOW. WE ARE GOOD TO GO.
YOUR MOM AND I ARE REALLY DAMN GOOD AT WHAT WE DO. YOU HAVE TO TRUST US.
TRUST YOU? THAT'S WHAT YOU'VE GOT FOR ME? FINE THEN.
LET'S JUST GET THIS OVER WITH.
LET'S GET PAID. LET'S GET VENGEANCE.

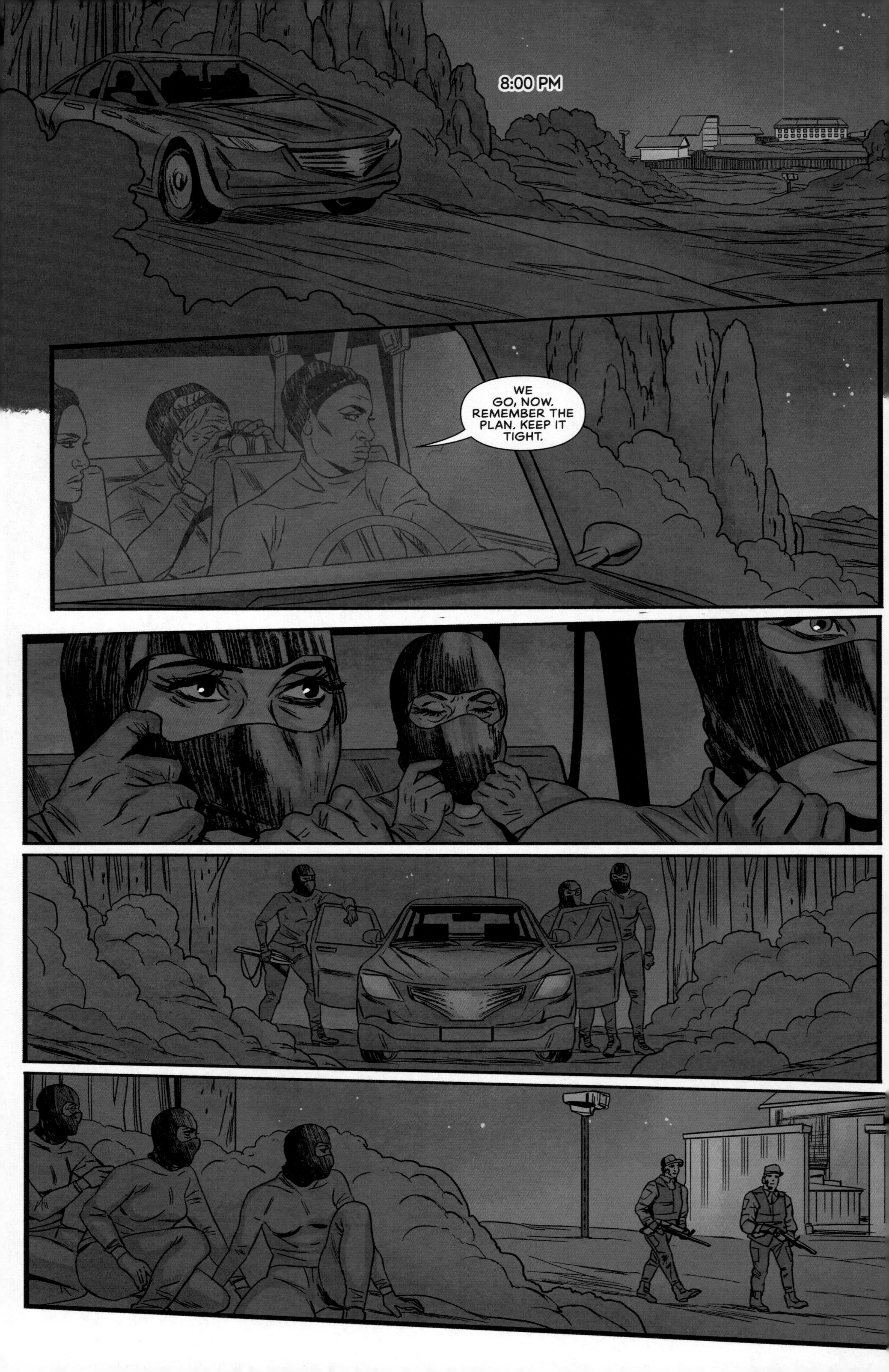
8:00 PM
WE GO, NOW. REMEMBER THE PLAN. KEEP IT TIGHT.

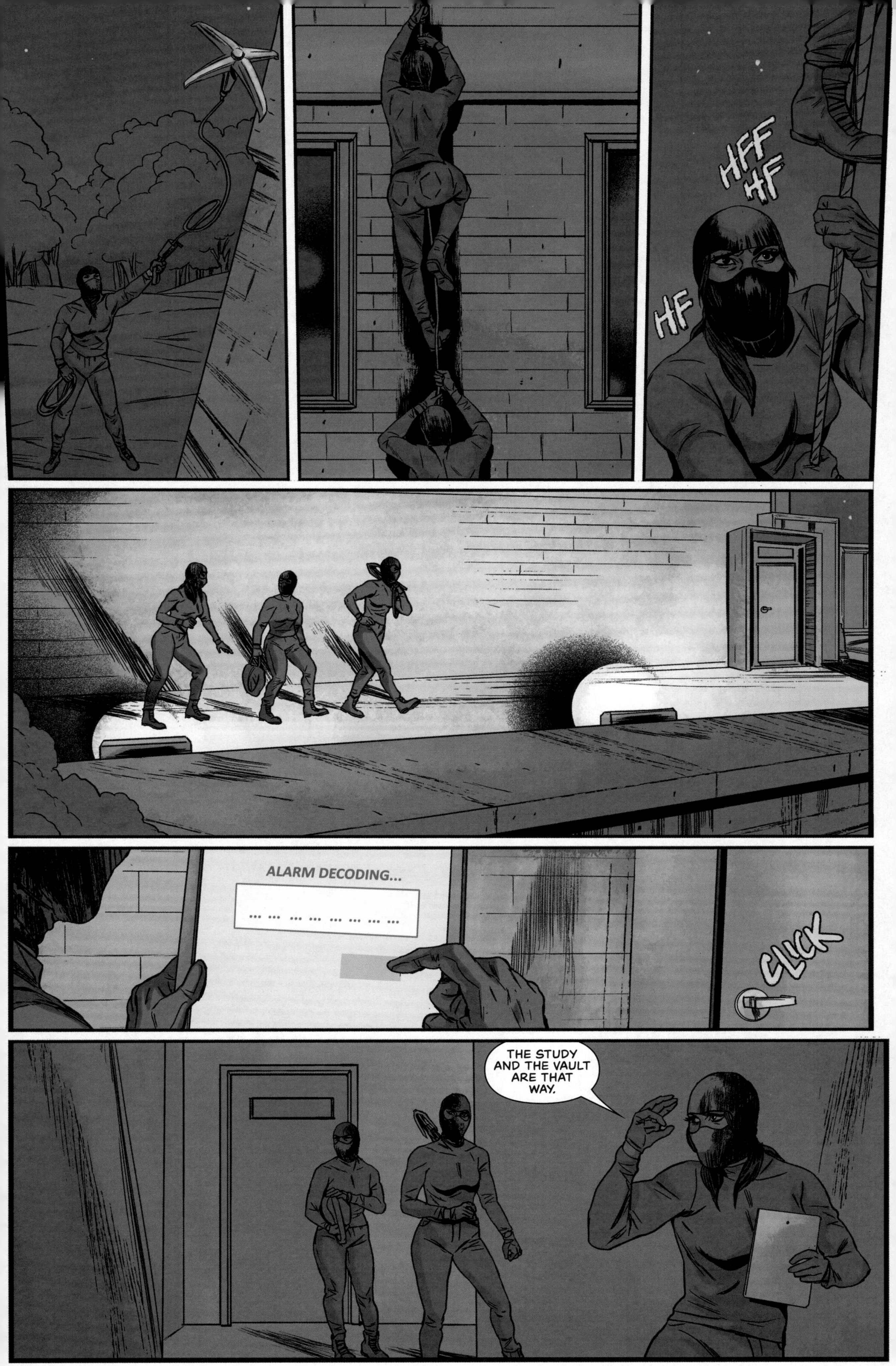
HFF HF
HF
ALARM DECODING...
... ...
CLICK
THE STUDY AND THE VAULT ARE THAT WAY.

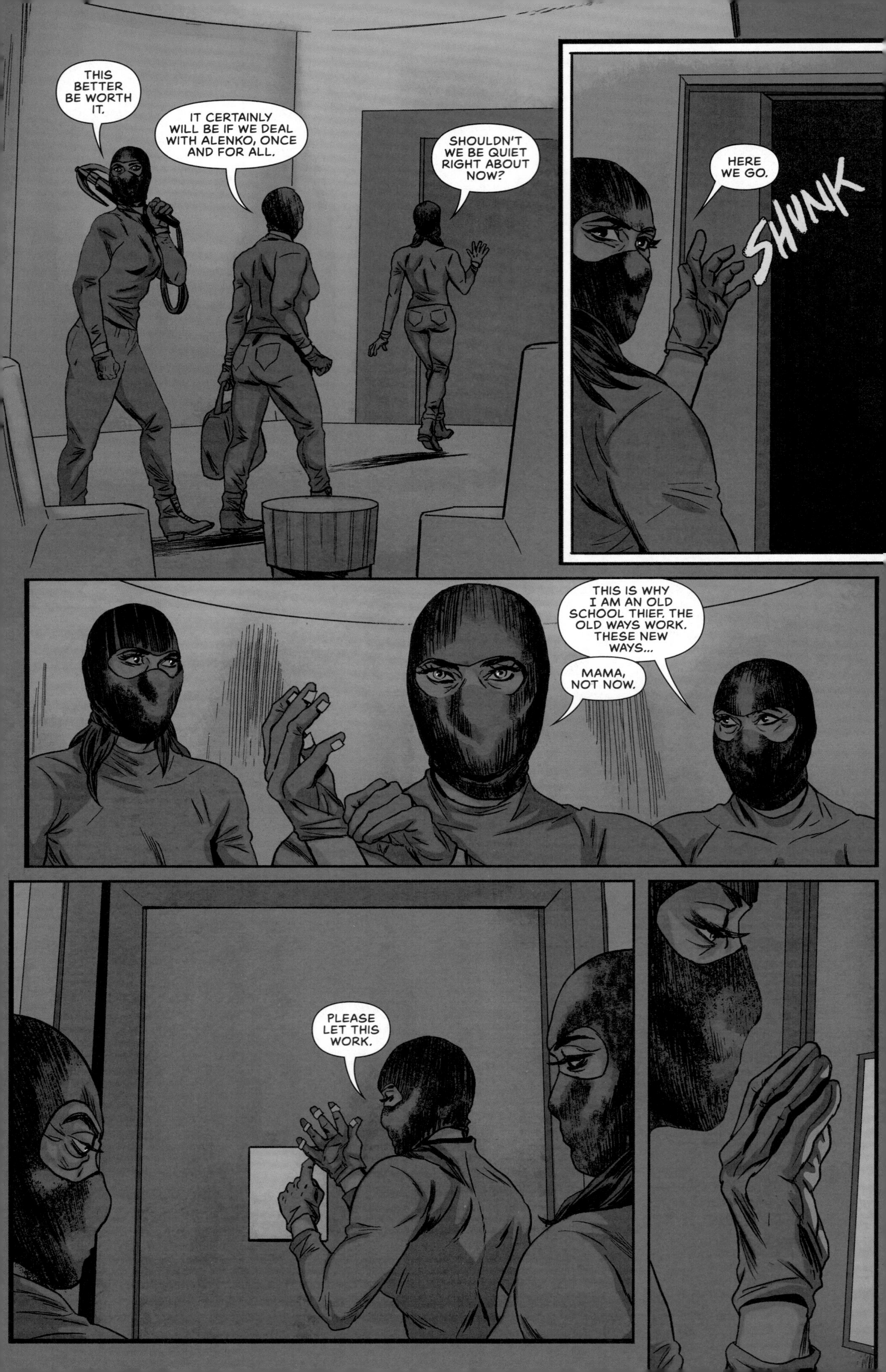
THIS BETTER BE WORTH IT.
IT CERTAINLY WILL BE IF WE DEAL WITH ALENKO, ONCE AND FOR ALL.
SHOULDN'T WE BE QUIET RIGHT ABOUT NOW?
HERE WE GO.
SHUNK
THIS IS WHY I AM AN OLD SCHOOL THIEF. THE OLD WAYS WORK. THESE NEW WAYS...
MAMA, NOT NOW.
PLEASE LET THIS WORK.

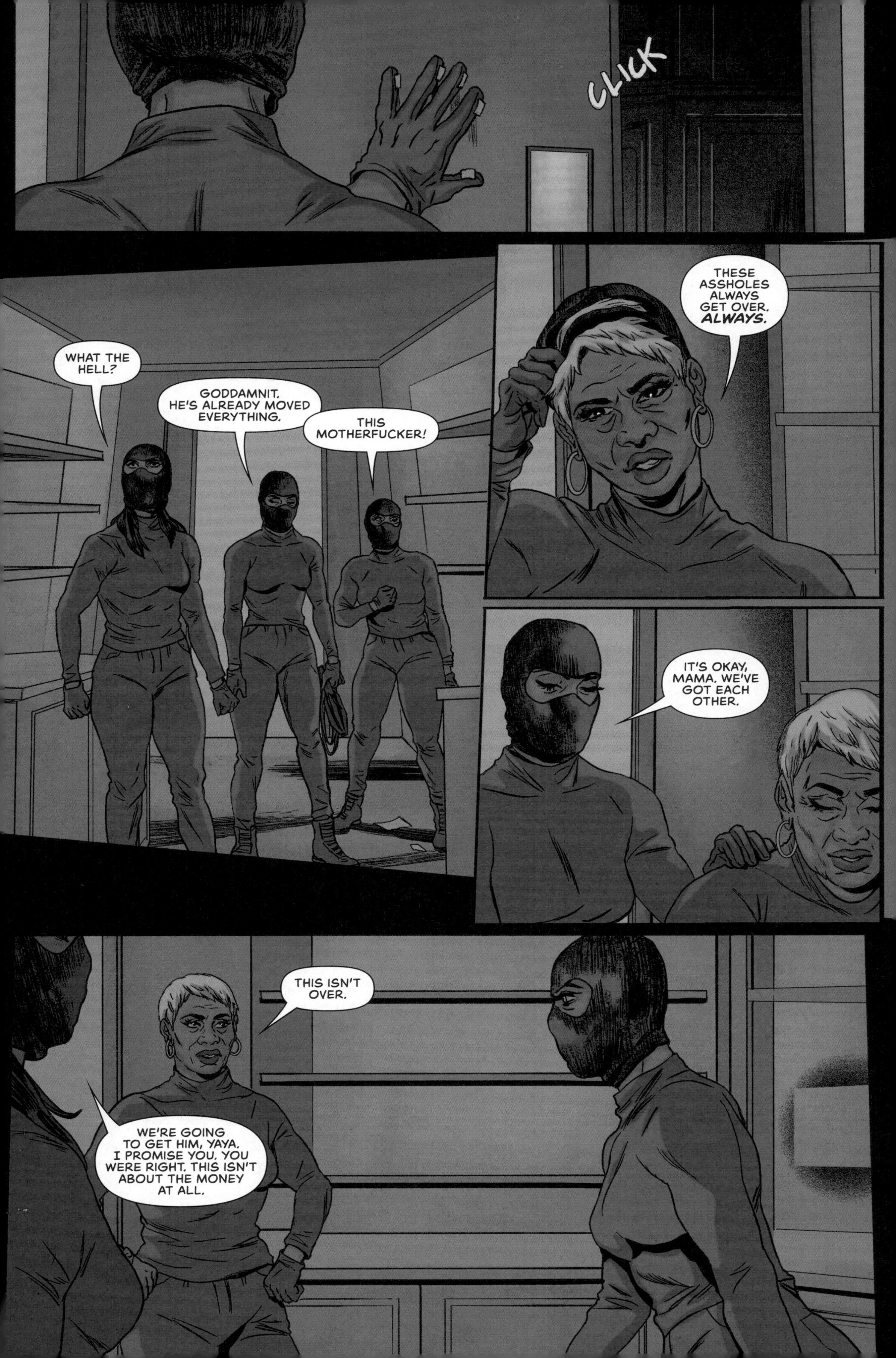

CLICK
WHAT THE HELL?
GODDAMNIT. HE'S ALREADY MOVED EVERYTHING.
THIS MOTHERFUCKER!
THESE ASSHOLES ALWAYS GET OVER. ALWAYS.
IT'S OKAY, MAMA. WE'VE GOT EACH OTHER.
THIS ISN'T OVER.
WE'RE GOING TO GET HIM, YAYA. I PROMISE YOU. YOU WERE RIGHT. THIS ISN'T ABOUT THE MONEY AT ALL.

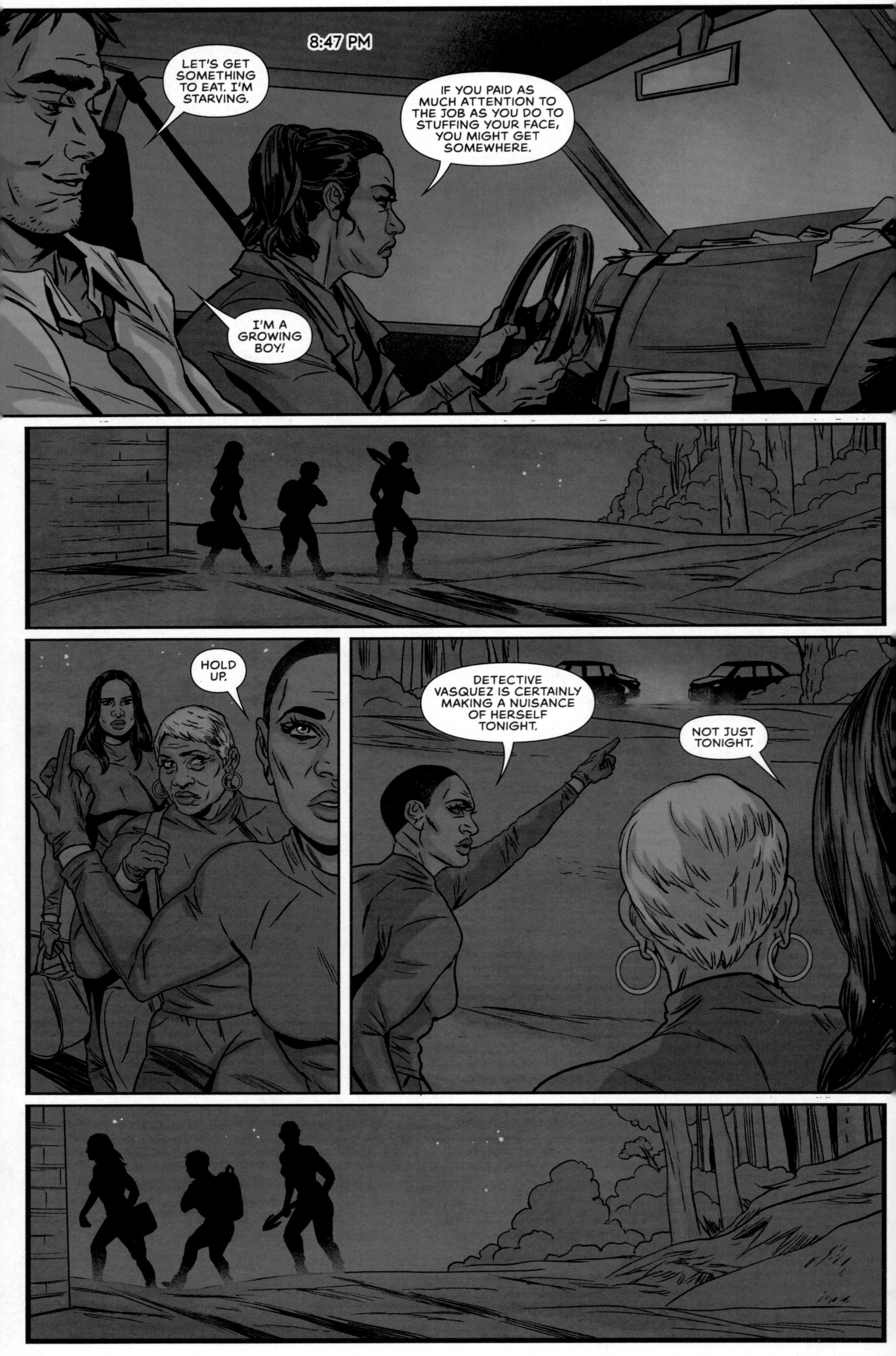
8:47 PM
LET'S GET SOMETHING TO EAT. I'M STARVING.
IF YOU PAID AS MUCH ATTENTION TO THE JOB AS YOU DO TO STUFFING YOUR FACE, YOU MIGHT GET SOMEWHERE.
I'M A GROWING BOY!
HOLD UP.
DETECTIVE VASQUEZ IS CERTAINLY MAKING A NUISANCE OF HERSELF TONIGHT.
NOT JUST TONIGHT.

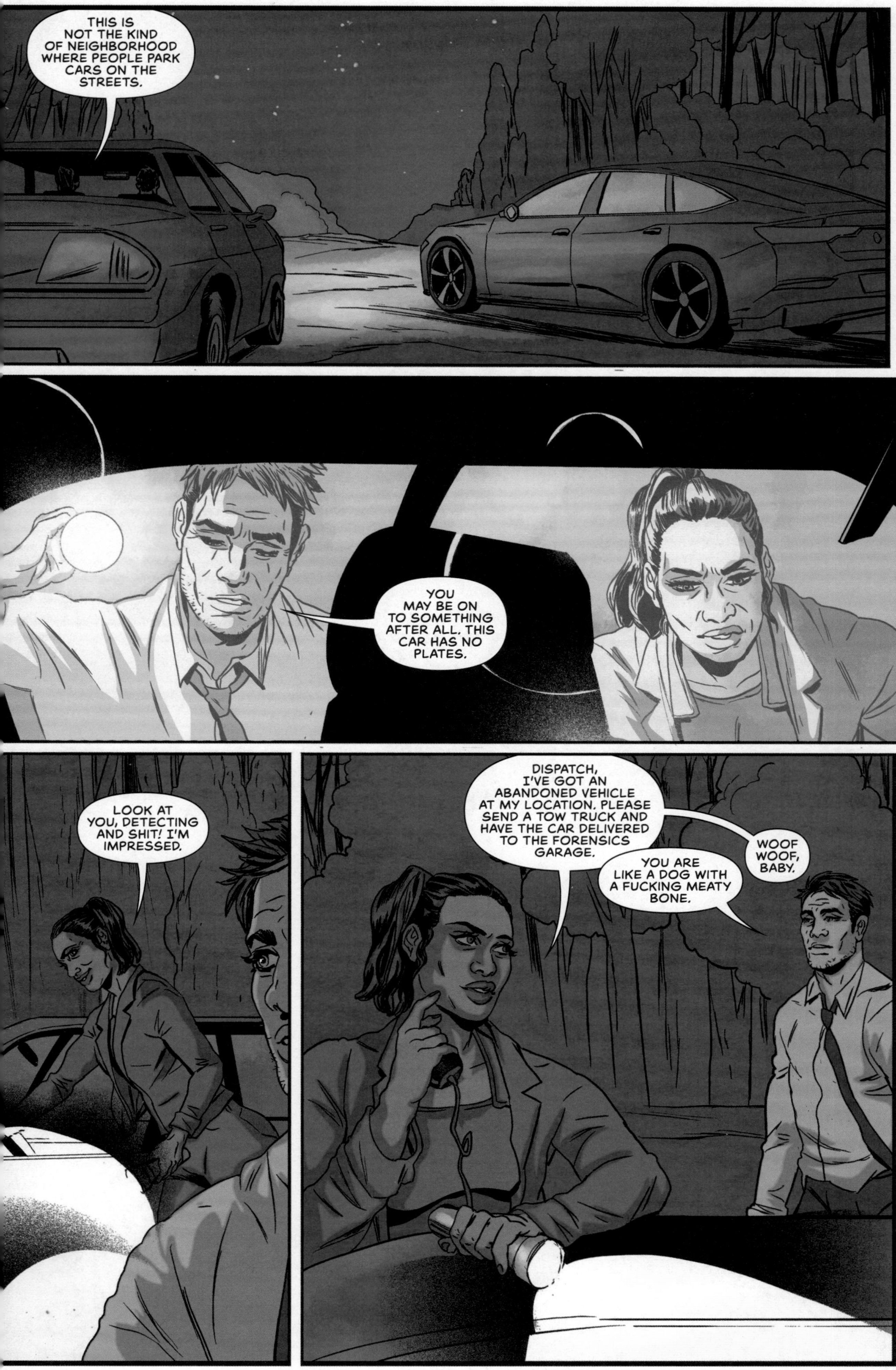
THIS IS NOT THE KIND OF NEIGHBORHOOD WHERE PEOPLE PARK CARS ON THE STREETS.
YOU MAY BE ON TO SOMETHING AFTER ALL. THIS CAR HAS NO PLATES.
LOOK AT YOU, DETECTING AND SHIT! I'M IMPRESSED.
DISPATCH, I'VE GOT AN ABANDONED VEHICLE AT MY LOCATION. PLEASE SEND A TOW TRUCK AND HAVE THE CAR DELIVERED TO THE FORENSICS GARAGE.
YOU ARE LIKE A DOG WITH A FUCKING MEATY BONE.
WOOF WOOF, BABY.

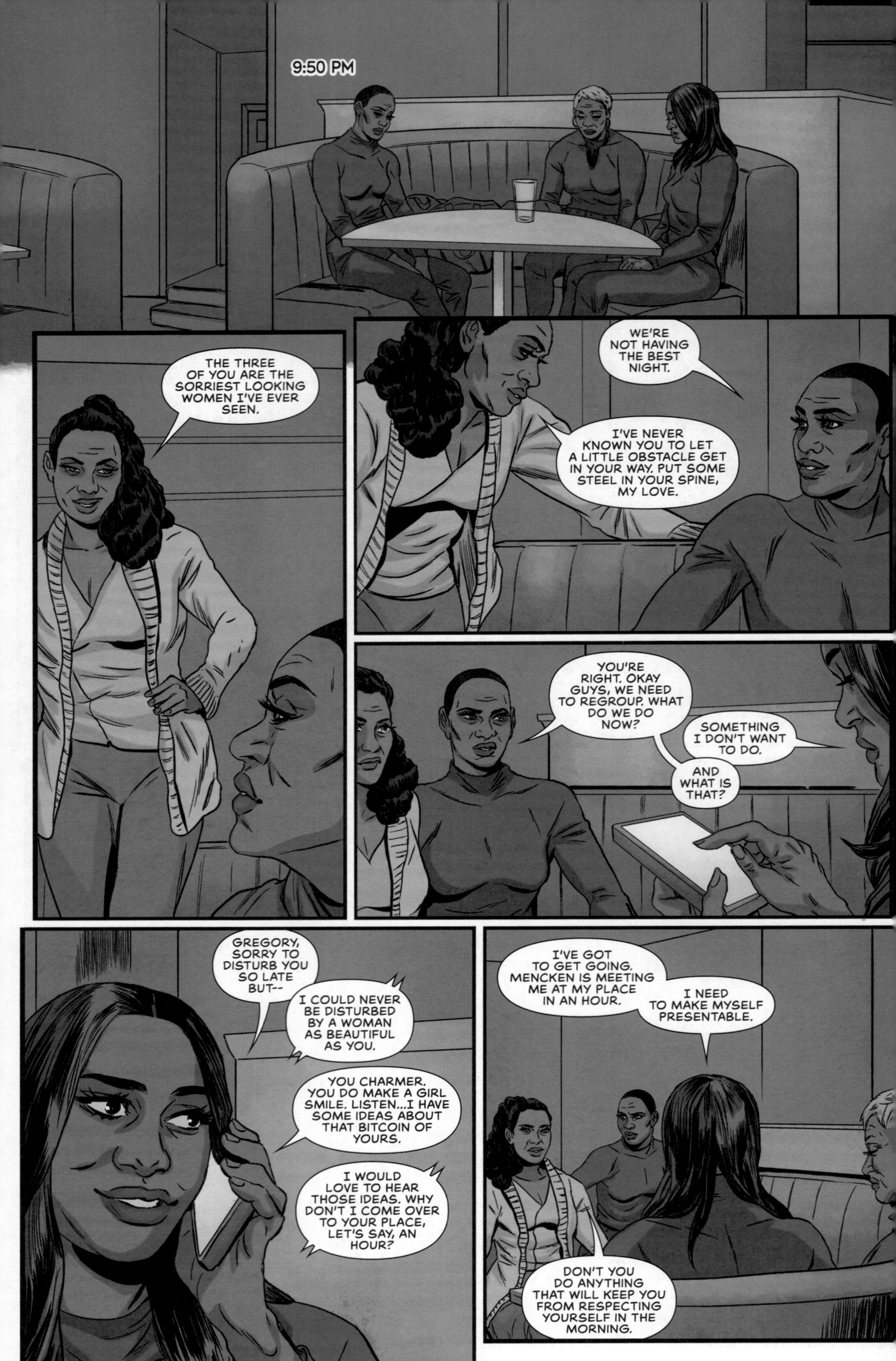
9:50 PM
THE THREE OF YOU ARE THE SORRIEST LOOKING WOMEN I'VE EVER SEEN.
WE'RE NOT HAVING THE BEST NIGHT.
I'VE NEVER KNOWN YOU TO LET A LITTLE OBSTACLE GET IN YOUR WAY. PUT SOME STEEL IN YOUR SPINE, MY LOVE.
YOU'RE RIGHT. OKAY GUYS, WE NEED TO REGROUP. WHAT DO WE DO NOW?
SOMETHING I DON'T WANT TO DO.
AND WHAT IS THAT?
GREGORY, SORRY TO DISTURB YOU SO LATE BUT--
I COULD NEVER BE DISTURBED BY A WOMAN AS BEAUTIFUL AS YOU.
YOU CHARMER. YOU DO MAKE A GIRL SMILE. LISTEN...I HAVE SOME IDEAS ABOUT THAT BITCOIN OF YOURS.
I WOULD LOVE TO HEAR THOSE IDEAS. WHY DON'T I COME OVER TO YOUR PLACE, LET'S SAY, AN HOUR?
I'VE GOT TO GET GOING. MENCKEN IS MEETING ME AT MY PLACE IN AN HOUR.
I NEED TO MAKE MYSELF PRESENTABLE.
DON'T YOU DO ANYTHING THAT WILL KEEP YOU FROM RESPECTING YOURSELF IN THE MORNING.

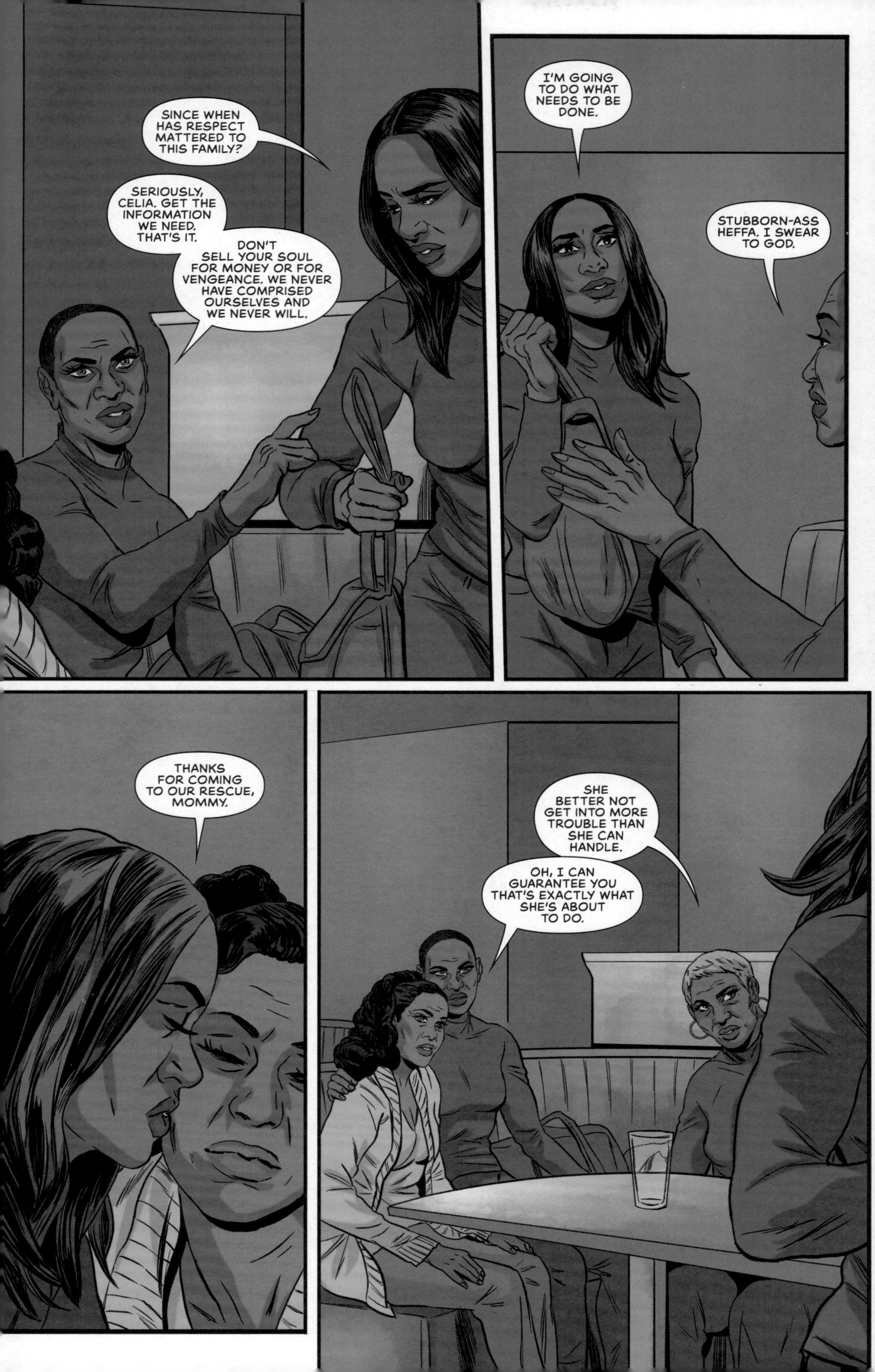
SINCE WHEN HAS RESPECT MATTERED TO THIS FAMILY?
SERIOUSLY, CELIA. GET THE INFORMATION WE NEED. THAT'S IT.
DON'T SELL YOUR SOUL FOR MONEY OR FOR VENGEANCE. WE NEVER HAVE COMPRISED OURSELVES AND WE NEVER WILL.
I'M GOING TO DO WHAT NEEDS TO BE DONE.
STUBBORN-ASS HEFFA. I SWEAR TO GOD.
THANKS FOR COMING TO OUR RESCUE, MOMMY.
SHE BETTER NOT GET INTO MORE TROUBLE THAN SHE CAN HANDLE.
OH, I CAN GUARANTEE YOU THAT'S EXACTLY WHAT SHE'S ABOUT TO DO.

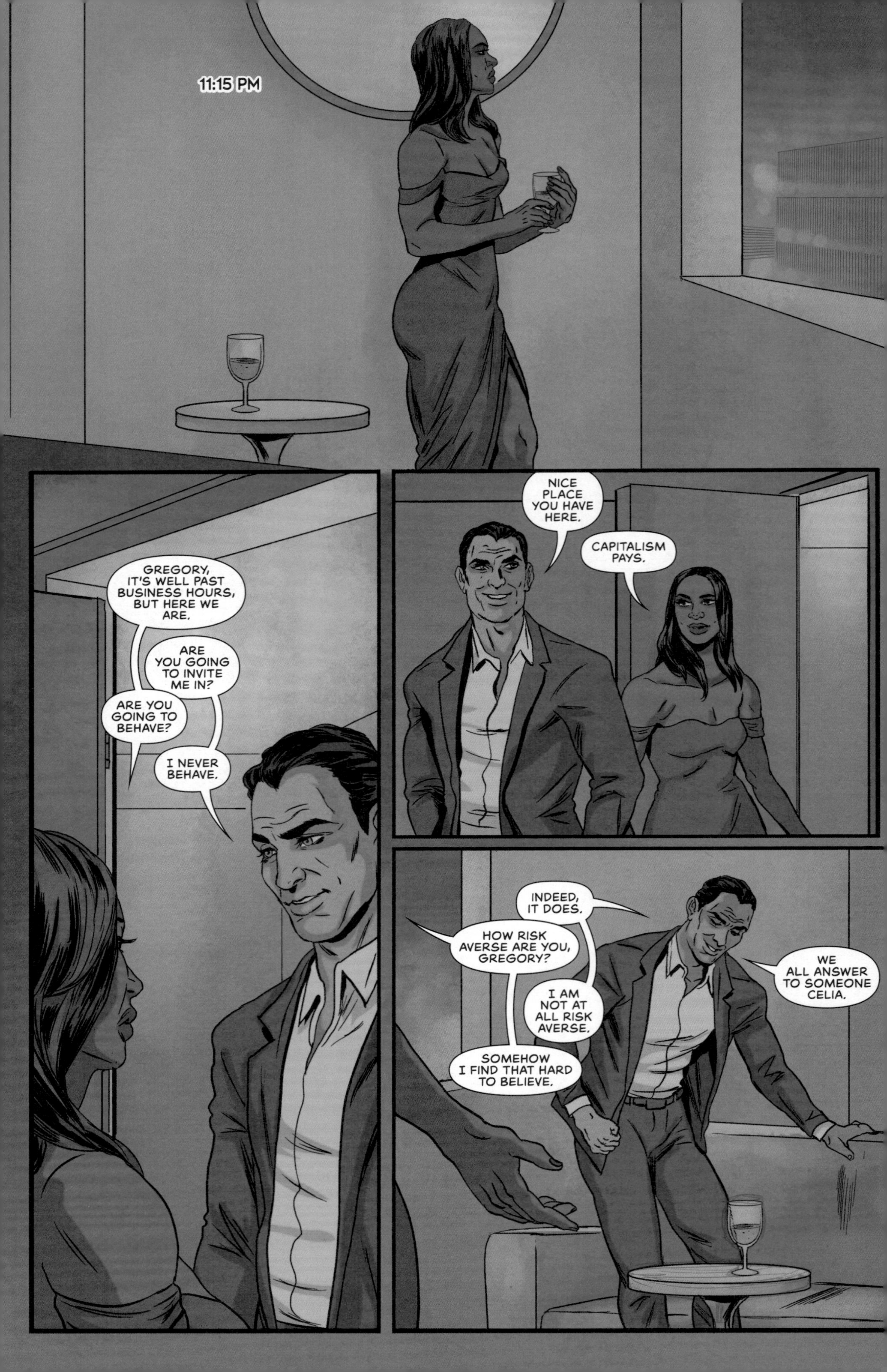
11:15 PM
GREGORY, IT'S WELL PAST BUSINESS HOURS, BUT HERE WE ARE.
ARE YOU GOING TO INVITE ME IN?
ARE YOU GOING TO BEHAVE?
I NEVER BEHAVE.
NICE PLACE YOU HAVE HERE.
CAPITALISM PAYS.
INDEED, IT DOES.
HOW RISK AVERSE ARE YOU, GREGORY?
I AM NOT AT ALL RISK AVERSE.
SOMEHOW I FIND THAT HARD TO BELIEVE.
WE ALL ANSWER TO SOMEONE CELIA.

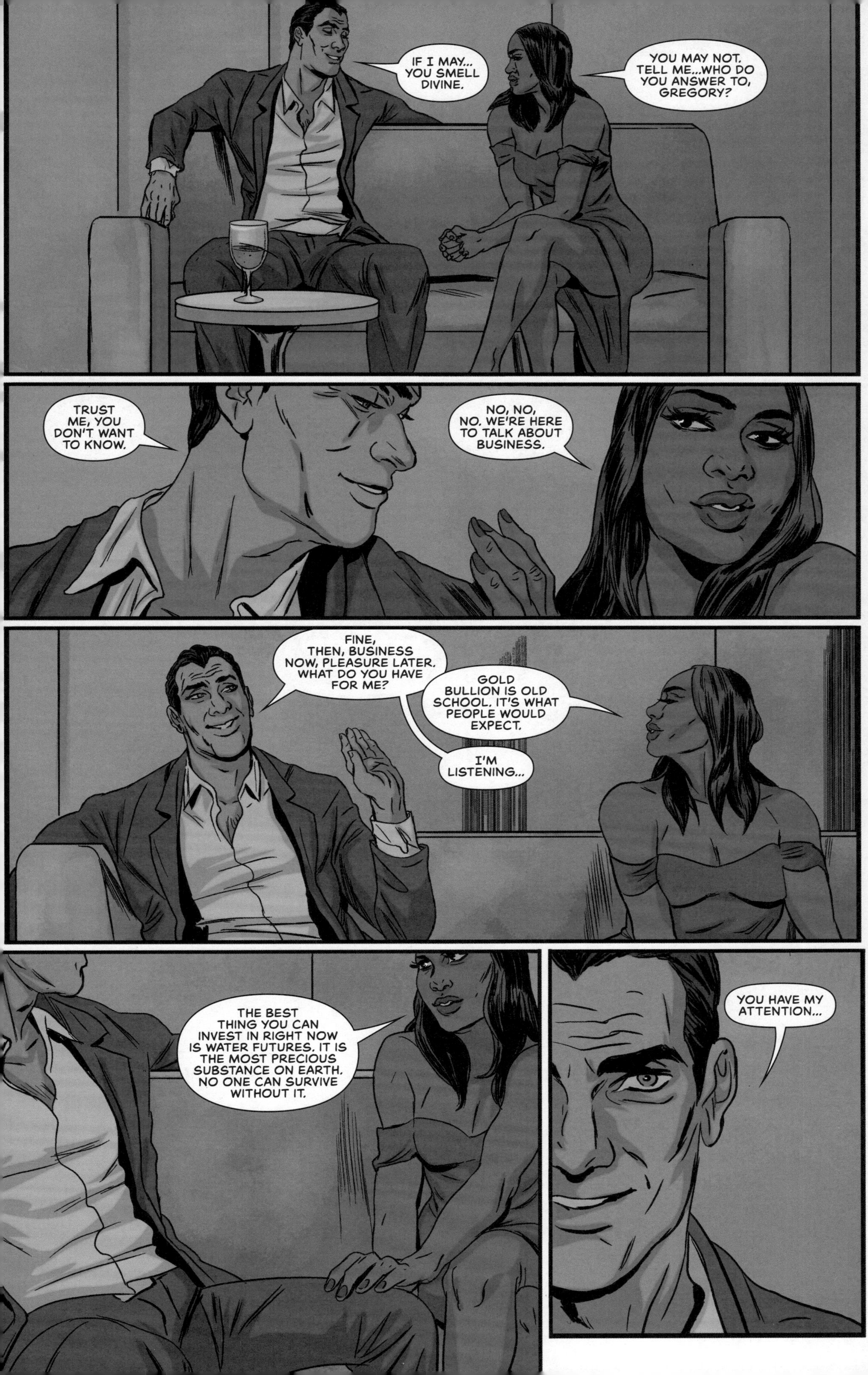
IF I MAY... YOU SMELL DIVINE.
YOU MAY NOT. TELL ME...WHO DO YOU ANSWER TO, GREGORY?
TRUST ME, YOU DON'T WANT TO KNOW.
NO, NO, NO. WE'RE HERE TO TALK ABOUT BUSINESS.
FINE, THEN, BUSINESS NOW, PLEASURE LATER. WHAT DO YOU HAVE FOR ME?
GOLD BULLION IS OLD SCHOOL. IT'S WHAT PEOPLE WOULD EXPECT.
I'M LISTENING...
THE BEST THING YOU CAN INVEST IN RIGHT NOW IS WATER FUTURES. IT IS THE MOST PRECIOUS SUBSTANCE ON EARTH. NO ONE CAN SURVIVE WITHOUT IT.
YOU HAVE MY ATTENTION...

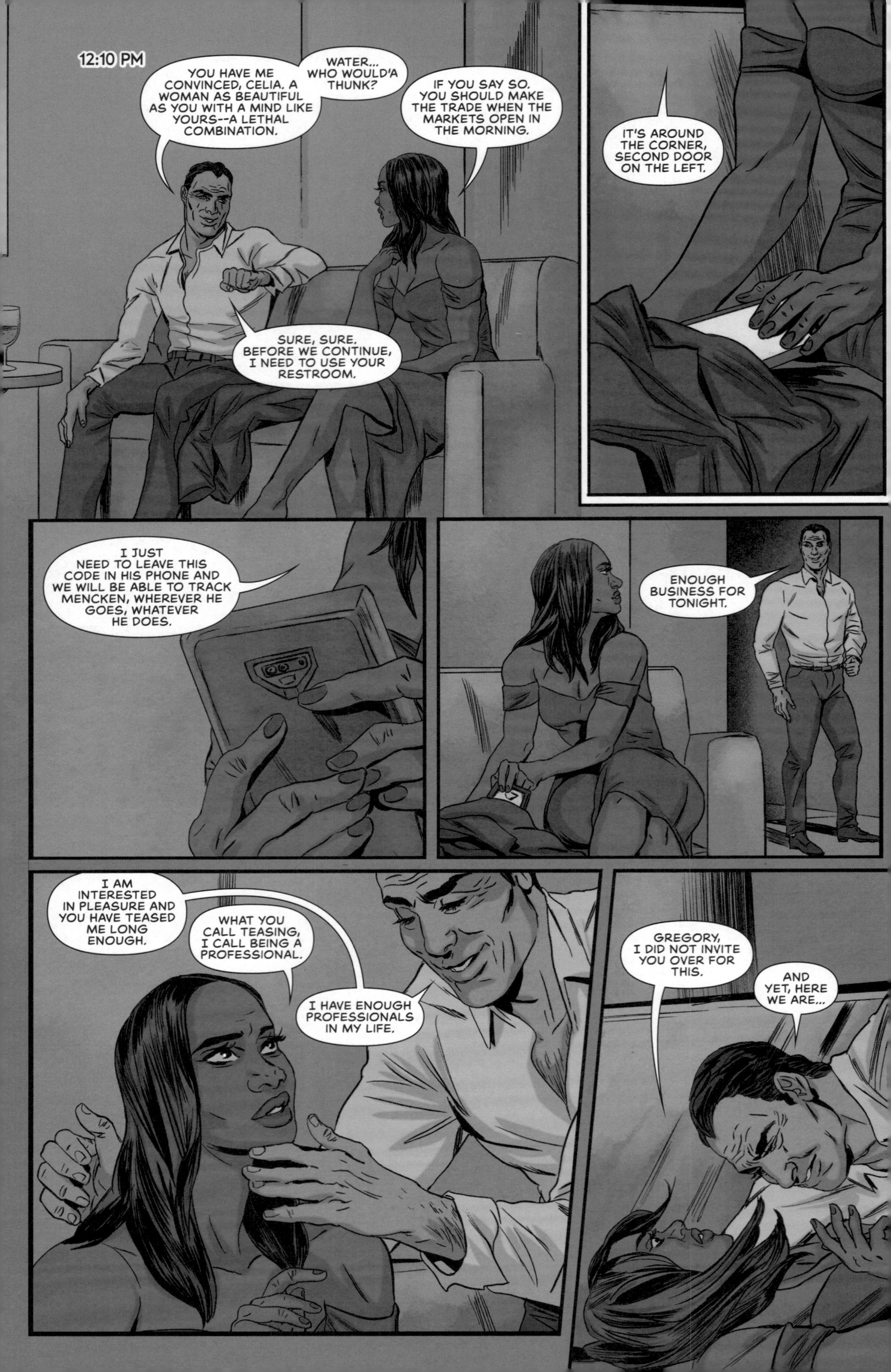
12:10 PM
YOU HAVE ME CONVINCED, CELIA. A WOMAN AS BEAUTIFUL AS YOU WITH A MIND LIKE YOURS--A LETHAL COMBINATION.
WATER... WHO WOULD'A THUNK?
IF YOU SAY SO. YOU SHOULD MAKE THE TRADE WHEN THE MARKETS OPEN IN THE MORNING.
SURE, SURE. BEFORE WE CONTINUE, I NEED TO USE YOUR RESTROOM.
IT'S AROUND THE CORNER, SECOND DOOR ON THE LEFT.
I JUST NEED TO LEAVE THIS CODE IN HIS PHONE AND WE WILL BE ABLE TO TRACK MENCKEN, WHEREVER HE GOES, WHATEVER HE DOES.
ENOUGH BUSINESS FOR TONIGHT.
I AM INTERESTED IN PLEASURE AND YOU HAVE TEASED ME LONG ENOUGH.
WHAT YOU CALL TEASING, I CALL BEING A PROFESSIONAL.
I HAVE ENOUGH PROFESSIONALS IN MY LIFE.
GREGORY, I DID NOT INVITE YOU OVER FOR THIS.
AND YET, HERE WE ARE...

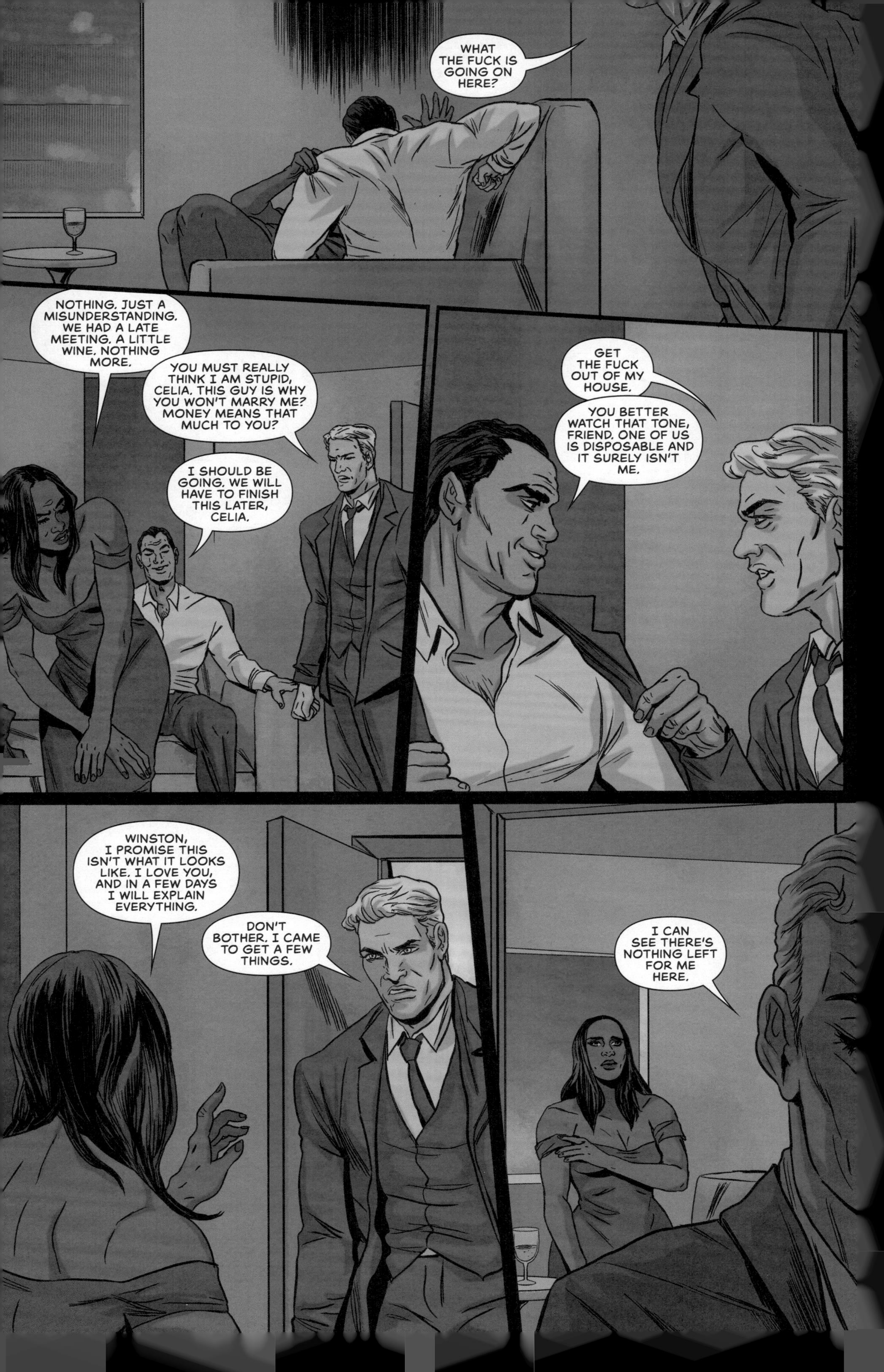
WHAT THE FUCK IS GOING ON HERE?
NOTHING. JUST A MISUNDERSTANDING. WE HAD A LATE MEETING, A LITTLE WINE. NOTHING MORE.
YOU MUST REALLY THINK I AM STUPID, CELIA. THIS GUY IS WHY YOU WON'T MARRY ME? MONEY MEANS THAT MUCH TO YOU?
I SHOULD BE GOING. WE WILL HAVE TO FINISH THIS LATER, CELIA.
GET THE FUCK OUT OF MY HOUSE.
YOU BETTER WATCH THAT TONE, FRIEND. ONE OF US IS DISPOSABLE AND IT SURELY ISN'T ME.
WINSTON, I PROMISE THIS ISN'T WHAT IT LOOKS LIKE. I LOVE YOU, AND IN A FEW DAYS I WILL EXPLAIN EVERYTHING.
DON'T BOTHER. I CAME TO GET A FEW THINGS.
I CAN SEE THERE'S NOTHING LEFT FOR ME HERE.

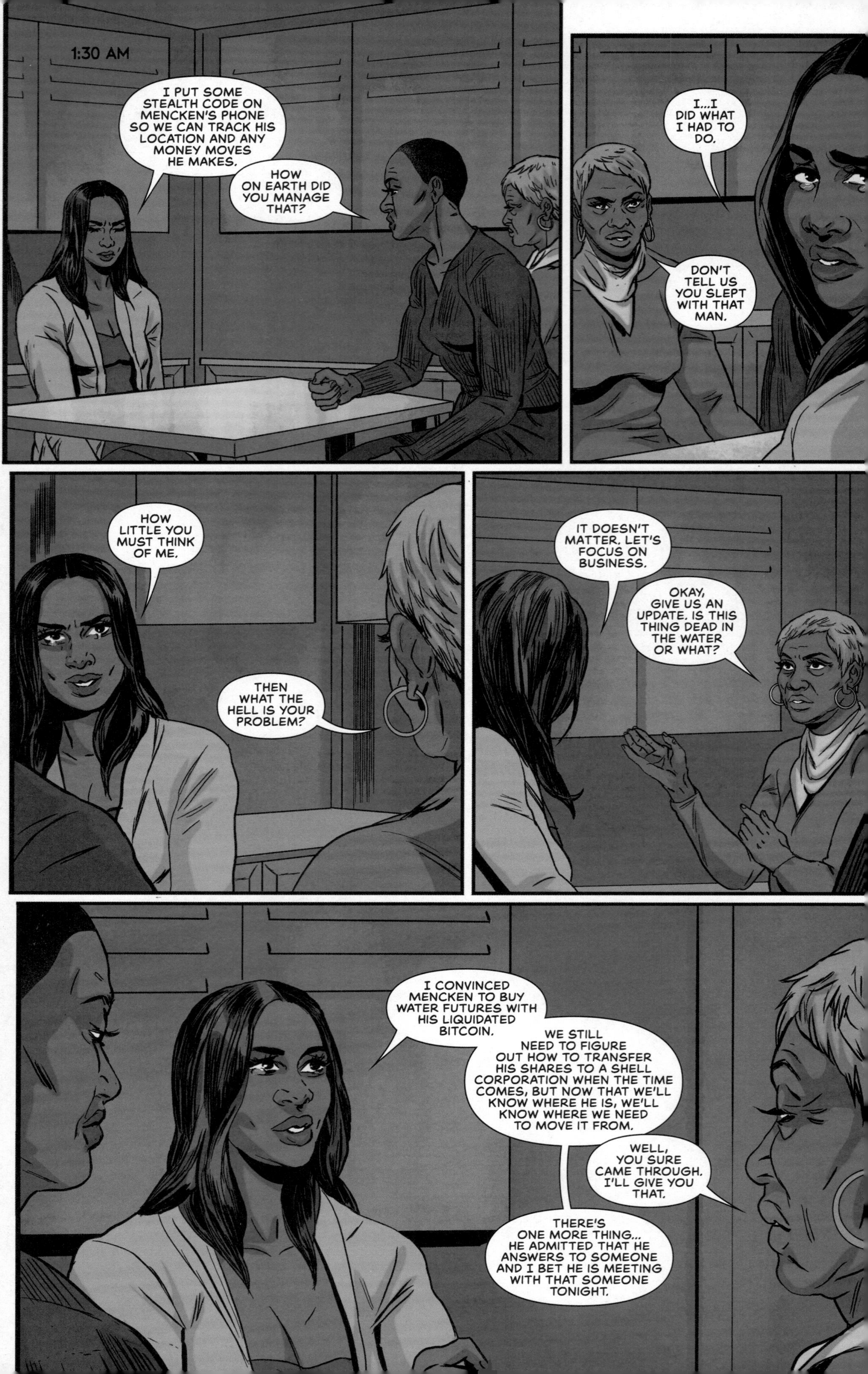
1:30 AM
I PUT SOME STEALTH CODE ON MENCKEN'S PHONE SO WE CAN TRACK HIS LOCATION AND ANY MONEY MOVES HE MAKES.
HOW ON EARTH DID YOU MANAGE THAT?
I...I DID WHAT I HAD TO DO.
DON'T TELL US YOU SLEPT WITH THAT MAN.
HOW LITTLE YOU MUST THINK OF ME.
THEN WHAT THE HELL IS YOUR PROBLEM?
IT DOESN'T MATTER. LET'S FOCUS ON BUSINESS.
OKAY, GIVE US AN UPDATE. IS THIS THING DEAD IN THE WATER OR WHAT?
I CONVINCED MENCKEN TO BUY WATER FUTURES WITH HIS LIQUIDATED BITCOIN.
WE STILL NEED TO FIGURE OUT HOW TO TRANSFER HIS SHARES TO A SHELL CORPORATION WHEN THE TIME COMES, BUT NOW THAT WE'LL KNOW WHERE HE IS, WE'LL KNOW WHERE WE NEED TO MOVE IT FROM.
WELL, YOU SURE CAME THROUGH. I'LL GIVE YOU THAT.
THERE'S ONE MORE THING... HE ADMITTED THAT HE ANSWERS TO SOMEONE AND I BET HE IS MEETING WITH THAT SOMEONE TONIGHT.

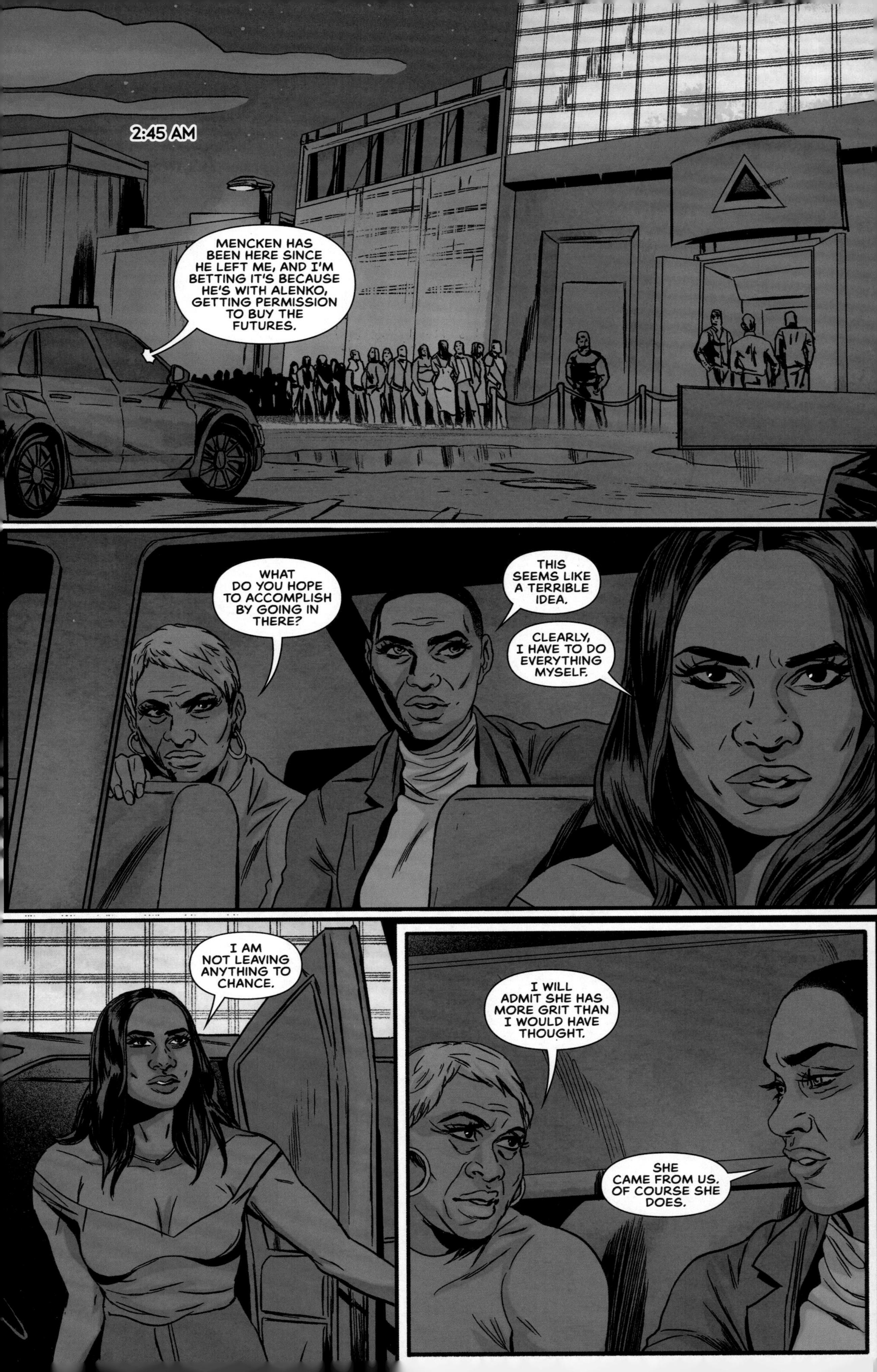
2:45 AM
MENCKEN HAS BEEN HERE SINCE HE LEFT ME, AND I'M BETTING IT'S BECAUSE HE'S WITH ALENKO, GETTING PERMISSION TO BUY THE FUTURES.
WHAT DO YOU HOPE TO ACCOMPLISH BY GOING IN THERE?
THIS SEEMS LIKE A TERRIBLE IDEA.
CLEARLY, I HAVE TO DO EVERYTHING MYSELF.
I AM NOT LEAVING ANYTHING TO CHANCE.
I WILL ADMIT SHE HAS MORE GRIT THAN I WOULD HAVE THOUGHT.
SHE CAME FROM US. OF COURSE SHE DOES.

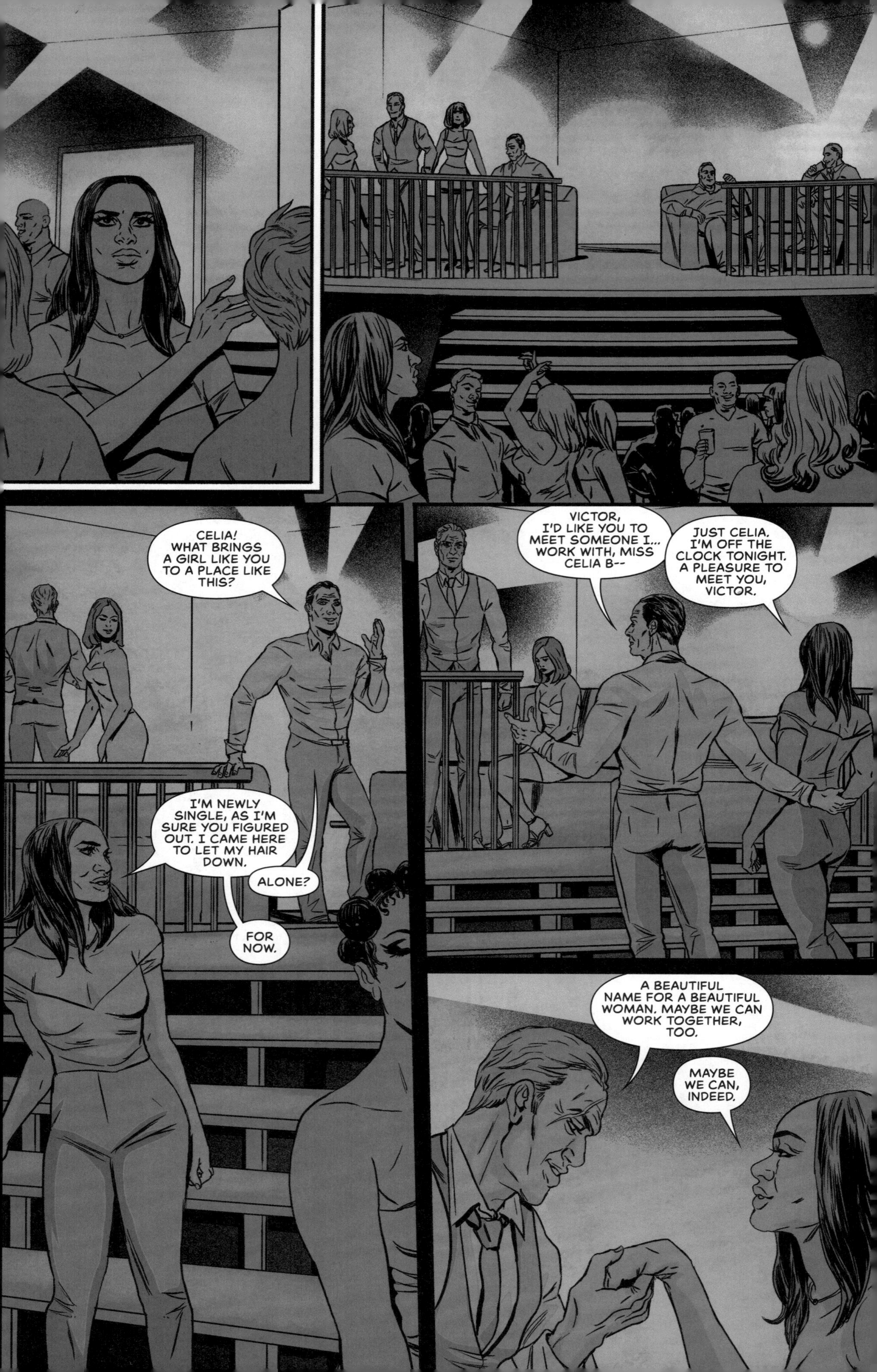
CELIA! WHAT BRINGS A GIRL LIKE YOU TO A PLACE LIKE THIS?
I'M NEWLY SINGLE, AS I'M SURE YOU FIGURED OUT. I CAME HERE TO LET MY HAIR DOWN.
ALONE?
FOR NOW.
VICTOR, I'D LIKE YOU TO MEET SOMEONE I... WORK WITH, MISS CELIA B--
JUST CELIA. I'M OFF THE CLOCK TONIGHT. A PLEASURE TO MEET YOU, VICTOR.
A BEAUTIFUL NAME FOR A BEAUTIFUL WOMAN. MAYBE WE CAN WORK TOGETHER, TOO.
MAYBE WE CAN, INDEED.

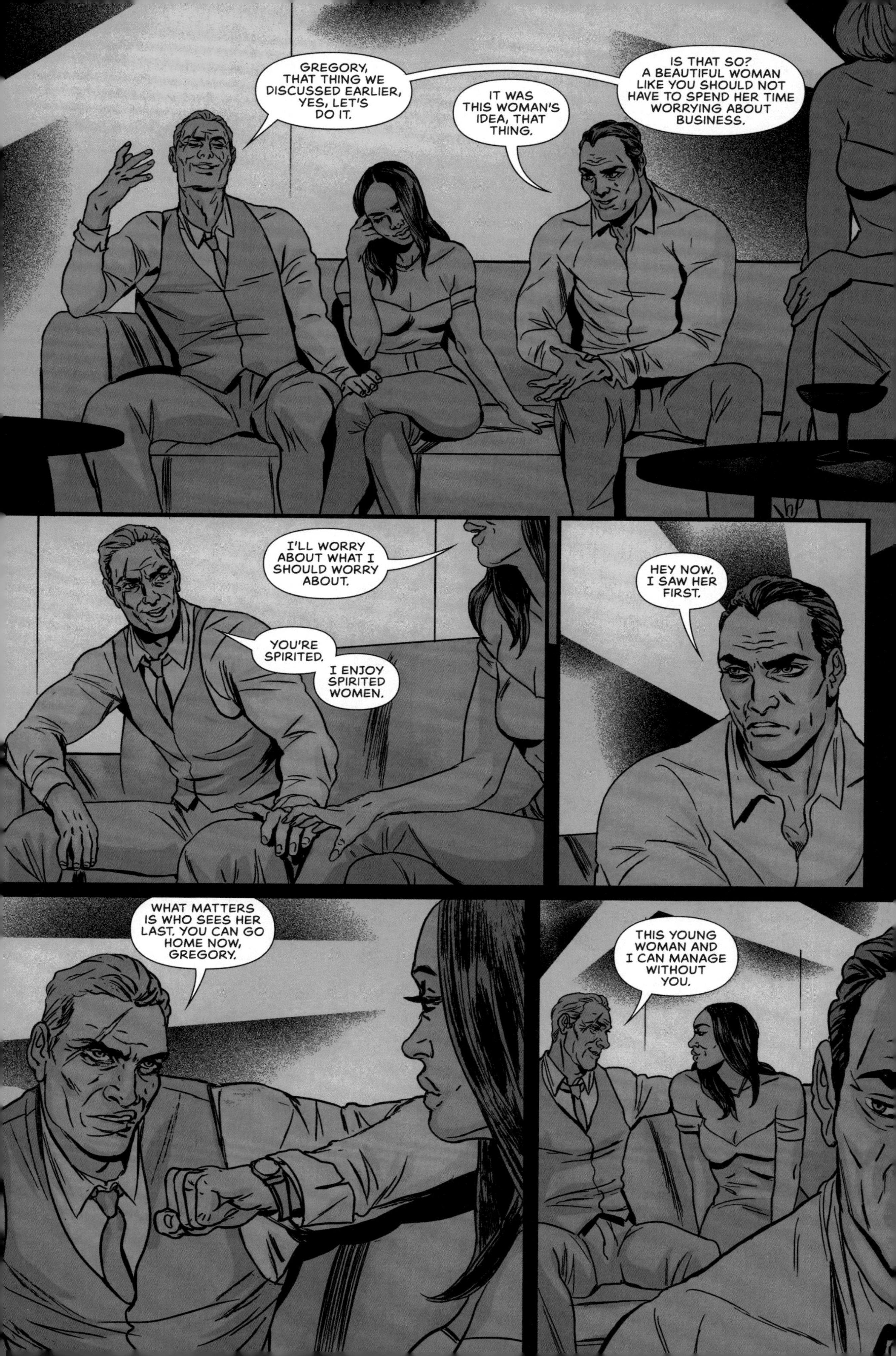
GREGORY, THAT THING WE DISCUSSED EARLIER, YES, LET'S DO IT.
IT WAS THIS WOMAN'S IDEA, THAT THING.
IS THAT SO? A BEAUTIFUL WOMAN LIKE YOU SHOULD NOT HAVE TO SPEND HER TIME WORRYING ABOUT BUSINESS.
I'LL WORRY ABOUT WHAT I SHOULD WORRY ABOUT.
YOU'RE SPIRITED.
I ENJOY SPIRITED WOMEN.
HEY NOW. I SAW HER FIRST.
WHAT MATTERS IS WHO SEES HER LAST. YOU CAN GO HOME NOW, GREGORY.
THIS YOUNG WOMAN AND I CAN MANAGE WITHOUT YOU.

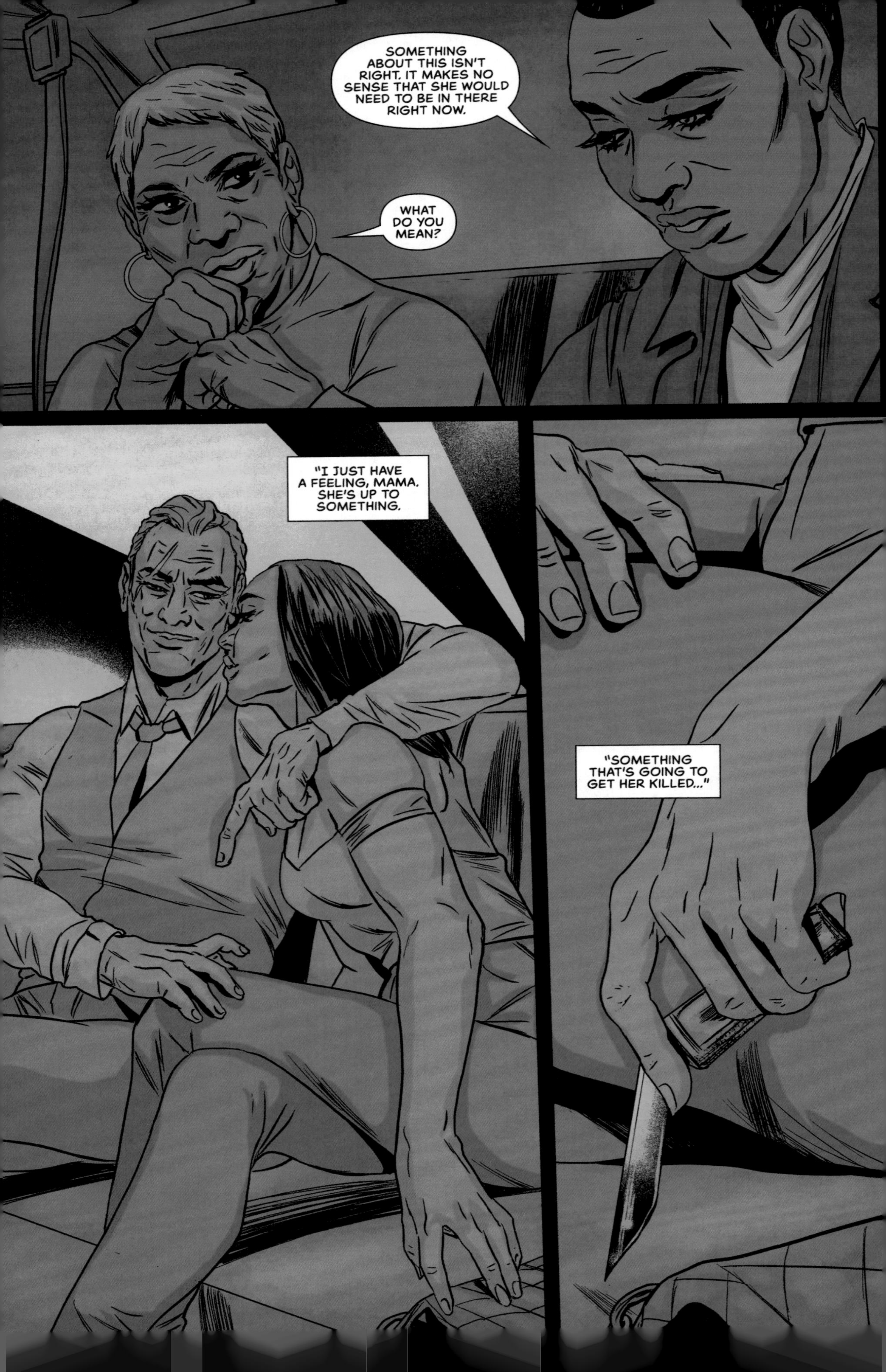
SOMETHING ABOUT THIS ISN'T RIGHT. IT MAKES NO SENSE THAT SHE WOULD NEED TO BE IN THERE RIGHT NOW.
WHAT DO YOU MEAN?
"I JUST HAVE A FEELING, MAMA. SHE'S UP TO SOMETHING.
"SOMETHING THAT'S GOING TO GET HER KILLED..."

CHAPTER 6

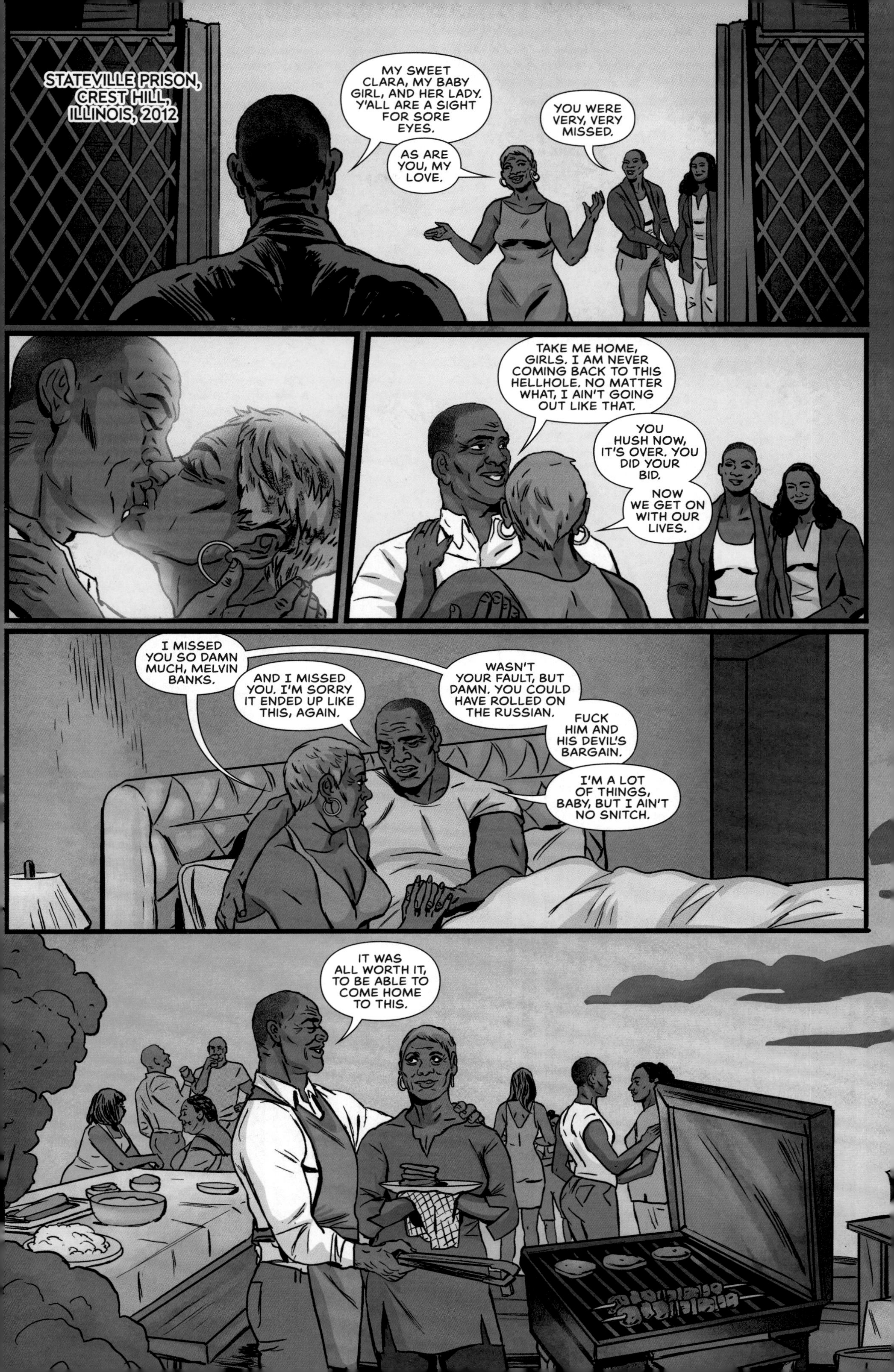
STATEVILLE PRISON, CREST HILL, ILLINOIS, 2012
MY SWEET CLARA, MY BABY GIRL, AND HER LADY. Y'ALL ARE A SIGHT FOR SORE EYES.
AS ARE YOU, MY LOVE.
YOU WERE VERY, VERY MISSED.
TAKE ME HOME, GIRLS. I AM NEVER COMING BACK TO THIS HELLHOLE. NO MATTER WHAT, I AIN'T GOING OUT LIKE THAT.
YOU HUSH NOW, IT'S OVER. YOU DID YOUR BID.
NOW WE GET ON WITH OUR LIVES.
I MISSED YOU SO DAMN MUCH, MELVIN BANKS.
AND I MISSED YOU. I'M SORRY IT ENDED UP LIKE THIS, AGAIN.
WASN'T YOUR FAULT, BUT DAMN. YOU COULD HAVE ROLLED ON THE RUSSIAN.
FUCK HIM AND HIS DEVIL'S BARGAIN.
I'M A LOT OF THINGS, BABY, BUT I AIN'T NO SNITCH.
IT WAS ALL WORTH IT, TO BE ABLE TO COME HOME TO THIS.

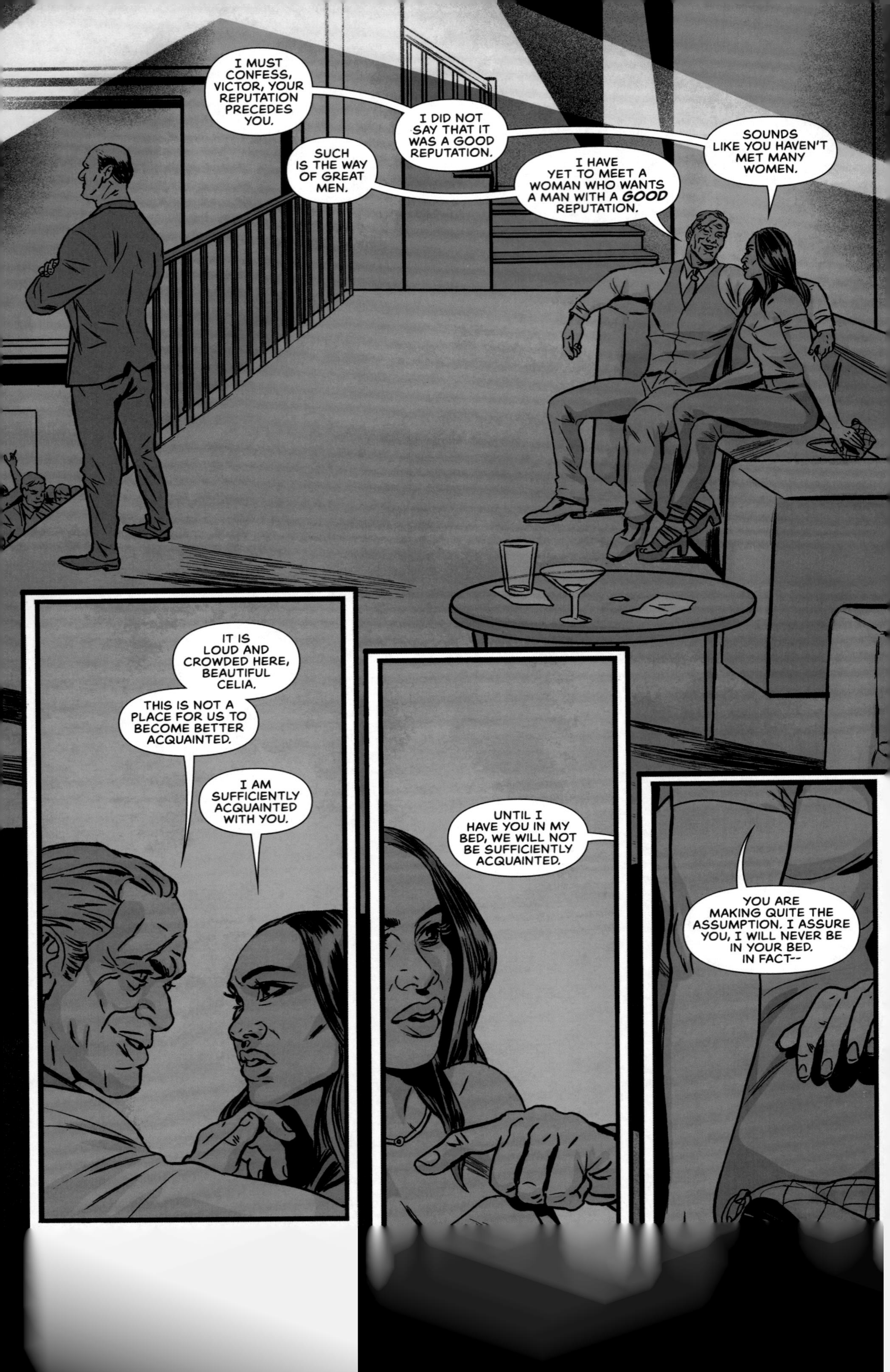
I MUST CONFESS, VICTOR, YOUR REPUTATION PRECEDES YOU.
SUCH IS THE WAY OF GREAT MEN.
I DID NOT SAY THAT IT WAS A GOOD REPUTATION.
I HAVE YET TO MEET A WOMAN WHO WANTS A MAN WITH A ***GOOD*** REPUTATION.
SOUNDS LIKE YOU HAVEN'T MET MANY WOMEN.
IT IS LOUD AND CROWDED HERE, BEAUTIFUL CELIA.
THIS IS NOT A PLACE FOR US TO BECOME BETTER ACQUAINTED.
I AM SUFFICIENTLY ACQUAINTED WITH YOU.
UNTIL I HAVE YOU IN MY BED, WE WILL NOT BE SUFFICIENTLY ACQUAINTED.
YOU ARE MAKING QUITE THE ASSUMPTION. I ASSURE YOU, I WILL NEVER BE IN YOUR BED. IN FACT--

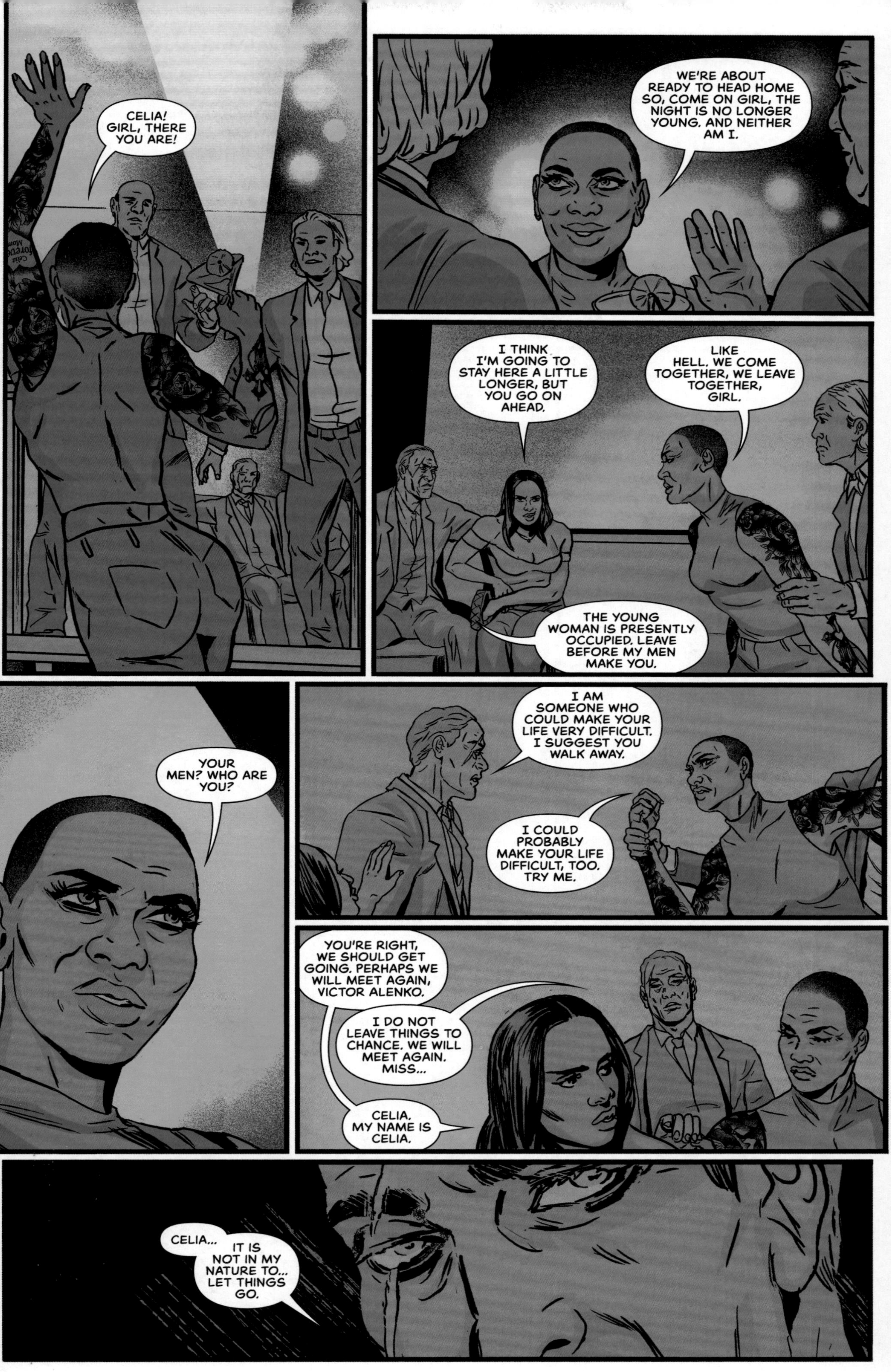
CELIA! GIRL, THERE YOU ARE!
WE'RE ABOUT READY TO HEAD HOME SO, COME ON GIRL, THE NIGHT IS NO LONGER YOUNG. AND NEITHER AM I.
I THINK I'M GOING TO STAY HERE A LITTLE LONGER, BUT YOU GO ON AHEAD.
LIKE HELL. WE COME TOGETHER, WE LEAVE TOGETHER, GIRL.
THE YOUNG WOMAN IS PRESENTLY OCCUPIED. LEAVE BEFORE MY MEN MAKE YOU.
YOUR MEN? WHO ARE YOU?
I AM SOMEONE WHO COULD MAKE YOUR LIFE VERY DIFFICULT. I SUGGEST YOU WALK AWAY.
I COULD PROBABLY MAKE YOUR LIFE DIFFICULT, TOO. TRY ME.
YOU'RE RIGHT, WE SHOULD GET GOING. PERHAPS WE WILL MEET AGAIN, VICTOR ALENKO.
I DO NOT LEAVE THINGS TO CHANCE. WE WILL MEET AGAIN, MISS...
CELIA, MY NAME IS CELIA.
CELIA...
IT IS NOT IN MY NATURE TO... LET THINGS GO.

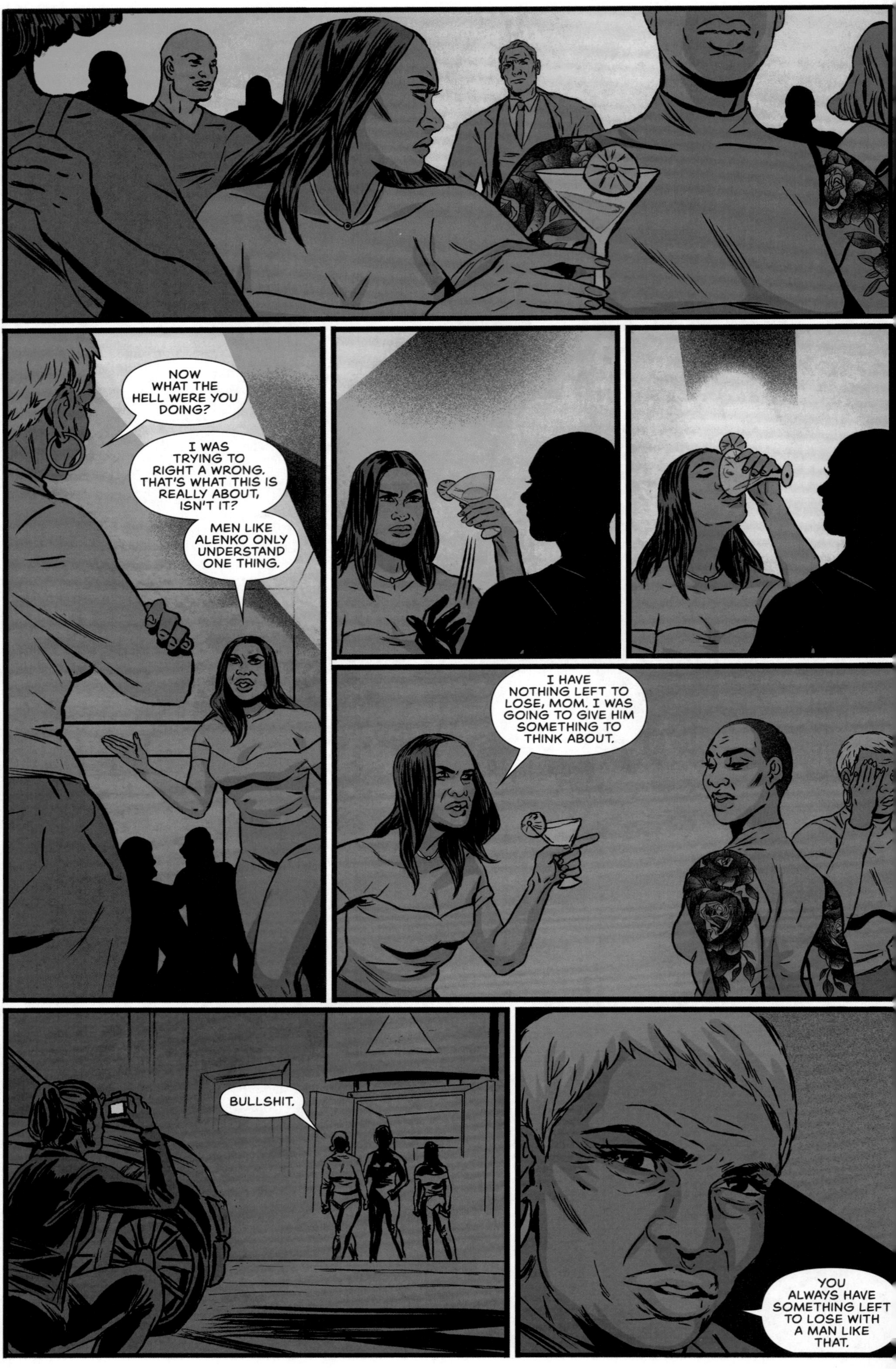
NOW WHAT THE HELL WERE YOU DOING?
I WAS TRYING TO RIGHT A WRONG. THAT'S WHAT THIS IS REALLY ABOUT, ISN'T IT?
MEN LIKE ALENKO ONLY UNDERSTAND ONE THING.
I HAVE NOTHING LEFT TO LOSE, MOM. I WAS GOING TO GIVE HIM SOMETHING TO THINK ABOUT.
BULLSHIT.
YOU ALWAYS HAVE SOMETHING LEFT TO LOSE WITH A MAN LIKE THAT.

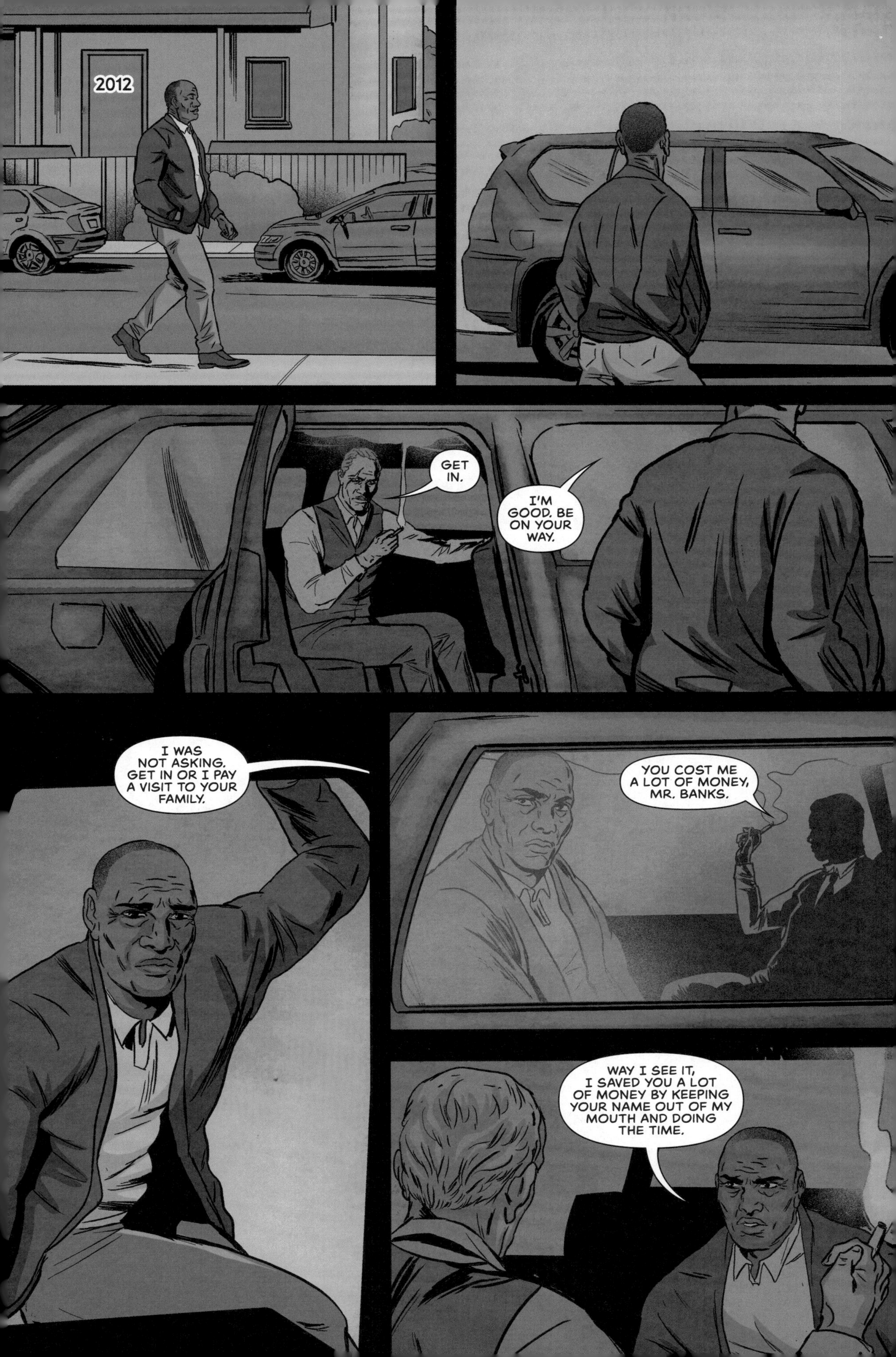
2012
GET IN.
I'M GOOD. BE ON YOUR WAY.
I WAS NOT ASKING. GET IN OR I PAY A VISIT TO YOUR FAMILY.
YOU COST ME A LOT OF MONEY, MR. BANKS.
WAY I SEE IT, I SAVED YOU A LOT OF MONEY BY KEEPING YOUR NAME OUT OF MY MOUTH AND DOING THE TIME.

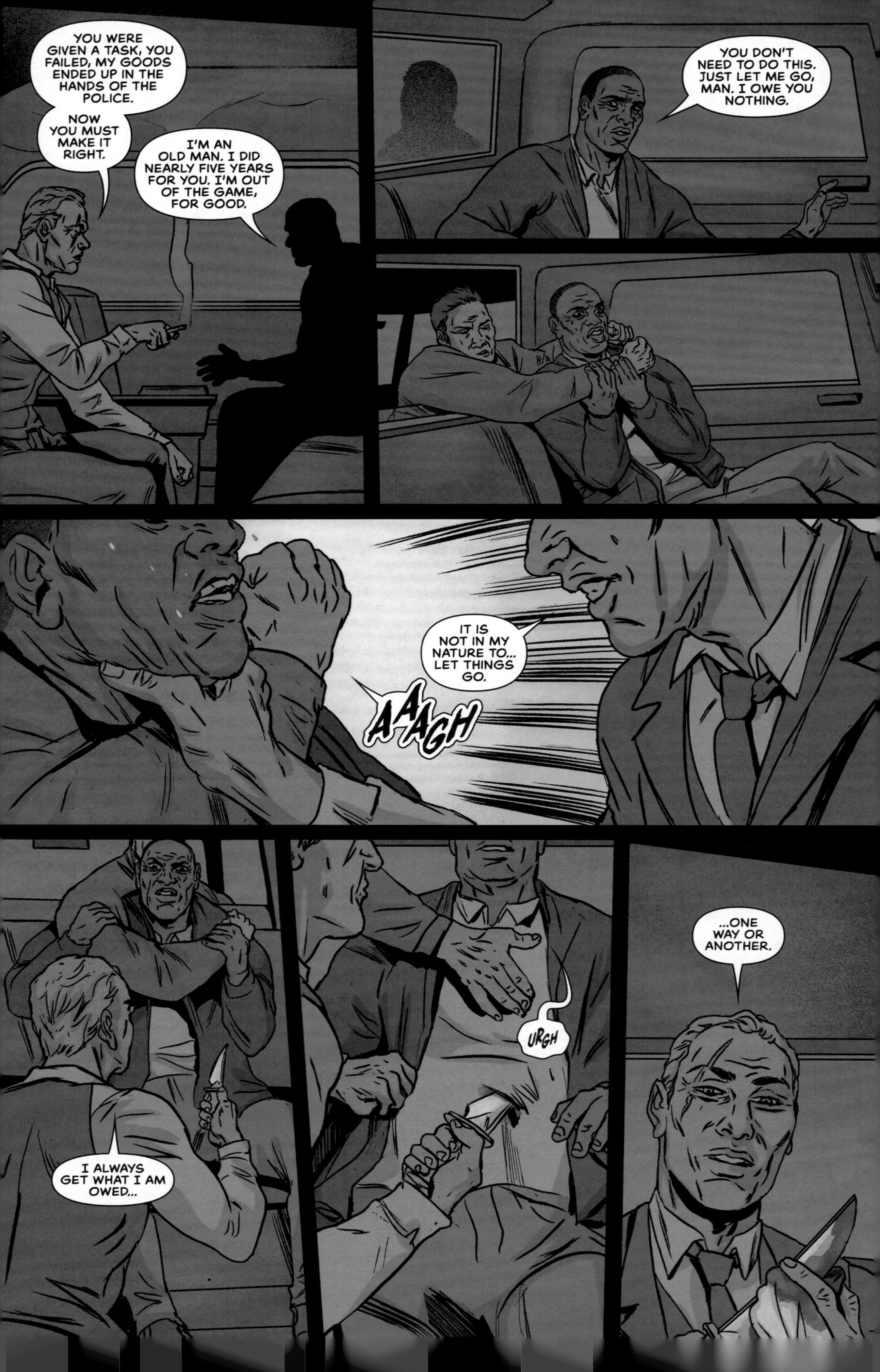
YOU WERE GIVEN A TASK, YOU FAILED, MY GOODS ENDED UP IN THE HANDS OF THE POLICE.
NOW YOU MUST MAKE IT RIGHT.
I'M AN OLD MAN. I DID NEARLY FIVE YEARS FOR YOU. I'M OUT OF THE GAME, FOR GOOD.
YOU DON'T NEED TO DO THIS. JUST LET ME GO, MAN. I OWE YOU NOTHING.
IT IS NOT IN MY NATURE TO... LET THINGS GO.
AAAGH
I ALWAYS GET WHAT I AM OWED...
URGH
...ONE WAY OR ANOTHER.

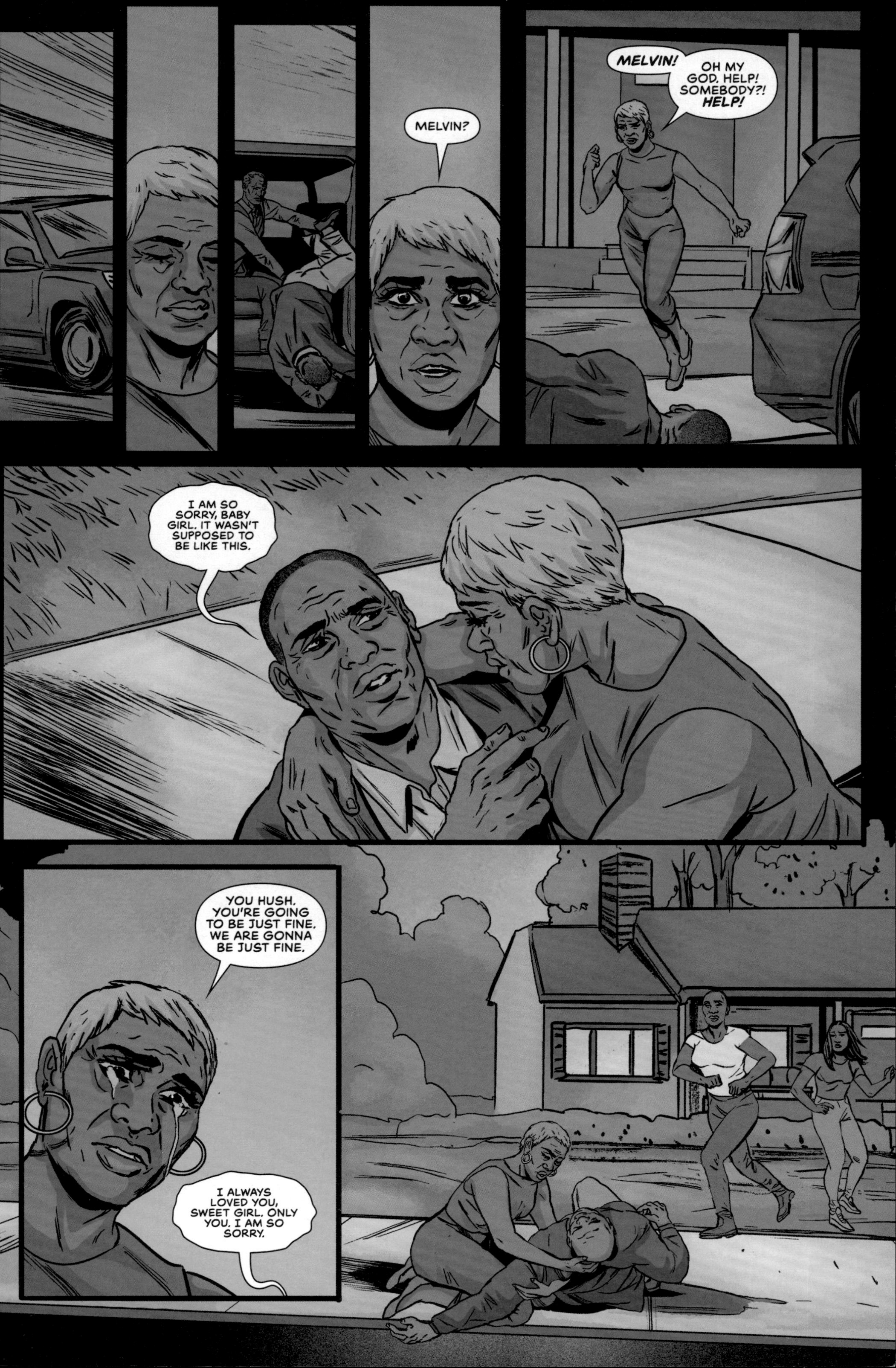
MELVIN?
MELVIN!
OH MY GOD. HELP! SOMEBODY?! HELP!
I AM SO SORRY, BABY GIRL. IT WASN'T SUPPOSED TO BE LIKE THIS.
YOU HUSH. YOU'RE GOING TO BE JUST FINE. WE ARE GONNA BE JUST FINE.
I ALWAYS LOVED YOU, SWEET GIRL. ONLY YOU. I AM SO SORRY.

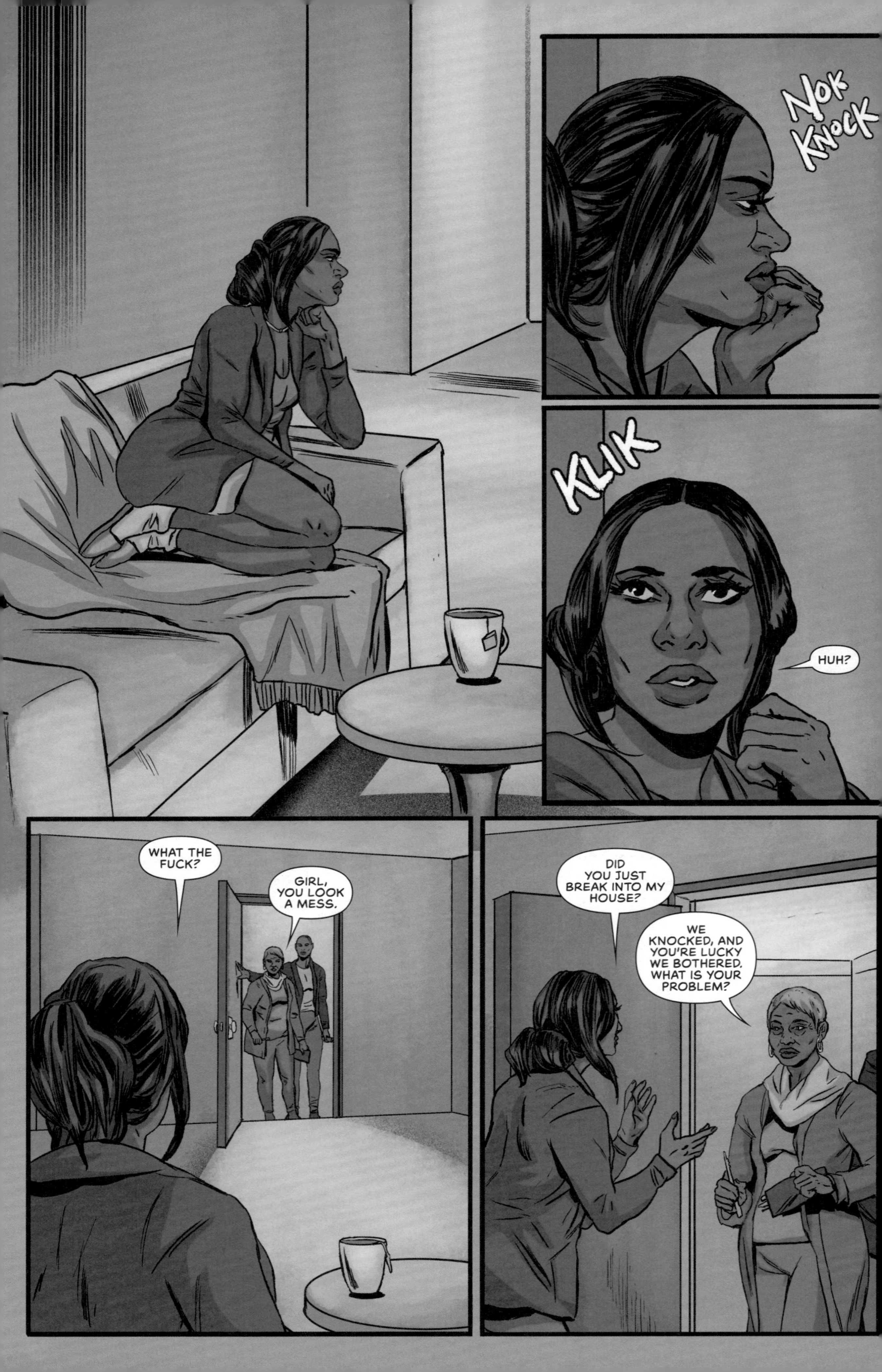
NOK KNOCK
KLIK
HUH?
WHAT THE FUCK?
GIRL, YOU LOOK A MESS.
DID YOU JUST BREAK INTO MY HOUSE?
WE KNOCKED, AND YOU'RE LUCKY WE BOTHERED. WHAT IS YOUR PROBLEM?

EVERYTHING IS MY PROBLEM. WE TRIED TO GET ONE OVER AND WE FAILED. THE MAN I LOVE THINKS I'M CHEATING AND WANTS NOTHING TO DO WITH ME.

VASQUEZ IS WAITING FOR US TO SLIP UP.

ENOUGH! YOU ALWAYS ASSUMED STEALING WAS EASY. NOW YOU KNOW IT ISN'T. WASH YOUR FACE, THEN DO WHATEVER COMPUTER THINGS YOU ARE GOING TO DO TO GET US OUR DAMN MONEY.

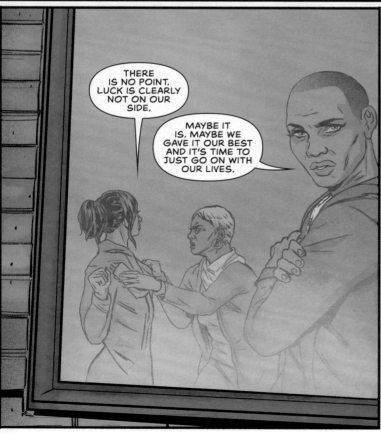

THERE IS NO POINT. LUCK IS CLEARLY NOT ON OUR SIDE.

MAYBE IT IS. MAYBE WE GAVE IT OUR BEST AND IT'S TIME TO JUST GO ON WITH OUR LIVES.

LIKE HELL. GET IT TOGETHER.

STEALING HAS NOTHING TO DO WITH LUCK AND EVERYTHING TO DO WITH SKILL, WHICH WE HAVE, IN SPADES.

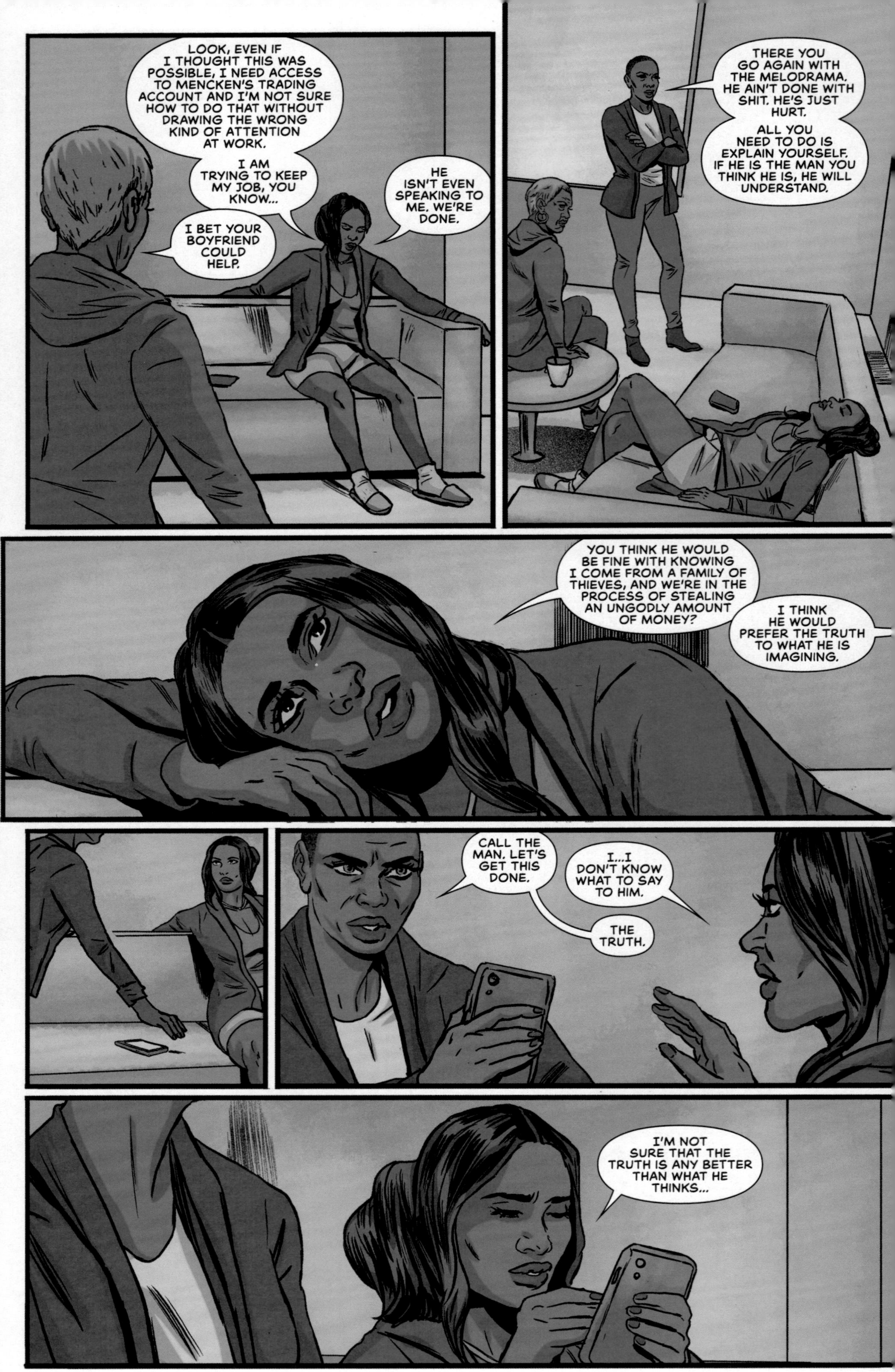
LOOK, EVEN IF I THOUGHT THIS WAS POSSIBLE, I NEED ACCESS TO MENCKEN'S TRADING ACCOUNT AND I'M NOT SURE HOW TO DO THAT WITHOUT DRAWING THE WRONG KIND OF ATTENTION AT WORK.
I AM TRYING TO KEEP MY JOB, YOU KNOW...
I BET YOUR BOYFRIEND COULD HELP.
HE ISN'T EVEN SPEAKING TO ME, WE'RE DONE.
THERE YOU GO AGAIN WITH THE MELODRAMA. HE AIN'T DONE WITH SHIT. HE'S JUST HURT.
ALL YOU NEED TO DO IS EXPLAIN YOURSELF. IF HE IS THE MAN YOU THINK HE IS, HE WILL UNDERSTAND.
YOU THINK HE WOULD BE FINE WITH KNOWING I COME FROM A FAMILY OF THIEVES, AND WE'RE IN THE PROCESS OF STEALING AN UNGODLY AMOUNT OF MONEY?
I THINK HE WOULD PREFER THE TRUTH TO WHAT HE IS IMAGINING.
CALL THE MAN. LET'S GET THIS DONE.
I...I DON'T KNOW WHAT TO SAY TO HIM.
THE TRUTH.
I'M NOT SURE THAT THE TRUTH IS ANY BETTER THAN WHAT HE THINKS...

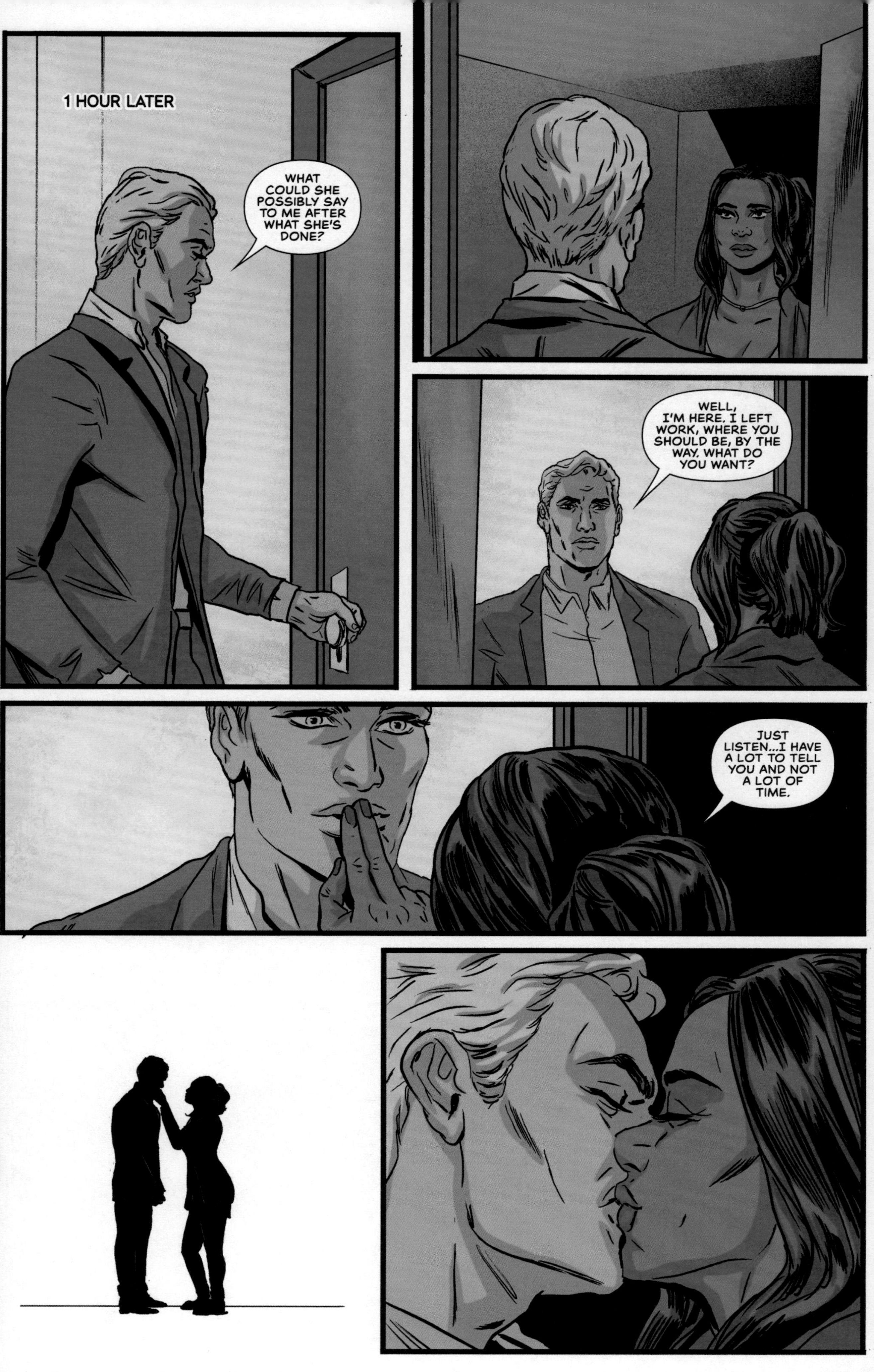
1 HOUR LATER
WHAT COULD SHE POSSIBLY SAY TO ME AFTER WHAT SHE'S DONE?
WELL, I'M HERE. I LEFT WORK, WHERE YOU SHOULD BE, BY THE WAY. WHAT DO YOU WANT?
JUST LISTEN...I HAVE A LOT TO TELL YOU AND NOT A LOT OF TIME.

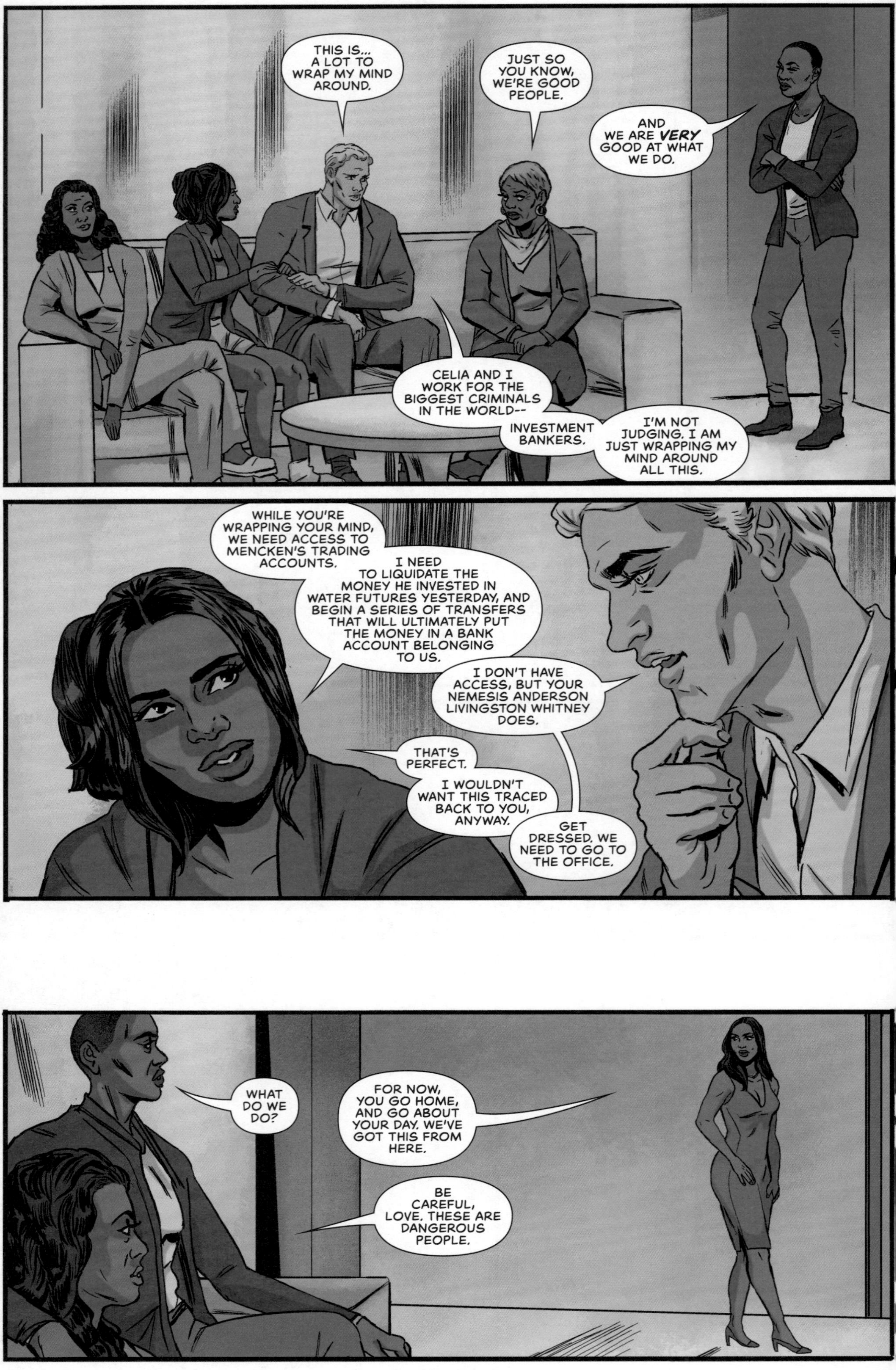
THIS IS... A LOT TO WRAP MY MIND AROUND.
JUST SO YOU KNOW, WE'RE GOOD PEOPLE.
AND WE ARE *VERY* GOOD AT WHAT WE DO.
CELIA AND I WORK FOR THE BIGGEST CRIMINALS IN THE WORLD--
INVESTMENT BANKERS.
I'M NOT JUDGING. I AM JUST WRAPPING MY MIND AROUND ALL THIS.
WHILE YOU'RE WRAPPING YOUR MIND, WE NEED ACCESS TO MENCKEN'S TRADING ACCOUNTS.
I NEED TO LIQUIDATE THE MONEY HE INVESTED IN WATER FUTURES YESTERDAY, AND BEGIN A SERIES OF TRANSFERS THAT WILL ULTIMATELY PUT THE MONEY IN A BANK ACCOUNT BELONGING TO US.
I DON'T HAVE ACCESS, BUT YOUR NEMESIS ANDERSON LIVINGSTON WHITNEY DOES.
THAT'S PERFECT.
I WOULDN'T WANT THIS TRACED BACK TO YOU, ANYWAY.
GET DRESSED. WE NEED TO GO TO THE OFFICE.
WHAT DO WE DO?
FOR NOW, YOU GO HOME, AND GO ABOUT YOUR DAY. WE'VE GOT THIS FROM HERE.
BE CAREFUL, LOVE. THESE ARE DANGEROUS PEOPLE.

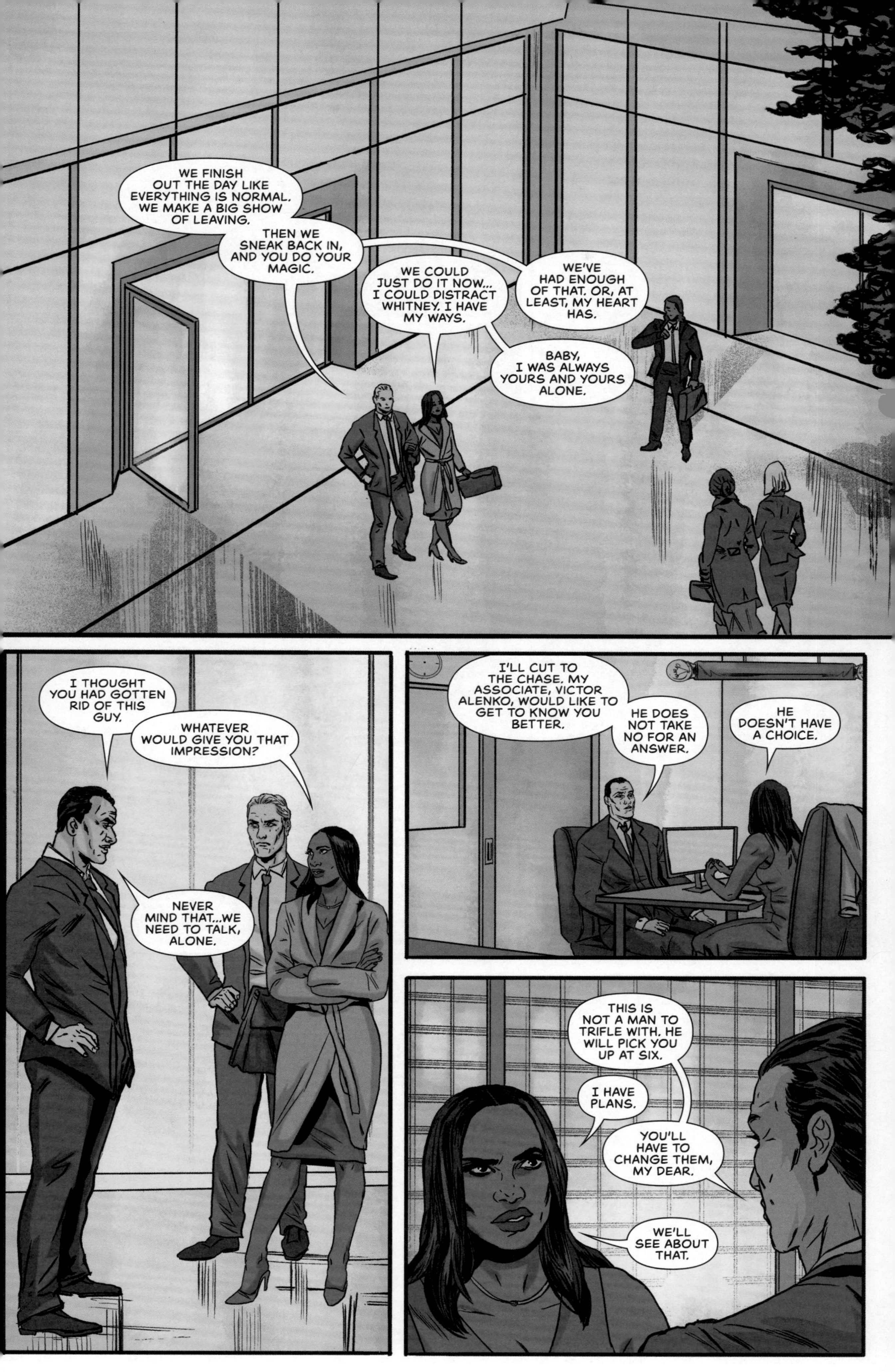
WE FINISH OUT THE DAY LIKE EVERYTHING IS NORMAL. WE MAKE A BIG SHOW OF LEAVING.
THEN WE SNEAK BACK IN, AND YOU DO YOUR MAGIC.
WE COULD JUST DO IT NOW... I COULD DISTRACT WHITNEY. I HAVE MY WAYS.
WE'VE HAD ENOUGH OF THAT. OR, AT LEAST, MY HEART HAS.
BABY, I WAS ALWAYS YOURS AND YOURS ALONE.
I THOUGHT YOU HAD GOTTEN RID OF THIS GUY.
WHATEVER WOULD GIVE YOU THAT IMPRESSION?
NEVER MIND THAT...WE NEED TO TALK, ALONE.
I'LL CUT TO THE CHASE. MY ASSOCIATE, VICTOR ALENKO, WOULD LIKE TO GET TO KNOW YOU BETTER.
HE DOES NOT TAKE NO FOR AN ANSWER.
HE DOESN'T HAVE A CHOICE.
THIS IS NOT A MAN TO TRIFLE WITH. HE WILL PICK YOU UP AT SIX.
I HAVE PLANS.
YOU'LL HAVE TO CHANGE THEM, MY DEAR.
WE'LL SEE ABOUT THAT.

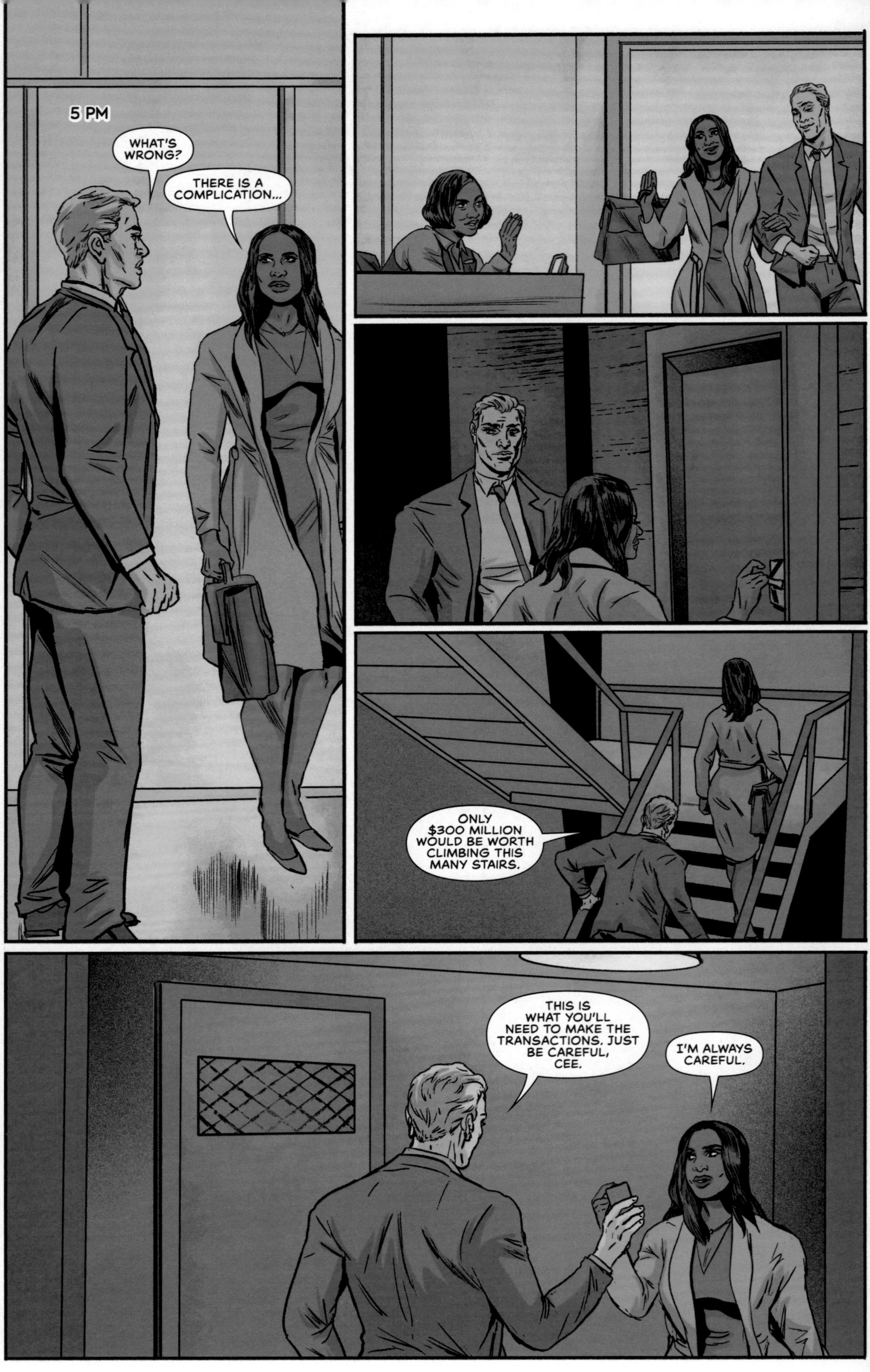
5 PM
WHAT'S WRONG?
THERE IS A COMPLICATION...
ONLY $300 MILLION WOULD BE WORTH CLIMBING THIS MANY STAIRS.
THIS IS WHAT YOU'LL NEED TO MAKE THE TRANSACTIONS. JUST BE CAREFUL, CEE.
I'M ALWAYS CAREFUL.

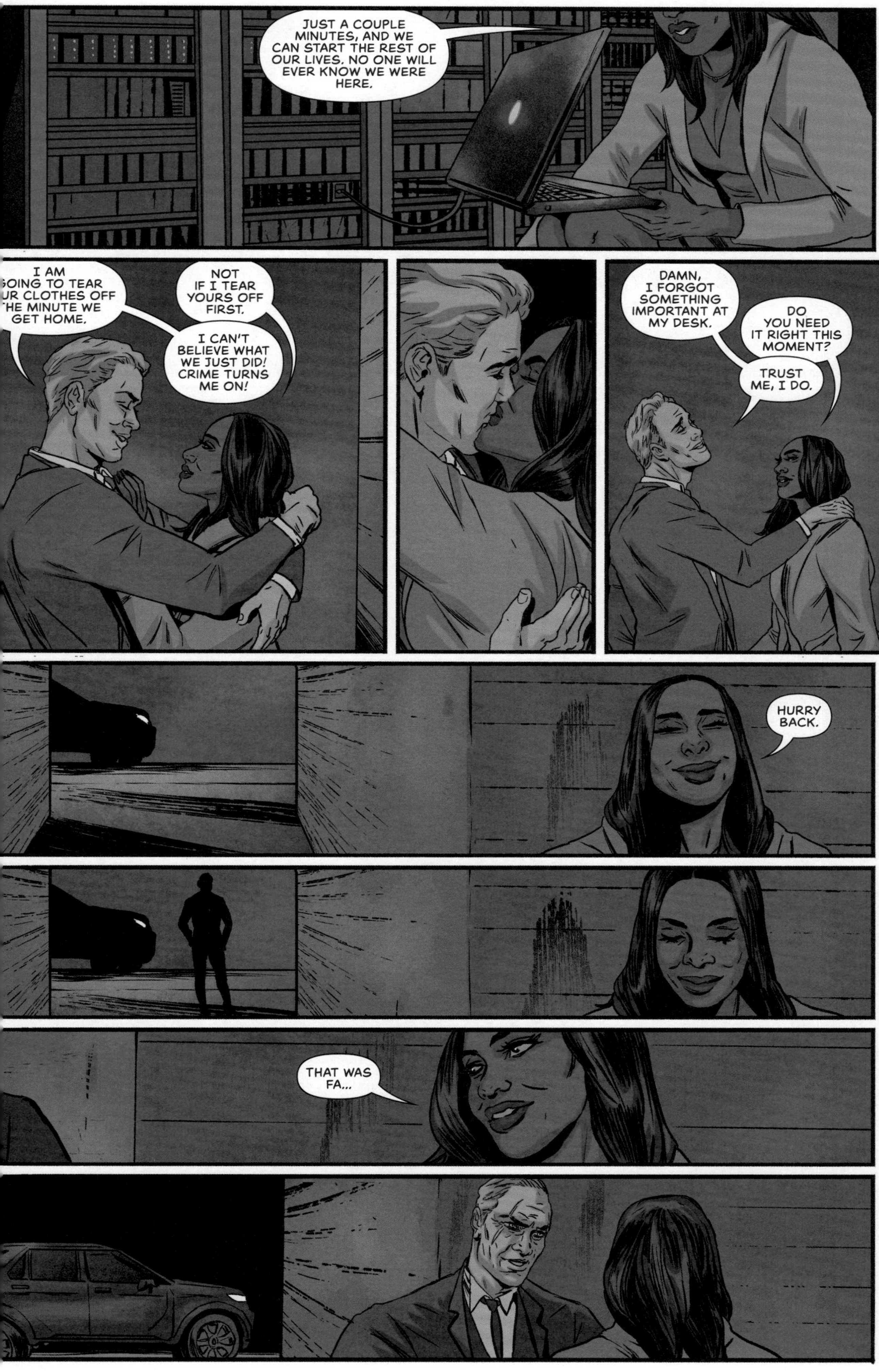
JUST A COUPLE MINUTES, AND WE CAN START THE REST OF OUR LIVES. NO ONE WILL EVER KNOW WE WERE HERE.
I AM GOING TO TEAR YOUR CLOTHES OFF THE MINUTE WE GET HOME.
NOT IF I TEAR YOURS OFF FIRST.
I CAN'T BELIEVE WHAT WE JUST DID! CRIME TURNS ME ON!
DAMN, I FORGOT SOMETHING IMPORTANT AT MY DESK.
DO YOU NEED IT RIGHT THIS MOMENT?
TRUST ME, I DO.
HURRY BACK.
THAT WAS FA...

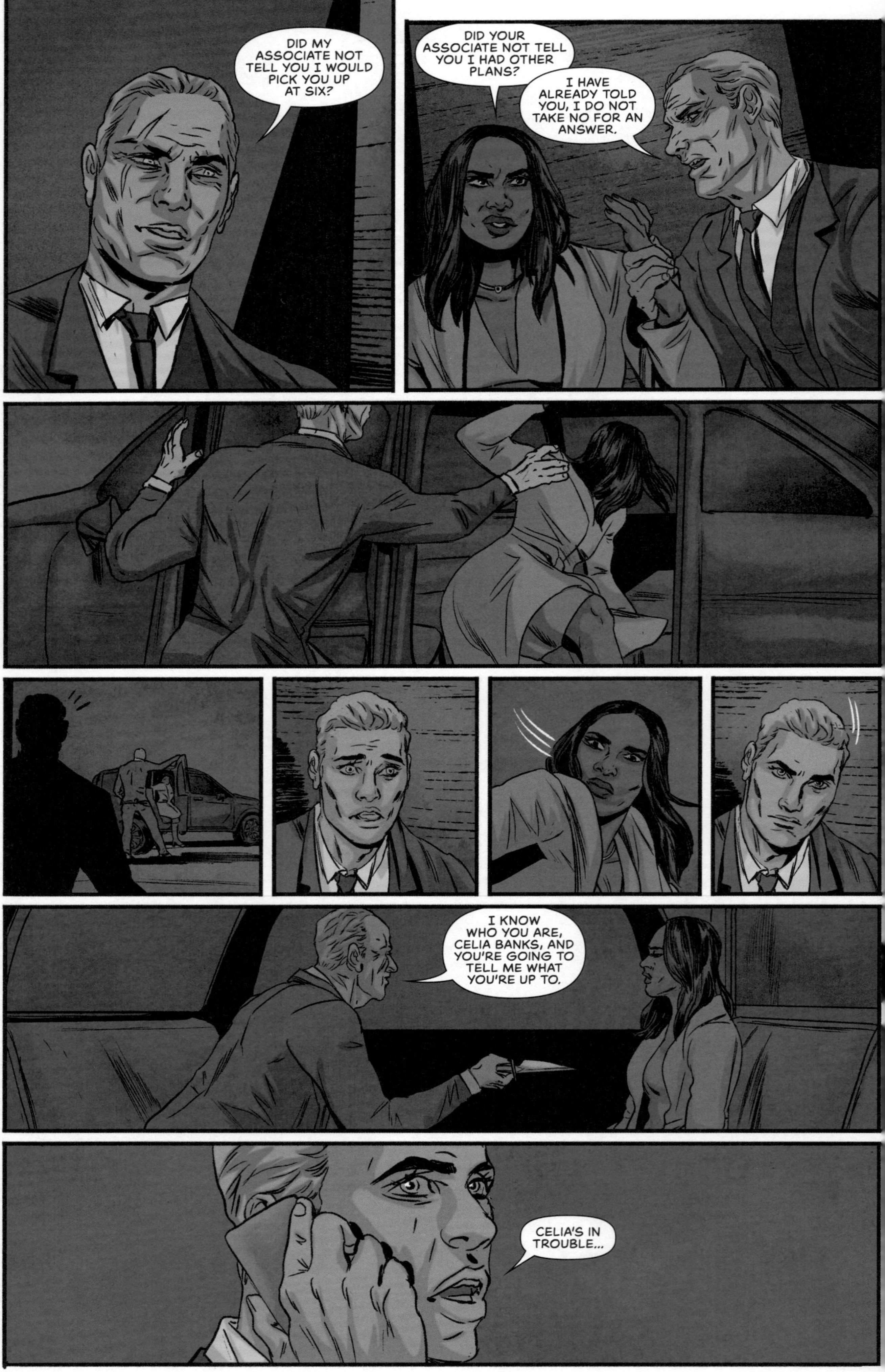
DID MY ASSOCIATE NOT TELL YOU I WOULD PICK YOU UP AT SIX?
DID YOUR ASSOCIATE NOT TELL YOU I HAD OTHER PLANS?
I HAVE ALREADY TOLD YOU, I DO NOT TAKE NO FOR AN ANSWER.
I KNOW WHO YOU ARE, CELIA BANKS, AND YOU'RE GOING TO TELL ME WHAT YOU'RE UP TO.
CELIA'S IN TROUBLE...

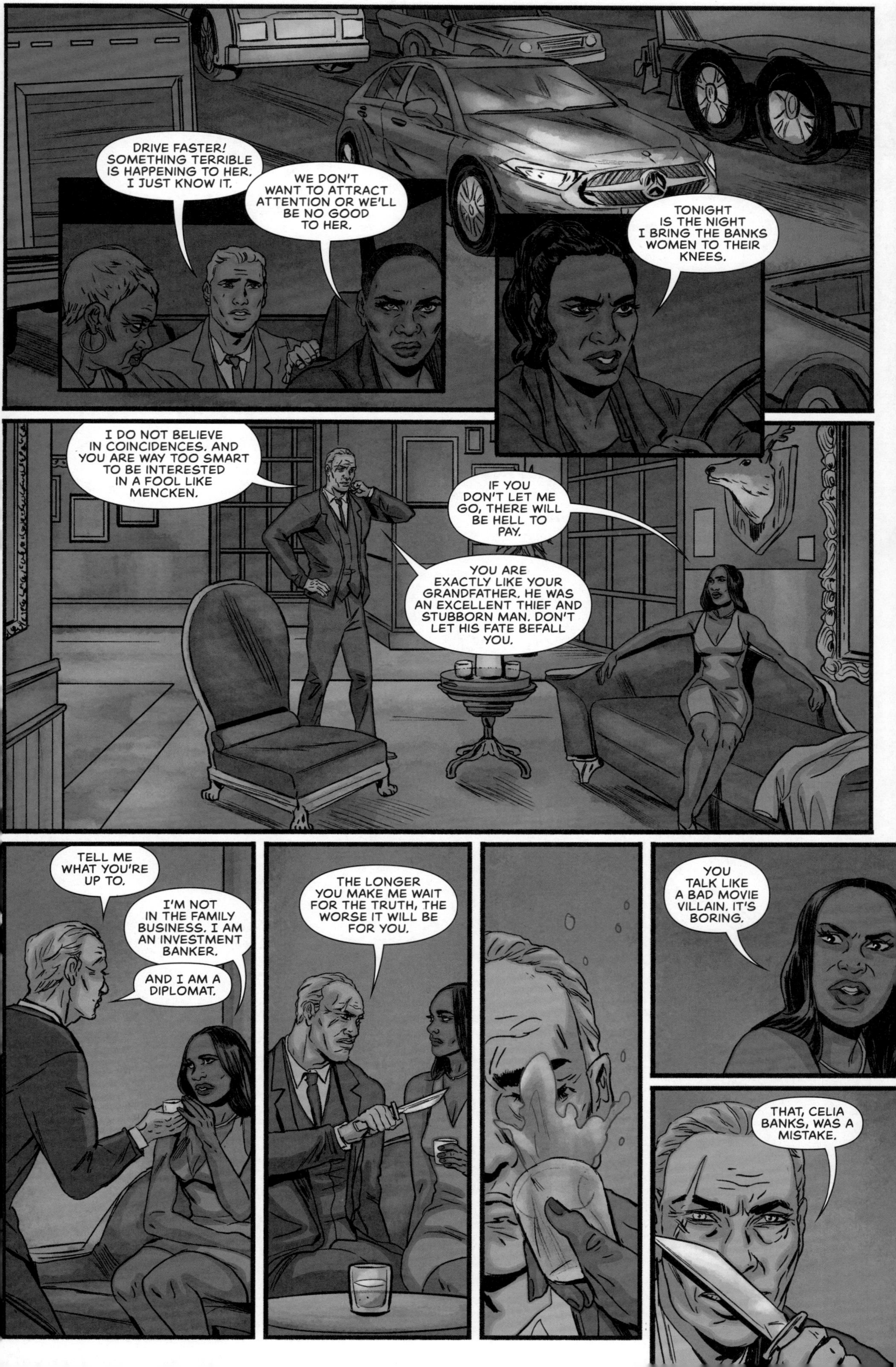
DRIVE FASTER! SOMETHING TERRIBLE IS HAPPENING TO HER. I JUST KNOW IT.
WE DON'T WANT TO ATTRACT ATTENTION OR WE'LL BE NO GOOD TO HER.
TONIGHT IS THE NIGHT I BRING THE BANKS WOMEN TO THEIR KNEES.
I DO NOT BELIEVE IN COINCIDENCES, AND YOU ARE WAY TOO SMART TO BE INTERESTED IN A FOOL LIKE MENCKEN.
IF YOU DON'T LET ME GO, THERE WILL BE HELL TO PAY.
YOU ARE EXACTLY LIKE YOUR GRANDFATHER. HE WAS AN EXCELLENT THIEF AND STUBBORN MAN. DON'T LET HIS FATE BEFALL YOU.
TELL ME WHAT YOU'RE UP TO.
I'M NOT IN THE FAMILY BUSINESS. I AM AN INVESTMENT BANKER.
AND I AM A DIPLOMAT.
THE LONGER YOU MAKE ME WAIT FOR THE TRUTH, THE WORSE IT WILL BE FOR YOU.
YOU TALK LIKE A BAD MOVIE VILLAIN. IT'S BORING.
THAT, CELIA BANKS, WAS A MISTAKE.

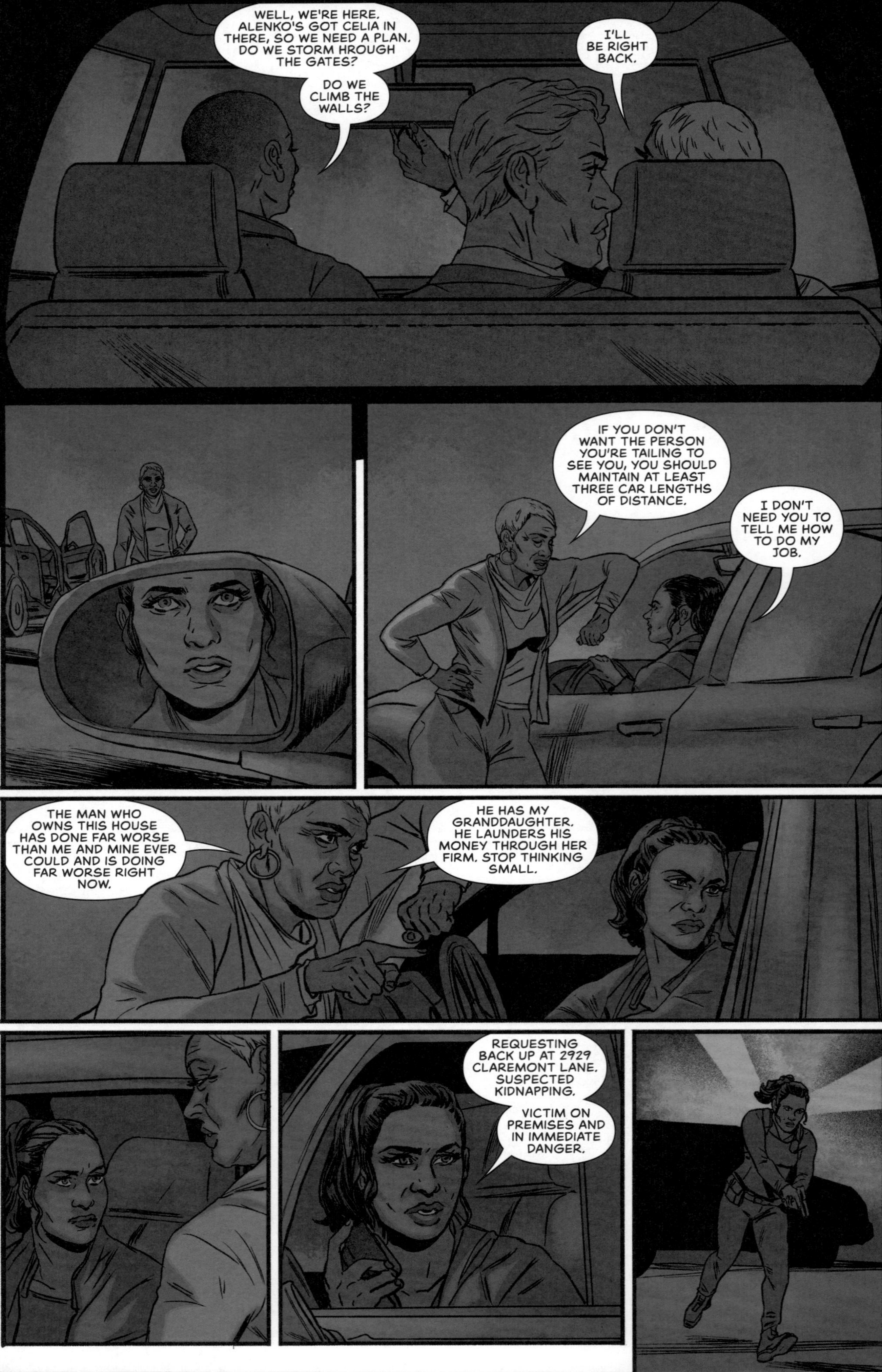

WELL, WE'RE HERE. ALENKO'S GOT CELIA IN THERE, SO WE NEED A PLAN. DO WE STORM HROUGH THE GATES?
DO WE CLIMB THE WALLS?
I'LL BE RIGHT BACK.
IF YOU DON'T WANT THE PERSON YOU'RE TAILING TO SEE YOU, YOU SHOULD MAINTAIN AT LEAST THREE CAR LENGTHS OF DISTANCE.
I DON'T NEED YOU TO TELL ME HOW TO DO MY JOB.
THE MAN WHO OWNS THIS HOUSE HAS DONE FAR WORSE THAN ME AND MINE EVER COULD AND IS DOING FAR WORSE RIGHT NOW.
HE HAS MY GRANDDAUGHTER. HE LAUNDERS HIS MONEY THROUGH HER FIRM. STOP THINKING SMALL.
REQUESTING BACK UP AT 2929 CLAREMONT LANE. SUSPECTED KIDNAPPING.
VICTIM ON PREMISES AND IN IMMEDIATE DANGER.

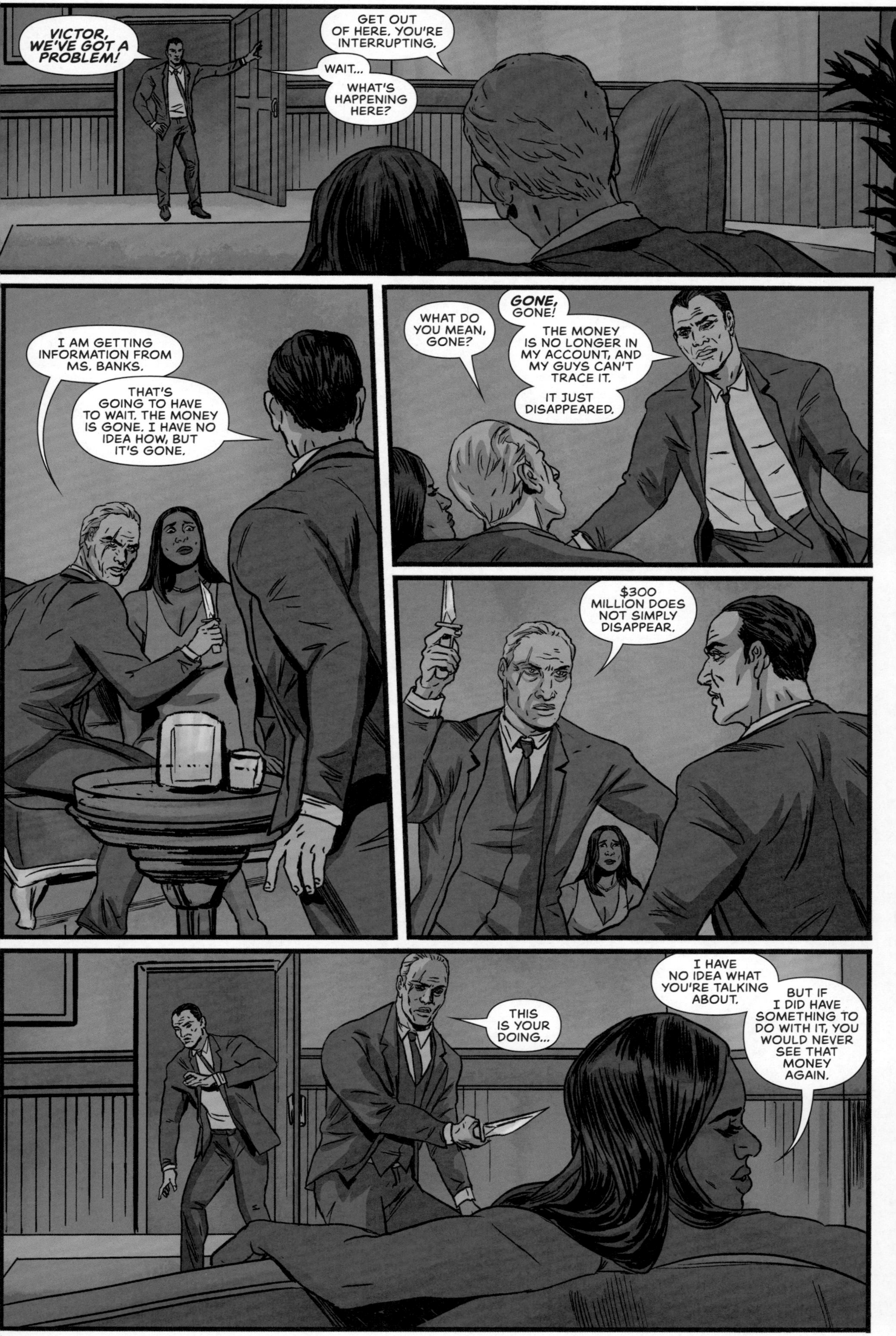
VICTOR, WE'VE GOT A PROBLEM!
GET OUT OF HERE. YOU'RE INTERRUPTING.
WAIT...
WHAT'S HAPPENING HERE?
I AM GETTING INFORMATION FROM MS. BANKS.
THAT'S GOING TO HAVE TO WAIT. THE MONEY IS GONE. I HAVE NO IDEA HOW, BUT IT'S GONE.
WHAT DO YOU MEAN, GONE?
GONE, GONE!
THE MONEY IS NO LONGER IN MY ACCOUNT, AND MY GUYS CAN'T TRACE IT.
IT JUST DISAPPEARED.
$300 MILLION DOES NOT SIMPLY DISAPPEAR.
THIS IS YOUR DOING...
I HAVE NO IDEA WHAT YOU'RE TALKING ABOUT.
BUT IF I DID HAVE SOMETHING TO DO WITH IT, YOU WOULD NEVER SEE THAT MONEY AGAIN.

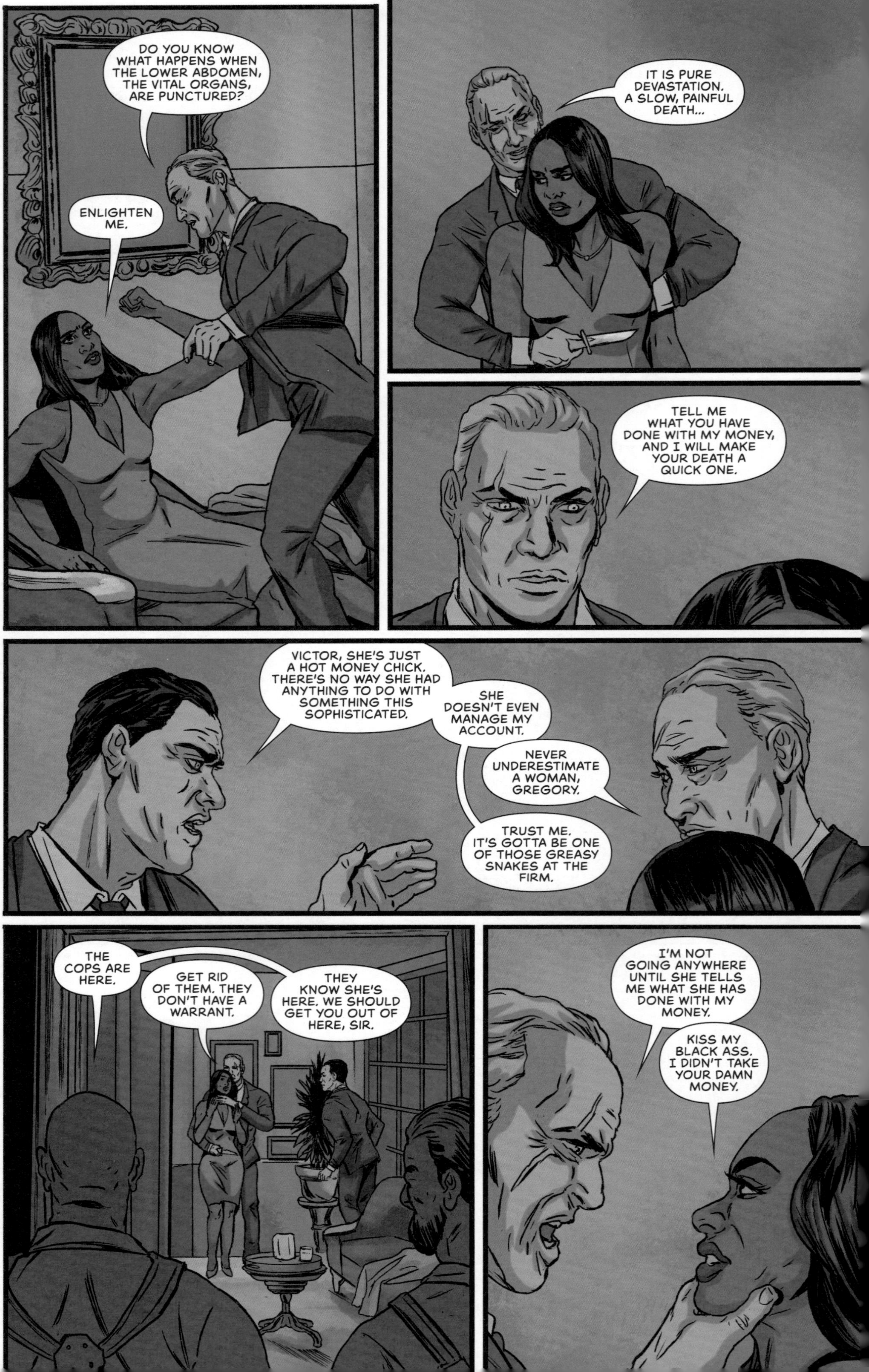
DO YOU KNOW WHAT HAPPENS WHEN THE LOWER ABDOMEN, THE VITAL ORGANS, ARE PUNCTURED?
ENLIGHTEN ME.
IT IS PURE DEVASTATION. A SLOW, PAINFUL DEATH...
TELL ME WHAT YOU HAVE DONE WITH MY MONEY, AND I WILL MAKE YOUR DEATH A QUICK ONE.
VICTOR, SHE'S JUST A HOT MONEY CHICK. THERE'S NO WAY SHE HAD ANYTHING TO DO WITH SOMETHING THIS SOPHISTICATED.
SHE DOESN'T EVEN MANAGE MY ACCOUNT.
NEVER UNDERESTIMATE A WOMAN, GREGORY.
TRUST ME. IT'S GOTTA BE ONE OF THOSE GREASY SNAKES AT THE FIRM.
THE COPS ARE HERE.
GET RID OF THEM. THEY DON'T HAVE A WARRANT.
THEY KNOW SHE'S HERE. WE SHOULD GET YOU OUT OF HERE, SIR.
I'M NOT GOING ANYWHERE UNTIL SHE TELLS ME WHAT SHE HAS DONE WITH MY MONEY.
KISS MY BLACK ASS. I DIDN'T TAKE YOUR DAMN MONEY.

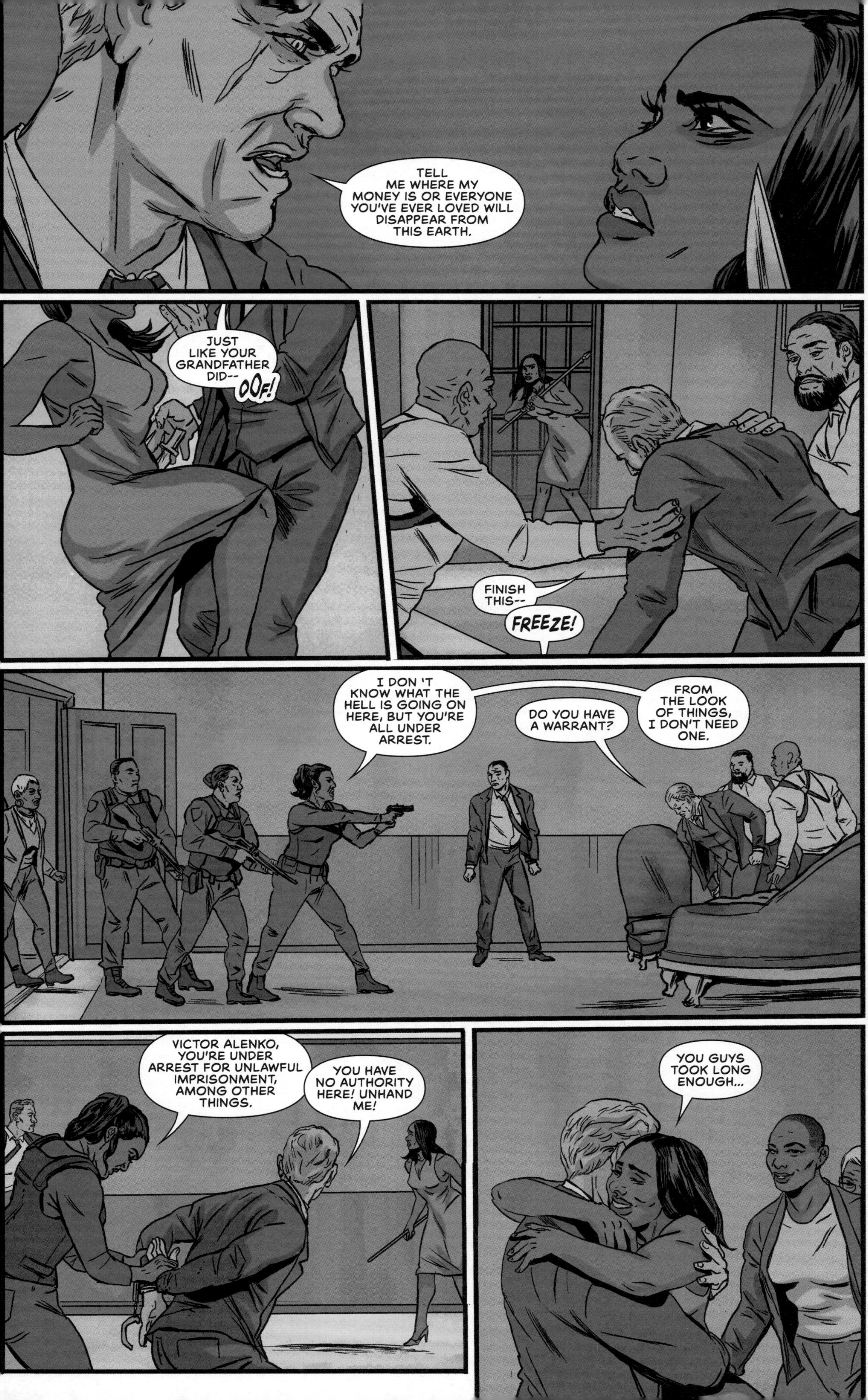
TELL ME WHERE MY MONEY IS OR EVERYONE YOU'VE EVER LOVED WILL DISAPPEAR FROM THIS EARTH.
JUST LIKE YOUR GRANDFATHER DID--
OOF!
FINISH THIS--
FREEZE!
I DON 'T KNOW WHAT THE HELL IS GOING ON HERE, BUT YOU'RE ALL UNDER ARREST.
DO YOU HAVE A WARRANT?
FROM THE LOOK OF THINGS, I DON'T NEED ONE.
VICTOR ALENKO, YOU'RE UNDER ARREST FOR UNLAWFUL IMPRISONMENT, AMONG OTHER THINGS.
YOU HAVE NO AUTHORITY HERE! UNHAND ME!
YOU GUYS TOOK LONG ENOUGH...

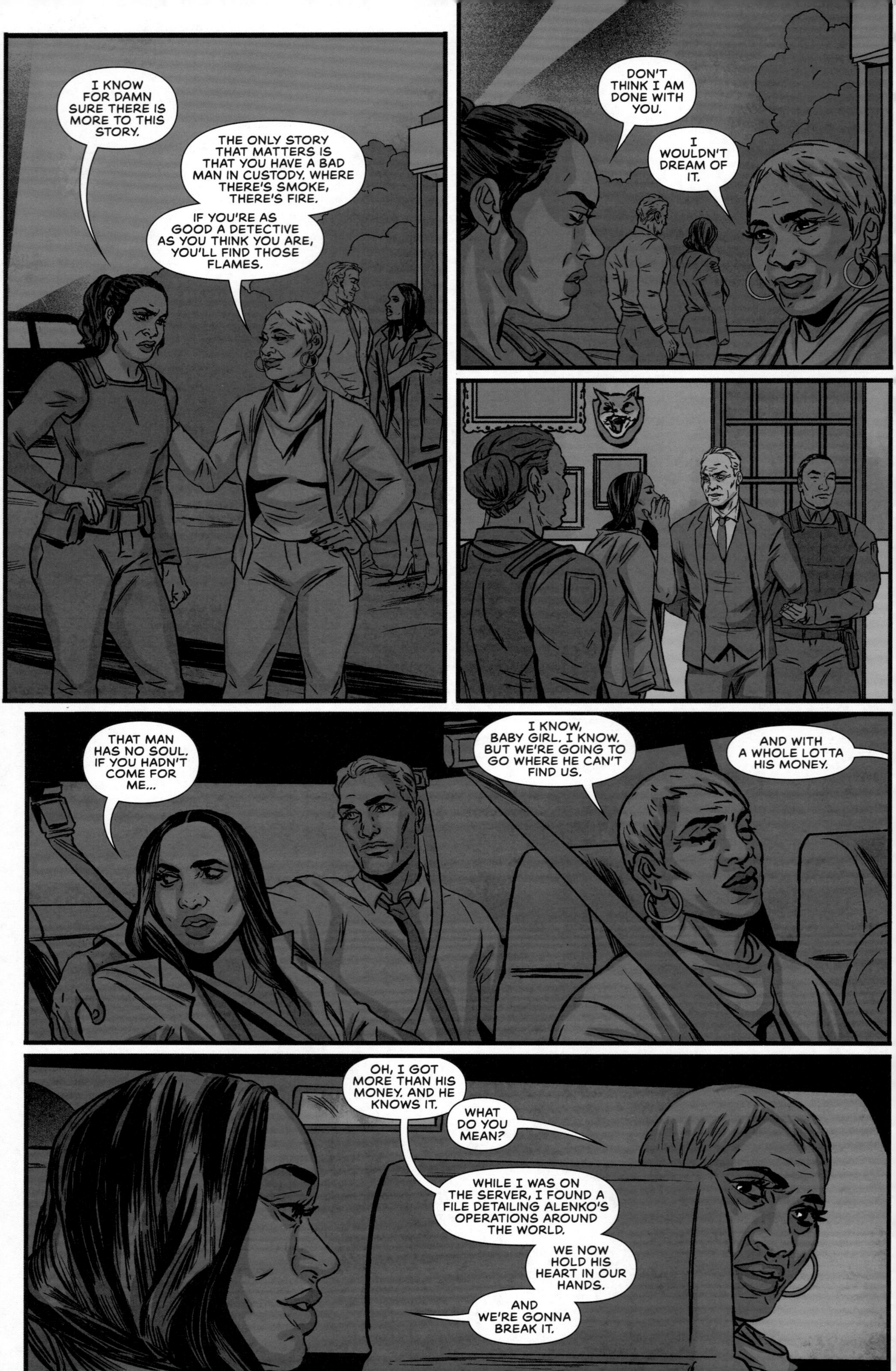
I KNOW FOR DAMN SURE THERE IS MORE TO THIS STORY.
THE ONLY STORY THAT MATTERS IS THAT YOU HAVE A BAD MAN IN CUSTODY. WHERE THERE'S SMOKE, THERE'S FIRE.
IF YOU'RE AS GOOD A DETECTIVE AS YOU THINK YOU ARE, YOU'LL FIND THOSE FLAMES.
DON'T THINK I AM DONE WITH YOU.
I WOULDN'T DREAM OF IT.
THAT MAN HAS NO SOUL. IF YOU HADN'T COME FOR ME...
I KNOW, BABY GIRL. I KNOW. BUT WE'RE GOING TO GO WHERE HE CAN'T FIND US.
AND WITH A WHOLE LOTTA HIS MONEY.
OH, I GOT MORE THAN HIS MONEY. AND HE KNOWS IT.
WHAT DO YOU MEAN?
WHILE I WAS ON THE SERVER, I FOUND A FILE DETAILING ALENKO'S OPERATIONS AROUND THE WORLD.
WE NOW HOLD HIS HEART IN OUR HANDS.
AND WE'RE GONNA BREAK IT.

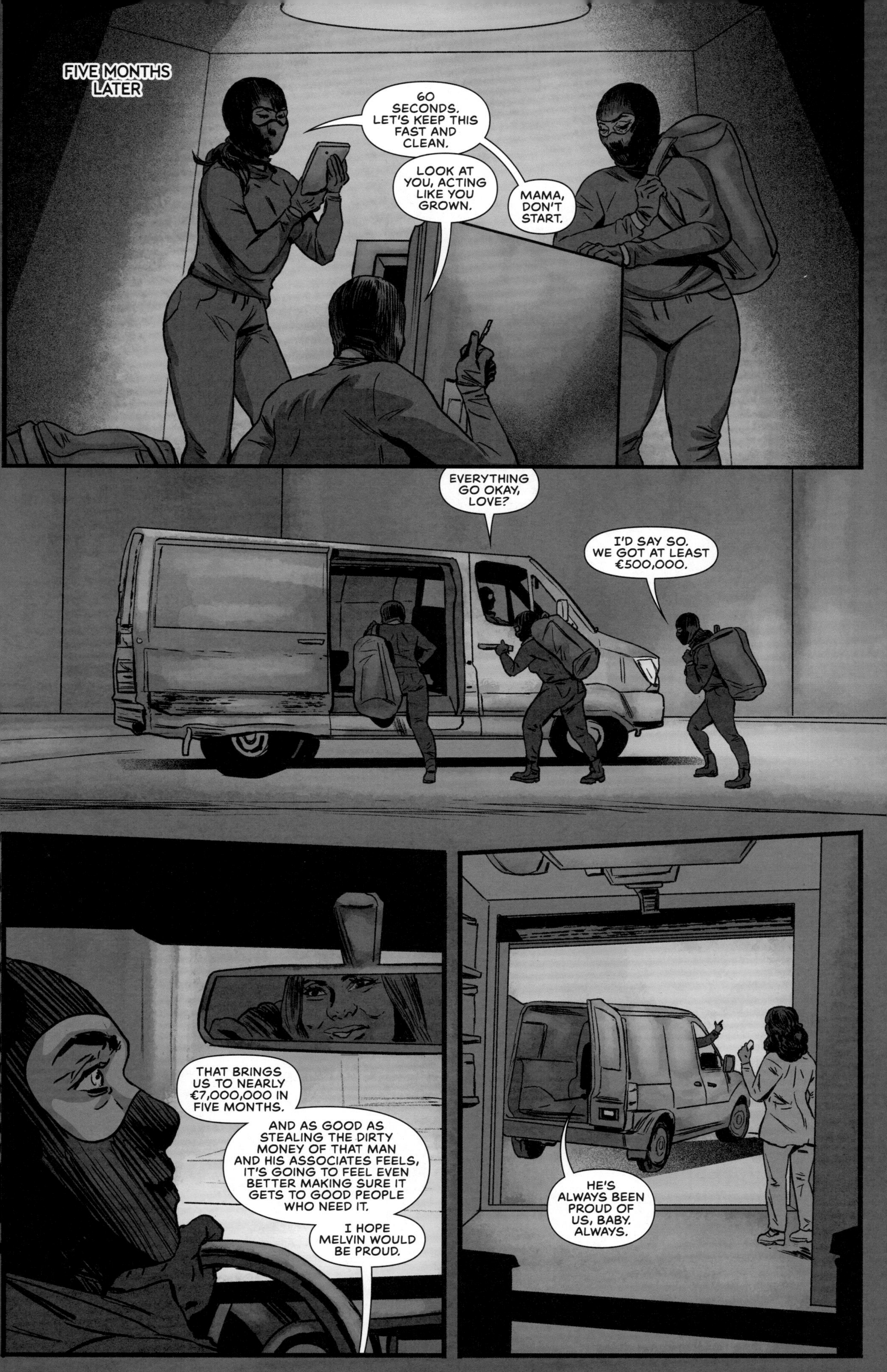

FIVE MONTHS LATER
60 SECONDS. LET'S KEEP THIS FAST AND CLEAN.
LOOK AT YOU, ACTING LIKE YOU GROWN.
MAMA, DON'T START.
EVERYTHING GO OKAY, LOVE?
I'D SAY SO. WE GOT AT LEAST €500,000.
THAT BRINGS US TO NEARLY €7,000,000 IN FIVE MONTHS.
AND AS GOOD AS STEALING THE DIRTY MONEY OF THAT MAN AND HIS ASSOCIATES FEELS, IT'S GOING TO FEEL EVEN BETTER MAKING SURE IT GETS TO GOOD PEOPLE WHO NEED IT.
I HOPE MELVIN WOULD BE PROUD.
HE'S ALWAYS BEEN PROUD OF US, BABY. ALWAYS.

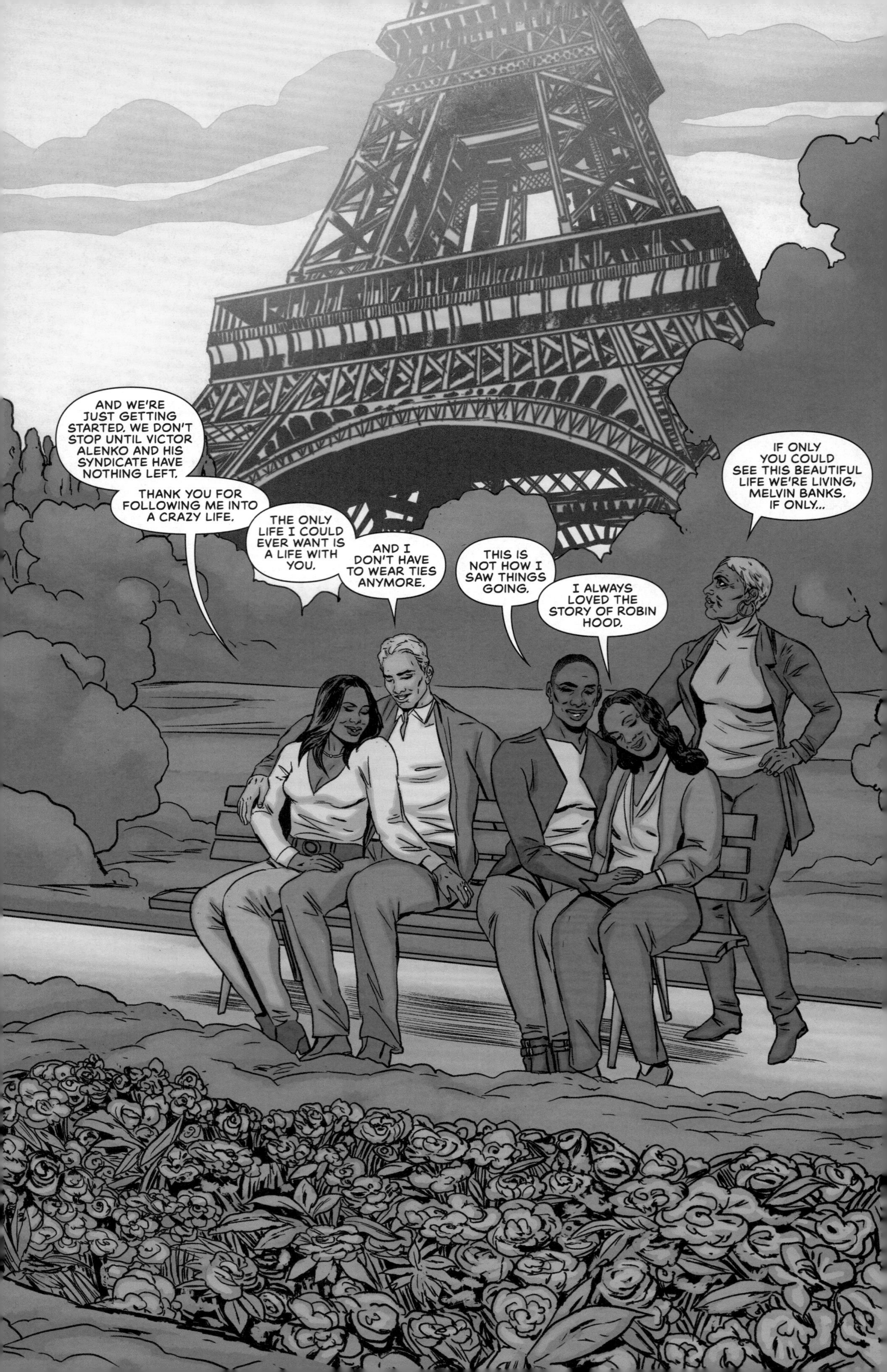
AND WE'RE JUST GETTING STARTED. WE DON'T STOP UNTIL VICTOR ALENKO AND HIS SYNDICATE HAVE NOTHING LEFT.
THANK YOU FOR FOLLOWING ME INTO A CRAZY LIFE.
THE ONLY LIFE I COULD EVER WANT IS A LIFE WITH YOU.
AND I DON'T HAVE TO WEAR TIES ANYMORE.
THIS IS NOT HOW I SAW THINGS GOING.
I ALWAYS LOVED THE STORY OF ROBIN HOOD.
IF ONLY YOU COULD SEE THIS BEAUTIFUL LIFE WE'RE LIVING, MELVIN BANKS. IF ONLY...

ORIGINAL COVER ART BY
MING DOYLE

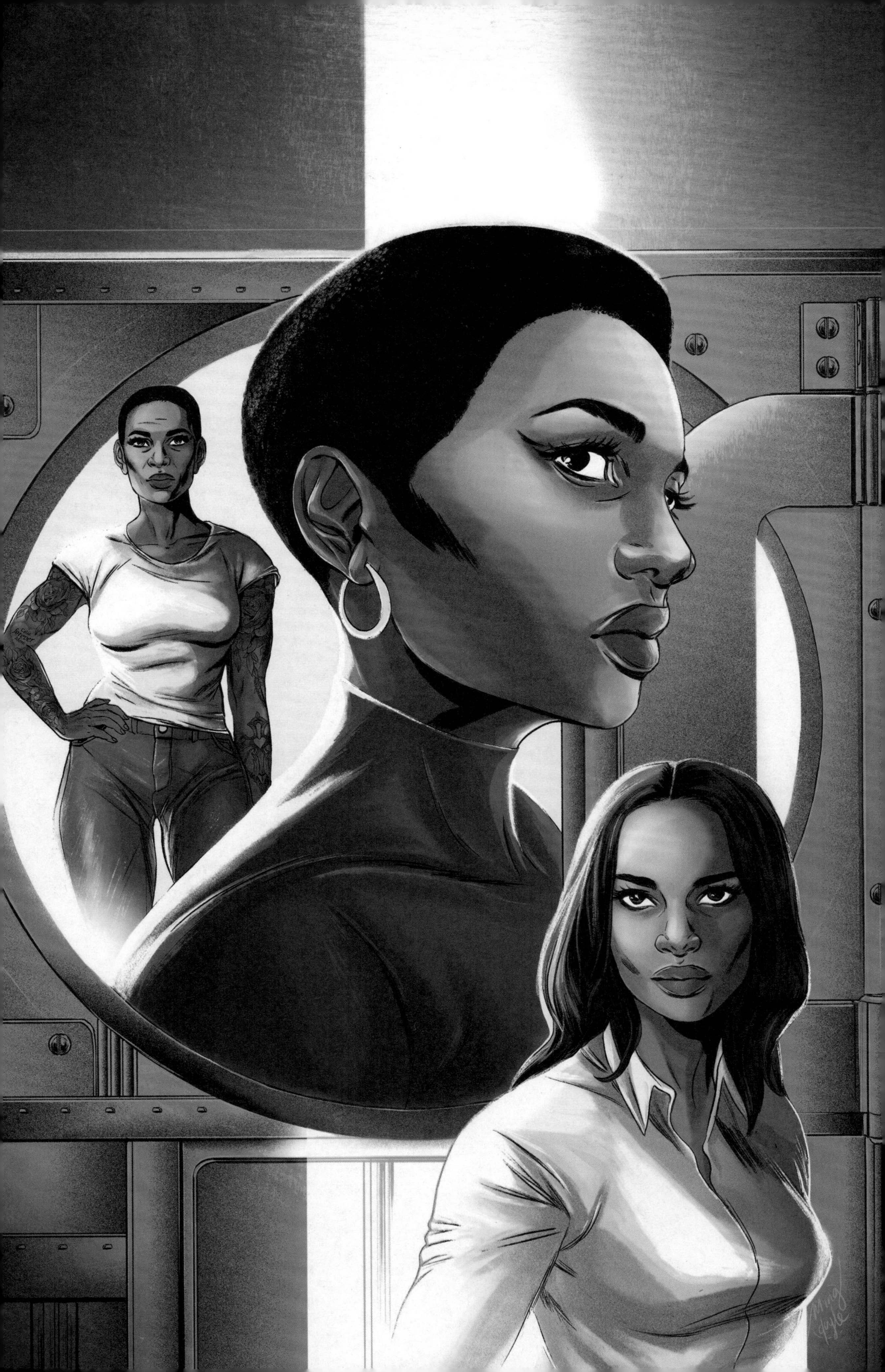

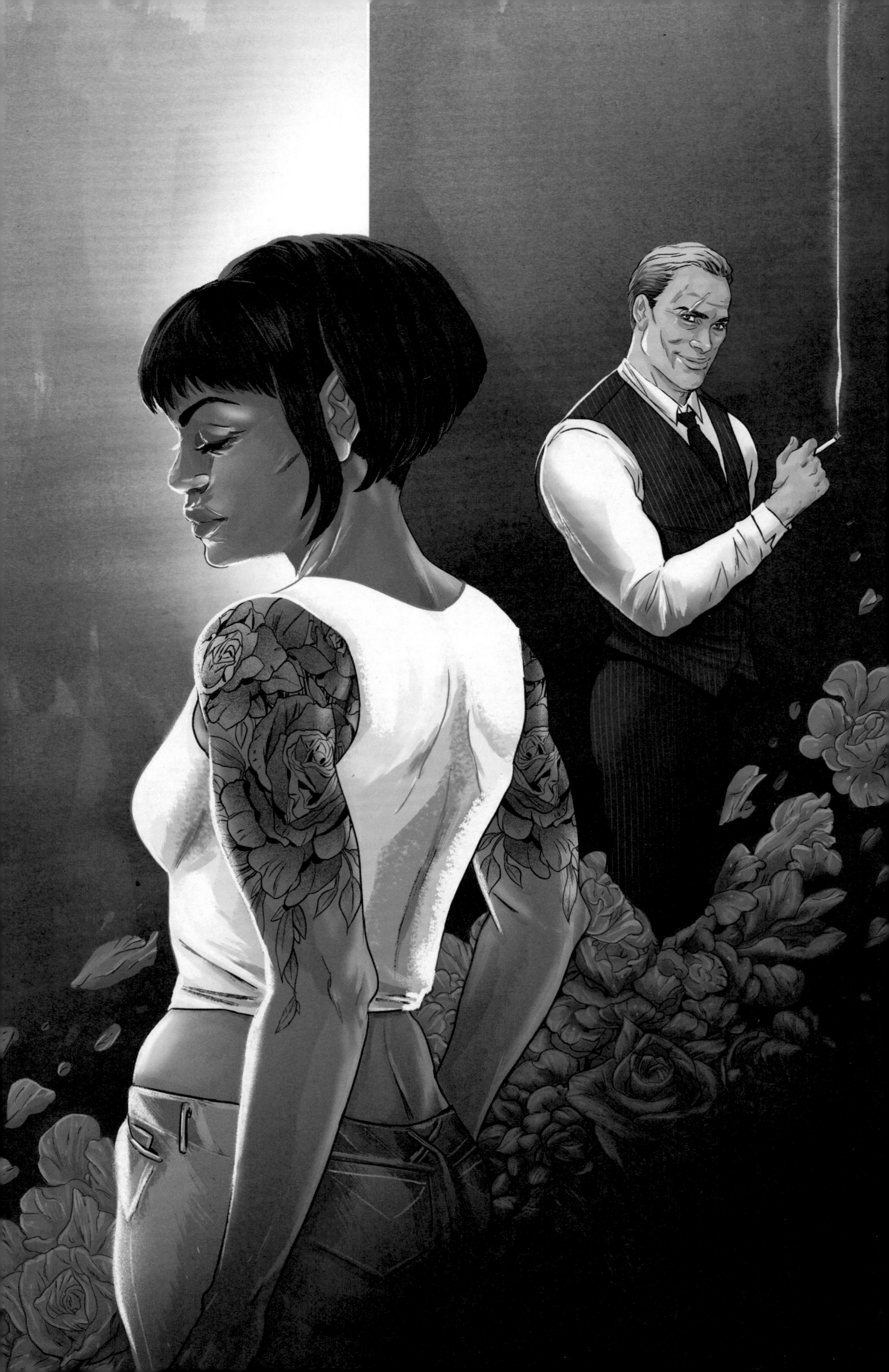

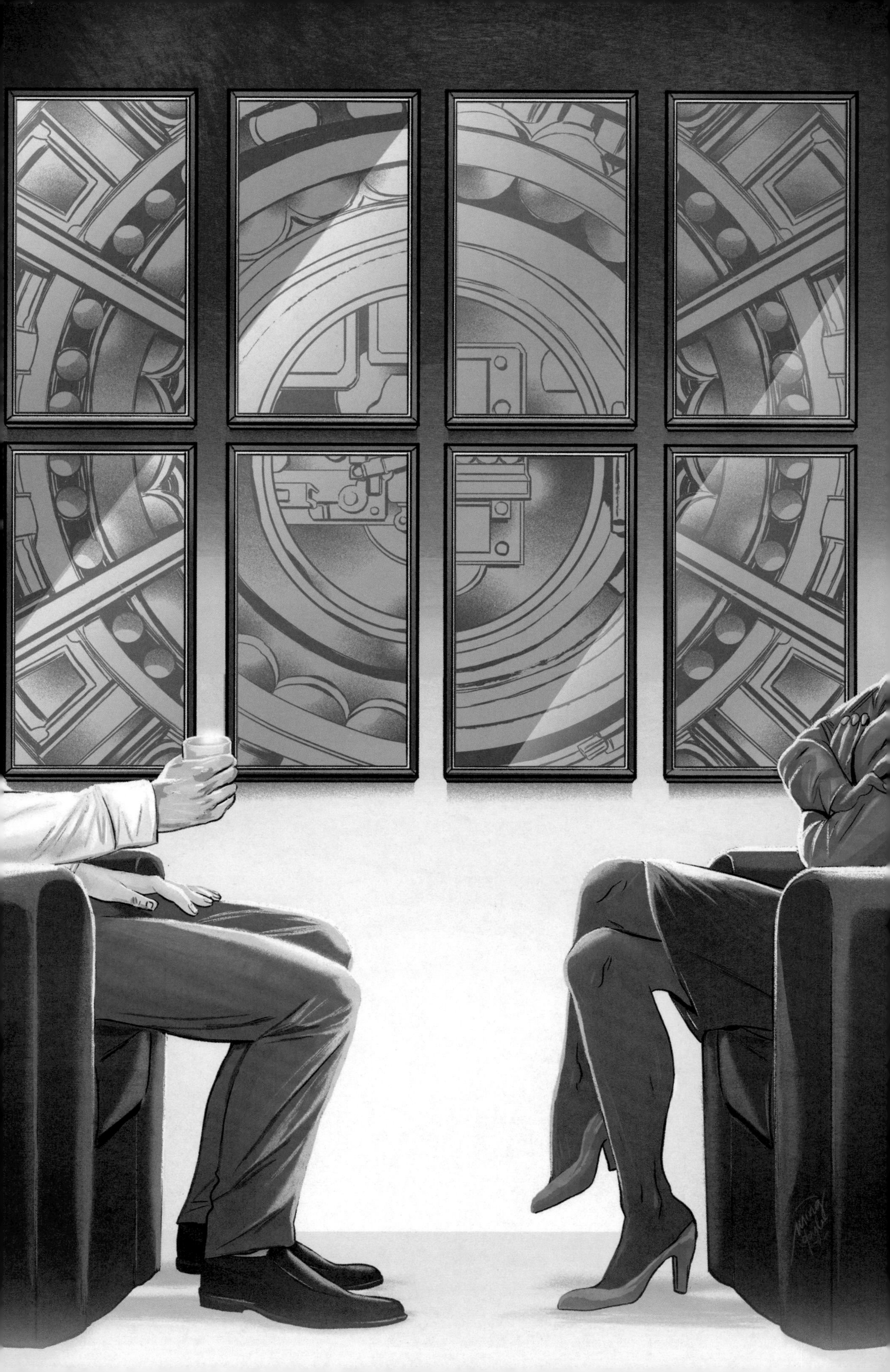

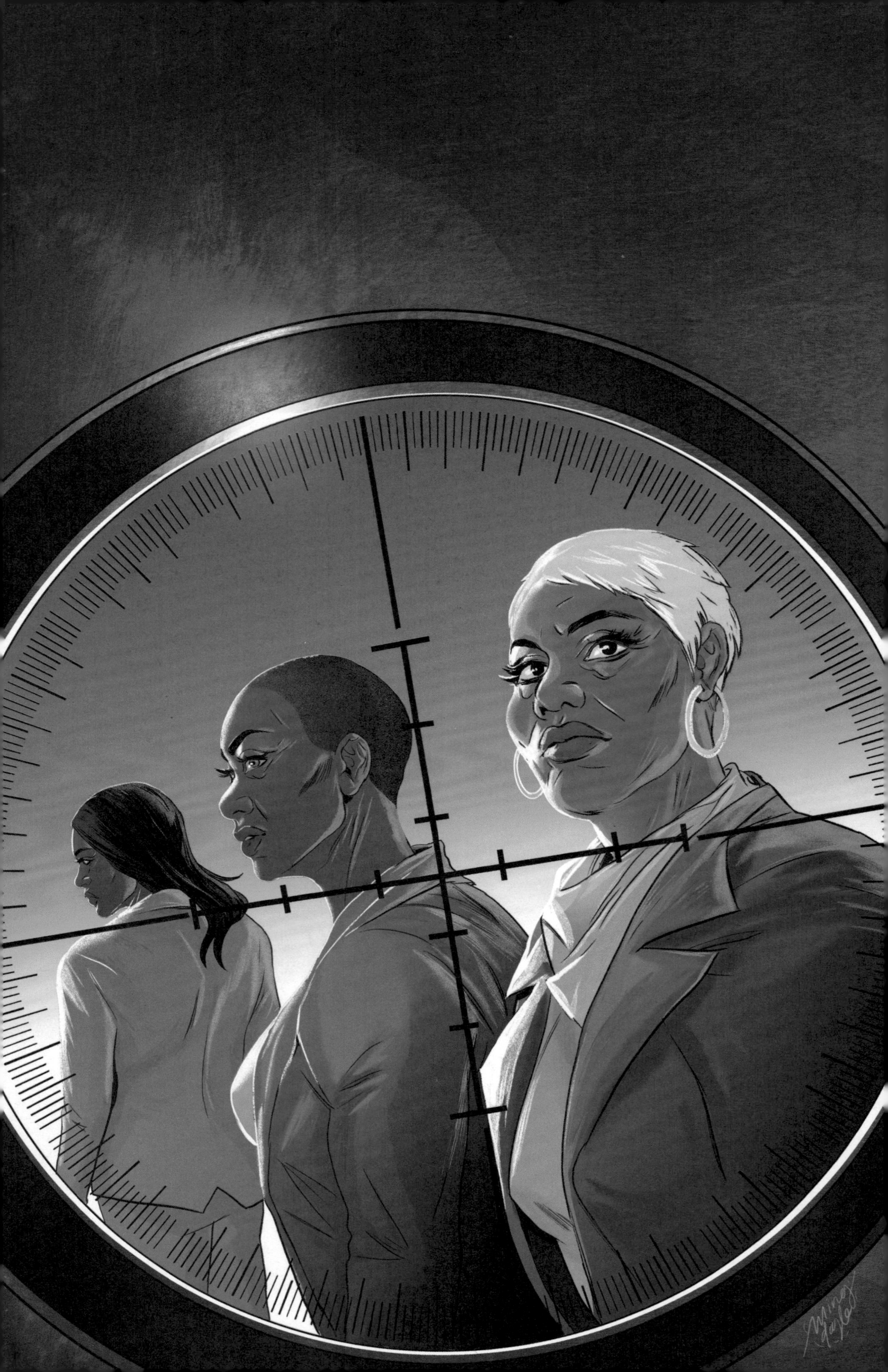

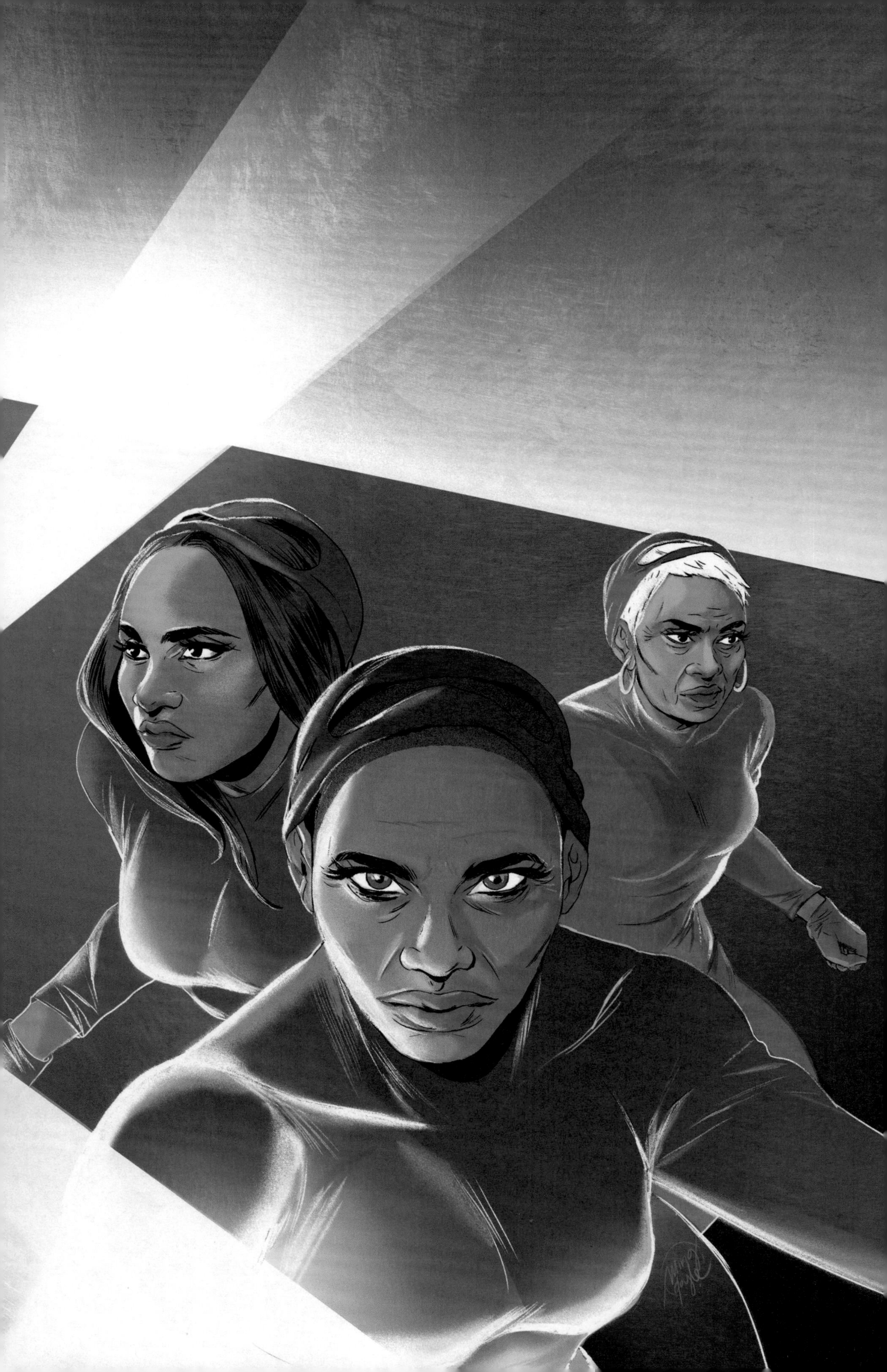

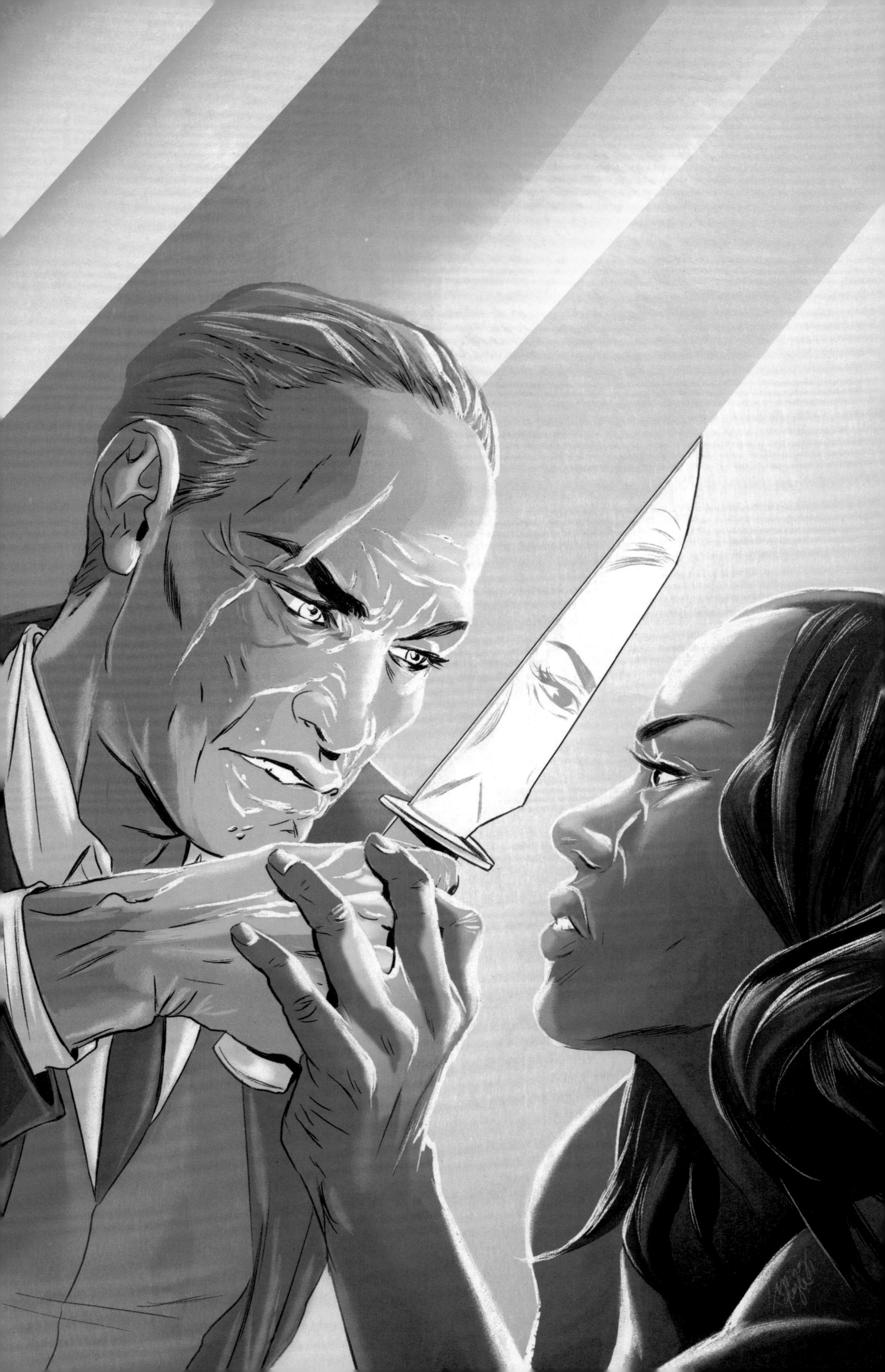

CREATORS

ROXANNE GAY | WRITER

Roxane Gay's writing appears in BEST AMERICAN MYSTERY STORIES 2014, BEST AMERICAN SHORT STORIES 2012, BEST SEX WRITING 2012, A PUBLIC SPACE, MCSWEENEY'S, TIN HOUSE, OXFORD AMERICAN, AMERICAN SHORT FICTION, VIRGINIA QUARTERLY REVIEW, and many others. She is a contributing opinion writer for *The New York Times*. She is the author of the books AYITI, AN UNTAMED STATE, *The New York Times* bestselling BAD FEMINIST, the nationally bestselling DIFFICULT WOMEN and *The New York Times* bestselling HUNGER.

MING DOYLE | ARTIST

Ming Doyle was born in Boston to an Irish-American sailor and a Chinese-Canadian librarian. In 2007 she earned her BFA from Cornell University with a dual concentration in Painting and Drawing. She has been working as a freelance illustrator and comic book artist ever since. She is known for her work on THE KITCHEN (now a feature film starring Melissa McCarthy, Tiffany Haddish, and Elizabeth Moss), MARA, CONSTANTINE: HELLBLAZER, ANATOMY OF A METAHUMAN, and GIRL OVER PARIS.

JORDIE BELLAIRE | COLOR ARTIST

Jordie Bellaire is an Eisner Award-winning colorist best known for her work on BATMAN, VISION, and PRETTY DEADLY. Aside from coloring exciting projects, she's currently living a dream, writing BUFFY THE VAMPIRE SLAYER for Boom Studios.

ARIANA MAHER | LETTERER

Ariana Maher is a comic book letterer who works with both independent imprints such as Little Foolery and publishers such as Image Comics, Dynamite Entertainment, and Skybound. Recent projects include EVE OF EXTINCTION, JAMES BOND 007, RINGSIDE, SFEER THEORY, FLAVOR, and Outpost Zero.

SEBASTIAN GIRNER | EDITOR

Sebastian Girner is a German-born, American-raised comic editor and writer. His editing includes such series as DEADLY CLASS, SOUTHERN BASTARDS and THE PUNISHER. He lives and works in Brooklyn with his wife.